SPECIAL MESSAGE TO READERS

THE ULVERSCROFT FOUNDATION
(registered UK charity number 264873)
was established in 1972 to provide funds for
research, diagnosis and treatment of eye diseases.
Examples of major projects funded by the
Ulverscroft Foundation are:

- The Children's Eye Unit at Moorfields Eye
  Hospital, London
- The Ulverscroft Children's Eye Unit at Great
  Ormond Street Hospital for Sick Children
- Funding research into eye diseases and treatment
  at the Department of Ophthalmology, University
  of Leicester
- The Ulverscroft Vision Research Group, Institute
  of Child Health
- Twin operating theatres at the Western Ophthalmic
  Hospital, London
- The Chair of Ophthalmology at the Royal
  Australian College of Ophthalmologists

You can help further the work of the Foundation
by making a donation or leaving a legacy. Every
contribution is gratefully received. If you would like
to help support the Foundation or require further
information, please contact:

THE ULVERSCROFT FOUNDATION
The Green, Bradgate Road, Anstey
Leicester LE7 7FU, England
Tel: (0116) 236 4325

website: www.ulverscroft-foundation.org.uk

ABANDONED IN DEATH

Three young women have gone missing. They're all pretty, mid-twenties — someone clearly has a type. But no one links their disappearances until the first — Lauren Elder — is found lying peacefully on a bench in a children's playground. She is neatly dressed with a wide black velvet ribbon covering where her neck has been precisely slit. Her hands are folded over a childish sign on which is written in black crayon — 'Bad Mommy!'.

Lt Eve Dallas and her team are brought in to investigate Lauren's murder and uncover the links to the other two women. Can they find out enough about the missing women and unmask their captor before they kill again . . . ?

J.D. ROBB

♦

ABANDONED IN DEATH

Complete and Unabridged

LARGE
PRINT

ISIS
Leicester

First published in Great Britain in 2022 by
Piatkus
An imprint of
Little, Brown Book Group
London

First Isis Edition
published 2022
by arrangement with
Little, Brown Book Group
London

*A catalogue record for this book is available
from the British Library.*

ISBN 978-1-39912-541-3

Mother is the name for God
in the lips and hearts of little children.
WILLIAM MAKEPEACE THACKERAY

Though this be madness,
yet there is method in 't.
WILLIAM SHAKESPEARE

1
BEFORE

The decision to kill herself brought her peace. Everything would be quiet and warm and soft. She could sleep, just sleep forever. Never again would she hide in the dark when the landlord banged on the door for the rent she couldn't pay.

Or climb out a window again, to take off. Again.

She wouldn't have to give blow jobs to some sweaty john to buy food. Or the pills, the pills she needed more than food.

The pills that made everything quiet, even the pain.

Maybe she'd even go to heaven, like it looked in the books in Bible study where everything was fluffy white clouds and golden light and everyone smiled.

Maybe she'd go to hell, with all the fire and the screaming and eternal damnation. Taking a life, even your own, was a big sin according to the Reverend Horace Greenspan, the recipient of her first BJ — payment and penance when he'd caught her lip-locked with Wayne Kyle Ribbet, and Wayne Kyle's hand under her shirt.

The experience had taught her, at age twelve, it was better to receive than give payment for such tedious services.

Still, suicide ranked as a bigger sin than blowing some grunting asshole for traveling money or a handful of Oxy. So maybe she'd go to hell.

But wasn't she there already?

1

Sick, half the time sick, and her skin on fire. Sleeping in her car more often than in a bed. Driving from one crap town to the next.

Trading sex in steamy alleys for pills.

It wasn't going to get better, not ever. She'd finally accepted that.

So she'd take the pills, enough of the pills so the quiet went on and on and on.

But before she did, she had to decide whether to take her little boy with her. Wouldn't he be better off, too?

She shifted her gaze to the rearview mirror to watch him. He sat in his grubby Spider-Man pj's, half-asleep as he munched from a bag of Fritos she'd grabbed from a machine when she'd pumped all but the last few dollars of her money into the gas tank. They kept him quiet, and she needed the quiet.

She hadn't had time — or just hadn't thought — to grab anything when she'd scooped him out of bed. She had money — nearly gone now — and pills — far too few of them — stuffed in her purse.

They didn't have much anyway, and what they did have she'd shoved into a trash bag weeks before. She had another couple of outfits for the kid — nothing clean. But she'd nearly gotten busted trying to lift a T-shirt and jeans for him from a Walmart in Birmingham.

If she got busted they'd take her kid, and he was the only thing completely hers. She'd wanted the best for him, hadn't she? She'd tried, hadn't she? Five years of trying after the asshole who got her pregnant told her to fuck off.

She'd done her best, but it wasn't enough. Never enough.

2

And the kid was no prize, she had to admit. Whiny and clingy, Christ knew, carrying on so she'd lost babysitters when she'd tried serving drinks or stripping it off in some hellhole.

But she loved the little son of a bitch, and he loved her.

'I'm thirsty, Mommy.'

Thirsty, hungry, tired, not tired. Always something. She'd seen motherhood as something holy once. Until she'd learned it was nothing but constant drudgery, demands, disappointments.

And she wasn't good enough, just like everyone had told her all her damn life.

She slowed enough to pass the bottle of Cherry Coke between the seats. 'Drink this.'

'Don't like that! Don't like it! I want orange soda pop! I want it! You're a bad mommy!'

'Don't say that. Now, don't you say that. You know it hurts my feelings.'

'Bad Mommy, Bad Mommy. I'm thirsty!'

'Okay, okay! I'll get you a drink when I find a place to stop.'

'Thirsty.' The whine cut through her brain like a buzz saw. 'Thirsty *now*!'

'I know, baby darling. We'll stop soon. How about we sing a song?' God, her head felt like a soggy apple full of worms.

If she could be sure, absolutely sure, she'd die from it, she'd swerve into an oncoming car and be done.

Instead, she started singing 'The Wheels on the Bus.' And when he sang with her, she was, for a moment, almost happy.

She'd put one of her pills in his drink, that's what she'd do. He'd sleep — she'd given him a portion of a

3

pill before when she'd needed him to sleep. But she'd give him a whole one, and wouldn't he just drift away to heaven?

He could have a puppy, and friends to play with, and all the toys he wanted. Orange soda pop by the gallon.

Little boys, even bratty ones, didn't go to hell.

She pulled off the highway and hunted up a twenty-four-hour mart. She parked well back from the lights where insects swarmed in clouds.

'You have to stay in the car. If you don't, I can't get you a drink. You stay in the car now, you hear? Be quiet, be good, and I'll get you some candy, too.'

'I want Skittles!'

'Then Skittles it'll be.'

The lights inside were so bright they burned her eyes, but she got him an orange Fanta and Skittles. She thought about sliding the candy into her purse, but she was too damn tired to bother.

It left her with less than a dollar in change, but she wouldn't need money where she was going anyway.

As she crossed back to the car, she dug out a pill from the zipped pocket in her purse. Thinking of puppies and toys and her baby darling giggling with the angels, she popped the tab and slipped it into the can.

This was best for both of them.

He smiled at her — sweet, sweet smile — and bounced on the seat when she came back.

'I love you, baby darling.'

'I love you, Mommy. Did you get my Skittles? Did ya? Are we going on another 'venture?'

'Yeah, I got 'em, and yeah, you bet. The biggest adventure yet. And when we get there, there'll be angels and flowers and puppy dogs.'

'Can I have a puppy? Can I, can I, can I? I want a puppy now!'

'You can have all the puppies.'

She looked back at him as he slurped some of the drink through the straw she'd stuck in the pop top. Her little towheaded man. He'd grown inside her, come out of her. She'd given up everything for him.

No one in her life had ever loved her as he did.

And she'd ruined it.

Windows open to the hot, thick air, she drove, not back to the highway, but aimlessly. Somewhere in Louisiana. Somewhere, but it didn't matter. She drove, just drove with the sweaty air blowing around her. Away from the strip malls, away from the lights.

He sang, but after a while his voice had that sleepy slur to it.

'Go to sleep now, baby darling. Just go to sleep now.'

He'd be better off, better off, wouldn't he be better off?

Tears tracked down her cheeks as she took a pill for herself.

She'd find a place, a dark, quiet place. She'd down the rest of the pills, then climb in the back with her baby boy. They'd go to heaven together.

God wouldn't take her away from her baby darling or him from her. He'd go to heaven, so she would, too. The God in Bible study had a long white beard, kind eyes. Light poured right out of his fingertips.

That was the way to heaven.

And she saw a light instead of the dark. It seemed to shine above a small white church sitting by itself on a little hill. Flowers bloomed around it, and grass grew neat and smooth.

She could smell it all through the open window.

5

Dazed, half dreaming, she stopped the car. This was heaven, or close enough. Close enough for her baby darling.

She carried him to it like an offering to the kind-eyed God with his white beard, to the angels with their spread wings and soft smiles.

He stirred as she laid him down by the door, whined for her.

'You sleep now, my baby darling. Just sleep.'

She stroked him awhile until he settled. He hadn't had enough of the drink, she thought, not enough to take him all the way to those angels and puppies. But maybe this was the best. Close to heaven, under the light, with flowers all around.

She walked back to the car that smelled of candy and sweat. He'd spilled the drink, she saw now, when he'd fallen asleep, and the Skittles were scattered over the back seat like colorful confetti.

He was in God's hands now.

She drove away, drove and drove with her mind floating on the drug. Happy now, no pain. So light, so light. She sang to him, forgetting he no longer sat in the back seat.

Her head didn't hurt now, and her hands didn't want to shake. Not with the night wind blowing over her face, through her hair. And the pill doing its magic.

Was she going to meet her friends? She couldn't quite remember.

What classes did she have in the morning?

It didn't matter, nothing mattered now.

When she saw the lake, and the moonlight on it, she sighed. There, of course. That's where she needed to go.

Like a baptism. A cleansing on the way to heaven.

Thrilled, she punched the gas and drove into the water. As the car started to sink, so slowly, she smiled, and closed her eyes.

NOW

Her name was Mary Kate Covino. She was twenty-five, an assistant marketing manager at Dowell and Associates. She'd started there straight out of college, and had climbed a couple of rungs since.

She liked her job.

She mostly liked her life, even though her jerk of a boyfriend had dumped her right before the romantic getaway she'd planned — meticulously — like a campaign.

Yesterday? The day before? She couldn't be sure. Everything blurred. It was June — June something — 2061.

She had a younger sister, Tara, a grad student at Carnegie Mellon. Tara was the smart one. And an older brother, Carter, the clever one. He'd just gotten engaged to Rhonda.

She had a roommate, Cleo — like another sister — and they shared a two-bedroom apartment on the Lower West Side.

She'd grown up in Queens and, though her parents had divorced when she'd been eleven, they'd all been pretty civilized about it. Both her parents had remarried — no stepsibs — but their second round was okay. Everybody stayed chill.

Her maternal grandparents — Gran and Pop — had given her a puppy for her sixth birthday. Best present

7

ever. Lulu lived a happy life until the age of fourteen when she'd just gone to sleep and hadn't woken up again.

She liked to dance, liked sappy, romantic vids, preferred sweet wines to dry, and had a weakness for her paternal grandmother's — Nonna's — sugar cookies.

She reminded herself of all this and more — her first date, how she'd broken her ankle skiing (first and last time) — every day. Multiple times a day.

It was essential she remember who she was, where she came from, and all the pieces of her life.

Because sometimes everything got twisted and blurred and out of sync, and she started to believe him.

She'd been afraid he'd rape her. But he never touched her that way. Never touched her at all — not when she was awake.

She couldn't remember how she'd gotten here. The void opened up after Teeg ditched her, and all the shouting, and the bitching, her walking home from the bar, half-drunk, unhappy. Berating herself for haunting the damn stupid bar he owned, putting in hours helping out four, even five nights a damn stupid week.

For nothing but one of his killer smiles.

Then she'd woken up here, feeling sick, her head pounding. In the dark, chained up — like something in a horror vid — in a dark room with a cot.

Then he'd come, the man, looking like someone's pale and bookish uncle.

He turned on a single light so she saw it was a basement, windowless, with concrete floors and walls of pargeted stone. He had sparkling blue eyes and snow-white hair.

8

He set a tray holding a bowl of soup, a cup of tea on the cot and just beamed at her.

'You're awake. Are you feeling better, Mommy?'

An accent, a twangy southern one with a child's cadence. She needed to remember that, but in the moment, she'd known only panic.

She'd begged him to let her go, wept, pulled against the shackles on her right wrist, left ankle.

He ignored her, simply went to a cupboard and took out clothes. He set them, neatly folded, on the bed.

'I know you haven't been feeling good, but I'm going to take care of you. Then you'll take care of me. That's what mommies do. They take care of their little boys.'

While she wept, screamed, demanded to know what he wanted, begged him to let her go, he just kept smiling with those sparkling eyes.

'I made you soup and tea, all by myself. You'll feel better when you eat. I looked and looked for you. Now here you are, and we can be together again. You can be a good mommy.'

Something came into those eyes that frightened her more than the dark, than the shackles.

'You're going to be a good mommy and take care of me the way you're supposed to this time. I made you soup, so you eat it! Or you'll be sorry.'

Terrified, she eased down on the cot, picked up the spoon. It was lukewarm and bland, but it soothed her raw throat.

'You're supposed to say *thank you*! You have to tell me I'm a good boy!'

'Thank you. I — I don't know your name.'

She thought he'd kill her then. His face turned red,

his eyes wild. His fisted hands pounded together.

'I'm your baby darling. Say it! Say it!'

'Baby darling. I'm sorry, I don't feel well. I'm scared.'

'I was scared when you locked me in a room so you could do ugly things with men. I was scared when you gave me things to make me sleep so you could do them. I was scared when I woke up sick and you weren't there, and it was dark and I cried and cried.'

'That wasn't me. Please, that wasn't me. I — You're older than me, so I can't be your mother. I didn't —'

'You go to hell for lying! To hell with the devil and the fire. You eat your soup and drink your tea or maybe I'll leave you all alone here like you left me.'

She spooned up soup. 'It's really good. You did a good job.'

Like a light switch, he beamed. 'All by myself.'

'Thanks. Ah, there's no one here to help you?'

'You're here now, Mommy. I waited a long, long time. People were mean to me, and I cried for you, but you didn't come.'

'I'm sorry. I . . . I couldn't find you. How did you find me?'

'I found three. Three's lucky, and one will be right. I'm tired now. It's my bedtime. When you're all better, you'll tuck me into bed like you should have before. And read me a story. And we'll sing songs.'

He started toward the door. 'The wheels on the bus go round and round.' He looked back at her, the face of a man easily sixty singing in the voice of a child. 'Good night, Mommy.' That fierceness came back into his eyes. 'Say *good night, baby darling*!'

'Good night, baby darling.'

He closed the door behind him. She heard locks

10

snap into place.

She heard other things in the timeless void of that windowless room. Voices, screaming, crying. Sometimes she thought the voices were her own, the screams her own, and sometimes she knew they weren't.

But when she called out, no one came.

Once she thought she heard banging on the wall across the room, but she was so tired.

She knew he put drugs in the food, but when she didn't eat, he turned off all the lights and left her in the dark until she did.

Sometimes he didn't speak with the child's voice, the accent, but with a man's. So reasonable, so definite.

One night, he didn't come at all, not with food, not to demand she change her clothes. She had three outfits to rotate. He didn't come to sit and smile that terrifying smile and ask for a song or a story.

She'd die here, slowly starving to death, alone, chained, trapped, because he'd forgotten her, or gotten hit by a car.

But no, no, someone had to be looking for her. She had friends and family. Someone was looking for her.

Her name was Mary Kate Covino. She was twenty-five.

As she went through her daily litany, she heard shouting — him. His voice high-pitched, like the bratty child he became when upset or angry. Then another voice . . . No, she realized, still his, but his man's voice. A coldly angry man's voice.

And the weeping, the begging. That was female.

She couldn't make out the words, just the sounds of anger and desperation.

She dragged herself over to the wall, pressed against

11

it, hoping to hear. Or be heard.

'Please help me. Help me. Help me. I'm here. I'm Mary Kate, and I'm here.'

Someone screamed. Something crashed. Then everything went quiet.

She beat her fists bloody on the wall, shouted for someone to help.

The door to her prison burst open. He stood there, eyes wild and mad, his face and clothes splattered with blood. And blood still dripping from the knife in his hand.

'Shut up!' He took a step toward her. 'You shut the fuck up!' And another.

She didn't know where it came from, but she shouted out: 'Baby darling!' And he stopped. 'I heard terrible sounds, and I thought someone was hurting you. I couldn't get to you, baby darling. I couldn't protect you. Someone hurt my baby darling.'

'She lied!'

'Who lied, baby darling?'

'She pretended to be Mommy, but she wasn't. She called me names and tried to hurt me. She slapped my face! But I hurt her. You go to hell when you lie, so she's gone to hell.'

He'd killed someone, someone like her. Killed someone with the knife, and would kill her next.

Through the wild fear came a cold, hard will. One to survive.

'Oh, my poor baby darling. Can you take these . . . bracelets off so I can take care of you?'

Some of the mad fury seemed to die out of his eyes. But a kind of shrewdness replaced it. 'She lied, and she's in hell. Remember what happens when you lie. Now you have to be quiet. Number one's in hell, so number two can clean up the mess. Mommy cleans up messes. Maybe you'll be lucky number three. But if you're not quiet, if you make my head hurt, you'll be unlucky.'

'I could clean up for you.'

'It's not your turn!'

He stomped out, and for the first time didn't shut and lock the door. Mary Kate shuffled over as close as she could. She couldn't reach the door, but at last she could see out of it.

A kind of corridor — stone walls, concrete floor — harshly lit. And another door almost directly across from hers. Bolted from the outside.

Number two? Another woman, another prisoner. She started to call out, but heard him coming back.

Survive, she reminded herself, and went back to the cot, sat.

He didn't have the knife now, but a tall cup. Some sort of protein shake, she thought. He'd pushed one on her before. Drugged. More drugs.

'Baby darling —'

'I don't have time now. She ruined everything. You drink this because it has nutrition.'

'Why don't I make you something to eat? You must be hungry.'

He looked at her, and she thought he seemed almost sane again. And when he spoke, his voice sounded calm and easy. 'You're not ready.' When he stroked a hand over her hair, she fought not to shudder. 'Not nearly. But I think you will be. I hope so.'

She felt the quick pinch of the pressure syringe.

'I don't have time. You can drink this when you wake up. You have to be healthy. Lie down and go to sleep. I'm going to be very busy.'

13

She started to fade when he walked to the door. And heard the bolt snap home when she melted down on the cot.

* * *

He had a plan. He always had a plan. And he had the tools.

With meticulous stitches — he was a meticulous man — he sewed the neck wound on the fraud. Over the wound he fastened a wide black velvet ribbon.

It looked, to his eye, rather fetching.

He'd already cut her hair before bringing her — with so much hope! — to this stage. Now he brushed it, used some of the product to style it properly.

He'd washed her, very carefully, so not a drop of blood remained, before he'd chosen the outfit.

While he worked, he had one of Mommy's songs playing.

'I'm coming up,' he sang along with Pink, 'so you better get this party started.'

Once he had her dressed, he started on her makeup. He'd always loved watching her apply it. All the paints and powders and brushes.

He painted her nails — fingers and toes — a bright, happy blue. Her favorite color. He added the big hoop earrings, and he'd already added the other piercings, so fit studs into the second hole and the cartilage of her left ear.

And the little silver bar in her navel.

She'd liked shoes with high, high heels and pointy toes, even though she mostly wore tennis shoes. But he remembered how she'd looked at the high ones in store windows, and sometimes they went in so she

14

could try them on.

Just pretending, baby darling, she'd told him. Just playing dress-up.

So he slipped her feet into ones she'd have wished for. A little tight, but it didn't matter.

And as a final tribute, spritzed her body with Party Girl, her favorite scent.

When he was done, when he'd done his very best, he took a picture of her. He'd frame it, keep it to remind him.

'You're not Mommy, but I wanted you to be. You shouldn't have lied, so you have to leave. If you hadn't, we could've been happy.'

Number two and number three were sleeping. He hoped number two had learned a lesson — you had to learn your lessons — when he'd made her clean up the mess.

Tomorrow, he'd cut her hair the right way and give her the tattoo and the piercings. And she'd see all she had to do was be a good mommy, and stay with him always, take care of him always.

And they'd be happy forever.

But the Fake Mommy had to leave.

He rolled her out on the gurney — a man with a plan — out through the door and into the garage. After opening the cargo doors, he rolled her — with some effort — up the ramp and into the van.

He secured the gurney — couldn't have it rolling around! — then got behind the wheel. Though it was disappointing, he'd known he would probably go through more than one before finding the *right* one, so he already knew where to take her.

He drove carefully out of the garage and waited until the doors rumbled down closed behind him.

It had to be far enough away from the home he and Mommy would make so the police didn't come knocking to ask questions. But not so far away he had to take too much time getting there.

Accidents happened.

It had to be quiet, with no one to see. Even at this time of night in New York, you had to know where to find quiet. So the little playground seemed perfect.

Children didn't play at three in the morning. No, they did not! Even if they had to sleep in the car because the mean landlord kicked them out, they didn't play so late.

He parked as close as he could, and worked quickly. He wore black coveralls and booties over his shoes. A cap that covered his hair. He'd sealed his hands, but wore gloves, too. Nothing showed. Nothing at all.

He rolled the gurney right up to the bench where good mommies would watch their children play in the sunshine.

He laid her on it like she was sleeping, and put the sign he'd made with construction paper and black crayon over her folded hands.

It said what she was.

Bad Mommy!

He went back to the van and drove away. Drove back and into the garage, into the house.

He had the house because she'd left him. He had the house because she'd given him the deed and the keys and the codes and everything.

But he didn't want everything. He only wanted one thing.

His mommy.

16

In the quiet house he changed into his pajamas. He washed his hands and face and brushed his teeth like a good boy.

In the glow of the night-light, he climbed into bed.

He fell asleep with a smile on his face and dreamed the dreams of the young and innocent.

17

2

In the shallow light just beyond dawn, Lieutenant Eve Dallas badged through the police barriers to study the body on the bench.

A tall woman, and lean with it, Eve took in the details. The position and condition of the body, the distance of the bench from the street, from buildings.

A faint breeze stirred air that, while morning cool, teased of summer. It fluttered around Eve's cap of choppy brown hair and stirred some cheerful scent from a concrete barrel of flowers by the bench.

For once her partner had beaten her to the scene, but then Detective Peabody lived only blocks away. Peabody, in her pink coat and cowboy boots, heaved out a sigh.

'Really close to home.'

'Yeah.' Eve judged the victim as mid-twenties, Caucasian female. She lay peacefully and fully dressed with her hands folded over a childish sign that deemed her a Bad Mommy.

'Run it down for me,' Eve said.

'First on scene responded to a flag-down at approximately zero-six-forty-five. A female licensed companion got out of a cab on the corner, walked down toward her apartment.' Peabody pointed west. 'When she passed the bench, she saw the victim. She assumed sidewalk sleeper, and states that since she had a really good night, she was going to leave a few bucks on the bench. And when she started to, realized, not sleeping. Started to tag nine-one-one, then saw the cruiser make the turn, so she flagged the cops down. We've got all her info, so Officer Steppe escorted her home.'

'Did you ID the vic?'

'Lauren Elder, age twenty-six. She lived on West Seventeenth. Cohab, Roy Mardsten, filed a missing persons on her ten days ago. She tended bar at Arnold's — upper-class bar on West Fourteenth Street — I've been there. She didn't come home from work the night of May twenty-eighth. Detective Norman, out of the four-three, caught it.'

'TOD, COD?'

'Hadn't gotten that far. McNab — here he comes.'

Eve glanced over to see Peabody's main dish, Electronic Detectives Division's hotshot, jog toward them.

The strengthening sun couldn't hold a candle to the orange-glow tee under a floppy knee-length jacket the color of irradiated plums matched with baggies of mad colors that might have been spray-painted by insane toddlers.

His sunny ponytail swung; his forest of ear hoops sparkled.

'No cams on this area,' he told them. 'Low security, quiet neighborhood. Sorry.'

'Since you're here, you can knock on doors with the first on scene. See if anyone saw her dumped here.'

With her record on, Eve crouched, opened her field kit. 'Victim's identified as Elder, Lauren, female, age twenty-six, missing since May twenty-eight. And held against her will by the look of the marks on her right wrist and left ankle. Her clothes appear undisturbed. If there was sexual assault, the killer dressed her again.'

Frowning, Eve sniffed, leaned closer, sniffed again. 'She's wearing perfume.'

'Full makeup, too,' Peabody commented. 'Perfect makeup, and her hair's unmussed.'

'Yeah, nail polish looks fresh. A woman held against her will isn't usually so worried about appearance. He fixed her up, that's how it went. Bad Mommy. She doesn't look like a mom, does she? More like the let's-party type. Maybe mommy's a sexual deal here.'

Frowning again, she pulled out microgoggles, bent down to the midriff exposed by the short, glittery top. 'This belly bar thing? I think that's recent. It's still a little red. ME to confirm, but that looks fresh to me. Why does anyone stick holes in their navels?'

'If I had those abs . . .'

Eve spared Peabody a glance. 'Odds are she didn't get a choice about the piercing.' With one finger, Eve loosened the black ribbon. 'Or having her throat cut.'

'Jesus, he stitched her back up.'

'And carefully. Definitely the dump spot. He didn't do all this to her here. And there's your COD.' She took out a gauge. 'TOD twenty-two-twenty. Perfume's stronger up by the throat. Let's see if we can get a sample for the lab.'

'I'm betting there's product in her hair.' With a sealed finger, Peabody touched the victim's hair. 'Yeah, it's got setting gel, maybe spray, too. To hold that spiky style.'

'We've got Harvo, Queen of Hair and Fiber. She'll nail that down. Our perp left us a lot. We can ID the makeup, any hair gunk, maybe the nail polish. Let's find out if these are her clothes, because maybe not.'

Curious, she pried off one of the shoes. 'A little tight. Not her size. Same polish on the toes, and perfect. She's really clean, too. No way you can be shackled for over a week and stay this clean and shiny. So he washed her. Maybe they can ID what he used on her.'

'I'm not seeing any other injuries. Nothing to indicate he knocked her around.' Peabody secured a swab, bagged it.

'Let's turn her over.'

Together they rolled the body.

'Tattoo, lower back. A big butterfly, blue with yellow markings. This is fresh, too, Peabody. It can't be more than a few days old. It's not all the way healed.'

'It looks professional. I mean it sure doesn't look like a home job. A way of branding her?' Peabody wondered. 'The tat, the piercing.'

'Maybe. Making her into some image. This is what I want, so this is how you'll look. Is she blond in her ID shot?'

'Yeah, but her hair's longer, past her chin. Smooth bob in the ID shot.'

Peabody shook back her own dark hair with the red tips, brought up the photo on her PPC. 'And see? The makeup's more subtle, more natural. Nothing on here, since I'm looking for identifying marks, like a tat.'

'Image somewhere in the perp's head,' Eve concluded. 'And she was adjusted to fit it. Her next of kin's in Flatbush.' Eve scanned the details on Peabody's handheld. 'Both parents. We'll take the wit, the cohab, then do the notification. Let's call in the sweepers and the morgue, then we'll get a follow-up statement from the LC.'

Eve stepped back, looked at the playground, the climbing things, the sliding things, the spinning things.

'This is going to be Bella's playground when Mavis and Leonardo move into the new house. And you and McNab. Hell, number-two kid when it gets here.'

21

'Yeah, like I said, close to home.'

Eve's eyes narrowed. 'We're going to bust the killer's ass for murder, and we're going to bust it for screwing with Bella's playground.'

The witness couldn't add anything, so they drove to the victim's apartment.

'Decent security,' Eve noted, studying the building. She bypassed the buzzers, mastered through the locks into a small lobby. 'Clean. We're going to three.' And ignoring the set of elevators, took the stairs.

'She worked at Arnold's four years.' Peabody read off the data as they climbed. 'College before that, hospitality major. Busted for disorderly conduct twice. Looks like college protests. No marriages, this was her first official cohab. Parents — married twenty-nine years — in Flatbush. She was the oldest of three. Brothers, age twenty-four and twenty. Oldest is in grad school, youngest in college, and both list their primary address with the parents.'

Eve heard the mumble of morning shows behind closed doors when they came out on three. Otherwise, the floor was nearly as quiet as the stairway.

She pressed the buzzer on 305. No palm plate, no door cam, she noted, but solid locks and a Judas hole.

She saw the shadow pass over the peep.

Those locks snapped open quickly. Roy Mardsten stood about six-two in bare feet. He wore suit pants and a dress shirt still untucked, and held a mug that smelled like fake coffee.

He wore his gold-streaked black hair in short dreads that crowned his rawboned, dark-skinned face. His eyes, wide, deep, latched onto Eve's.

He said, 'Lauren.'

'Mr. Mardsten, I'm Lieutenant Dallas —'

'I know who you are. I've seen you in court. I saw the vid. I know who you are. Lauren. God, Lauren. Say it fast. Please, say it fast.'

She'd already broken his world, Eve thought, and said it fast.

'I regret to inform you Lauren Elder is dead.'

His hand went limp. Instinctively Eve reached out, grabbed the mug before the contents spilled. 'Can we come in?'

'I knew. I knew, but I hoped. I kept thinking, she's so strong and smart and . . . But I knew because she'd never just — I need to . . . '

He turned, walked to one of the two chairs in a compact living area. A ruthlessly clean one with a small sofa, a few tables, a lot of street art. A pair of windows, uncurtained but privacy screened, looked out over the street.

He sat, seemed to shrink into himself, then got up again to circle the room. 'I can't. Just can't. I need . . . '

'Mr. Mardsten.' Peabody spoke gently. 'Could I get you some water?'

'No. No. Nothing. Lauren. Lauren. She didn't come home. She didn't answer her 'link. Buddy said she left at two-thirty. Night shift, she had the night shift, so I was sleeping, and it was morning before I knew she didn't come home. I went to bed and she didn't come home.'

He turned back, those wide, deep eyes full of tears. 'I was sleeping.'

Not shock, Eve thought, because some part of him had known. But grief, overwhelming.

'Can we sit down, Roy?'

'I should've waited up.'

'It wouldn't have mattered.' Taking his arm, Eve led

23

him back to the chair. She set his coffee on the table beside him, took the second chair. 'I'm sorry for your loss, Roy, and we're going to do everything we can to find who hurt Lauren. We need your help.'

'It's only a few blocks to walk. We got this place because it's only a few blocks.'

'How long have you lived here?' Peabody asked, though she'd already read the data.

'Six months. We — we started seeing each other a year ago, a year in March, and we got this place together. We . . . ' He shut his eyes, ignored the tears that tracked down his cheeks. 'Doesn't matter. She matters. What happened? What happened to Lauren?'

'You're a law student?' Eve asked.

'Yeah. Yeah. I'm working at Delroy, Gilby, and Associates this summer, and taking a couple of night classes so I can get my degree this fall.'

'What kind of law?'

'Criminal. I want to work for the PA, I want to prosecute criminals.' Heat burned through the tears. 'Now more than ever. I know I have to pull myself together. I know I have to answer questions. I know how this part works, but please, please, tell me what happened to Lauren.'

'If you understand how this works, you know we're in the very beginning stages of the investigation. We can surmise Lauren was abducted on the night of May twenty-eighth. You filed a missing persons report.'

'Detective Norman.'

'Yes, and we'll coordinate with him.'

'He said she left the bar like Buddy said. They were the last ones, they closed. And they left, and he walked to the subway, and she started home. Buddy wouldn't hurt her, okay? He's a friend, and they checked, they

24

checked the cams in the subway and everything. And he — the detective — couldn't find anybody who saw her after.'

'He would've asked, but I'm asking, do you know of anyone who'd want to hurt her? An ex?'

'No. I mean she dated before me, but we've been together more than a year, and people move on. She wasn't stressed about anything or anyone. She never said anything about somebody bothering her or watching her. There was nothing. She'd have told me.'

He picked up the coffee, set it down again. 'Did he — they — Was she raped?'

'The medical examiner will determine that, but she was fully dressed. What was she wearing when she went to work?'

'Detective Norman asked that. They have kind of a uniform at Arnold's. So black pants, a white shirt. She wore her black low-tops because she's on her feet behind the bar.'

'Jewelry?'

'Ah . . . I gave her a ring when we moved in. Not like an engagement ring because we weren't ready for that. But a silver band, a thumb ring, so that, and her wrist unit. Her parents gave her a nice one last Christmas. She isn't much for a lot of it, but she usually wore these little ruby studs, shaped like hearts. Ruby's her birthstone, and her grandparents gave them to her when she turned twenty-one.'

'One for each ear?'

'Yeah. She's kind of conservative.'

'So, no other piercings, no tats?'

'Lauren?' A ghost of a smile came and went. 'Oh no. Wait.' He jerked up. 'Maybe it's not her? You're not sure it's Lauren?'

25

'I'm sorry, we're sure.'

'How? I mean how did she die? What did they do to her? I'm not going to fall apart again, okay? I need to know.'

'There were abrasions and lacerations on one of her wrists and one of her ankles that indicate she was restrained for some time. My on-scene examination indicates a severe neck wound caused her death.'

'They . . . they cut her throat.' He closed his eyes, then covered his face. 'One second, give me a second. Her family. I have to tell her family. We talk every day. They're going crazy, and I have to tell them.'

'We're going to notify her family when we leave here. It's best if we tell them. Could we see the bedroom?'

'The bedroom? Oh, sure. I have a little office, too. It's more of a closet, but you can look in there. I can open the comp for you. You can look at anything that will help.'

'We appreciate that.'

He rubbed his eyes; Eve saw his shoulders tremble before he stiffened them.

'I need to contact my supervisor. She gave me her personal contact when Lauren went missing. I need to tell her I'm not coming in.'

'That's fine.'

'When can I see her? When can we — her family and I — see her?'

'I'll let you know as soon as that's cleared. Roy, the ME? She couldn't be in better hands.'

'I remember from the vid, and I've seen him in court, too. You'll find who did this. You'll find who treated her this way.'

When they left, Eve had a good sense of her victim.

Lauren Elder had close family ties. Her mother had done several of the street scenes on the walls, and she kept a photo of her family on her dresser — a beach vacation scene from the background — and with everyone mugging for the camera.

She'd kept her clothes — a little on the conservative side, Peabody had confirmed — ordered in the closet she'd shared with her cohab. She hadn't gone for a lot of frills, a lot of sparkles. Her ambitions had run to one day owning her own bar. She'd kept a memory book of photos — family, her circle of friends, co-workers — so loyal and sentimental.

She'd lived within her means, and kept a careful record of tips — considerable, which led Eve to believe she'd been good at her job.

No nail polish and minimal makeup in her supply.

Whoever the killer had wanted her to be, she hadn't matched the image inside.

'They made a nice place.' Peabody settled in for the drive to Brooklyn. 'You can tell most of the furniture's family castoffs, but they made it nice. I don't think he's going to be able to stay there now. It's too much them.'

'He's been waiting for us to knock on the door since she went missing. He wasn't ready, because you never are, but he's been waiting for us.'

Her family wouldn't be ready, either, she thought.

'Contact Detective Norman, fill him in, and get his files. We'll need to talk to the staff at the bar, so let's see if we can set that up, at least to start with Buddy, since he was the last we know of who saw her.'

'Buddy's his actual birth name. Buddy James Wilcox. Who names their kid Buddy?'

'Buddy's parents. She had a routine,' Eve continued,

and whipped around a slow-moving mini. 'Roy said she'd had the seven-to-closing shift for the last eight months. They'd try to grab dinner together about six, and she'd head to work by six-forty-five. He'd head to his night class at the same time. Except for Sundays when they both had off, Mondays for her, and Saturdays for him. Some Saturdays he'd hang out at the bar for a while, but mostly he studied. Work nights, she walked home between two-fifteen and two-thirty. Same route. Three blocks north, one east.'

'She was nabbed on that route.'

'Did he get lucky or did he know her routine? He knew, that's how I see it. She was a type he wanted. Need a consult with Mira, but that's what plays. Her age, coloring, build. Something about her hit the marks, and he could do the rest with the clothes, the tat, the hair.'

'He kept her for ten days,' Peabody added. 'Plenty of time to make those adjustments.'

'The tat, at least, is fresher than ten days. I think.'

'A good-sized tat, with detail,' Peabody pointed out. 'Had to take a couple of hours.'

'Precise work, maybe a pro. But is she going to stay still while you're poking all those needles into her flesh?'

Even the thought of it had Eve's back muscles quivering.

'You could strap her down, but there'd be movement if she was conscious.'

'I'm going to get a tat.'

In reflex, Eve nearly hit the brakes. 'What? Why? What?'

'Not right now this minute. I have to decide on what and where. Just a little one.' Peabody held up her thumb and index finger to indicate an inch or two.

28

'I'm down to the back of my shoulder or my ankle. Something girlie maybe.'

'Something girlie, carved into your living flesh. Forever.'

'That's why it has to be the exact right symbol or image.'

'Tiny needles injecting ink into your body. Which you pay for. On purpose.'

'Maybe a thistle — Scottish symbol — because McNab. But maybe a rainbow.'

'You could do two rainbows. One on each ass cheek.'

'Or a crescent moon with a little star,' Peabody continued, unperturbed. 'Those are my top contenders right now. It's a big decision.'

'Yeah, paying somebody to pump ink into your skin's a big one. Now, let's move on from voluntary self-mutilation and back to murder.'

'Self-expression. Body art.'

'Whatever.' The entire conversation just weirded her out. Murder, at least, Eve understood.

'We'll see what Elder's tox says, but I think it's a safe bet she was drugged for a good portion of those ten days. Still, you need a nice private place to do all of that. You need transport.'

'Private residence, or exceptional soundproofing in a multiunit. With a multiunit you'd need a private entrance. Someplace to keep a vehicle. Maybe a private garage for the whole deal.'

'Did she know the killer? From the bar, her old neighborhood, her new one? He rolls up — 'Hey, Lauren.'.'

'Bartenders are usually friendly types. It's part of the job. But why would she willingly get in a vehicle when she's only blocks from home?'

29

'Check the weather the night she went missing. Otherwise, maybe he lured her in. 'Hey, Lauren, take a look at this.' Or he's parked along the route, maybe looks like he needs help with something. Or just grabs. He got her into the vehicle. No head wounds that showed on scene, but if he bashed her that could've healed up, and Morris will find it. Jabbed her with a drug, that's more likely.

'Jab, load her in, drive away.' Eve played it out like a vid in her head. 'It wouldn't take half a minute.'

'Partly cloudy, no precipitation, low of sixty-two on May twenty-eighth.' Peabody lowered her PPC. 'Not the kind of night you'd jump into a vehicle for a couple of blocks.'

She'd walk the route, Eve thought. Family notification had to come first, but she wanted to walk in Lauren's footsteps, see what she'd seen.

'If she didn't know him, how did he choose her? He had to see her to want her, had to want her to choose her. At the bar? Is he from the neighborhood? Say he spots her, studies her, decides on her. Maybe he starts parking the vehicle along the route so she gets used to seeing it. Doesn't think anything of it.'

She rolled it around and around as she crossed the bridge into Brooklyn.

'Who's Mommy? That's going to matter. If it represents a sexual thing, he'd rape her. Or she'd rape her if the killer's female. If Mommy's Mommy, that's fifty-fifty.'

'Ew.'

'Didn't Octopus have a mommy deal?'

'Octopus? I don't think they screw with their mothers. Do they know their mothers? How do they know?' Peabody wondered. 'They all have weird heads and

30

tentacles.'

'No, the guy with the complex, and the mother banging and the eyes.'

'Oedipus. I think. I think Oedipus.'

'Octopus, Oedipus, all creepy. So maybe the perp wants to bang his mom, but mom isn't all about that, so he creates a substitute. Or she was, and that fucked him up, so a substitute. Or it's some other mom deal, and he doesn't want to bang her.'

'Why kill her once you create her?'

'She's not the real deal. And she's not banging him right, or giving him what he needs. She's not the original. He was always going to kill her.'

'Why do you think?'

'Because he's shithouse crazy, Peabody. You don't do all this unless you're shithouse crazy. Ten days, ten months, whatever, the crazy's going to crack through the control eventually. The perfection of the tat, the piercings, the makeup, the hair, the clothes. That's control, precision. So he's got to have that, but under it? Shithouse crazy.'

And following that logic, Peabody turned to Eve. 'He's going to need another substitute.'

'Yeah, so let's hope he doesn't already have one picked out.'

Eve followed her in-dash directions to a pretty house with a pretty yard on a block of pretty houses and yards.

'Father's a mechanic — owns his own place,' Peabody began.' Mother's an artist — you saw some of her stuff in the vic's apartment. She runs a local gallery. I'd guess both the sibs are home from college for the summer. Somebody's probably home.'

'Let's find out.'

31

Eve got out of the car and prepared to destroy someone else's world.

★ ★ ★

By the time they'd finished, the emotional overload had a headache trying to drill through the crown of her head. She programmed coffee, black for her, regular for Peabody.

'They reminded me of my family.' Peabody let out a sigh. 'Not Free-Agers, but they're tight. They'll get through it, but nothing's ever going to be exactly the same.'

'You can check out the couple of ex-boyfriends they gave us. If nothing else, it'll block that avenue. We'll take the bar next, then you can split off, check out the exes, for what it's worth. I'll take the morgue. Morris should have at least started on her by the time I get there.'

'Need to close off the avenue,' Peabody agreed, 'but I can't see either of the exes they gave us. I think we're looking for older.'

So did she, but Eve glanced over at her partner. 'Why?'

'It's that control and precision. It's not that somebody in their twenties or early thirties can't have it, and we've dealt with younger organized killers, but you add the control and precision with needing, almost for sure, a private space, a vehicle. And the killer could be female. Daughters have mom issues, too. She'd have to be strong enough to load a struggling or unconscious woman into a vehicle. Unless we have a team. And it could be. Siblings even.'

'Siblings.' Eve considered it. 'Both obsessed,

severely pissed or sexually attracted to their mother? Not impossible. Interesting even. Easier for two to do the snatch and grab, the transporting. But the kill was one stroke from the look of it. Then again, the second could have done the sewing up. You'd think that and the ribbon covering the wound could be signs of remorse, then the sign contradicts that. The sign was like a kid's printing, and with the thing.'

'Crayon.'

'Right. A kid thing. Made her pretty — or his/her/ their version of pretty. Dressed her up, put her near a playground — another kid thing. Who's Mommy? His/her/their mommy. Is she still alive, already dead?'

'Mommy didn't have much fashion sense,' Peabody commented. 'I mean her clothes were just tacky.'

'Cheap. Maybe she couldn't afford better ones. The jeans were ripped.'

'I've seen pictures of my granny in jeans with holes in the legs. When she was younger.'

'A Free-Ager thing? Don't all you guys sew? Wouldn't she sew up the holes or whatever?'

'I don't know. Maybe it was a thing. I'll check into it. But the top — really short — and all spangles, the shoes — really dressy, and tacky, out of style — shoes with the weird jeans? Comes off kind of slutty, especially with the overdone makeup.'

Fashion might not have been Eve's area of expertise — by a long shot — but she followed Peabody's line.

'Mommy could've been kind of slutty — which may be part of the issue. Or he/she/they see her that way. Or he/she/they want Mommy to be slutty. I really need to talk this out with Mira. We've got to find the logic in the shithouse crazy, so we need a shrink.'

33

With the manager's cooperation, they spent an hour at Arnold's interviewing coworkers. More tears, no new information, and more confirmation of Eve's sense that the victim had a solid, happy life, enjoyed her job, her circle.

The bar struck her as solid as well, if a little pretentious. It wasn't the casual neighborhood place you'd belly up for a brew, but where you'd take a date to impress, or a client to ply with a fancy drink served in a fancy glass on a table with low lights flickering in a little potted plant.

It served tidbits like organic squash blossoms and goat cheese truffles. She couldn't see ever being hungry enough to put either in her mouth.

When she said so, outside the bar, Peabody shook her head.

'They're pretty terrific, and the pancetta crisps are totally mag. You could make a meal.'

'You make a meal. Later. Go into Central, check out the exes, update Detective Norman, and get me a time slot with Mira. I'm going to walk the vic's route and back before I hit the morgue.'

They split off, and Eve walked in the not-quite-warm late-spring sunshine. She saw some tourists, who never seemed to know how to actually walk on a sidewalk, several kids and babies in various pushcart things, a man walking a pair of tiny, hairless dogs who could've passed for large rats.

They yip-yip-yipped, darting at her boots as she passed, and the man scolded them in sugary tones.

'Now, now, Sugar and Spice, be good doggies.'

She saw well-maintained homes, tidy buildings,

34

busy shops, restaurants with patrons sitting outside in the spring air sipping drinks or having lunch.

A few homes had front yards separated from the pedestrians by fences more ornamental than functional. Flowers bloomed or spilled out of pots on doorsteps. A team of three efficiently washed the windows on a duplex. A woman carrying a pair of market bags hurried up to the door of another.

Traffic streamed by, almost pleasantly.

It was hard to beat New York in the spring. Nothing could beat it for her at any time, but spring added some shine.

She stopped in front of the victim's apartment again. Roy still had the privacy screens engaged. In the apartment below his, a woman sat on the windowsill, busily washing the window.

It seemed to be the day for it.

As she started back, she decided a decent vehicle parked along the route wouldn't cause attention. A beater, now, would, but a decent ride, a clean one, who'd notice?

And the vic's block — especially the vic's block — would be quiet at night. Almost entirely residential, and the restaurants would be shuttered, the bakery and deli closed.

A five-minute walk at night, a couple minutes more if she'd taken it at a stroll. Less if she'd jogged it.

Home base, familiar. No worries.

And in seconds — it would only have taken seconds — everything changed.

And all because, Eve was sure of it, she'd looked just enough like someone else.

Bad Mommy.

3

Eve walked the long white tunnel of the morgue, bootsteps echoing. Her thoughts focused on the victim, and that last walk toward home. Odds were she'd been at least a little tired, and likely moving briskly.

Young, in familiar territory, heading home in the night quiet of a good neighborhood.

An easy mark for someone with a plan in place.

The questions remained: Why the plan? Why her?

She pushed through one of the doors to Morris's domain and saw he had his sealed hands inside the chest cavity of her victim.

Music murmured, something with a lot of low-note brass and a woman singing about love lost.

He looked up, smiled. 'An early start on the day for you, and a very early end for her.'

He wore a blue suit, a bold color that told her his mood hit high. He'd matched it with a shirt the color of ripe pears and a tie that blended the two tones in subtle swirls. He'd braided his long, dark hair in some complicated pattern that formed a coil at the back of his neck.

He weighed an internal organ with easy efficiency.

Eve moved closer, looked down on the body, naked and open now.

'I think her end, in a lot of ways, happened the night of May twenty-eighth.'

'The lacerations and contusions on the wrist and ankle. Some would meet that date, some are more recent. Shackled, and the cuffs would be an inch and

36

three-quarters wide. Some other minor contusions, as you can see — the other ankle, the knees, elbows.'

'The other ankle, from banging into the shackle.'

'Yes. And the others, minor, as I said. Not consistent with violence. He didn't beat her, and he didn't rape her. There's no sign of sexual assault, or consensual sex, not recent.'

Morris walked over to a sink to rinse the blood off his hands. 'She's very clean. Her hair, her body, recently and thoroughly washed — her hair styled. The makeup, as you can see, very carefully applied.'

'I think he had an image, and she was like a doll, you know?'

With a nod, Morris walked to his mini-friggie, took out a tube of Pepsi for both of them. 'I do, and had the same thought. She was a form, and he used that form to create the image he wanted. Both the makeup and hairstyle are dated, as was the clothing.'

'Were they?'

Now he grinned as he opened the tubes, handed her one. 'For someone who dresses so well, you have a sketchy knowledge of fashion and its history.'

'Roarke's always putting stuff in my closet. How dated?'

'Turn of the century, I'd guess, or the first few years of it. But it shouldn't be difficult to get a solid time frame.'

'Where'd he get them? Did he have them already, and she fit the build, the size?' Frowning, Eve circled the body. 'Maybe. Mostly fit, because the shoes were too small.'

'Correct there. She'd have been closer to a size eight than the seven and a half of the shoes he put on her.'

'Tougher to gauge a shoe size than clothes, I'd

37

think. Jeans were a little tight. You can see where they dug in.'

'Again slightly off her size.'

'So he already had them, or just needed her to be the size he wanted.'

'Possibly. I can tell you that other than being dead, she was healthy. No sign of illegals abuse, alcohol abuse. Her last meal, consumed about five hours before TOD, consisted of a few ounces of grilled chicken, some brown rice and peas.'

'So he kept her fed.'

'And hydrated. She drank tea.'

'No signs of torture.'

'None, but I've sent the contents to the lab, and we'll have a tox report shortly, I hope. The tat, the belly piercings, the third ear and the ear cartilage piercings were done within the last seventy-two hours. She was alive for those. But her nails? This is a fresh mani-pedi. These nails were recently shaped. Postmortem.'

Maybe somebody who worked on the dead in funeral and memorial venues. Somebody who fixed them up like they were just sleeping for the mourners. Maybe.

'Bad Mommy — that's what he wrote, left on her.'

'Yes, I saw the recording.'

'She doesn't look like the standard image of Mommy, right?'

'They come in all shapes and sizes.'

Eve drank absently, gave a flickering thought to her own. Far from standard. 'I guess so. If the victim was a surrogate, we'd be looking for someone about this build, likely this coloring, with the tat, the piercings, who was in this general age range — or looked like it — around the turn of the century.'

She circled the other way.

'Or he just wanted to play with a doll, and has an old-fashioned sense of style.'

She stopped. 'The neck wound and repair.'

'No hesitation marks. One quick stroke. Smooth, sharp blade. About four inches long. I'd look for a folding knife. A good, sharp pocketknife.'

Now her eyes narrowed. 'A pocketknife.'

'Smooth, short, straight blade. No jags, no angles. He faced her to kill her. A left to right slice, so right-handed.'

Nodding, she ran it through her head. 'Makes sense. Why would he have a knife — a sharp — sitting around anywhere near a woman he's holding against her will? Pocketknife.'

She pulled her own out of her pocket, hit the button to flip out the blade. 'But you're carrying it, you're done with her, just take it out. It's more of the moment. She does or says something, hasn't done or said something. He's pissed, and swipe. Done.'

'A single slice, no hesitation marks, so yes, it could be in the moment. The stitching, now, is precise, like the rest of his work. Careful and meticulous. I sent the thread to the lab. It may be upholstery thread — stronger and thicker than what you'd use to sew on a button, for instance. And the needle would be the same, thicker, likely longer than a standard sewing needle. More like what I'll use to close this Y-cut.'

'Not medical-grade thread, but maybe some medical skills?'

'Or sewing skills. Or — sorry for the ors,' he said with a smile. 'Someone taking their time.'

'Yeah, or that or that. Or he's just obsessively

precise. No sex, no violence, no torture. What did he want from her? What did he want with her? Maybe the obvious. A mommy.'

Morris laid a hand on the victim's shoulder. 'Now she'll never get the chance to decide if she wants to be one.'

'No, she won't. She has family, and a cohab. They'll want to see her.'

'I'll contact them when she's ready.'

'Okay. Thanks for the tube.'

'Anytime. Dallas? She was left at the playground near the house — the house our friends will live in.'

'Yeah. I'm on that.'

'I'm sure you are. We look after strangers who become ours every day. And we look after family. If Mavis needs anything, let her know I'll be there.'

'I will. She doesn't fit the image. She's smaller, and Christ knows what color her hair will be on any given day. And she's pregnant. But the pregnant thing makes her a mommy.'

'He doesn't want someone else's mommy though, does he?'

'I don't think so. Still, I'm on it.'

Or would be, she told herself as she started out. She had to get to Central, set up her board and book. Think. She had questions for Mira.

She considered going by the lab, lighting a fire under Berenski, maybe giving Harvo a nudge.

Too soon, she admitted. She'd give them twenty-four hours, then she'd light fires and give nudges.

As she pulled into Central, Peabody tagged her.

'Mira can squeeze you in now if you're on your way back.'

'I am back.'

40

'She's got a short window now, otherwise —'

'I'm taking now.' Eve zipped into her slot. 'I'll run it down for her, send her the report later.'

'I'll tell her admin you're on your way. Hey, ask about the baby.'

'What baby?'

'The admin's new grandbaby. Make nice,' Peabody said before Eve could object or complain, 'and she may make nice next time you need a window with Mira.'

'Stupid,' Eve muttered as she crossed to the elevators. 'Babies don't have anything to do with homicide and profiling. Unless they do, and they don't on this.'

'Just try it. It won't hurt much.'

'So you say.' Eve cut her off and jumped in the elevator.

Since she figured now meant now, she stayed on even when cops and techs and who the hell knew squeezed on.

On Mira's floor, she shouldered her way through the pack and out. Breathed in clear air as she moved quickly to Mira's outer office, and the dragon at the gates.

Mira's admin sat imperiously as always at her desk, ear-link on as she worked on whatever the hell she worked on.

She shifted her icy gaze up, pinned Eve with it.

'Dr. Mira has only twenty minutes.'

'I'll make it quick.' She started to go straight in, then mentally rolled her eyes, ground her teeth. 'Anyway, congratulations on the grandchild thing.'

The ice melted into a kind of dreamy mist. 'Thank you.' She lifted a framed photo from her desk. 'Isn't she gorgeous?'

41

Eve saw what appeared to be the result of a strange mating of a trout and a very angry, possibly constipated old man. She said, 'Wow.'

'So precious. Twenty minutes,' she repeated, but the misty dreamy remained.

Eve stepped in where Mira sat behind her own desk, keyboarding. She held up a finger. 'I need one more minute to finish answering this. Have a seat.'

Because she wasn't ready to sit, Eve just stood, studying the shelves that held Mira's memorabilia, awards, photos. More babies and kids, but none with that fishy newborn look.

'Sorry,' Mira said after a moment. 'It's already a day.'

'No problem, and I appreciate you fitting me in.'

'You wouldn't ask if you didn't need.' Rising, Mira walked to her AutoChef on her high, skinny heels the color of perfectly cooked salmon.

They matched her suit with its knee-skimming skirt that showed off excellent legs. She wore a triple chain with pale blue stones that exactly matched the buttons of the suit jacket.

It never failed to astonish and baffle Eve that anyone managed that coordination, especially as consistently as Charlotte Mira.

She expected to smell the lightly floral tea Mira preferred, and instead scented good, strong coffee.

'Coffee.' Eve almost sighed it.

'I need it.' With a smile, Mira handed Eve a cup before she took a seat in one of her blue scoop chairs. 'As I said, a day. And you're having one yourself. A body, Peabody said, left in the playground near the new house. Have you spoken with Mavis?'

'Not yet. It's on the list.'

42

'Which is long.'

'It is. I'm just back from the field so haven't written it up yet.'

'So you'll tell me.'

'Female, Caucasian, twenty-six, a bartender walking the few blocks home after closing.'

Still standing, she ran through it all as the department's top profiler listened.

She pulled out her 'link, called up the crime scene record to show Mira the body, the message left.

'It looks like it was written with a crayon.'

'The lab'll confirm.'

Nodding, Mira studied the images.

'The look? The way he dressed her, styled her? It reminds me of my mother's sister — my aunt — back when I was a child. Photos of her from that time frame. She was, according to my mother, a bit of a wild child.'

'Morris said the clothes were outdated.'

'Yes. To my eye as well.'

'You'd be two who'd know.'

With a smile, Mira brushed back a wave of her mink-colored hair. 'It's a . . . hard look, again to my eye. The makeup, the hairstyle. Hard rather than edgy or overtly sexy. Certainly not traditionally or classically maternal. At the same time, it's all so very exacting. A lot of care went into creating this look. It mattered. She — the woman he, or she, sought to re-create — mattered. There's as much love here as hate. Maybe more.'

'He kept her for ten days, had to have chosen her, known her basic routine. All that takes time and care.'

'It does,' Mira agreed. 'She fit the outline, either physically or by lifestyle. She worked in a bar, perhaps the one she represented worked in a bar. Or worked nights. Certainly something about the victim sparked this need to take her, keep her, try to make her into the original.'

'The mother.'

'Almost certainly the killer's mother or mother figure.'

Mira sat back again, sipping her coffee as she chose her words.

'No sexual aggression or rape, no physical violence beyond the abduction and the killing blow. I agree she must have been drugged when the tattoo and the piercings were done — and these markings will reflect the original. A woman, most likely, at least in her upper seventies — to fit the fashion he chose, potentially older. She's either dead or has broken ties with the killer. Assuming mother, the killer would be at least late fifties. He shows control, patience, organized behavior, maturity.

'If this is his first, and you'll check for like crimes, there's a trigger. A betrayal by the mother figure, her death, her abandonment, remarriage. Something that drove him to need to replace and re-create.'

'She didn't measure up — the victim. Or he killed her to punish the original because she did, in his mind, measure up. Why sew up the killing wound and hide it under the ribbon?'

'It's all so tidy,' Mira added. 'A hard look, but so clean, so perfect. There may be remorse here, but it strikes me as more likely leaving an open wound is incomplete, untidy, and even the stitches would spoil the image. He's angry with her — she's bad — but she still represents Mother. Precise, controlled, a perfectionist with the maturity to plan it out, but the lettering on the sign?'

'Like a kid's. Not precise.'

'The child in him — the angry child — lashed out. The mature tidied it all up. He's psychotic, with a mother obsession that drove him to — in his mind — matricide.'

'He'll kill her again.'

'Almost certainly. The love/hate, the rage/need, all must be met. The killer's a man or woman likely at least fifty-five, and I think more likely at least sixty, and his mother figure was Caucasian, blond at the time he's re-creating, with a build that closely matches the victim's. She liked to party — or he sees her that way, he remembers her, from childhood, that way. He wants her back as much as he wants to destroy her. He didn't give her a wedding ring.'

'People don't always go for those.'

'More so, much more so, in the era I believe he's re-creating. Unmarried woman, widowed or divorced. The father isn't important to him. It's only her. It's only them. He won't have siblings. Or had no relationship with them, has none now. The killer isn't in a relationship, lives alone. He may have a skilled job. If indeed the killer is male, he's asexual or impotent.'

'I'm leaning male.'

Mira set aside her coffee, recrossed her legs. 'Why?'

'From what I've seen, mothers and daughters have — generally — a different sort of dynamic than mothers and sons. A guy's more likely, it seems to me, to deify or demonize the mother figure. I feel like if the killer was the daughter — or saw herself that way — there would have been some violence on the vic. You know, 'You ruined my life, you bitch.' And there wouldn't've been so much effort put in to make

45

her look, you know, pretty.'

Mira sat back. 'I completely agree. I wouldn't rule out the female, and there I'd look for someone the people who think they know her describe as meek and unassuming, quiet, diligent.

'In either case, this is someone scarred in childhood who's carried those scars, and — again if this is the first kill — recently experienced a trigger.'

'Okay.' Talking it through gave Eve a picture. Not clear and exact, not yet, but a picture. 'I'll get you the report, the record, the lab results as they come in.'

'It's fascinating. Tragic for all involved, but fascinating. The power of motherhood, for good or ill.' Mira's soft blue eyes held on Eve's. 'You understand that.'

'Yeah. The last thing I'd want to do is re-create mine.' She started to push to her feet, then stopped. 'She didn't abuse the kid — the killer. If she had, he'd have paid her back. There'd be signs of payback. Physical abuse or sexual abuse.'

'Abuse, if it applies, may have been emotional.'

'Yeah, there's that.' Now she stood. 'I appreciate the time.'

'I'm glad I had it. It is fascinating, Eve. You'll search for more missing women?'

'On the list,' she said.

She took the glides up for the breathing room and thinking time. She needed to dive into every detail of the victim's appearance, every step her killer had taken to create her.

Missing persons, female, between twenty and thirty to be safe, she considered. In the last month, to fully cover it. Start with a search using the victim's basic physicality.

Finding the 'mother,' the original, had to be one of

46

the top priorities. She had some ideas how to start on it, but it would take time.

If the killer abducted another surrogate, time narrowed.

And on a personal level, she needed to talk to Mavis.

She smelled the brownies the minute she swung into Homicide.

And there in her bullpen, her damn good cops — including her partner — scarfed down brownies as Nadine Furst, bestselling writer, Oscar-winning screenwriter, and, more relevant, award-winning on-air reporter for Channel Seventy-Five, leaned her well-toned butt on Peabody's desk.

'I assume the population of New York, including all tourists and visitors, is alive and well.'

Jenkinson, her senior detective, brushed a crumb from his atomic-yellow tie. Eve found herself surprised one of the grinning green frogs hopping over it hadn't flicked out a tongue to capture it first.

'Just a real quick break, boss. They're double fudge.'

'Break's over. Nadine, I don't have time for you. Peabody, my office.'

Peabody hustled after her, but Eve heard the bright click of Nadine's skyscraper heels in pursuit.

'Busy,' Eve snapped without looking around. 'Take off before I charge you with bribing police officers.'

'Give me one minute — and don't close the door in my face. One minute, and I'm gone if that's what you want. Either way, you get the brownie I saved you in my purse.'

The scent of chocolate could have weakened the strongest spine, but the friendship weighed on the scale. The friendship existed because while Nadine would pursue a story like a dog pursues a rabbit, she cared about truth.

'Let's see the brownie.'

Nadine reached into a stop-sign-red bag the size of Brooklyn and took out a little pink bakery box. Eve opened it, nodded at the brownie within, then set it on her desk.

'One minute, clock's ticking.'

'Mavis. I sat on that same damn bench with you at that playground after Mavis gave me a tour of that big, rambling, strange, and wonderful house she and Leonardo, Bella, and the new one when it gets here are making into a home. Where Peabody and McNab are making theirs. He left that woman's body on that bench, where Bella's played, and will play.

'They're my family, too.'

There was truth, Eve acknowledged, absolute and pure.

'Okay. Then get out and let me do my job.'

'Give me something. Not to air,' Nadine said quickly. 'I hit the story this morning — my first day back, by the way, post-book tour — and I've got enough for a follow-up report.'

Which, Eve thought, explained the camera-ready. Streaky blond hair carefully styled, perfect makeup, the sharp white suit, the red-and-white-striped heels.

'I can help. You know I can. I'll give you a blanket off-the-record until you give me the go. I'll want a one-on-one, when it's appropriate, and I'll hound you until I get it, but this isn't about the story. Give me something I can dig into. Something I can get my team to research. We're good, you know we are.'

Eve eased back on the corner of her desk. 'I'm going to send you a picture of a tattoo. The killer inked the victim a couple days before he killed her. Lower back.

We're looking for a woman with that tattoo in that place — a woman between twenty and thirty, White, blond, about five-five and a hundred and twenty-five. I'll give you the ID shot of the vic. There'll be a resemblance. The tat may have been done in the last decade of the twentieth century or anytime since.'

'What is it, the tat?'

'Butterfly.'

'That's it? Jesus, Dallas, do you know how many people get butterfly tats?'

'You want easy or you want to help?'

Nadine let out a huff of breath. 'Send me the pictures. We'll get started.'

'She'll have a navel piercing,' Eve added. 'Three piercings in the left ear, two lobe, one cartilage. Remember, it's most probable the victim bore some resemblance, build, coloring. Same age range.'

'All right, that's helpful. And without a lot of luck, this won't be quick, but we'll push. You think the killer more or less replicated someone. Mavis isn't at all physically like the victim.'

'No, but I'll talk to her anyway.'

'Okay. I've got to get to Seventy-Five, do the follow-up. I'll start the team on this. I'll be working it, too.' She looked at Peabody, smiled. 'It's a great house. An original — or it sure as hell will be when you're done with it.'

'I'm in love with it.'

'Don't blame you a bit. I'll be in touch,' she said to Eve, and started out.

'Nadine?' Eve waited a beat. 'Thanks.'

'No thanks when it's family.'

Peabody cleared her throat after Nadine left. 'I only had half a brownie, 'cause loose pants, and because

49

she had just enough time to tell me she wanted to help before the rest of the bullpen swarmed.'

'If she finds the original Bad Mommy with what I gave her, it's a miracle. But she may pull it off. We also search. I want you to start a search for missing women, using the vic as a template. Stretch it to between twenty and thirty, and in the last month. And contact Norman.'

'I did. He wants to come in, talk face-to-face. He'll bring the files.'

'Give him the go there. I'm going to run like crimes, but if he did this before in New York, we'd already know. Not impossible he did it elsewhere, so we'll nail that down. He fed her, Peabody. A few hours before he killed her, she had a solid, healthy meal. No signs of sexual abuse or torture.'

She needed to put up her board, start her book, but she thought about mothers and daughters, mothers and sons. What did she know, really? Observations, not personal experience. Personal experience didn't count when your mother had been a monster.

'Describe your mother,' she said to Peabody. 'Not physically. What's the first word that comes to mind?'

'Love. She loves. We love her back.'

'Next word.'

'Ah. Strong. She's loving, yeah, but she's strong. Tough when she needs to be.'

'Third and final word.'

'Tolerant.' Peabody's shoulders lifted and fell. 'Tolerance is a basic element of being a Free-Ager. That's offset by the strong. No bullshit from us kids, but tolerant of personal choices that cause no harm to others.'

'Would you use those same three, in that order, for

your father?'

'Love first, tolerant next. And he's strong, sure, but the top three? I'd probably say playful. He's just . . . cuddly. How does that help?'

'Just trying to form directions. Male or female. I lean, as does Mira, toward male. Potentially asexual or impotent. I bet you fought with your mother more than your father.'

'Well, yeah, I guess. Yeah. I mean, like, lipstick and mascara aren't tools of Satan, and at thirteen —'

'Don't need the details. Your brothers probably fought more with your dad.'

'Probably. I mean, Free-Agers, so disputes are usually talked to death, or solved through meditation or mediation. But yeah, my brothers would claim Dad was harder on them than my sister and me, and I can attest Mom was harder on my sister and me — but piddly stuff.'

'And I bet if I did a survey in the bullpen, the percentages would agree. Not a hundred percent, but that's the more general dynamic.

'Okay, get out, get started. Let me know when Detective Norman gets here.'

Alone, Eve started the search for like crimes first. That could run while she set up the rest. Then she contacted Detective Yancy, the police artist she respected most, to ask for a meeting.

Finally, she set up her board, adding Morris's report when it came in, the sweepers' report. And with that visual aid, she started her murder book.

Once done, she sent copies to Mira and to her commander.

It had to be done, she told herself, and, taking out her 'link, tagged Mavis.

51

Today's hair was a soft sort of lavender and mad curls. Solid joy all but leaped through the screen and kissed Eve on the mouth. Somewhere in the background somebody banged. Saws buzzed.

'Hey, Dallas! Things are happening. Roarke's going to try to come by later. You should, too.'

'Maybe. Mavis —'

'Trina just dropped by. Bellamina's showing off her room. Some of the crew's over in Peabody and McNab's place. Things are happening there, too. It's a mega, mag, mutual happening.'

'I bet. Mavis —'

'You have your serious face on. Something's happening there, too, and it's not good.'

'You haven't heard any media reports today.'

'Who's got time for all that when it's all this? This is the really good stuff. What's the bad?'

'I don't want you to worry.'

'Shit, oh shit, maybe me and Number Two should sit down.'

'This is just a precaution, okay? A woman was killed, and her body left on a bench at the playground, the one near you.'

'Oh no, oh God. When?'

'Last night — well, early this morning. It's my case, Mavis, and Peabody and I are all over it. I've even got Nadine doing some research.'

'The poor woman.' Mavis's eyes, dyed a deep purple, filled. 'Was she a neighbor?'

'She worked the stick at Arnold's, lived a few blocks from there.'

'I know that bar. It's classy.'

'He wanted a type, and he may want another. You're not the type.' She thought of Trina, the much-dreaded stylist. 'Neither's Trina if she's coming and going a lot. But I want you to take precautions. Don't take Bella to that playground until I have more on this. And you could bring in the security detail you use for gigs. They're good. Just a precaution.'

'What did he do to her? No, don't tell me.' Closing her eyes, she breathed deep. 'I have to think of Number Two. No bad vibes allowed. I think we've got most of the security installed that McNab and Roarke worked out, but I'll ask Roarke when he gets here later.'

'Good, that's good. Just . . . don't go out walking, you and Bella, by yourselves right now.'

'You think he lives around here?'

Not panic, which Eve had feared, but icy anger.

'I don't know, but he spent enough time in that neighborhood to choose the dump site. And the bar and the vic's place aren't that far. I need some time to work the case.'

'And not worry about me. Don't. We'll be careful. Nobody's going to touch my babies, and Number Two goes wherever I go, right? Get the bastard, Dallas.'

'Count on it.'

'I do. Come by if you can. We're going to be here all day.'

'I'll try. And I'll keep you in the loop as much as I can.'

The faintest smile crossed Mavis's face. 'He sure made a mistake using our playground. Pissed off Lieutenant Dallas.'

'Damn right. I'll talk to you later.'

'Cha.'

She sat a minute, ridiculously relieved Mavis hadn't fallen apart. And equally relieved to be sure her oldest friend would take every precaution.

Off the list, she thought.

Then she rose, rolled her shoulders. She programmed coffee, sat again.

And nibbling on her brownie, drinking her coffee, she studied her board.

4
BEFORE

She didn't know where she was or how she got there. She remembered nothing before waking on the ground, surrounded by trees, with the sun pushing through the thick canopy of leaves and covering her like a blanket soaked in hot water.

And shivering, shivering despite that smothering blanket of heat.

Everything hurt, and her head pounded sickly even as her stomach churned. When she pushed up to her hands and knees, her pounding head spun, and her stomach revolted.

Sweat slicked her skin as she vomited up the vile.

Weeping, she crawled away, then just curled into a ball, waiting to die.

But she didn't.

Chills racked her so her teeth clacked together, and, when they passed, more sweat poured, ran down her body like a river. The sickness cycled back until there was nothing left, and she lay exhausted, throat burning.

And somehow she slept.

She woke burning with fever, racked with chills, and this time prayed to die.

Without sense or purpose, she managed to gain her feet, took a few stumbling steps. When she fell, she waited for the sickness to come again, but there was only pain and that terrible heat.

So she pushed to her feet again. She saw nothing to tell her where she was, which way to go, so she walked blindly.

She couldn't say how long she walked, forced time and again to stop and rest. She feared she walked in circles. She saw birds, squirrels, knuckles of trees poking out of brown water. And the things that swam in it, silently.

But not another human being.

She knew she was a human being, a girl, a woman, but beyond that she had nothing to anchor her.

She didn't remember driving into the lake, or the sudden wild panic that had her fighting her way out of the submerged car, swallowing water, thrashing her way to the surface.

She certainly didn't remember a little boy left sleeping and alone in front of an empty church.

She was alone, and too sick, too tired to think of before.

She fell asleep again, and woke in the dark, woke freezing this time.

The air — so thick — seemed to clog her lungs so her breathing wheezed. And the wheezing led to horrible spells of agonizing coughing.

Insects buzzed around her, biting until every inch of her skin burned and itched. She scratched and scratched until she bled, and the blood drew more to bite and swarm.

She tried calling out, but her voice was a croak, no louder than the frogs.

She walked and wept, walked and wept. And finally just walked, shuffling like a zombie, and jolting at each sound.

The hoot of an owl, the rustle of leaves. She waited

for something to leap out of the dark and consume her.

She thought she heard something else, something familiar.

A car.

She knew there were cars in the world. She knew she wore red sneakers, sneakers coated in mud. She knew, because she'd run her hands over it, she wore her hair short. But she couldn't bring an image of herself into her mind.

If she had a mirror — she knew what a mirror was! — would she know herself?

She tried to walk in the direction she thought she'd heard a car. Someone would help. If she could find someone, someone would help. Water, someone would give her water. She was so thirsty.

She had no sense of time, of distance.

She followed snatches of moonlight.

She knew the moon, the sun, flowers, buildings, trees — why were there so many trees? She knew cats and dogs and hands and feet.

Her feet ached and ached. Her head felt as big as the moon and pulsed with pain.

Delirious, she muttered to herself things she remembered and found the word for the body of water she nearly fell into.

Swamp.

She wanted to drink it, but knew the things that swam in swamps.

Alligators, snakes.

She walked the other way. What did it matter? She'd walk until she died.

And then, like a miracle, she stumbled out onto a road.

She knew what a road was, and cars traveled on them.

She walked, limping now, as her shoes rubbed blisters on her feet. But no car traveled this road. Maybe she was the only person left in the world.

Maybe there'd been a nuclear war. She knew what that was, sort of. Everything blew up. But there was still a road, and trees.

As dawn began to break, she gave up, gave in to exhaustion, and simply dropped down on the road. She curled into herself and let the darkness come.

* * *

On his way home from a graveyard shift at the ER, Dr. Joseph Fletcher had the top down, the radio blasting. Both ploys to keep him alert after a long, hard night.

He loved his work, had always wanted to be a doctor, and he'd chosen emergency medicine. But there were nights he wondered why he hadn't listened to his parents and gone into private practice.

Of course, he knew why. He helped more people, often desperate people, on any given night than he might have in a week in a posh office.

He was thinking about a long cool shower and his big soft bed when he rounded the final curve before home and nearly ran over the figure crumpled in the road.

He had to slam the brakes, swerve. He nearly lost control of the BMW Roadster he'd treated himself to when he got his degree. Gravel spit from the wheels when he hit the shoulder, and he fishtailed but managed to stop without ending up in the gully.

Grabbing his medical bag, he was out of the car in

seconds and running.

When he dropped down beside her, he feared the worst, but he found a pulse. And when he began to check for injuries, she stirred.

She opened her eyes, bloodshot, swollen, and glazed with shock.

Her voice came out in a hoarse croak, but he heard her.

She said, 'Help me.'

NOW

Eve read the tox report on her victim and got a picture of those last hours. As she copied it to Mira, added it to her book and board, Peabody buzzed through.

'Detective Norman's here, Lieutenant.'

She considered her office, the single ass-biting visitor's chair, and decided to give Norman a break. 'Let's take it to the lounge. I'm right behind you.'

After a last look at her board, she started out.

'One second, LT.' Santiago hustled over to her. 'If you can sign off on this, Carmichael and I can close it out.'

She scanned the report on the suspect in a bludgeoning death — her spouse — and her confession thereto.

'Looks like good work between brownie breaks.' She scrawled her signature and kept going.

She found Peabody and Detective Norman already at a table with crap coffee. A scatter of other cops took their break, or used the quieter space for work.

Norman looked young. Since she'd already looked

him up, she knew he was only a couple years older than Trueheart, her youngest detective.

He had smooth, golden brown skin, deep-set dark eyes that spoke of some Asian in his DNA. He wore his hair close cropped with hints of gold among the black. He had a skinny build inside a black suit and a dull gray tie knotted at the base of his long neck.

As well as young, Eve thought he looked miserable.

She sat. 'Detective Norman, thanks for coming in. I'm Lieutenant Dallas.'

He offered his long, slender hand — and a solid grip with it. 'Lieutenant. I brought all the files on Lauren Elder. I was working with Detective Marlboro on this case — she's senior — but she's on vacation.'

'Okay, why don't you just run it through for us.'

'Yes, sir. Roy Mardsten, who identified himself as Elder's cohab, reported her missing on the morning of May twenty-ninth. Detective Marlboro and I caught the case, and though it had been less than twenty-four hours, and Elder an adult, Mardsten expressed urgency. Elder wasn't answering her 'link, and he'd checked with her coworkers — I have a list in the files — and her family. He'd contacted her friends, and had also contacted local hospitals.'

He paused to gulp at some coffee. 'We interviewed him, and there was no indication he and Elder had any relationship difficulties. This was confirmed by interviews with neighbors, coworkers, family. Her coworker Buddy Wilcox was the last to see her at approximately zero-two-thirty-seven when they closed the bar, Arnold's, where they both worked. The door cam confirms both of them exiting at this time. He stated Elder intended to go straight home, indicated no distress, and was in fact joking with him as they

60

closed for the night. They stood on the sidewalk for a minute, according to his statement, talking. Then she walked in the direction of her residence, while he traveled in the other direction to catch the subway to his own. We have security footage of him on the train platform, time stamped at zero-two-thirty-seven, and getting on the train two minutes after.'

He let out a long breath. 'We concluded Elder had been abducted between her workplace and her residence. Her routine was the same when she worked the night shift. She traveled the same route, and in general, between zero-two-twenty and zero-two-thirty.'

'You concluded it would have been possible for someone to note this routine.'

'Yes, sir. We interviewed former relationships, bar regulars, neighbors, and canvassed her route. The thing is, Lieutenant, there was nothing. We looked into finances, her family's, her cohab's, but even if this had been for ransom, there wasn't really enough there. The cohab's family's got some, but why take her? Nobody saw her after she left the bar. We didn't find a trace of her. Our EDD tracked her 'link from the bar to 16 West Seventeenth.'

'A half block from her apartment building.'

'Yes, sir. It went dead, just dead, so they concluded her abductor disabled it. But he didn't discard it, or if he did, someone picked it up before we caught the case. No, sorry, before Mardsten walked the route, which he did the next morning when he woke to discover she hadn't come home, when she didn't answer his tags, and he was unable to connect.'

'Smart. Close to home. She was less likely to be on any sort of alert that close to home.'

'That's what Marlboro said. She was young and

pretty, so we pushed at the idea of snatching her for the sex trade. We pursued that, and, honestly, sir, every line we could think of. Marlboro figured she was a little over the edge age-wise for the sex trade — they tend to like them younger — but we pushed. Marlboro told me, before she left, we'd probably never find the body.'

Now he stared down at his hands. 'But you did. Sorry, it's my first homicide. I kept hoping — even though you know the odds — she'd just turn up. I keep thinking there had to be more we could've done.'

'It's not my first homicide, Detective. I'm going to tell you that you did everything you could.'

He looked up, big, expressive eyes in a thin face. 'Do you know why? Why her especially?'

'The why is most likely her general physical appearance and age range, and that routine. The killer didn't luck upon her. He stalked her.'

'We looked into that. Nobody we interviewed saw any strange vehicles in the area. No one stated she'd complained about being followed or harassed.'

'He's probably been in the bar a time or two. Not enough to be a regular, not enough to be noticed. His vehicle's likely nondescript but higher end. It blended with the neighborhood. He was ready for her, and knows enough to have disabled her 'link rather than just tossing it.'

Planning, Eve thought again. Control and planning.

'He took it,' she continued. 'Leave no trace. It's possible she knew him, but with what we've learned, the possibility of that's low. He drugged her. Even on the night he killed her he mixed a tranq — basically a soother — in her tea. He kept her restrained and

62

submissive.

'You did your job, Detective.'

'Is there anything I can do? I know I don't work murders — or not yet — but if there's legwork or drone work, I can do it on my own time.'

He should let it go, Eve thought. But it was damn hard to let go of your first. 'I'm going to copy you on our file. We're looking into other missing persons, looking at women who have a similar appearance and age range. If your lieutenant signs off, you could help with that.'

'I'll have him contact you, and I appreciate it.' He passed her a disc, sealed. 'That's everything. I haven't contacted Marlboro. It's her first real break, with her family, in almost a year. But if you think —'

'If we need her input, I'll let you know.'

'Okay. Thanks. I'd better get back.'

Eve sat where she was as he walked out.

'He'll be a good cop if he sticks,' she said to Peabody. 'Anyway, we know the abduction spot, and that's new. We'll take another look at it, but I've got Yancy coming in.'

'Yancy?'

'Yeah. Walk and talk,' Eve said as she rose. 'Keep pushing the missing persons, for now, but I'm going to clear it with Norman's LT and let him hit that area. But tag McNab and ask him if disabling a 'link is enough to kill any chance of tracing it. And how that works.'

'Sure.'

'Because here's the thing. There are recyclers along that route. Why not park near one, disable the vic, then toss the 'link into a recycler? I'm betting the 'link would've been crushed before morning. And even if it

63

wasn't, it would be by the time the cops started looking.'

'Maybe he did know her, and contacted her on it.'

'And we won't dismiss that. But what are the odds he knew her, knew how to contact her, and she fit all his requirements? I don't buy anyone being that lucky. We'll see when the recyclers along her route run and when the contents are picked up.'

She saw Yancy get off the elevator across from Homicide. With his dark curls and vid-star face he looked more like an artist than a cop. Eve knew he hit both on the mark.

'Good timing.'

'Soonest I could break loose,' he told her.

'Works.' As she turned into the bullpen, Jenkinson and his eye-watering tie crossed to her.

'We maybe got a break in the DeBois hit. Got a woman coming in says she saw the whole thing, and she'll spill it for protection and immunity.'

'Where's she been for the last three days?'

'She says hiding out. Reineke ran her. She's a former high-rent LC who got booted when she failed the standard illegals screening.'

'See what she's got. You better get a prosecutor on tap in case.'

'Got that covered. His brother did him, Dallas, I know it in my bones. But he's a slippery bastard. She sounded scared enough, so maybe she's got something that'll give us a better grip. If she does, we'll need a safe house for her.'

'I'll clear it. Keep me up.'

She led the way into her office. 'Rich wheeler-dealer ends up stabbed a couple dozen times in his fancy penthouse — private entrance and elevator. Security

64

feed's taken. Set up to look like a botched burglary, but it comes off as a botched botch, and Jenkinson liked the brother for it from the jump. Only he's alibied tight — smug with it. Alibi's his wife and a couple of other assholes. Anyway.'

She shoved her hands through her hair. 'Peabody, coffee.'

'How do you want it, Yancy?' Peabody asked him.

'If it's the real stuff, black's good.'

'Here's our vic.' Eve gestured to her board. 'You can see the killer went heavy on the hair and facial enhancements — that's postmortem. Our angle is he picked her, and, after holding her for ten days, killed her, then made her up to represent someone else. His or her mother or mother figure.'

'Pretty young for it.'

'Yeah, so mother from back a ways. Mira dated her outfit to around the turn of the century, or a few years after. That confirms Peabody and Morris's fashion take.'

'Okay. Thanks,' he added when Peabody handed him a mug of coffee. 'So, with this line, Mom could be hitting eighty or so.'

'If she's still alive, yeah. To pursue this angle, we need a better fix on the mother figure. ID her, we have a strong shot at IDing the killer.'

'You want me to use the victim as the base, age her to around eighty, give you the most likely image. I'm not going to promise face recognition on it. All kinds of variables, Dallas. She could've had work done, or lived the kind of life that leaves marks.'

'Or she could've died sixty years ago,' Eve put in. 'Or any time between then and now. I'm using the current image to try to match the potential subject at this age range — but that's before universal ID. We've got to use driver's licenses, passports — and it's going to be a slog. She might have had neither.'

'There's a tat.'

'Also inked after abduction, so we have that identifying mark on the mother figure. What I want, if you can do it, is age reproduction analyses, a decade-by-decade, from this point to now. Best probable.'

'Huh.' Sipping coffee, he moved closer to the board. 'Interesting. I need more photos. Different angles. Vids would be good. It wouldn't hurt to get some of the victim younger, too. Even with that, it'll take awhile. I can comp-generate a lot of it, work with a holo for a three-sixty, but I'll need to finesse that, punch it up for any chance at facial recognition. Even then . . . But I can give you the best approximation.'

'We'll get more pictures, some vids. Peabody.'

'I'll contact her family, her cohab.'

'Whatever they've got have them send to me and to Yancy.'

'On it.'

'How long's awhile?' Eve asked Yancy when Peabody went out.

'I've got a couple things to clear up, but I can probably start on it before end of shift. I've got to figure a week — three days in a squeeze — to give you everything you want, and that's if I don't have too much else land on my desk.'

'How about you start at the high end, the oldest version, first. I haven't yet found any like crimes, nothing that matches this. Mira figures a trigger. The mother figure let him down, crossed him, or maybe died on him, and he's trying to replace her with this image.'

'Young, kind of glamorous.'

66

'Glamorous?'

'To a kid, right? He'd have been a kid if this was his actual mom — given her age, and how long ago. All the sparkly stuff — top, shoes, the makeup and all. Seems like a kid might think of that as glamour. Fancy. Shiny.'

She flashed back to playing with her mother's makeup — pretty colors, shiny — and getting knocked on her ass for it.

'Yeah, I get that. I'll keep working the lower age range, you start with the high. And I appreciate anything you can get me.'

'Frosty assignment. Never tried anything quite like it.' He handed her the empty coffee mug with his dreamy smile. 'I'll go clear up my currents and get started.'

When Yancy left, she sat down and considered that memory flash. What had she been — four, five, six when Stella walked out on Richard Troy the last time? She couldn't be sure, those memories remained vague. But had she thought Stella pretty, even glamorous?

Probably. What else had she had to compare?

Had she had shiny clothes?

Probably.

She remembered the smells — sex and smoke — and the smell of the powders and paints — like candy. Perfume.

She'd smelled perfume on the body.

So he remembered the smells, too. Childhood smells.

Had he lived his life with this woman, or had she walked out on him like Stella had on her?

She rose, paced to her skinny window.

In New York, or somewhere else?

Bad Mommy. Hadn't Stella been her template for motherhood, Stella and the array of foster mothers that followed, for a very long time?

Bad Mommy would've been her judgment, too.

Had the killer been in the foster system? Another angle, but one she couldn't begin to dive into without a better time frame. And she'd started out in Dallas. Like the killer, she'd ended up in New York.

No way to know, yet, where the killer had started his journey.

The next thought had her heading out of her office.

'I'm going up to EDD, tapping Feeney,' she told Peabody.

'I'm on with Norman.' Peabody jiggled her 'link. 'We may have a couple missing persons who fit the basics.'

'Nail them down, and we'll take them when I get back.'

Taking the glides, she thought it through as she went. Another long shot, maybe, but worth pushing.

Once she got this rolling, she'd get back in the field, check out these other missing women, hit all the victim's contacts. Hair salon, health clinic, dentist, the shops she frequented regularly. Someone might have noticed something.

She walked into the crazed and colorful world of EDD. It was Jenkinson's ties on steroids.

Though she didn't see McNab bouncing in his cube, she saw plenty of others in equally wild gear bopping and hip-swiveling as they worked.

She turned toward what she knew would be the brown, baggy calm of Feeney's office.

Found it empty.

68

'Hey, Dallas.'

She looked around, and nearly didn't recognize him. The moment's blankness might have been caused by the blinding purple baggies and the exploding aurora borealis on his shirt.

He'd let his hair grow long enough so he could pull it back in a stubby tail, and had streaked the blond with spring-grass green.

Jamie Lingstrom, Feeney's godson, and the kid — well, college kid now — who had the distinction of being the only person she knew who'd ever — almost — gotten through Roarke's home security.

'Is it something in the air up here,' she wondered, 'that turns colors nuclear?'

'Energy boost.'

'Sure. What are you doing here?'

'Summer intern. Just grunt work, but it's a start.' He looked around EDD as if he'd entered paradise. 'I rotate. Two days a week here, three with Roarke. Next week, reverse it.'

'Roarke? You're interning with Roarke?'

'Low rung, but it's iced supreme. Best of both worlds.'

She eyed him. 'Getting a leg up in both so you can straddle them.' She had to admire the strategy. 'Smart.'

'Gotta explore to know where to plant the flag, check me? So, if you're looking for the Cap, he and McNab are in the field. You got something I can —'

'Callendar,' she said, naming another detective she knew and had worked with.

'She's buried right now.' Jamie shifted his weight, subtly, to block Eve. 'I just finished what the Cap laid

69

on me, so I can take what you've got.'

She considered the fact that what she wanted done equaled the gruntiest of grunt work. The work of an apprentice drone.

He fit the bill.

'Where's your ring in this circus?'

'Down around here.' He led the way through the maze, did a fist bump, finger wiggle with a female with a cascade of blue braids, and ended up in a cube so small and tight if she'd tried to squeeze in with him, she'd have had to bring herself up on inappropriate conduct charges.

'I need a long-range ID search.'

'I'm your man.'

'By default, and when Feeney gets back, you clear this with him. Female, Caucasian, no age range at this time. I have an identifying mark. I want you to use that data, check criminal records. You're going back to the year 2000. No, make it 1990.'

His eyes widened. 'No bull?'

'No bull. Start in New York.'

'Start?'

'Yeah. Start in the city, then the boroughs, then the state. You don't get a hit, move on.'

'To what?'

'Another state.' She pulled out her PPC, ordered up the photos she wanted. 'What's your code? No, here, just copy it over yourself.'

He took her handheld. 'Dallas, she looks pretty dead.'

'She is. I'm not looking for her, but who she represents to the person who killed her.' She hesitated, then reminded herself she'd connected with Jamie not so much through Feeney as through Alice.

His sister, his murdered sister.

So she ran through the basics.

'Butterfly tat, that's a solid. Okay, I'm all over it and back again.' Faster than she could have thought it, he transferred the photos to his unit.

And looked, Eve thought, not daunted by the impossibility of the assignment but energized.

'Clear it with Feeney,' she repeated as she took back her PPC.

'No prob. I got this. Yo to Roarke.'

'Yeah.' Even as she turned away to escape the carnival, Jamie was bopping to the beat.

5

Back in the bullpen, at Peabody's desk, Eve studied the two missing women's data. Anna Hobe, age twenty-four, single, worked at Mike's Place, a karaoke bar. Lower West. She lived alone, in an efficiency just under six blocks from her workplace.

Seven days missing, Eve noted, reported by her manager when she didn't show up for work, her 'link didn't respond, and the coworker who talked the building super into letting her in found the apartment empty.

Becca Muldoon, age twenty-five, a dancer at Honey Pot, a Lower West Side strip joint, eight days missing. Single, reported by roommate.

'We'll take Hobe, have Norman take Muldoon. We'll hit her workplace and residence. Get the files transferred. Give me five.'

She went into her office, added some notes to her book. She printed out Hobe's photo, held it next to Elder's. Same coloring, a similarity in features. And from the data, likely a similarity in build.

Muldoon, now, she thought as she studied that printout, she'd put closer to the Bad Mommy. But that came from the facial enhancements Muldoon wore in the ID shot.

With a quick search she found one of Muldoon's professional shots on her social media. Curvier, definitely bustier.

Would he adjust for that? she wondered.

Either way, they struck her as candidates.

72

She pinned them up, grabbed her jacket.

'Let's move, Peabody,' she said as she walked through the bullpen.

'Norman's already heading out,' Peabody told her. 'He contacted the lead on the Muldoon case, and they're meeting up at the strip club. Eight days,' Peabody added. 'If he grabbed her, she's running out of time.'

'I think the probability's lower on Muldoon. Yeah, maybe he always wanted backups, alternates, but is he going to grab one right after the other? Higher probability — maybe — because she more closely matches what he created — her face. But her build's different. She wouldn't fit in what he dressed Elder in.'

'Buys to fit her.'

'Yeah, easy enough. She's got a couple of tats already. A snake — a cobra — going down her left hip, and a dragonfly on her right tit. What does he do about that? Leave them, remove them, just cover them up? If he's seen her in the club, he knows that. But, other side, she's already got the navel piercing, which would also be in view when she's working.'

'It caught me she looks more like what he did with Elder than Hobe does. But Hobe looks more like Elder before he worked on her.'

'Exactly. What does he want, Peabody?' Eve asked as they crossed the garage level to Eve's car. 'The good mommy or the bad one?'

Peabody considered it as she climbed in. 'He kills the bad mommy, so it could follow he wants the good one. It would weigh on Hobe more than Muldoon.'

'That's how I see it. If it was only about punishment, he'd have hurt Elder. Messed her up, smacked her around. He took what he wanted, and he took her

73

after observing her, watching her routine, planning it out. If he's taken another, he did it the same way.'

As she drove out, pushed through traffic, Eve thought it through. 'That's not to say he didn't have more than one at the same time on his radar. If he's taken another — and if he hasn't, he will — he likely had a gauge on her for a while.'

'He'd almost have to, right? If neither of these pans out, if he's still in the stalking phase, that's one thing. But if either of these, potentially both, are targets, he had to have picked them and studied them for a while.'

'And how does he pick them? You can't pick what you don't see. We don't have a pattern yet, we're assuming one.' Though it troubled her to assume, her instincts continued to demand it.

'Mavis doesn't fit the pattern — the assumed pattern. I talked to her,' Peabody added. 'She said you had, and asked her to bring in her security guys. She did, and that's just a good idea considering the proximity of the dump site to the apartment and the house. But she doesn't fit, Dallas. She's smaller, and coloring — if we take hair and eyes? Mavis is all over the place. She doesn't have a real routine, either, and she'd usually have Bella, or Bella and Leonardo, or Trina with her when she goes anywhere. Or me and McNab.'

All true, Eve thought, and all reassuring. But she had to think on the dark side — the killing side.

'He knew the playground. He didn't pick the dump site on impulse. He scoped it out, or he knows it because he lives or works in the neighborhood. Add the mommy thing. She's already a mommy.'

'Because of Bella, and she's already showing some with Number Two.'

74

'He could've seen her — them — in that playground.' And it gnawed at her, Eve admitted. Gnawed away at her. 'What does he want? A good mommy. She fits there. She's a damn good one.'

'Okay, that ups my worry level. McNab and I will stick close.'

'Stick close but keep the worry level low. She doesn't fit. It's just . . . Friends are a pain in the ass more than half the time.'

'Aw.' Peabody beamed a smile. 'That's down from what you probably thought a couple of years ago. That would've been more like eighty percent, not fifty.'

'I said more than half. Eighty's more than fifty. Contact Hobe's building super, get him or her to clear us into her apartment. We'll walk her route once we check at the bar.'

'Already did. See? Friends are handy.'

Eve flicked a glance over as she rounded a turn. 'That would come under *partner*. Partners are a pain in the ass about a quarter of the time.'

Eve spotted a slot in a loading zone about a block from Mike's Place and decided to grab it rather than take time to hunt another.

She flipped on her On Duty light.

'Decent neighborhood,' she decided when she got out. 'Not as quiet or high on the scale as Elder's.'

'More crowded, dingier,' Peabody agreed. 'Not as close to home,' she added.

'A solid walk from Elder's, but if you're hunting the area, this fits.' She paused at a crosswalk as vehicular traffic pushed by and pedestrian traffic crowded in.

'Maybe bars are part of it. If there's a pattern, bars might be part of that. Maybe the mother worked at a bar.'

'Worked at one,' Eve agreed, 'or spent a lot of time drinking in them.'

When the light changed, they joined the flood.

'According to the report, Hobe worked till twelve-fifty or clocked out at twelve-fifty. She walked a few blocks with a coworker — the same one who checked her apartment. Coworker peeled off to go another half block south to her residence. It was raining, so they were walking fast. Hobe's building doesn't have door cams, but she would need to code in. She didn't.'

Eve stopped in front of Mike's Place. It boasted a bright red door and a wide glass window filled with neon. The name of the bar, a figure of some guy with a mic and an arm raised. Under him, it announced: KARAOKE! NIGHTLY!

Eve considered working in a karaoke bar versus getting eaten by sharks. The sharks came close to winning.

She stepped inside, relieved the *Nightly!* hadn't yet begun.

A few asses snuggled in stools at the bright red bar. A scatter of people slumped at shiny silver tables. Those struck her as primarily tourists worn out from shopping — likely for things they could just as easily find at home.

The stage — all silver and red — remained, thank Christ, empty.

Clean, she noted, and it probably packed them in at night with people who thought they could sing, those who wanted to humiliate their friends by making them sing, or those who couldn't resist a mic once they had a few drinks in them.

A single waitress navigated the tables in high red heels, a short black skirt, white shirt, and red bow tie.

She served one of the tables what looked like decent bar food and a carafe of white wine.

Eve crossed to the bar, where a lone bartender in a MIKE'S PLACE T-shirt pulled a draft brew.

'Ladies.' He had smooth dark skin, shoulder-length braids, and a killer smile. Eve imagined his tip pull proved awesome. 'You can have your pick of tables or pull up a couple stools and keep me company.'

To give him a break, Eve discreetly palmed her badge.

She watched the killer smile fade.

'Oh crap. Is this about Anna? Did you find her? Is she okay? What —'

'We haven't located Ms. Hobe. We're here to follow up on the pending investigation.'

'It's been days. It's been, like, a week.'

'Were you working the night she went missing?'

'Yeah. I mean, I was on the stick till about eleven. She had another couple hours on, so she was here when I left.'

'Can we get your name?'

'Yeah sure. Bo — I'm Bo Kurtis — with a K. Look, Anna and I worked together the last four years — I've been here six. We even sort of dated a few years ago. Nothing major, and it didn't, you know, happen for either of us. I just want to get that out there. We're friends.'

Eve slid onto a stool and took him through the usual questions, ones she knew he'd have answered before.

'Honest to Jesus, she wouldn't have just walked away. She liked working here. She could sing, and she'd get up there sometimes with some of the customers. She liked living in New York. She came here not long before she got the job — from upstate. She

77

really liked living in the city, liked her apartment. It's small, but she liked it. She had friends, man.'

'No relationship?'

'Not right now. I mean, sure, she dated. She just liked people. Nothing serious going. Like I told the other cops, I never saw or heard of anyone hassling her. This isn't that kind of place, and Mike, well, he wouldn't put up with that shit. People get lit up, sure, but they don't come into a karaoke bar looking for trouble.'

'Where is Mike?'

'He's in the back. He's been sick about this. You want me to get him?'

'Yeah, why don't you do that.'

'Give me a sec. They're signaling me down the bar. We don't get busy until about eight, but you gotta keep the customers happy.'

He went down, flashed that smile again. Once he'd taken care of the fresh drinks, he slid into a door on the side of the bar.

The man who came out with Bo would've made two of him.

Built like a linebacker with shoulders wide as a redwood, he had a shaved head and soft, worried blue eyes. He wore a pale gray suit with an open-collar white shirt, and stuck out a hand that gripped — and swallowed — Eve's.

'I'm Mike, Mike Schotski. What can I do to help, Detective?'

'Lieutenant. Lieutenant Dallas and Detective Peabody. We're following up on —'

'Wait.' He held up one of those meaty hands, and the worry flashed into alarm. 'I know you. The book, the vid. Jesus, you do murders. Anna —'

'Mr. Schotski, we haven't found Anna. We're pursuing a possible connection between Ms. Hobe's disappearance and another case.'

'The girl at the playground this morning. I've been keeping an ear out since . . . Sorry.' He took a breath, visibly steadied himself. 'Let's get a table. What can we get you to drink?'

Since she calculated he needed a little more settling, Eve asked for a Pepsi.

'Make mine a diet,' Peabody said as Mike gestured to a table.

'I had a moment this morning with the report — I didn't catch the girl's name at first. I just caught a flash on-screen when they put up her picture. She looks a little like Anna. Once I focused in I could see it wasn't her, but that little flash?'

He looked away, shook his head. 'Stopped my heart.'

'Bo told us he couldn't think of any reason Anna might have decided to take off,' Eve began. 'That she gave no indication she was worried about anything or anyone.'

'That's a fact. Thanks, Bandi.' He gave the waitress who brought the drinks — a sparkling water for him — a quick smile. 'She liked the work here. You can tell when somebody's just putting in time, and she wasn't. And I'm damn sure she'd have told me if anybody was bothering her, if she had worries. If not me, she'd've told Liza.'

'Liza Rysman? The coworker she left with?'

'That's right. They're good friends — most who work here get pretty tight, you know. I run a happy place. Hey, Bo, give Liza a tag, ask her to come in and talk to these officers. Save you time,' he said to Eve.

79

'She just lives a couple blocks away, and she's worried sick. We all are.'

'We appreciate that.'

'I don't know what we can tell you that we haven't told the other cops. I've gone over that night again and again, trying to see something. I'm not always in the front of the house, but I spend most of my time out here once things get hopping. Anna and Liza left together, right around one. We close at one on Wednesdays — midweek, slower business. Since they live close, and I like knowing neither of them walk it alone that time of night, I try to mesh their schedules.'

'Did you see them leave?'

'I saw Anna right before. It was raining, so I asked if she had an umbrella. She just gave me a poke, said how she wouldn't melt. She had her walking shoes on.'

'Walking shoes?'

'The girls wear heels and short skirts — better tips.' He gave a shrug. 'That's the way it is. A lot of them keep the work shoes here, in the back, change into them when they come in, out of them when they clock out. She had on her walking shoes, the little skirt. It wasn't a hard rain, so I didn't push it.'

He ran a hand over his smooth dome. 'I keep thinking, if I had, if she'd had a damn umbrella, she maybe could've used it to beat him off or something.'

'Him?'

Those worried eyes met Eve's. 'Somebody grabbed her. I know it in my gut. Someone like Anna — happy, steady — they don't just up and go, leave everything. Somebody's got her.'

'Would she have gotten in a vehicle with someone, willingly?'

80

'Anna? No, just no. She's friendly, personable, but not stupid, right?'

'Someone she knew? 'Hey, Anna, how about a lift home? It's raining.'.'

'I don't think so, and I've thought that one around, too. She only had a few blocks left after Liza turned off. She had a routine on work nights. Walk home, get in her jams — pajamas — pull out her bed, and watch a little screen to wind down. She'd say how she'd be conked in about twenty after the wind-down most nights. She'd say how she loved this place, loved hanging and working and singing and being, but after, she needed her little nest and her quiet time.'

'Getting in a vehicle with somebody puts off the nest and the quiet.'

'Yeah, so I don't think she would.'

Eve ran him through, and when Liza rushed in, did the same.

It gave her a good picture of the missing woman, and a very bad feeling.

'If it was a mugging,' she began as she and Peabody started to walk the route, 'a rape, a combo of those, her body would've turned up by now. That's high probability.'

'The rain gave him more cover,' Peabody put in. 'Maybe another reason he didn't wait to grab her. But if he had two at the same time? That's two to control, two to feed.'

'He's got to have the space. Maybe he wanted two so they could compete, so he could judge which was the right one, or better one.' Eve shook her head, paused at the point where Liza would have separated, walked her own way home.

'Liza's taller, more muscular. A yard of dark hair,

81

mixed race. Wouldn't fit for him. Anna Hobe? You can see why Mike had that flash moment when Lauren Elder's photo popped on-screen. They're a type. Slim, young blondes. It's not going to be a coincidence two slim, young blondes who work nights at a bar and walk home late went missing within days of each other.'

'He's got her.'

'And within walking distance of each other. Yeah, a solid hike, but only about six blocks.

'This is his hunting ground.' Eve stopped again a half block from Hobe's building. 'Here's a good spot to park, to wait. Between the streetlights, in the rain. Her head's down, she's walking fast. Maybe bash her, but a quick-acting drug — quick jab — that's easier, cleaner. Has to be quick. She's what — a hundred and fifteen pounds? So bundle her into the vehicle and drive away. But then you've got to get an unconscious woman out of the vehicle and into your place.'

'You'd want privacy if you could get it.'

'A garage maybe,' Eve said as they walked again. 'I can't see driving her out of the city to hold her, then back in to dump her. Adds risk. Nothing strikes me as the behavior of a risk taker. It's need and it's anger, but he doesn't want to be caught. He's not after the thrill.'

She studied Hobe's building. Decent, but right on the edge of it. The street-level door required buzzing in from the inside or a code swipe. Even without a master she calculated she could — thanks to Roarke's tutelage — gain access in under two minutes.

Though tempted, she used her master. 'Tag up the super.'

'Doing that now. Hobe's on four.'

Eve gave the single elevator a suspicious glance and pushed open the door to the stairs. 'He can meet us there, or just give verbal permission for us to enter.'

The stairway didn't hit disgusting, but it came close. No smell of piss or puke — her line of disgust — but it held a stale, sour stench. And the lack of sound-proofing meant she heard someone trying — and failing — to play a keyboard, some kid screeching he wanted *Mongo, now! Mongo, now!*, and the blast of someone's screen — a comedy, she assumed, given the hysterical laughter.

'He's on his way up,' Peabody said as her boots clomped on the steps. 'Sounds like he just wants to nose his way in.'

'He'll be disappointed.'

They came out on four. No keyboard, no screeching kid or hysterical laughter. But she clearly heard some-one behind a door talking — on a 'link, she assumed, as the conversation was one-way — in a voice that screamed Brooklyn, to someone named Margie about someone named Sylvie, who, apparently, was a queen bitch.

'I was okay living in an apartment,' Eve remem-bered. 'You're okay living in one.'

'Sure, but it's a solid building, clean building, and it has good soundproofing.'

'Still, you start thinking about all the people breath-ing and farting and banging together in the same group space. I had a neighbor who poisoned her hus-band with a pie she told him not to eat because she knew he would if she told him not to. Stuff like that.'

'I never really thought about stuff like that until now — thanks — and find myself only more grateful I won't be living with the breathing, farting, banging, and poisoning in a few months.

'What kind of pie?'

'Cream of cyanide. It did the job.'

The elevator squeaked open after giving a distinct creak and rumble that she felt justified her choice of stairs.

The man who stepped out still had a scatter of teenage acne on his pointy face, and a lot of brown hair falling over his forehead into his eyes. He wore a tight white T-shirt and black skin pants over thick, bulging muscles.

'You the cops?'

'We're the cops.' Eve held up her badge. His eyes told her he'd recently enjoyed some Zoner, the smoke from which still clung to his clothes like a sickly-sweet body spray.

'You're not the cops who were here before.'

'Because we're different cops. You can let us in, or you can make us get a warrant. If you choose the second option, I'll get a second one for your place.'

'What for?'

'Because we're the cops, and you were stupid enough to come up here still stinking of Zoner smoke. Between that and the 'roids you're popping, it'll really screw up the rest of your day. Let us in, go away, and we won't have to waste our time or the city's resources.'

'Try to do somebody a favor.' He unlocked the door, but when he started to open it, Eve blocked him.

'We'll take it from here.'

'Rent comes due, I can haul her stuff outta there.'

'Try it, and I'll screw up more than one of your days.'

He gave her a hard look, then turned to stalk off. He lost the impact, as the elevator door had creaked

84

closed again. He stomped to the stairs, let the door bang shut behind him.

'There's a dumbass for you,' Eve commented, and opened the door.

It smelled stale — not like the stairwell, but from disuse. A fine layer of dust thinly coated a small table by the door where a vase held flowers that had withered and died.

A dark green couch, one Eve assumed opened into a bed, faced a large wall screen. Two stands with drawers, one on either side of the couch, held lamps.

On a long, low cabinet under the screen sat photos, a decorative bowl, a small pink stuffed bear. She'd set up an eating area outside a galley kitchen — a café-style table, two chairs. A trio of candles sat in the center.

Art ran to posters of music artists, and Mavis rocked out of one of them. On closer inspection Eve saw Mavis had signed it.

Sing Out, Anna!
Mavis Freestone

'Aw, man.' Peabody blew out a breath. 'Why does that make it harder?'

'Closer to home. Looks like she collected the posters and signatures. They're all signed. She kept a tidy nest, everything has a place and purpose. Check the bathroom and kitchen. It's already been done, but we look again.'

No house 'link, and she knew the lead investigator had already taken the single tablet found in the drawer beside the bed into his EDD. She found clothes, a kit for doing nails, a box of concert and vid stubs, a small collection of costume jewelry.

Cold weather clothes she found separated out, organized. Clothes Eve feared Anna Hobe would never put on again.

She went through the room, and it occurred to her the entire space was smaller than her home office.

But it had been hers, Eve thought. She'd made it friendly and comfortable.

'Monthly birth control,' Peabody announced. 'Some drugstore brand skin and hair care, same with makeup. Nothing high-end. Really clean. Well, a little dusty now, but her towels are folded or hung up. She's got candles on the sink. No illegals, no prescription meds.'

'Organized,' Eve said as Peabody moved into the kitchen. 'She likes her space, knows how to make the most of it. Condoms in the bedside drawer. Box is nearly full.'

Nothing here, Eve thought. Nothing here to tell us where or how. Nothing here but a life on pause.

'No dishwasher, and no dishes in the sink or the rack. Everything's put away. Some leftover Chinese in the friggie, some cheese, snack food, water, crap coffee, creamer, an open bottle of white wine. The AC's busted, so she wasn't using that.'

Nothing here, she thought again.

'Let's talk to some of the neighbors, then hit some of the local take-out/delivery. Maybe we'll jog something the primary didn't shake out before.'

She checked the time. 'After, I'll take you to the house. You can let McNab know.'

'We'll stick with Mavis.'

Eve looked back at the poster. 'Yeah. He's not going

86

to want her, but yeah. Stick close.'

They hit on the way out as Peabody held open the door for a woman carrying a couple of market bags and a giant purse in the shape of a sunflower.

'Thanks.'

'Do you live here?' Eve asked.

The woman waggled her entry swipe. 'Who's asking?'

Eve held up her badge.

'Oh. Yeah, right there. What's the problem?'

'Do you know Anna Hobe?'

'Yeah, some. Lives upstairs, works over at Mike's Place. Is she in trouble? Listen, these are heavy.'

'Let me give you a hand.' Peabody took one of the bags.

'Okay, fine. What about Anna?' she said as she moved to her apartment door, juggled the remaining bag and purse to swipe, then unlock the dead bolt. 'I know her to say hi to.'

'Miss Hobe's been missing since the early hours of June first,' Eve told her.

'What?' The woman glanced back as she pushed the door open. Her amber-tinted sunshades slid down her nose. 'What do you mean, missing?'

'As in no one's seen her.' Eve stepped into the apartment — and colorful chaos.

A flowered tote bag sat on a small square table outside a small kitchen area. A carry-on bag sat open, its contents jumbled on a couch covered with red flowers over a sky-blue background. A cloth bag in front of the open bathroom door exploded with laundry.

'You've been away,' Eve concluded.

'Yeah — so sorry about the mess. Got in really late last night — our flight was delayed — and I had to go

87

back to work this morning, so I haven't had time to unpack or, well, anything.'

She set her market bag on the short kitchen counter, did the same with the one she took from Peabody.

'When did you leave, Ms . . . .'

'Rameriz. Joslyn Rameriz. I left on the first. A group of us friends rented a villa right on the beach in Costa Rica. It was just freaking mag.' She began to unload staples — a quart of nondairy creamer, fake egg mix, a couple of bananas.

'I take it no one from the NYPSD has interviewed you previously regarding Ms. Hobe.'

'No, first I've heard. Missing.' Rameriz paused to pull out the tie holding her sun-streaked brown hair back, then scrubbed her hands through it. 'She doesn't seem like the type to go missing, but I guess I don't know what that type is, exactly. I know Anna to say hi, like I said, and some of my gang would go into Mike's every couple-three weeks. It's a fun place. Maybe she just took off.'

Shaking her head, she scrubbed at her hair again. 'But if I think about it, she doesn't seem like the type to take off.'

'What type does she seem like?'

'I don't know. Regular.' Her pretty, sharply angled face with its vacation tan slowly registered concern. 'Jeez, you don't think something really happened to her?'

'She was last seen leaving her place of employment at approximately one A.M. on the morning of June first. She hasn't been seen since, hasn't returned to her apartment, and her 'link has been disabled. Yes, we're investigating the possibility something really happened to her.'

88

'Okay, listen, sorry.' Now Rameriz rubbed at the back of her neck. 'Long, weird day back at work, and I'm still on vacation time, so I'm a little slow here. I don't know the last time I saw her, and — oh yeah, yeah, I do.'

She shot up a finger. 'There's an abso craphole of a laundry station in the basement. We were both down there a couple days before I left. I mean we passed each other — she was coming in as I was leaving — commented on the craphole. I said how I was going to Costa Rica, and she said like wow, and have fun. Just like that.'

'Did she ever, in passing, mention any problems, someone who bothered her?'

'No, not to me. I mean we didn't cross paths all that much, and she mostly worked nights.'

'You left on the first, how about the night before? What were you doing around one A.M.?'

'Usually, I'd've been conked, but with the trip, I was still packing, mostly. And getting myself worked up because I was excited, and I get nervous when I fly, and I was sure I was going to forget something I'd absolutely had to have. So I . . . '

She blew out a breath. 'Okay, we're not supposed to smoke in the building — as if the Zoner freak super would notice. But I was worked up, so I lit up an herbal because they smooth me out. I cracked the window. It was raining, but it was kind of nice. A little cool, the rain, so I, like, sat on the windowsill awhile and smoothed out.'

'So you were sitting in the open window. Did you notice anything, anyone?'

'No. I mean, what's to notice? I noticed it was rainy — not like pouring or anything, but raining, so

89

I thought how it would be all sunny and hot the next day, and I'd be looking out at the water instead of the street. And cute monkeys and parrots instead of some guy standing in the rain like a dumbass.'

'What guy?' Eve interrupted.

'I don't know. Some guy.'

'Show me the window.'

Rameriz stepped back. 'You want to see my bed-room window. Everything's really a mess because —'

'It takes me days to unpack and get everything straightened up when I take a trip.' Peabody aimed a sympathetic smile. 'The more fun I had, the longer it takes.'

'Right?' Rameriz let out a laugh. 'So don't judge.' She led the way down the short hall that led to the bathroom, and the bedroom to the left of it. With a window facing the street on the far side of the build-ing.

6

Eve ignored the big open suitcase on the floor and the clothes spilling out of it and went straight to the window.

The way the window angled offered a reasonably decent view.

'Tell me about the guy.'

'Just a guy. I only noticed because I was kind of looking down that way and saw him when he got out of the car.'

'What kind of car?'

'I don't know. Honestly. Maybe it was a van, or an all-terrain. It was dark, and it was raining, and I think I just noticed because he got out and walked over to stand on the sidewalk.'

'Did you see his face?'

'No. Maybe he had a hoodie on. Or a hat. Or a hat and a hoodie. I wasn't paying attention, just thinking, Look at that idiot standing in the rain, then — Yeah, yeah, Darlie tagged me up because she was packing and all worked up, too, so we talked awhile, calmed each other down while we finished packing. Then I went to bed.'

'Did you leave the window open?'

'No — man you don't want to do that. I closed and locked it before I went to bed.'

'Where was the guy when you closed it?'

'Gone. Yeah! Yeah, he was gone. Pretty sure. I guess the car or van or whatever was, too. I didn't notice.'

'What time did your friend tag you?'

'Oh, I don't know. I was smoking an herbal and, okay, drinking a brew. Just to smooth myself out because —'

'Can we check your 'link?'

'Well, ah, sure. I guess.' Dubious, Rameriz took her 'link out of her back pocket. 'I'll just, you know, go back to that night, okay?'

She swiped back, shifting her weight, frowning as she swiped. 'Yeah, here we go. Darlie tagged me at twelve-fifty-three. After midnight, so on the day we were leaving. She knew I'd be up because —'

'How long did you talk?'

'Oh . . . Wow, twenty-six and a half minutes. It didn't seem that long.'

'Did you sit in the window while you talked?'

'No. I'd about finished the herbal, so I put it out, and we set our 'links down so we could talk while we both finished packing. Then it was like, 'See you in a few hours, yay!' and I went to bed.'

'Are you certain you saw a male?'

'A male? Oh, a guy.' Rameriz bit her lip, crinkled her eyes. 'Well, I don't know, but I thought guy.'

'How about the vehicle? Ever notice it before? Maybe when you sat in the open window?'

'Honestly, I don't know. It was a car or maybe a van, black maybe. I only noticed the guy — probably a guy — because he's just standing in the rain.'

Eve took her through it all again to try to nudge out some details. She let the sympathetic, cajoling Peabody have a shot.

By the time they left she had a vague headache, but knew where the killer had parked his (most likely his) car/van/AT. That was maybe black or just dark.

'Closer to the building than I thought,' Eve decided

92

as they stopped at the area Rameriz approximated. 'The timing? He's parked, and waiting, just before she's off shift, he gets out of the vehicle. To wait for her. He could watch through the windshield, but he'd need to keep the wipers on to see through the wet. Maybe he just got out to be ready.'

'If Rameriz had stayed where she was another few minutes, she might've seen the grab.'

'Yeah. Even with the dark, the rain, the distance, she might've seen enough to give us something to pull. But she didn't. Let's have some uniforms do another canvass of the building, and the others in this area. Maybe somebody else they missed on the first rounds was looking out at the rain. Notify Norman.'

'I'll get it started. You know, Dallas,' Peabody continued as they walked, 'one A.M.'s a world away from two-thirty. If it hadn't been raining, if it had been a nice night, there might've been — likely would've been — more people out, more windows open.'

'Yeah. Option One, he took advantage of the weather, moved up his schedule to grab her on an early closing night at Mike's. Option Two, he wanted her enough to take the risk. And the option that combines both? Lauren Elder wasn't working out the way he thought. One thing's clear. He's got her, and he's had her for a week.'

Since they'd already passed end of shift, Eve decided to take the work home. After a detour.

She drove to Mavis's strange new house, and found relief when the gate stayed securely closed.

'I got it!' Nearly bouncing in her seat, Peabody took out her 'link, tapped in a code. 'We're going to have your ride tagged for entry when the security's complete,' she said as the gate slowly opened. 'Can't do

Roarke's because he's got a zillion rides.'

The first thing Eve noticed was the grounds that had been neglected, overgrown into a tangle of God knew what, had been cleared. On either side of the drive green sprouts poked up through what looked like piles of straw.

'Landscapers seeded the lawn, after they cleared out the overgrowth. Had to take out some trees — just dead — but we're going to plant others, and more, and have a veg garden out back. Leonardo bought a lawn tractor.'

'A lawn tractor.'

Eve visited a strange image of the fashion designer with his shining braids and one of his flowing outfits plowing a field.

'For maintenance,' Peabody explained. 'Mowing the grass, sucking up leaves. And we're going to expand the little garden shed. And see, see? They already tore up and redid the flooring on the front porches. It wasn't safe. Doing the back next, we hope.'

The house still looked strange and rambling to Eve's eye, but not as strange since it no longer looked as if it grew up inside some urban jungle.

The minute she stopped the car, Bella ran out the open front door.

The kid wore pink overalls over a flowered T-shirt, little pink work boots, and had a hard hat — pink of course — over her spill of golden curls.

'Das! Pee-oddy!'

''Pee-oddy'?'

'She's getting closer.' Peabody popped out, snatched Bella up for a hug and a toss.

Mavis bounced out — and Eve hoped she'd keep her hair that shade of purple for a while. Just in case.

She wore a snug white tee that said NUMBER TWO! with an arrow pointing down at her tiny baby bump. Rather than work boots she wore blue skids with yellow, calf-skimming skin pants.

'You made it!' She all but flung herself into Eve's arms. 'We have grass!'

'Yeah, I see. It's green and everything.'

'Come in, come see!' She grabbed Eve's hand to drag her forward. 'Roarke and McNab are here. They're upstairs doing something with the security and the communication and entertainment and all that. The inspector's coming in the morning.'

'Oh God! Are we ready?'

'Everybody says so. Right, Job Boss?'

Bella grinned, tapped her hard hat. 'Oss!'

'Ba-ba-ba-boss.'

'Bababa! Oss!'

'We'll keep working on that,' Mavis said as Bella laughed like a lunatic and leaped toward Eve.

She grabbed Eve's face in both hands, babbled madly.

'She's juiced up,' Mavis told her.

'When isn't she?'

'She's juiced because . . . Ta-da-de-da!'

Mavis spread out her arms, twirled in circles.

Eve noted some walls had come down and — better — all the hideous wallpaper in her sight line. Some walls apparently would go back up, and inside their framework lived the new guts that would run security and the rest.

'It looks bigger. It was already big.'

'Roomier, more open. It'll be function city, too, when it's done. We got more samples, Peabody.'

'I wanna see!'

95

Bella wiggled down to run, to lead the way through what Eve remembered as a labyrinth and now presented as — yeah, roomier, more open. And into what had been an ugly nightmare of a kitchen.

It seemed the gut job Roarke had deemed it had been accomplished. Most of the wall leading out to the now-cleared backyard was glass.

'They installed the accordion doors!'

Mavis did another dance. 'Surprise! And check this!'

She tapped a code on her 'link, and the doors silently folded in and away. 'It'll be voice command, too, when it's all done. Is that frosted or what?'

'Frost supreme,' Peabody agreed, and took Mavis's hand. 'We're going to have the most fabulous gardens. I've got so many ideas.'

'And over there' — Mavis pointed — 'Play Town. Ken, the secondary job boss after Bellamina who's fallen hard for her, drew up this magomaniac play/adventure house. Roarke gave it the okay, so they're going to build it.'

'Roarke?'

Mavis turned to Eve. 'He's Supervisor of All.'

'Ork,' Bella said, and sighed like a woman in love.

'Over here, that'll be the hang-out area.' Mavis circled the kitchen. 'And there, kind of a cozy place, like for breakfast, and back here . . . Roarke calls it a butler's pantry. We're not getting a butler, unless it's Summerset.'

'He's yours.'

Mavis spun to Eve with a laugh. 'As if.'

'No, seriously. I'll make him your housewarming present. I'm supposed to do that, right?' she asked Peabody. 'Do the present thing?'

'Housewarming presents aren't usually human beings.'

'We can have a debate on whether or not Summerset's human, but either way, I'll make an exception.'

'Someshit,' Bella announced, and Eve nodded at her.

'You got that right, kid.'

'Check these samples, Peabody, and give me your what-what. I got Trina's, but I need more votes.'

'You guys do that. I'm going to find . . . Ork.' And escape from tile samples.

'Take the back stairs,' Mavis suggested. 'We're leaving them in. I'm digging deep on having back stairs.'

When Eve reached the second floor, she noted the absence of ugly wallpaper, and more walls down to studs.

And through the studs the colorful McNab working on a handheld, the towering Leonardo in what she supposed passed as work clothes in his world — the flowing blue-and-red-striped shirt over blue baggies — and Roarke, still in his king-of-the-business-world suit.

Or maybe Supervisor of All.

He did something with those long, clever fingers to something inside the open studs. 'Try it now, Ian.'

'And we are up! We are green all the way! Woot! My man!' He gave Roarke a high five, then offered his palm for a low one to Leonardo. 'This system will rock it up, down, sideways, inside, and out.'

'And the house, the grounds, my girls, they'll be safe.'

'They will, yes.' Roarke gave Leonardo a pat on the shoulder. 'I promise you.'

'That's all that matters.'

Roarke looked through the studs, the odd wire, and smiled at Eve right up into those wonderful wild blue eyes. 'Nothing matters more. Lieutenant.'

'He's not going to look at Mavis,' Eve said as she walked forward. 'I've got a line on him, and she doesn't fit. I just want to be careful.'

Leonardo crossed to her, folded her in. 'They're my world.'

'They're a really big chunk of mine. Just steer clear of the playground until we've got him.'

'We will. Bella's so in love with the house, it's her playground for now.'

'Job Boss,' Eve said, adding a smile in hopes it took the worry from his eyes. And it did.

'She runs the show. We've got wine. I'll go open a bottle.'

She started to beg off. She wanted to get home, get back to work — but she caught Roarke's eye.

'Sure. We'll have a glass before we take off. Everything echoes.'

'Sometimes Mavis wanders around singing. It's wonderful. I can already see us here. I already see it.'

Eve slowed her pace so she fell well behind Leonardo and McNab. 'I really can't stay long. There's another missing woman, and he has her.'

'We won't.' Roarke took her hand. 'They need this, need just a moment with you here.'

She did her best to shift gears. 'Can you already see it?'

'Actually, I can. It's going to be a colorful, creative, and surprisingly functional home.'

'And safe.'

'Safe as our own. Trust me on that.'

'I do.'

When they reached the kitchen area, McNab poured wine into disposable cups, and Leonardo mixed some sort of sparkling drink for Mavis.

'To welcoming friends who are family into our home.' Leonardo hauled Bella onto his hip, handed her a sippy cup.

'And when it's finished,' Mavis continued, 'Leonardo, Bella, Peabody, McNab, and me? We're going to throw the mother of all parties.'

Eve watched Bella's eyes go dreamy as she sucked on the little protrusion on the side of the cup. 'What's in that thing?'

'Water.' Leonardo nuzzled his girl. 'With a vitamin fizzy tab.'

Conversation headed into tile samples, and choices of sinks, and, oddly to Eve, doorknobs. She didn't object when Mavis tugged her outside.

'I know you gotta book it.'

'Yeah, but when you throw the mother of all parties, I'm going to use the power of my will to put a moratorium on all homicides, suicides, and suspicious deaths for one damn night.'

'Bet you will. Don't worry about me, Dallas. I'm heading out tomorrow for a gig in Atlanta the next night. Security team's with me,' she added. 'And because he's still a little freaked, Leonardo's going, too.'

'I'm sorry I freaked him.'

'He freaks if I break a nail these days. My honey bear loves me. And don't be sorry, it means Bella's going so I don't have to miss her for a couple of days. I'm going to miss this, though — the house, the crew, the big magalicious mess of it. I'm so into it. Who'da thought, right? But the gigs are part of why I have to get so into. I feel abso-poso forking serene.'

She turned to Eve, beaming. 'Another who'da thought.'

'It looks forking good on you.'

'Totally does.'

When Mavis wrapped an arm around Eve's waist, Eve took the moment. And gave it.

When the moment passed, she left her friends with their tile samples and doorknobs.

Roarke drove home so she could check on any progress.

'No other witnesses popping up.' She frowned at her 'link. 'We were lucky to hit on one with Hobe.'

'I take it Hobe's the missing woman.'

'Yeah. We coordinated with the detective who caught the Lauren Elder case when she was reported missing. I had him and Peabody do searches for others in that age group, with that basic physical description.'

Because he invariably provided an exceptional sounding board, she went back to the beginning — the body on the bench of the playground — and caught him up.

'The Bad Mommy message. You held that back from the media.'

'Yeah.'

'And it's key.'

'Has to be. I pulled Nadine, and she's doing a deep dive to try to find the original.'

'Who you believe existed, and would've been in that age range, with that physical description, shortly after the turn of the century.'

'Due to fashion — how he dressed her, did her hair, makeup — according to Morris, Mira, and Peabody.'

'A long time to mourn, or hate, or obsess.'

'Yeah, it is.'

She watched a small group of tourists, announcing their status in matching I ❤ NEW YORK tees, gawking up at an airtram — and the street thief who slid through them like butter.

'By the time I stop, you get out, he'd be two blocks gone,' Roarke commented.

Eve looked back, noted he'd already turned a corner. 'Yeah.'

'They might as well wear shirts that say: I Heart Pickpockets. Anyway. Mira figures some sort of more recent psychic break. Mommy kicked it, or kicked him, or something just snapped.'

He wove his way through traffic — miserable traffic — with far more calm than she would have.

'And both women worked at bars — late shift. So you'd deduce the mother did as well.'

'It's possible. Or their work, and the timing, made them easier to grab.'

'He had to look for them first, find candidates that suited his specific needs. But, at least for these two women, he didn't look at other late shifts. Not at licensed companions, at any who work at twenty-four/sevens or building security or maintenance and so on. Which . . . ' He glanced over at her. 'You've factored in.'

'I factored it in, and deduce the probability the mother worked in a bar, or frequented them regularly, is high. It doesn't get us closer to finding Anna Hobe before he kills her.'

'A handful of hours ago, no one knew Anna Hobe had been taken, was being held, by the same person who abducted, held, and killed Lauren Elder.'

'He held Elder for ten days before he killed her.

101

He's had Hobe for seven already.'

Coming fast up on eight, Eve thought.

'He left Elder where we'd find her, and quickly. He has a vehicle. He could have taken the body out of the city, buried her. He has somewhere private enough to hold women. He could have dismembered her, dumped her in a tub of lye. Shit, weighed her down and dumped her in the river. All kinds of ways to dispose of her, to at least stretch out the time between killing and discovery. But he didn't.

'He wanted us to find her. Wanted to see the media reports.'

'You think Hobe doesn't have the ten days.'

'I think he stepped up his schedule, taking Hobe so soon after Elder. Maybe because of the rain, good cover. Maybe because he didn't want to put all his eggs in one box. Maybe because Elder already wasn't working out for him.'

'Two are more difficult to hold than one, so I agree there was some need or reason. It's basket for the eggs, not box.'

She turned in her seat. 'I've seen eggs in boxes. With the little . . . ' She outlined a dip in the air with a hand. 'To hold them in.'

'You gather them up from the hens in a basket.'

'How do you know that? When's the last time you snatched an egg from a chicken, ace?'

'That would be on the far side of never, but I watched my cousin gather them up on the farm in Ireland.'

'Don't they get pissed off? The chickens. Like, 'Hey, that's my egg, you fuckhead.' What's Irish for *fuckhead*?'

'*Fuckhead* translates to all languages. Young Sean

told me they, for the most part, go broody — don't ask me why — but occasionally one might object and have a go at you.'

'I'd brood, too, if I worked to push out an egg and somebody snagged it to make an omelet. Anyway, now I'm thinking about exactly where eggs come from, so I have to erase this entire conversation from my memory bank.'

He only smiled as he turned, and the gates of home opened.

And home stood, fanciful as a castle, its towers and turrets stone gray against the summer-blue sky. Bright things dotted the lush green grass — artfully placed beds of flowers, blooming shrubs and bushes. Trees spread their quiet evening shade.

She thought of Mavis again, in a house not as massive but in its way just as fanciful. And she'd feel this way, Eve thought, probably just this way when she came home from a gig and saw the house she'd made her home.

Welcomed, and grateful.

And her mind shifted to what Elder and Hobe might have felt as they'd walked from work, one in the clear, one in the rain, toward what they'd made home.

'They were nearly there.'

Roarke parked, looked at her.

'He caught them at their most vulnerable, nearly there, when you're just thinking about getting inside, shaking off the day. Or night in their case. Did he think of that? I think so. He's not stupid. A lot, maybe most, criminals are. Just dumb as a basket of rocks. He's not.'

He started to tell her it was a box of rocks, but saw that winding around, and let it go.

103

'Is that what you think when you come through the gates? Getting inside and shaking off the day?'

'Depends, I guess. Because if I'm working one, I usually know it'll take awhile to shake it off. Don't you?'

'I do, yes.' He didn't say his first thought, always, was: Is she home? Is she safe?

She didn't need to hear that.

They went inside together, where Summerset, bony in black, stood with the fat cat at his feet. Galahad pranced over to ribbon through Eve's legs, through Roarke's, and back again.

'Barely late and together,' Summerset observed.

'A bit of tweaking the internals at Mavis's house,' Roarke told him.

'Ah. On schedule there?'

'We are, yes. You should drop by again.'

'Be sure I will.'

'Thoughts, Lieutenant?' Summerset asked as she started up the stairs.

'What? On the house? It's better without the scary wallpaper and nightmare kitchen.'

'A point of agreement. I'll mark the calendar.'

He sort of got her that time, Eve thought as she continued up. But she'd been thinking of home and work and not of giving him a nice little jab.

Next time.

'I need to set up my board and book.'

'Understood.' The cat shot by them because he also understood.

'And I'm hoping I've got some lab reports. All that makeup, the hair products, and she was wearing perfume. I could smell it. Then there's the jewelry he put on her. And the tat.'

104

She glanced over as they turned into her office. 'Forgot, I gave Jamie the tat.'

'Sorry, what?'

'EDD's new part-time intern. Part-time because you finagled getting him part-time interning for you. Long shot, like Nadine coming up with an ID on the mother figure, but it'll keep him busy.'

'If memory serves, he's working in Cybersecurity at my headquarters tomorrow.'

'Your memory always serves. Cybersecurity. Clever of you, keeping it close to cop work.'

'And the head of that division tells me what I already knew. The boy's a bloody genius. Be grateful he didn't decide to tread my earlier path. If he and I had partnered up back in the day? Ah.' Roarke let out a sentimental sigh. 'The possibilities.'

'Cop here. Still a cop standing right here.'

'Darling Eve, you can't fault a man for imagining.'

'Imagine me busting your ass and slapping the cuffs on you.'

Now he grinned, now he grabbed her. 'A different sort of imagining altogether.'

She struggled away from the kiss — after a minute. 'Put a pin in that imagining. I've got work.'

'Since you do, I'll leave you to it, and finish up a few things.' He walked over, opened the doors to her little balcony. 'Then we'll have a meal.'

He stood there a moment in the open doorway with the light streaming in and a gentle breeze, a warm one, playing with all that black silk hair. Stood there, she thought, all tall and lean in his perfect suit, one hand in his pocket.

On her button, she realized. He carried that damn button like a magic charm.

Then he turned, and those wildly blue eyes met hers. His lips — those gorgeously sculpted lips — curved.

'What?'

'I would've busted you,' she said. 'Or worked my ass off trying. I think I'd've busted you in the end. But, damn it, I'd have fallen for you. I'd have fallen for you, and busted you anyway. And you'd have really screwed up my life.'

'If you'd have busted me — and there we strongly disagree — I believe my life would've been considerably more screwed. Especially since I'd have fallen for you as well.'

He walked back to her, ran his hands down her arms, back to her shoulders. 'Isn't it a lovely twist of fate we met at a time neither of us had to put our considerable skills to that test?'

'You were a murder suspect when we met.'

He shook his head, ran a finger down the dent in her chin. 'You knew better. You have those considerable skills and knew better.'

'Yeah, I did. I could fall for a thief, but not a cold-blooded murderer. Which is why you'd have screwed up my life when I busted you on all the other stuff.'

He smiled, gave her a light kiss. 'Not a chance, Lieutenant,' he said as he walked away.

Chance, she thought. Probably. Maybe fifty-fifty. If she'd made it her mission in life.

But she'd made catching killers her mission in life. So she walked to her command center, opened operations, and picked up the mission where she'd left off.

7

She wrote up the interviews with the bartender and Mike, with Liza, updated her home copy of her murder book. Programmed coffee, set up her board with the addition of Anna Hobe, the timeline.

Since the lab hadn't come through, she put her boots on her command center, studied her board, and drank the coffee.

No like crimes, she thought. That didn't mean he hadn't grabbed someone at some other time, experimented . . . .

Didn't fit. Just didn't. Too exact, too precise.

The tat, the piercings, the clothes, the message.

But . . .

'Maybe he killed the mother,' Eve said when Roarke came back in. 'Maybe he snapped, killed the mother, disposed of *that* body. Now he's trying to replace her.'

'That's a cheerful thought.' Like her, he studied the board. 'There's a slight resemblance between Elder and Hobe, but you have to look for it. It's really more the type. Pretty blondes, early twenties, and, from the height and weight listed here, the same basic body type.'

'We have another, a stripper, missing. I gave her to Detective Norman, but I don't see it. She's got three times the tits and more ass.'

'I imagine she'd be grateful for the T&A for more than professional reasons if she knew.'

'She used to be an LC, but failed the screening. She had a habit, maybe still does. Elder and Hobe come

107

clean there. I think he wants clean. Bad Mommies are addicts, right? Wouldn't he see it like that? I don't know, but that's how I see it. Still, I want to find her.'

She stared at the hole in her desk unit. 'Nothing from the lab. Maybe I'll tag Harvo, give her a poke.'

'Lieutenant, she's bound to be home or out with friends at this point in the evening. Possibly enjoying a good meal. It's time we did the same.'

He strolled into the kitchen. The cat, who'd sprawled over Eve's sleep chair, perked up, leaped off, strolled — very nonchalantly — after Roarke.

She listened with half an ear as Roarke informed the cat he knew bloody well he'd already had his evening meal. And being a trained investigator, deduced Roarke would cave and give Galahad a handful of cat treats anyway.

He carried in two domed plates, walked over to set them on the table by the window.

'He had to get the makeup from somewhere,' she said as Roarke walked back to select a bottle of wine from the wall cabinet. 'It was, you know, the full shot.' Eve waved a hand in front of her face.

'So I can see from the crime scene photo. And heavy-handed at that.'

'Yeah. The clothes are probably vintage. Lab has to confirm, but if everyone says they're way out of date, that's likely. How long does makeup last?'

He popped a cork. 'I have no idea, but doubt half a century or so.'

She shot a finger at him as she rose to circle the board. 'That's what I think. Maybe he snaps, kills the mother. Snaps bigger, and hatches this insane idea of replacing her.'

'Wouldn't she, following your current line, be — or

have been — in the neighborhood of eighty?'

'Yeah, but he doesn't want that mom. He wants the one he remembers from when he was a kid.' Absently, she took the wineglass he offered. 'The one who took care of him, made sure he ate, had clothes, all that. Or if she was abusive or messed up, his idealized version. The mother he wanted. And wants.'

Roarke took her free hand, drew her to the table.

She frowned down at the plates, the wine in her hand. Thought about the clothes on her back. 'I guess you're the good mom.'

'Careful where you step.'

He removed the domes.

She saw what she thought was some kind of chicken that managed to look a little crispy and moist at the same time, a scoop of herby rice — he'd snuck some peas in that. And those odd — and oddly tasty — purple carrots.

'It could be a kind of compliment. It is a kind of compliment,' she said as she sat. 'When it's not annoying.'

'Which would make you the child who has to be reminded, and often coaxed, to eat. What did you have for lunch?'

'I had a brownie.'

His eyebrows lifted. 'Really?'

'Good brownie.' She cut into the chicken, sampled it. And realized, yeah, it hit a pretty much empty stomach. 'Nice kick to this.'

She reached over to give his hand a squeeze before he lectured her. 'Thanks.'

'That's sneaky of you.'

'Yeah, but I also mean it. What did you have for lunch?'

'A chef's salad.'

'Why is it a chef's salad? Who's the chef? You don't cook a salad.'

He tapped his fork in the air in her direction. 'That's a weak way to change the subject.'

'Maybe. She caught me, Elder caught me. But it was the where. It was the playground, Roarke. I sat on that same damn bench with Nadine a few weeks ago. A two-minute walk from where Mavis and the rest of them are going to live. Sat there with kids running around. Chased off some asshole street thief and warned him I'd kick his ass if he ever came back where my friend's kid played. I meant it.

'How much worse is this?'

'I know.' He gave her hand a squeeze in return. 'She's going to white sage it.'

'What? Who and what?'

He smiled again. 'Mavis didn't mention it to you, I see. She's going to ask Peabody — with her Free-Ager cred — to white sage the playground once you find him and put him away. No doubt in her, absolutely none, you'll do just that.'

'What does that even mean? The sage thing.'

'It's a kind of purifying ritual. Banishes the negative energy.'

'Oh, for —' Eve cut herself off. 'Fine, good. Whatever works for her.' She scooped up some rice, then considered. 'Is it legal?'

'I don't see why it wouldn't be.'

'Okay then.' But she'd check. 'So, Jamie. What're you paying him?'

'Triple what he's making interning for Feeney.'

'Figured.' She smiled, drank some wine. 'He's going to end up a cop.'

110

'Odds are you're right, but a good taste of the private sector may change that. Still, if and when he decides on a cop's life, he'll know it's his calling, won't he?'

'Now who's sneaky?'

'We can say that's my calling. So, tell me what I can do.'

He would always ask, she knew, and would always mean it.

'Identify a woman who may or may not have existed about sixty years ago.'

'Challenging.'

'Well, seriously, I've got Jamie and Nadine pushing on that — and good luck to them. I'll dig at it myself, but . . . If she existed, and if she had a criminal record, and she had the tat — the identifying mark — at the time, maybe we hit. That would give us something to work off of. Did she have a kid? Who's the kid, where's the kid? And maybe she didn't have a bio kid. Maybe she fostered, or served as a mother figure in some other way.'

'Most of the time, the truth is simple. You have to look at all the angles and possibilities, but the simplest is the woman he's trying to re-create is or was his mother.'

'You thought Meg was yours until a couple years ago.'

'Another truth.' He thought it over as they ate. 'I never felt anything but fear and contempt for her, and certainly wouldn't have tried to re-create her. Why would I want back a woman who, it seemed to me, derived her greatest joy in making my life a misery?'

'So your truth would be that this woman who may or may not exist — and screw it, she existed — didn't do that.'

'First, we agree she existed. You don't do what was done to Elder over a phantom or illusion. The simplest answer is he, at one time at least, depended on her. Loved her, as children love their mothers.'

'That's not love.'

'Love flips to hate easily enough for some. And obsession. Wouldn't you say he wants what he had, or believed he had?'

'Yes. Or he wants what he thinks he should've had.'

'Ah.' Roarke lifted his wineglass in a toast. 'That rings of truth. Simple, impossibly complex, and truth.'

'It feels like truth to me. He stole what you should've had — Patrick Roarke. He took away, killed, a mother who loved you when you were too young to remember her, replaced her with Meg. Bad Mommy.'

'So he did, and Christ knows Meg was as bad as they come. You wonder if the woman he tried to re-create was taken from him, or him from her.'

Eve picked up her wine, studied it before she took a small sip. 'People say *raising kids*. It's weird to me because they say *raising crops*, right? But that's the term.'

'I suppose because you plant, and tend, and protect, and take pride in watching what you tend grow.'

'Okay, well, people like Meg, like Stella, they're not interested in raising anything or anyone. It's about the pleasure in abusing the weaker, smaller. Neglect, that's second nature. Why isn't it first nature?' She frowned over it. 'It's their nature to neglect and abuse, so I'm saying first nature.'

He loved her mind. 'As you like.'

'I've wondered if she — this mother figure — raised him, and if she raised him, if she was a major part of his life through adulthood, why would he hunt young

112

women? If she recently died, or they had some sort of break, if — because he's certainly capable — he killed the original, why the replication of the young mother?'

She looked out the open doors at the deepening sky, the ending of the day.

'It's possible, sure. Possible he craves that return to the innocence of childhood, and I circle back to that. But if the timeline is accurate, if the look and the clothes he used weren't just some whim or convenience, he's old enough for Elder and Hobe to be his kids, not the other way around. But if he lost her during the timeline we believe, if she died, she left, went to prison, and he was taken away from her?'

'He could come to idolize her,' Roarke finished. 'Or insist his image of her be perfect. That's where you're leaning.'

'Maybe. Yes.' She rose to walk back to the board, and tapped the crime scene photo of the body on the bench, the swings and playground equipment in the background.

'This. He could've left her anywhere. He didn't dump her. He placed her, and here. Laid her out, very tidily, on this bench, at this playground. He's seen kids playing there, you bet your tight Irish ass, and mothers watching them. Happy place, family place. He was supposed to have happy family places like this, maybe did for a while. She was supposed to sit on a bench like this, watch him. I don't know, applaud when he hung from the bars or whatever.'

He got up, picked up his wine and hers. He handed her the glass as he joined her at the board. 'Keep going.'

'He didn't beat her, torture her — or not physically, as being shackled for ten fucking days is plenty

113

of torture. But he fed her, drugged her — you can bet your ass on that again — but he didn't starve her. He branded her, and yeah, penetrated her. You could look at the piercings that way. But he didn't rape her. He made her into the mother.

'And in the end, when she didn't satisfy his ideal, or his sick need, he killed her. But quickly — didn't draw it out. He used a sharp, but he didn't go into a rage and stab her, slice her up, mutilate her.'

'A clean kill.'

'Yeah, clean. Then he sewed up the wound. Look here.' She tapped the autopsy photo of the neck wound. 'Morris thinks maybe an upholstery needle and thread — lab to confirm. But look how careful and precise the stitching. Nothing sloppy there. That took time and care. Then he washed the body, dressed her, did the hair, the makeup, put perfume on her. He covered the wound with a ribbon, added the jewelry. He painted her nails.'

'All how he remembered her, and how, wouldn't you say, he thought she looked her best?'

Now she poked a finger at his chest. 'I would. I would say that exactly. The note? Kid's paper, crayon? You can see some of the anger there. That's not neat, but childish printing.'

'You're seeing him as two aspects of one person.'

'I damn well am. He's shithouse crazy. We get him, he's probably going in a mentally deficient max security facility. I can live with that. But he has to make a mistake — they always do, but I don't know if Hobe has time for that mistake. I don't know how to find him until he does, or until we find the woman, the mother, who he wants.'

'Isn't it possible Hobe will find a way to satisfy him,

114

to keep him using her, until he makes that mistake or you find the mother figure?'

'Sure. She'd have to be damn smart and even more self-possessed.'

Shake it off, she reminded herself. For a minute.

'I'll take care of the dishes. No, I'll do it,' she insisted when she saw him start to object. 'It'll give me time to clear my head. I want to push some of this at Mira, see how she thinks. I need to tell Peabody to meet me at the lab, and I'm leaving a message for Harvo that I need some answers when I come in, first thing in the morning.'

'Again, what can I do to help?'

'Financials, at least right now, don't play in.'

'And that's a pity for me.'

'He has to have a place. He knew that playground, so I think he lives or works, owns or rents a property in that area. Close enough he'd pass by it often enough to target it. He needs a place private enough where he can take these women, hold them.'

She circled the board. 'He wouldn't keep them drugged out or gagged the whole time, right? What would be the point? And he fed Elder. She was awake enough to eat a meal before he killed her. He knew the bars — he had to spot them to want them. Lower West, Tribeca, Chelsea, maybe Little Italy. Maybe. It's a big area. He has a vehicle. Doesn't mean he owns it, but he has use of one.'

'So I should start looking for a building — a house, a warehouse, garage — something secure enough he could keep prisoners. Which is what they are.'

'Owns or rents — single individual, most likely male. It's a big area and, hell, it may not be owned or rented in his name, but it's somewhere to look.'

115

'So I will.'

'Could be a workplace, if he runs it, and it has a private, secured area. It's a big area,' she said again.

'Then I'll get started.'

She dealt with the dishes, and it gave her time to clear her head, align her thoughts. After programming coffee, she sat at her command center to send some of those thoughts, some questions to Mira. She sent memos to Peabody, to Harvo.

Then she called up a map on her wall screen, and highlighted each point.

Elder's apartment, her workplace, the playground. Hobe's apartment and workplace.

He has a territory, she thought again, and her own territory fell into it. Where she once lived, where her friends now lived. Where she worked.

Did he pass by her old apartment building or walk past Cop Central? Maybe he got takeout from the same places she had once upon a time.

Or, she admitted, lived or worked just far enough away he had his own little spots.

Bits and pieces, that's all she had. So she gathered them together and worked to make them fit.

The mother, she thought again. It was all about the mother.

The mother was the key.

BEFORE

Joe took care of her in the big old house his paternal grandparents had left him when they'd died — died together as they'd lived together for sixty-eight years.

His parents had resented that, of course, though they'd had no love for the place. As they'd resented him for using the family money for his education, then settling for work in the ER instead of a more prestigious private practice.

She'd begged him not to take her to a hospital, not to call the police. He'd agreed primarily because besides dehydration, exhaustion, exposure, infected insect bites, her injuries were minor. He had the means and skills to treat her at home.

And he agreed because she'd seemed so desperate and fragile.

She didn't remember her name, or anything else. She had no identification or belongings other than the clothes on her back.

She knew she'd walked a long way, but couldn't tell him how long, or from what direction. When she'd hydrated, when she'd eaten the soup he heated for her, she seemed strong enough to shower — as she'd asked.

Still, he stayed right outside the bathroom door.

He put fresh sheets on the bed in the guest room, gave her one of his T-shirts to wear.

He treated the bites — the poor woman was covered with them. Treated the broken blisters on her feet. He gave her an antibiotic, and kept watch in case she had an allergic reaction.

She slept twelve hours and woke disoriented and a little feverish.

Citing a family emergency, he took off work for five days.

While she ate, slept, healed, he studied dissociative amnesia. When he thought her stable enough physically, he tried basic talk therapy, cognitive therapy, guided her through meditation techniques.

But none of his gentle prodding brought back any memory. She had no name, no past, no possessions. And seemed, as his studies had suggested was often common with her sort of memory loss, content not to remember.

'I don't care,' she told him.

She wore one of his shirts, and they sat in the sunshine in the garden he kept thinking about hiring someone to help him deal with.

'You need to know who you are. What happened to you. Where you come from. If you have family.'

'I don't care,' she said again. 'I feel like my life started when you found me, and everything before that was dark and hard and mean. I don't want any of it, Joe. I don't want to know if I was a terrible person or a nice one. You said there haven't been any reports on someone like me missing or in trouble.'

'No, but —'

'If no one cares enough to look for me, why should I care enough to look for them? You cared enough.' She smiled at him, reached for his hand. 'You saved me. I was so scared, so lost, so tired, so sick. So alone. And there you were.'

'Your memory could come back, anytime.'

'I don't care.'

She shook back her short, shaggy hair and lifted her face to the sun. 'You know how this feels? It feels free. It feels new.' Tipping her head back, she closed her eyes. 'It feels safe and warm. Will you let me stay?' She looked back at him. 'At least for a while. I could clean. I don't know if I can cook, but I can try. I could learn. I could weed the garden and cut the grass. I know you have to go back to work, and I feel stronger every day. I could help you take care of this beautiful old house.'

'Of course you can stay until you remember or you're just ready to go.'

She closed her eyes again, but kept the grip on his hand.

'I don't think I ever knew anyone like you. I don't think I could have and ever gotten so lost. You brought me back. I don't know from what, and I don't care, but you brought me back. Would you name me?'

'Listen, I —'

'I'd like to use a name you give me, to think of myself as that someone.' She smiled at him now, her color healthy again, the raw, red bites fading. 'A name you like, and I can try to be who she is.'

'You need to be who you are.'

She smiled again. 'It's just a name. I'd like to have one.'

'Violet. The first time I walked you outside, you picked some violets. You must like them.'

'Violet. It's pretty. It's perfect.' She held out a hand to shake. 'Hi, Joe. I'm Violet. It's nice to meet you.'

NOW

Mary Kate knew he'd come back. The rumbling sound overhead — the first time she'd thought thunder — meant he left or came back. She usually heard footsteps overhead shortly before or shortly after.

She figured he must have a job, so he left in the morning, came back at night. So it must be night. Or evening. Or screw it, the son of a bitch worked the

119

night shift and now it was morning.

Time of day didn't matter. Getting away meant everything.

She'd tried calling out after the first rumble of the day — or night. She'd banged on the door, called out her name. But she didn't think anyone remained behind the door across from hers, where she thought she'd heard someone crying and calling before.

She wanted there to be someone. She didn't care how selfish it was, she just didn't want to be alone.

When he brought her breakfast, he carried in a lamp. Though he placed it well out of her reach, he showed her — gleefully — that she just had to clap her hands to turn it on and off.

'Try it, Mommy! Try it!'

Terrified, she obediently clapped it on and off, on again while he giggled.

'I made you scrambled eggs and toast and a fruit cup so you'll eat a balanced breakfast. You should've told me it's important to eat a balanced breakfast.'

'Didn't I?'

He ticked his finger back and forth. 'Uh-uh. Now, after you eat, you can wash in the sink and change clothes. It's important to be clean. You shouldn't have let me get so dirty all the time.'

'No, I shouldn't have. That was a mistake. I'm sorry.'

His eyes glittered in a way that had her heart slamming into her throat. 'You made lots of them, didn't you?'

'Yes, and I'm sorry for all of them. I'm going to do much better.'

He said nothing, just studied her. She wondered who looked at her so deeply. The little boy or the man?

120

'We'll see,' the man said. 'Now, I made you tea and you have two tubes of water.'

He set the tray on the cot — everything disposable, she noted. Nothing with weight, nothing sharp — and still she wondered if she could somehow overpower him.

But even as she coiled to try, his eyes flashed to hers. The man's, she thought. The crazy man's, not the little boy's.

'I'm giving you a chance. You should make the most of it.'

He stepped back, out of reach. 'Eat what I give you or you'll do without.'

'Are you going? Can't you stay?' She had to swallow hard, force a smile to her face.

He'd moved to the door, but turned, gave her that hard look again.

'I have to work. I have responsibilities.'

'I . . . don't have anything to do. Shouldn't I have responsibilities? I should be taking care of you. Making your breakfast. A healthy, balanced breakfast.'

She couldn't be sure if she saw interest light in his eyes or something else.

'That's not on the schedule yet. You're number three. Number two comes first.'

'Oh.' Her hands shook, but she managed to lean over, grip the sides of the tray to set it on her lap. 'What about number one?'

'She was bad, had to be punished. I had to take her away and leave her like she left me. If number two keeps being bad, you'll get your turn.'

'Is there a number four?'

He smiled. 'Not yet.'

'Please, can't you —' But he went out, and the door

closed. The locks clicked.

She wanted to throw the tray across the room, but understood he'd hurt her if she did. She tried a few bites, waited to see if it made her sick or sleepy. If so, she'd flush it all down the little toilet. When she had no reaction, she ate cautiously, nibbles at a time. She needed to be strong.

She decided against the tea — too easy to drug — flushed it. But the water tube seals were intact.

She heard the footsteps and, not long after that, rumbling.

She tried the calling out, the screaming, the banging on the walls.

As she had before, she looked everywhere for any kind of weapon. To fight the fear, she washed up in the sink, changed into clothes neatly folded on a bench bolted to the floor.

The clothes always had buttons or a zipper down the side of the pants leg so she could fasten them with the shackles.

He wasn't stupid.

He'd made this place. He had a purpose. He was a sick, crazy old man, but, no, he wasn't stupid.

She couldn't be stupid, either.

For a while she tried, and failed, to pry and pull a pipe from the wall. She'd already tried to use the disposable spoon to turn the bolts in her shackles, but broke the spoon almost immediately.

The pipe wouldn't budge, and, frustrated, she slammed her fist against it. Metal banged on metal. Furious, she beat her shackles against the pipe, until she folded to the ground weeping.

Then she heard it, the answering sound. Metal against metal.

'I'm here! I'm here!' Shouting, she scrambled to her feet. 'I'm Mary Kate Covino!'

She thought, as she strained her ears, she heard a faint cry in return. So she tried again. 'Are you locked in? Who are you? I'm Mary Kate Covino!'

She did hear something! She couldn't make out the words, but she heard a voice. She tried shouting louder. 'Can you hear me? Bang once if you hear me.'

When the single bang sounded, she closed her eyes, and tears rolled down her cheeks. 'I'm Mary Kate Covino. Can you yell louder? Can you tell me your name?'

It came in a high, thin scream she could barely make out. 'Anna? You're Anna. Bang once for yes, two for no. One bang, okay, okay. Anna,' she said aloud. 'Are you chained up, too? One bang. God, God.' She sipped some water, cleared her throat, shouted, 'Do you know how long you've been here?'

Two bangs.

She leaned against the wall, tried to clear the fear. She shouted questions. Added three bangs for I don't know.

It felt like hours, she couldn't be sure, they communicated. Once in a while she made out a few words.

She learned the crazy man had grabbed Anna and locked her in a room just like hers. Chained up, no window, drugged.

When her voice gave out, she pushed her burning throat one last time. 'I'm sorry, Anna, I can't yell anymore. I have to rest, but I'm here.'

After the single bang in response, Mary Kate drank the last swallow of water, then crawled onto her cot.

She needed to rest, to think.

She wasn't alone.

8

When she couldn't find a new angle to probe, when she found herself circling the same path with the same results, Eve pushed away from her command center.

There was simply nothing more she could do. A part of her believed Anna Hobe's time was ticking down, but there was nothing she could do to stop that clock.

The lab, she thought as she walked to the board again. She had to hope the lab provided some leads, some data, some something she could get her teeth into.

It cycled through her brain again. Tattoo, piercings, makeup, hair products, perfume, clothes, shoes.

She'd given the lab rats a big goddamn bouquet of forensics. They'd better come through.

She walked into Roarke's office to find he'd switched to water while he worked. He'd shed his tie, his suit jacket. Rolled up his sleeves, tied back his hair.

How appalled would he be if he knew she thought of this as his Roarke-cop mode?

Very, she concluded, so she'd save that for when she wanted to annoy him.

'Anything I can use?'

'A large area,' he reminded her. 'With plenty of buildings, commercial, residential, a combination, rented, owned, condemned, in the rehab process, that could meet your criteria.'

'I'll take them.'

He glanced over at her, and immediately saw both

stress and fatigue. 'It would take you days if not weeks to vet all that fall into the general parameters. It'll take a bit more time to refine and eliminate some of the possibles.'

'It's going to be a single man.'

'Understood, but a single man may own or rent under another name, a business name, a false front or legitimate one. A single man may have recently broken ties and not yet changed the ownership or lease — or may be legally bound to hold said ownership or lease in a business name, a partnership — marriage or business — and so on. And you know all that as well as I do.'

Since she did, she walked to his window, back again, then dropped down on the slick new sofa he'd installed when they'd redone their offices.

He'd kept the portrait she'd given him for their first anniversary on the wall across from his command center. It made her feel a little sentimental to see the two of them under that arbor of flowers on their wedding day.

And reminded her, with a kind of jolt, their third — Jesus! — anniversary was coming up in a few weeks.

Which meant she had to come up with another gift.

It never ended.

She scanned his office as if an idea would jump out and dance. All she saw equaled attractive, efficient, stylish, and important.

And she realized she'd never really looked at his space from this angle. She'd never actually sat on this sofa.

He had shelves with stuff on them — artfully arranged. She noted the photograph he'd asked her for, and she'd hunted up. One of her in her Academy days. He had the medal the NYPSD had bestowed on him — their highest civilian honor. Some books — actual books because he liked actual books — held upright by a pair of what she thought were dragons.

And among the other bits and pieces, some of which looked old, some of which were likely priceless, the photo of his mother holding him when he'd been an infant.

The child she'd never had the chance to raise.

Personal, she thought. All of it. Things he kept at home rather than in his big, fancy office in Midtown.

Looked like she had to think of something personal.

She scanned the office again. It sure as hell didn't strike her he needed anything else in here.

'What's this wall color?' she wondered out loud.

He glanced up. 'Ah, some sort of sage, if I recall.'

'Like what Peabody's going to burn in the playground once we toss this asshole in a cage?'

'I couldn't say.' What he could do was switch the search to auto.

'Do you ever sit on the couch? I've never sat on this couch.'

He rose, walked over, sat. 'We're sitting on it now.'

'Your office is about three times the size of my office at Central.'

'Easily.'

'But it's smaller than mine here. Why is that?'

'First, because the original purpose of yours was to replicate your apartment so you'd give it up and live with me. And second, I don't need the room to gather up teams of cops, feed them, brief them as you often do here. Or need the room so we can sit for a meal

126

together.'

'You put in a lot of time over there, with teams of cops and without. Expert consultant, civilian.'

'I do.'

'I don't spend much in here, consulting or whatever.'

'You don't.'

'Do you want me to?'

He brushed a hand over her hair. 'I would very much appreciate no.'

She let out a short laugh. 'You don't think I could help negotiate a deal for a couple rings of Saturn or give input into the design of the next indispensable widget?'

'I think it's very fortunate the purchase of any of the rings of Saturn — which aren't on the market, by the way — or the design of the next indispensable widget aren't a matter of life and death, law and order, or justice served. But if they were, you'd find a way.'

'I think that's an insult wrapped in a compliment. Or the other way around.'

She started to get up; he tugged her back down. 'It occurs to me this very nice sofa has yet to be used to its full potential.'

Because sometime during the sitting she'd relaxed, she didn't object when he eased her back.

'For napping?'

'Some other time.' He released her weapon harness; she tugged the tie out of his hair.

'It's comfortable. We've got a big bed probably being used by a cat right now, but this is comfortable.'

'And roomy enough,' he added as he pressed his lips to the pulse point in her throat. 'Lights, twenty percent,' he ordered. When they dimmed, he looked down at her. 'Quieter. It's nice to have some quiet time with you.'

She smiled, raised her head to nip at his bottom lip. 'Bet it doesn't last long.'

'Is that a challenge or a request?'

She bit him again, not quite as lightly. 'Guess.'

He responded exactly as she wanted with a deep, dazzling, drugging kiss that washed the day away. If she could have gotten her hands between them, she'd have gone to work on his shirt buttons. Since she couldn't, she just wrapped around him.

Quiet time could wait. She welcomed the need and the wild, the demands and the desperation.

It felt right, it felt necessary, to just shove aside everything but their bodies, locked tight, their hearts, already drumming in tandem, their wants, already meshed.

She dragged his shirt out of his pants so her hands could rush under it to skin.

When he simply tore her shirt to get to hers, she let out a quick laugh that ended on a moan. Then his mouth was on her, taking, feeding, feasting. Everything in her reached for more so she arched against him, ground center to center.

Primal. After a day struggling to find logic inside insanity, she wanted the primal.

He reached for more, fighting to shove her harness, her tattered shirt off her shoulders. But she reared up, took his mouth with hers again until his blood burned.

He muttered in Irish, lost, lost in her, in the feel, the taste of her, in the need that radiated from her to lodge in him and spread, spread to scorching.

He pulled at her belt, and she ripped his shirt as he

had hers.

Half-mad, half-dressed, they grappled with clothes, and, in the rush, rolled onto the floor. He hit first, so she straddled him. Already breathless, she took him in.

Deep, deep, fast, crazed. Hips pumped as if life itself hung in the balance.

He filled her, as he'd filled so many empty spaces. Outside the window, the city lights spoke of the world she'd sworn to protect and serve. But here, here, this belonged to only them.

He rose up, wrapped around her as she had him. Their mouths met again, ravenous. When she arched back, when he watched her fly, when her body shook, and her cry of release was his name, he said hers and went with her.

They lay tangled in clothes or remnants thereof. She still wore one boot, with her pants leg trailing from it. He, she noted, had managed to get both his fancy shoes off, and his pants.

'I believe I guessed correctly.'

Even in her current sexual haze he made her laugh. 'I gave you a pretty big hint.'

'You did, and I believe you lured me over to the sofa so you could have your way with me.'

'Worked, too, though ways were had all around. This used to be a really nice shirt. Yours, too.'

'More where they came from. I do, however, believe we've earned the big bed. Galahad will have to make room.'

'We still didn't bang on that sofa.'

'We'll try again, sometime soon.'

She rolled to tug her pants up. 'We have to get rid of the evidence.'

'Evidence?'

'Torn shirts. We can't just dump them somewhere.'

He found it oddly endearing when she actually buttoned — two buttons — what was left of hers.

'Summerset will find them, so they must be destroyed.'

He held out her second boot before he picked up his clothes. 'I can promise he won't scold us, as he'll never mention it.'

'He'll know.'

Adoring her, he scooped her up and started to the elevator.

'You're still naked. Doesn't it bother you to just wander around naked?'

'I'm not wandering, I'm going to bed with my wife.'

'After we destroy the evidence.'

★ ★ ★

The child without a name had to kneel on the chair to reach all the pretty colors the mother used to get pretty. She wanted to get pretty, too, because she was scrawny and stupid and ugly. If she could be pretty, the mother would be nice to her.

She poked the brush into some of the pink powder, and dabbed and swiped it on her cheeks. It made her laugh.

Pretty!

She played with some of the glittery stuff and tried smearing it on her eyelids. Delighted, and she had few delights, she tried more colors. She wasn't sure of all their names, but she knew things had names.

She didn't.

She didn't know how old she was, had no concept

130

of years or age. She knew the concept of pain because it hurt when the mother or the father smacked her. And the concept of hunger when they forgot to feed her, or didn't feed her because she'd been bad.

She didn't understand bad except that she was, a lot.

She knew the concept of fear because she lived in it.

But sometimes the father tickled her to make her laugh. And sometimes his tickles hurt or made her feel scared and sick.

If she could be pretty, it would be good. It was good when she wasn't hungry and when they didn't lock her in the dark, when they didn't give her something that made her wake up feeling funny and wrong and in another place.

When you were pretty, people were nice to you. Like when the mother got all pretty, the father smiled and said things like: Stella, you're a knockout!

She could be a knockout with all the pretty colors.

For a while, she played with the tube of lipstick when she figured out how to wind it up, wind it down. She didn't know toys, but she embraced the game before she smeared the gooey stick over her lips.

Red! She knew that color. Red, red, red!

It tasted funny, but she didn't mind, because pretty!

Then the mother came in, and proud, she beamed in the mirror. And the fear came fast. It wasn't nice she saw in the mother's eyes.

She screamed the words that meant bad. Brat, bitch, goddamn fucker. The cracking slap against her thin, pink cheek snapped her head back. The pain burned, and the second slap knocked her off the chair. Her head smacked the floor so now the pain screamed like

131

the mother screamed.

She didn't know the concept of hate, but she saw it in the mother's eyes when hands gripped her, nails dug into her arms.

Shaking her, shaking her, then it felt like she flew. When she landed, hard, crying because crying was all she had, she was somewhere else.

Outside. But she wasn't allowed to go outside, not by herself, and hardly ever. She knew outside because it was out the windows. She sat on something with colors, and it wasn't hard like the floor.

She didn't know the names for them, but she saw swings and slides and springs with funny animals, climbing bars and carousels. Fascinated, she forgot the pain, the fear even as a line of blood dribbled from the corner of her red-slicked mouth.

Getting up, she bounced on the springy safety surface on her way to the swings. She pushed at one, watched it rock back and forth.

She saw the ladder to the slide, though she didn't know the words for them. Walking to it, she climbed up and stood for a minute, not sure what came next. Curious, she sat, and as she shifted, she started to slide. A quick snap of fear, and then the thrill. She landed on her butt on the springy surface, then scrambled up to do it again.

When she landed again, a woman stood there. She cringed, but never thought to run. They always caught you if you ran, and smacked and smacked.

But the woman crouched down.

'Figured it out, right? I guess you would have.'

She didn't see mean in the eyes. She saw sad. And her own. Her eyes.

'You're going to have to go back, and I'm sorry

132

about that. I can't stop it,' Eve told her, told herself. 'Not yet anyway.'

She didn't speak. You didn't talk to anybody but the mother or the father. Ever.

'You're going to get through it, and you're going to be okay.'

'I should never have let Richie talk me into having you.'

Eve stood, turned, putting herself between Stella and the child she'd been. 'Your mistake, but then, you didn't give it a lot of time before you took off. Left him to beat me and rape me.'

'He turned out to be a loser, just like you. I stuffed food in your mouth, changed your filthy diapers. What did you ever do for me?'

'Not a damn thing.' Wasn't it odd, wasn't it strange, Eve thought, Stella wore clothes very like — not exact, but very like — those of the dead woman on the bench.

'I hated you before you were born. And a skinny whelp like you wouldn't've been the moneymaker Richie figured. I copped to that pretty quick, and I had my own life to live.'

Eve gestured to the body on the bench. 'Somebody slit her throat.'

Stella looked back, shrugged. 'Probably deserved it.'

'She didn't. You're going to end the same way, a blade across the jugular. Some would say you deserved it, but I can't. I don't say it. You deserved a cage, and a long life inside it.'

'You wanted me dead. If you could've, you'd've killed me like you did Richie.'

'You're wrong about that, but everything about you

is wrong. Take another ride, kid,' she told the child standing frozen behind her.

'Can you take me home with you?'

'Not yet, sorry. She's going to make your life hell for a while, so take another ride first.'

When the child ran to the ladder, Eve turned to Stella again. 'I just figured something out. It was all going to happen anyway, the beatings, the torment, the rapes. But at least I didn't have you making it even worse. You did me a favor by leaving.'

'Fuck you.'

As the child let out a sound of joy on her way down the slide, Eve saw the backhand coming.

She let it come and knock her out of the dream.

Roarke had an arm around her, with his free hand stroking her face. 'Come back now,' he murmured as the cat butted his head against her side.

'I'm okay. I'm all right.' But she let her head fall to his shoulder as he pulled her in. 'It wasn't that bad. It wasn't one of the bad ones.'

'Could've fooled me. Us,' he corrected as Galahad tried to worm between them. Roarke eased back to give the cat room and studied Eve's face.

He'd called for lights at ten percent when he'd realized she'd been in the grip of a nightmare. He bumped them up to twenty now.

'You were crying in your sleep.' He brushed a tear away with a fingertip.

'It wasn't me. Or it was, but kid me.'

'You'll tell me. I'll get you some water, and you'll tell me.'

'Yeah. You're dressed,' she realized when he got up for the water. 'It's dark, and you're already in a suit. What time is it?'

134

'Nearly half-five. I have a holo meeting with Prague shortly.'

'Prague, sure, of course.'

'I'll reschedule it.'

'No, don't. It wasn't that bad.' She took the water. 'Really.'

'You'll tell me, then I'll decide whether to take the meeting or reschedule.'

'Okay, fine. It's all this mother stuff that kicked it off. Stella dream.'

In those eyes, those glorious blue eyes, she saw guilt and grief and fury.

'I should have realized this would stir that up.'

'Even you can't fix everything. I don't know how old I was. Older than Bella,' she began, and told him.

'In the end,' she said when she'd finished, 'it was a good thing for my subconscious to work out. Because in the end was truth, what I said to her. She did me a favor leaving. If she'd stayed, it would've been worse. If she'd stayed, I might not have gotten away.'

'You took yourself to the playground.'

'Yeah. Symbolic dead mother, throat slit, on the bench. And Stella, who ended the same way. It's logical.'

While the guilt and rage had eased during her telling of it, the grief for the child she'd been remained. He pressed his lips to her brow, just held them there.

'You gave yourself another trip down the sliding board.'

'Yeah. Well, I knew what was coming, so why not grab the fun for a second? I don't much get what's fun about sliding down a plastic tube, but I guess it seemed like the thing at the time.'

She sat back a moment, wished the water she'd

finished would miraculously reappear as coffee.

'I think I'm leaning toward his mother — the killer — dying or abandoning him as a kid. I think I may be leaning there because of yours dying, mine taking off. And I need to set that aside and work the facts and evidence.'

Though she seemed steady again, he stroked her hair. Couldn't seem to stop touching her.

'Your instincts are every bit as valuable as facts and evidence.'

'Usually I'd agree they're almost as valuable, but I need to keep some distance this time. You need to go to work, and you don't have a tie. You always have a tie.' She ran a hand down the front of his shirt. 'I'm okay,' she added, knowing he'd object. 'I'm going down to the gym, sweat the rest of this out. Go buy Prague.'

'I'm not after buying it.' He leaned down to touch his lips to hers. 'Just a piece or two.'

He picked up the tie he'd dropped when he'd rushed to her, and slid it under the collar of his shirt. 'What do you think Mavis would do if she came on Bella playing with her makeup?'

'Laugh. Then help her put more on.'

'And there you have it. I'll be an hour.'

'That works for me.'

She spent another minute in bed, stroking the cat. 'You know, between you and Roarke I ended up with a couple of solid moms. Not an insult,' she added, and gave him a good scratch before she got up.

She fed him, and if she indulged him with seared tuna he deserved it.

After pulling on shorts, a support tank, she rode down to the gym. A good sweat, she decided, because

136

in truth, seeing herself as a child, that helpless need, that helpless fear, unnerved her.

She programmed a five-mile obstacle course run, and, on a whim, on the streets of Prague. When she finished, dripping and satisfied, she spent another fifteen on resistance and power lifting before she stretched it out.

Her initial thought was to end the whole deal with a swim, but she found herself turning into the dojo.

She didn't like meditation. In fact, it usually annoyed the crap out of her. But she decided, considering all, to give it a shot.

She programmed five minutes with the master, sat on the mat, crossed her legs.

She breathed, exhaling tension (or trying to) as instructed. She let her mantra play in her head, which was — her secret — *fuck this, fuck this, fuck this.*

She pictured a blank screen, normally the best she could do before her mind started wandering to a case, or paperwork, or why chocolate wasn't one of the major food groups.

The blank screen turned a soft blue, began to ripple gently. She floated on it, just floated until the chimes sounded.

'You did well,' the master told her. 'Take the calm and clear into your day.' He put his hands together at his heart, bowed. 'Namaste.'

She bowed in return. 'Namaste.'

When she stepped out of the elevator, Roarke walked in.

'And here's timing,' he said.

'I went to Prague, too. Five-mile run, obstacles. You probably bought or already own some of what I ran through. Gonna grab a shower. Oh, hey.' She shoved at her hair as she walked toward the bathroom. 'I meditated for, like, five minutes. Okay, probably three before I got there, but that's two minutes and fifty seconds more than I've managed before.'

She hit the bathroom, called back, 'And I fed the cat. Don't let him bullshit you.'

Roarke glanced over at Galahad. 'It appears the lieutenant's back in form.'

When she came back, he sat, the stock reports muted on the wall screen, a tablet in hand and the cat across his lap. Breakfast, whatever he'd chosen, sat domed on the table.

She poured coffee, then lifted the lids to find he'd gone for the full Irish.

'You're worried I'll skip lunch again.'

'If you do' — he set the cat on the floor — 'you'll have a good breakfast in you.'

'I guess we're going to see the Irish next month, right?'

He looked up, met her eyes. 'I'd like to.'

'Fine with me.' She sat and started on the bacon. 'That quick trip to catch Cobbe doesn't really count. Where else?'

He rubbed a hand on her thigh. 'Where would you like to go?'

'You've got something in mind. You always have something in mind.'

'I thought you might enjoy Greece, play tourist among the ancient sites, then there's a villa on Corfu. Sun-washed beaches, olive groves, vineyards.'

'See, you always have something in mind. Your villa?'

He smiled. 'Not yet. We'll see how you like it.'

'Yeah, I'm going to be critical of a villa in Greece.

What were you working on? On the tablet.'

'Not work. I was looking at the final design for Mavis's studio.'

He picked up the tablet, brought it up for her.

'Seriously? It looks so . . .'

'Professional?'

'Yeah, it does. Sure, it's got Mavis all over it. The colors — lots of color in that . . . I guess it's a lounge or break area.'

'Energy, Mavis claims.'

'Play area for the kid, and the next one.'

'Kitchen area.' Roarke brought the view in. 'Full bath, half bath, a dressing area. That for when she wants to get into costume. But the equipment, the studio proper — state-of-the-art. And she's learned her art very well indeed.'

It shouldn't be such a surprise, Eve admitted, to see the Mavis mix of the colorful and foolish with the absolute solid.

'Back when, I never thought she was serious, working at the Blue Squirrel. She didn't sound serious, either. Not like now.'

'Suited her audience, got her attention. Her style's still very much her own.'

'Hobe has a poster of her, signed, personalized, on her wall. I didn't tell Mavis that.'

'No need, is there?'

'No. Mavis might've gone into Mike's Place, it's the kind of place she'd go for fun. Maybe even met Hobe at some point, but it doesn't connect. So no point in telling her.'

'I'll have a list of possible properties sometime today.'

'That'll be good. I'm counting on the lab giving

me something. Getting an early enough start I can hit there before Harvo or any of them get started on something else, so I can cut the line if I need to.'

She polished off most of the eggs. 'I need to check in with Norman about the stripper. She doesn't fit, but who says he can't adjust? I need something I can start pulling out and tying together.'

'It's been less than twenty-four hours.'

'Not for Hobe.'

She topped off her coffee, then took it with her into her closet. She half expected Roarke to come in, eyeball what she chose, but she heard him warning the cat to cease and desist.

She went for brown trousers, a navy jacket, and spotted a shirt that had needle-thin stripes of both.

How could he complain about that?

She hit on navy boots with brown laces she swore hadn't been in there the day before.

When she came out for her weapon harness, her badge, and the rest, he waited until she'd shrugged into the jacket.

'You look ready to roll, Lieutenant.'

'Because I am. That five miles set me up.'

'It might've been the meditation.'

'Hope not, because I don't think I can pull that off again. I think it was a, what do you call it, an aberration. Send me whatever you've got on that search. We can start slimming it down.'

'I'll do that.' He rose, pointed a finger at the cat when Galahad took a very casual step toward the table. Then pulled Eve in and kissed her. 'Take care of my cop.'

'I'll do that.'

9

Since she'd left too early for the ad blimps to fly, Eve drove through the relative quiet of traffic snarls and horn blasts. She kept the windows down because the day dawned balmy.

Glide-carts already did brisk business with cart coffee guzzled by pedestrians trudging their way to work. Airtrams carried more — to or from — as did the maxibuses that could never seem to do more than poke along.

Delis and bakeries had their doors open. She caught whiffs of bagels and pastries along with the cart offerings of fake egg pockets.

She spotted a couple of dog walkers, a jogger who ran in place at the corner waiting for the light, a guy in a business suit riding an airboard. And the woman, eyes down on her 'link, he'd have mowed down when she walked in front of him if he hadn't had damn good reflexes.

She shook her head when the woman shot up her middle finger at his back.

'Your fault, sister. Be glad you're not bleeding on the sidewalk.'

The first ad blimp of the day cruised over as she pushed through downtown traffic.

It hyped sales on beachwear, which made her think of sun-washed beaches in Greece.

'Told you you'd get through it,' she mumbled, thinking of the girl she'd been in the dream. 'Told you you'd be okay. I didn't tell you how one day between locking up bad guys you'd spend time in a villa in Greece.

'Life's just weird.'

She got to the lab just before the change of shifts, and considered her best approach. She could hit Berenski — lab chief — and nag him about the makeup and the rest. But Dickhead was Dickhead for a reason, and she hadn't thought of a bribe she might need.

She'd try Harvo first, and that would give her a good gauge on progress.

She found Harvo just settling in at her workstation. Her purple hair had a scatter of green highlights, maybe to match the purple low-tops with green laces. She'd continued the theme with purple pants and a green tee with a bright white *42* emblazoned on the back.

'Hey, Dallas, I figured you'd come in. We had a flood yesterday, but I got going on the hair, and I took the clothes.'

'Thought you might. Got anything?'

'Still running, but I can tell you her hair was cut within twelve of time of death. Fresh snips, both with scissors and a razor. Shampoo and conditioner under the styling gel and setting spray. You'll want the brands there, so I've got that going. She used a lightener, and highlights, but hadn't had that done in about two weeks.'

On her rolling stool, she zipped to the other end of her station.

'I can tell you the jeans are Hot Shot brand, Diva series, ultra-low-rise in size four. And I can tell you they discontinued the Diva series in 2015. The Hot Shot brand — definitely low-rent — went under altogether in 2024. I can tell you the jeans had been

142

washed, using Keep It Green organic detergent.'

'So you can tell me a lot.'

'Oh, I got more. The top, polyester blend, Sexy Lady brand — and that's a store brand, or was, from 2002 to 2006, when they went under after the owner shot her lover and the sexy lady he had on the side who happened to be her sister, and Lover Boy's first ex-wife. It was a pretty big scandal in Greenville, Tennessee, in 2005. Single shop,' Harvo added. 'Strip mall about twenty-five miles south of Nashville.'

'Tennessee.'

'Had to be bought there originally, and in the way back. A lot more recently, somebody repaired the loose sequins, sewed them back in place. I've got the data on the thread for you, but it's standard. Better workmanship on the repairs than the original.'

'He knows how to sew.'

'Gotta say yeah there. Also gotta say there are thrift stores all over hell and back where you could find these articles. Maybe your grandma's attic, too, but once he had them, he took care of them. The black ribbon,' she continued. 'Velvet, black, any good craft or fabric store.'

'Tennessee,' Eve repeated. 'It's a long way from there to here.'

'Yeah, but that top made the journey.'

Something let out a tuneful series of beeps.

'That's my girl!' Harvo zipped back to the other end of her counter. 'Display it, baby. So here we go. Shampoo's Pearl Drops, Ocean Breeze scent, same with the conditioner. That's a drugstore type brand, and been around since the late twentieth. Styling gel, same era, Lowell's brand, Super Hold, and same brand on the setting spray.'

Harvo spun her chair around to face Eve. 'Decent, affordable, and widely available. Nothing special there, sorry.'

'Everything adds. How about the shoes?'

'Dezi the newlywed's got the shoes. I got a gander, and he'll give you more, but I'm gonna say the way back, like the jeans and top. Not designer level, either.'

'I'll check with him. Who's got the makeup?'

'That would be my man Dawber. I know he got started on it yesterday. Listen, I got a need for the fizz. His cave's on the way to Vending, so I'll bop you over.'

'Appreciate it. I didn't know you were a baseball fan.'

'Not really.' Obviously baffled, Harvo cocked her head. 'Why?'

'Forty-two.' Eve pointed at Harvo's shirt. 'Jackie Robinson's number.'

'Oh, forty-two. No, man, forty-two's the answer to all the questions in the universe. *Hitchhiker's Guide*.'

While Eve pondered what hitchhiking, the number forty-two, and universal questions had in common, she recognized the clomp of Peabody's boots.

'Yo, Peabody,' Harvo hailed her. 'How's it hanging in rehab land?'

'Hanging, boss. You have to come check it.'

'Gonna, been up past the ass the last days. Got the hair products and clothes ID'd for ya. Reports to follow. Heading over to Dawberville and makeup. Solid forensic chemist there. If he doesn't have it nailed yet, it's because of the past-the-ass deal.'

Peabody fell into step with them. 'So, Douglas Adams fan.'

'Who isn't?' Harvo responded. She made a turn, then another.

144

Then paused outside one of the mini-labs where a man with neatly cropped gray hair stood, hands on hips, as he studied formulaic data on a screen and muttered to himself.

'Hey, Dawb-man.'

He looked momentarily off-balance when Harvo took a step into his area. Then circled a finger in the air in a wait-a-second motion, cocked his head, said, 'Let it rip, Ethel.'

He gave the screen a nod, turned.

He smiled, vaguely, at Harvo. 'You brought me company.'

'Dallas and Peabody.'

'Yes, I know. I've testified in a few of your cases.'

Eve placed him. Veteran lab rat who did solid work that held up in court. He wore pristine white sneakers, pressed khakis, a pale blue collared shirt, with a white lab coat.

'You need the beauty products, the scent.'

'I explained about the past-the-ass.'

He offered them a quiet smile. 'We have been very busy. But I have some partial results. I hope to have a full report by midday.'

'We'll take whatever you've got now.'

'Of course.'

'I'm out. Gonna grab a fizzy. I can swing back if anybody wants.'

'You know my weakness, but no, thank you.'

Harvo grinned. 'Dawber Rules. No food or drink in his cave. Cha, all.'

'If you'd just give me a —' He didn't finish as something buzzed, snagged his attention. He walked to a counter screen, nodded, nodded, leaned down to look at something in a microscope.

145

'Yes, yes, yes, that follows.'

He straightened again. 'Sorry. There are several products to identify. I'm fascinated you were able to smell perfume — actually eau de toilette. And preserving it helped, of course. There was only a minute sample, and very faded, but we have a match. It's called Party Girl. Not a perfume but, as I said, an eau de toilette. Inexpensive as compared to a perfume.'

'Widely available?'

'Why, yes, indeed. According to my data there was a perfume form in the 1990s and into the early 2000s, but only the more moderately priced toilet water is currently marketed and is targeted, primarily, to teens and young adults, with its notes of bergamot, vanilla, and patchouli. Now I've just gotten the full breakdown on the foundation product — the full-face enhancement?'

He gestured to his counter screen. 'It's actually a tinted moisturizer — two-in-one — brand name Toot Sweet — a play, I suppose, on the French?' He shrugged, smiled.

'Drugstore brand?' Eve asked.

'Well, you would find it there, in the beauty section. In other venues as well. Ah, food markets, beauty supply shops, online, of course. It fits with the bronzer, which is the same brand, in their Sun-Kissed shade. The blush, however, is Betty Lou brand, in Pop o' Pink.'

'Hey, that's the first blush I ever bought. It was Peachy — the shade for me — but it was Betty Lou.' Peabody sighed a little in nostalgia. Then straightened when Eve stared at her. 'Affordable. Accessible.'

'Yes, it is,' Dawber confirmed. 'I suspect when I'm finished with the eye enhancements, the lipstick — I can tell you it wasn't a lip dye — we'll find the same. Widely available, well-established products, affordable. But established and popular,' he continued, 'because they're inexpensive and dependable.'

Eve got the picture. The killer could have bought them damn near anywhere. Nothing special, nothing unique about them.

'When we find him, we'll find the products. You can establish the samples you have came from the products we'll find?'

'Absolutely. I still have highlighter, setting powder, the eyebrow color, eye shadows — four different shades, and those blended — eyeliner, mascara, lip liner, lipstick, the nail color.'

He offered that vague smile again. 'I'm afraid midday might be overly optimistic, but I'll do my very best.'

'I'll take what you get as you get it, and appreciate the effort.'

'It's what we do here.'

She didn't expect any revelations on the shoes, and found the same pattern when she hit the newlywed in charge. Off-brand, size seven and a half, manufactured in Cleveland and sold in discount shoe stores all over the country.

Between 2002 and 2004.

Rather than driving straight into Central, Eve pointed across the street. 'Drugstore. I want a look at the setup.'

'Chain stores like this usually have a big selection of makeup and hair products,' Peabody said as they started to the crosswalk. 'Trina gives me, like, a family discount on hair products, and I usually hit one of the beauty product centers for skin care and makeup, but I still browse through, usually pick up something because, well, you never know.'

'Never know what?'

They joined the throng at the light, where the business types looked bored or annoyed and the early tourists looked goggle-eyed.

'If you'll find the perfect lip dye, or the eye shadow palette of your dreams.'

'Yeah, I'm always on the hunt for those.' She shot Peabody a warning look as they crossed the street. 'We're not buying anything.'

'If I find the perfect lip dye, I can note down the name and get it later. Though that would mean several hours, maybe a day or more of my lips denied perfection.'

'Cops don't need perfect lips.'

'It's possible — not outside the realm of possibility — that my perfect lips could so dazzle a bad guy I'd have him cuffed, charged, and transported before he recovered.'

'When that happens, I'll personally buy you a lifetime supply.'

'I'm getting that on record,' Peabody said as they pushed through the doors. 'Over this way.' She gestured and took the lead past aisle after aisle of what Eve thought had nothing to do with drugs. Unless you considered candy a drug.

Which, maybe.

Or diapers and baby stuff, or cleaning and laundry products.

The far side of the store held a massive section on the drugs purported to make you look, smell, and feel better. The promise filled shelves, spin racks, and endcaps.

'There's a whole section for feet.'

'When your feet look and feel good,' Peabody proclaimed, 'you look and feel good.'

'Is that what's up with the invisible shoes? Do they have a deal with the foot product people?'

'That's a definite fad. All it takes is one stub of the toe, one blister, to ruin the look.'

In her element, Peabody selected a lip dye, scanned the packaging, and studied the result on-screen. She smiled, pursed her lips, shook her head.

'This is not the perfect lip dye.' Setting it aside, she picked a powder blush off a spin rack, repeated the process. 'This is a pretty good color, but not perfecto.'

'Stop it.'

Eve scanned the products, noted the names of the brands Dawber had given her. She saw a woman at another testing station. She had a cart loaded with diapers and baby paraphernalia, and said baby in a halter strapped to her chest.

She looked at Peabody with exhausted eyes. 'Does this do anything for me? Like make me look human? I'm ready to settle for looking human. I haven't had a full night's sleep in six weeks.'

Peabody shifted stations, studied the screen. 'It's a pretty color, a happy color. And you know what else?' She found an eye shadow, scanned it, held it up so it transferred to the woman's eyelids. 'I use something like this when I've had a stretch of long nights. It just brightens you up, right?'

'It really does.'

'You should treat yourself. Look what you did. This adorable baby.' Leaning over, Peabody cooed.

'I love him so much I could burst. It's just . . . my husband and I are going to try to go out to dinner — if we can stay awake long enough. My mother's going to watch Jonah.'

'Jonah.' Peabody cooed again, and the woman grabbed her arm.

'I used to know how to do this, but I have baby brain. Help me? It's been so long since I fixed myself up. I want some new products, and my brain's so tired I don't know where to start.'

'Oh, well . . . ' Peabody sent Eve a look. Eve just waved a hand and wandered the aisle.

'Exfoliant, and a brightening facial mask. Let's get that canvas prepped first.'

Eve found the hair products Harvo and Dawber had identified, did a kind of running tab in her head as she found various items the killer had opted to use on Lauren Elder.

As she wandered, studied, calculated, she watched other people browse the aisle. Some just wandered as she did, others went directly to their choices. Others tried the screens, rejected or added the product to their cart or handbasket.

When she'd had enough, she looked back to see Peabody and the woman she'd taken under her wing exchange hugs before the woman strolled off with her cart and kid.

'That was fun!' Peabody bounced in her boots. 'Londa and her husband are both teachers. She got pregnant on their honeymoon. They didn't really plan it, but they decided to go all in. This is their first time out as a couple since Jonah was born, so they're going to the Italian place where they had their first official date three years ago.'

'She told you all that, and bought all the stuff you said to buy, when she doesn't even know you?'

'She was just looking for, you know, some backup.'

Eve considered that as she, very definitely, led the way out. 'I only saw two males come into that section — one for hair junk, the other for some skin deal.'

'Oh, you get guys — it's still more a female area, I guess, but —'

'I'll bet you don't see many males load up on everything, like your new friend did today. The skin and hair gunk, the face gunk, eye and lips gunk, the smelly stuff. A man who did would stand out some, because it's not the usual. Somebody would notice your new friend, too, because she loaded up, and there's the baby thing, but a man filling a cart with all those products would absolutely get noticed.'

'Oh, I get you.' Peabody thought it through as they crossed the street again. 'So if he shopped brick-and-mortar, he probably didn't buy everything in one place. A little here, a little there. Takes more time, but who's going to notice some guy buying vitamins or cold meds and an eye palette or lipstick?'

'That screen thing you did. Can you do that online?'

'Sure, you just go to a site that has that feature and carries the products, call them up, virtually try them on.'

'How about a photo? Trying them on a photo?'

Peabody got in the car, strapped in. 'Jesus, that would be smart. Get a picture of Elder — maybe in advance. Grab one off her social media, or take one yourself while you're stalking her.'

'Use it to pick the products that most closely make her resemble the mother.'

'Sick and smart. He could've ordered everything online that way, or the bulk of it, hit a few other venues.'

151

'When we get the full list from the lab, we'll search what sites carry all of them, with the try-on function. That's a solid start. For the clothes, thrift stores, secondhand stores, vintage stores.'

She gave Peabody a brief rundown on Harvo's report.

'He knows how to sew,' she finished.

'Well, not really. He knows how to repair. A seam.' Peabody traced a finger over her neck. 'Or tack on a loose sequin, probably sew on a button. That's just basic.'

'I don't know how to sew on a button. Lots of people don't.' If she'd known how, Eve thought, Roarke wouldn't carry the gray button that had fallen off her suit the first time they met.

'It's basic,' Peabody insisted as Eve zipped through the last light and made the turn into Central's garage. 'He's good at repair — his stitches are precise. But making something's different. Like that top? You can buy sequined fabric and sew a pattern that simple together in like an hour if you know what you're doing. You dig it out of a thrift shop, the making one might cost more, but if it ended up in a vintage shop, you could make three for what it'll cost you.'

Frowning, Eve pulled into her slot. 'Why?'

'Vintage adds panache, quirk, and cost.'

'It adds panache, quirk, and cost to buy something somebody else got rid of — after they wore it — if they call it vintage instead of secondhand?'

'Yeah, if you're talking about something from ago.'

Eve sat a moment, running it around. 'He's going to need another outfit, since Elder didn't work out.'

She pushed open the door, kept running it as they crossed to the elevator. 'Your grandmother dies —'

152

'Oh, don't say that.'

'Not yours, Peabody. Somebody's. And somebody's grandmother has a bunch of clothes from back when. Where do you take them when you clean them out?'

'If it's me — and it's not me because my grannies are going to live forever — I keep something for sentiment, and/or offer something to friends or family who'd want a memento. Then I'd donate to a shelter.'

'You'd donate a spangly slut top and fancy-ass do-me shoes to a shelter?'

'Oh. Well.' Recalculating, Peabody got in the elevator with Eve. 'If the clothes are in decent shape, somebody — not me — could sell them or put them on consignment at a vintage shop. Make a little money, or a decent chunk, depending.'

'The top made it here from Tennessee. Maybe the first owner did, too.'

'You can buy vintage stuff online.'

Eve said, 'Shit,' not only because that rang true, but because other cops started crowding into the elevator.

'But,' Peabody continued, 'that's sort of a crapshoot, right? You can't be sure it's going to fit. You don't know how it feels until you can touch it. I mean people buy clothes online all the time because the return's easy. But a lot of vintage shops have no return or tough return policies. People might —'

She broke off, hustling after Eve when Eve shouldered her way out the door at the next stop.

'They might buy a vintage evening gown, right? Wear it to some deal, then want to send it back. So it's not as easy to return to specialty stores as it is to think: This sweater's itchy, or, It's too small in the bust — and return it.'

'The jeans were snug on Elder.'

153

'You want jeans to fit snug.'

'No, the waist was small on her. The waist hit way down here.' Eve tapped the side of her hand down her hip. 'Harvo called them low-rise. No, ultra-low-rise. They left that indentation because he had to force the buttons closed. She was slim, but the way they fit, that low on the hip, they were a little small. So were the shoes, but not by much. How would he know Elder's size? Did it just happen to be nearly the same as the mother's?'

'Elder would've been wearing shoes when he grabbed her.'

'That's right.' Eve shifted to Peabody on the glide. 'He might have bought those shoes after — and could only get them in the slightly too small. Maybe the rest of the clothes, too, but it was the fit of the jeans that threw the size off. A waist is going to be smaller than mid-hip.'

'We've got a better chance of finding the vendor if he bought the clothes in the last two weeks.'

'Yeah, we do, and we're going to get started on that. Let's start with vintage shops in the city first. He's not just looking for clothes, but a specific era, a specific size. Do a search, send me half. We work the 'links first, and follow up in the field.'

'This could be a break. His need to replicate, to be exacting about it. That limits his choices, so it narrows our search. I'll get it started.'

Peabody went straight to her desk. Eve noted Jenkinson's and Reineke's empty stations. 'Where's the tie?' she asked Baxter.

'Caught one. Woman beat to death during possible break-in.'

'Santiago and Carmichael?'

154

'Caught one, too. Guy took a header out of a ten-story window, Midtown South, landed on a delivery truck.'

'Because the truck was parked on the sidewalk?'

Baxter grinned. 'No, sir, boss. It was parked at the curb on West Fifty-seventh. So, physics and gravity being what they are, he either took a flying leap or got tossed.'

'At least he didn't land on a pedestrian.'

Eve hit her office for coffee, updated her board and book with the lab data. She snatched an incoming and saw Dawber had taken her at her word, and sent what he got when he got it.

She added the highlighter and setting powder, tones, brands, to her board and book.

Eve considered contacting Elder's mother, or her cohab, but decided to try the friend and coworker. A little less painful, maybe.

She ended the call as Peabody came in. 'Got the list. More than I figured just in the city — a lot more if you hit the other boroughs and the 'burbs, but some of the more standard secondhand shops have vintage sections, so —'

'Yeah, we'll want to include those. Elder. Size four or six, depending on the cut, according to her co-worker pal.'

'It's all about the cut,' Peabody agreed. 'Like if I wanted to try something ultra-low-rise? I don't even want to think about it. That style comes around again, I've gotta take a hard pass. I did look, and it did come around like for a couple years in the '30s — but with wide legs, like flared out from the knees down, so not the same.'

'Well, that sounds . . . incredibly ugly.'

'I'm going with you on that. And with my body type? I don't want to think about that, either. We've got ten each,' Peabody said, then turned as Detective Norman stepped into the open doorway.

He wore yesterday's suit with a navy tie.

'Sorry to interrupt. I wanted you to know Becca Muldoon showed up alive and well. I've just come from verifying that and getting her statement. She eloped. Took off to Las Vegas with a customer, got married, gambled, partied. She got back this morning, and is filing for divorce. Or not. It, she claims, depends.'

'Okay. Alive and well is good. I'm going to catch you up on where we are.' She stopped when her comp issued an alert. 'Hold that.'

She read it out, dragged her hands through her hair.

'We've got another missing woman, one who fits the physical parameters. Mary Kate Covino, age twenty-five. Works at a marketing firm though, regular hours. Not at a bar or club or joint, no night work. Still . . .'

'She could be Elder's sister, Dallas.'

'Yeah, she's just the type. Norman, if you're clear, I'd like you to start on a list Peabody's generated. We're going to go talk to Covino's roommate to start, but I don't want this list to hang too long. It could be a break.'

'I can be clear.'

'I'm going to fill you in,' Eve said as she rose, 'and drop you off at your house. And we'll keep you in the loop on Covino, one way or the other.'

'We can hope she's like Muldoon.'

'We can hope,' Eve agreed, but she didn't see it.

10

BEFORE

While Violet nursed the baby, she stroked her daughter's cheek with one finger. The sensation was so lovely, and if it felt oddly familiar, she set that aside.

As far as she was concerned, her life began the moment she'd opened her eyes on the road, in the dark, and seen Joe's face.

He was her world now. He and Joella. Her family.

She was Violet Fletcher, wife, mother — and oh, how she loved being both — the caretaker of Sweetwater, the lovely old home named nearly two hundred years before.

For weeks after he found her on the road, Joe checked religiously for reports of a missing woman, but no one looked for her. She knew, absolutely, no one would, because Violet hadn't existed before Joe.

In her heart, her mind, in every cell of her body, she believed Joe had brought her back to life. He'd taken care of her, had given her a home, and a purpose. A job at first, she thought now as the baby nursed and the sunlight beamed through the windows of the nursery.

A guest room once, one where she'd slept those first months during her recovery, during the days and nights she'd spent cleaning the house, tending the garden, learning to cook while Joe worked.

She'd learned, had worked hard, had been grateful and content to be only his housekeeper even as she'd fallen so completely in love with him.

Everything she did, the washing, the polishing, even the painting when he finally agreed to let her, she did with an open heart. She believed, absolutely, that purpose — to tend to Joe, to tend to the house — helped her heal.

Then, another miracle, he'd wanted her, and he'd loved her. She hadn't believed he could, or would. She'd taken the last name Blank, because her life before the moment he'd saved her was just that.

But on a perfect spring day, in the garden she'd help tend, she took his name, took his ring, and pledged her life to him.

To avoid questions, they'd made up a past for her — a spotty one, but it served. But the past meant nothing, and now she was Violet Fletcher, Dr. Joseph Fletcher's wife, mother of Joella Lynn.

When the baby slept, perfect mouth slack and milky, she tucked her in the crib in the nursery she'd painted a soft sweet green. She smoothed the downy cap of white-blond hair and thanked God or fate or the sheer luck that had put her in this place.

She vowed she'd be a good mother, a loving one, a fun one, a patient one, a caring one.

'I'll always be there for you,' she whispered, 'and so will your daddy. He's the best man in the world.'

While the baby napped, she stripped the master bed, put on fresh sheets, started the laundry. Joe, the sweet man, had offered, and more than once, to hire a cleaning service. But she loved tending the house, loved making it shine.

She was a homemaker now.

By the time evening set in, casting its shadows so the Spanish moss dripped from the oaks like art, she sat in one of the rockers on the wide veranda, the baby once more at her breast. Inside, the house sparkled, and a roast chicken browned in the oven.

She smelled roses and magnolia as she sipped from a glass of sweet tea. And smiled when the car turned in and drove toward the house.

Her heart just swelled as he got out of the car and started toward her.

'Welcome home, Dr. Fletcher.'

'No place I'd rather be, Mrs. Fletcher.' He bent down, kissed her, then touched his lips to Joella's head. 'Has she been a good girl today, Mama?'

'Best girl ever, Daddy. Sit for a minute, will you? Dinner's got awhile yet, and I brought out a glass for you.' When he did, poured himself a glass, she shifted the baby to her other breast.

'Tell me about your day.'

He reached for her hand, held it while they rocked on the veranda in air smelling of roses and magnolia.

NOW

Mary Kate woke in the dark. For a moment, one blissful moment, she thought she was home, in her own bed. She started to roll over, slide back into sleep. And her wrist shackle dug into her wrist as the chain reached its limit.

She remembered.

For one moment, one horrible moment, she fell into desperate despair. She was alone, held prisoner by some madman who thought he was a child about half the time.

159

No one knew where she was, so how could they find her?

She was supposed to be basking in the sun on a beach, romping in the ocean with Teeg, not chained up in some room by some crazy old man who wanted his mommy.

But no, no, Teeg had dumped her. The son of a bitch. And surely even if he hadn't, even if they'd gone to the beach, she'd have been home by now. Surely she'd been in this nightmare more than four days.

It felt like four weeks. Four years.

Someone had to be looking for her by now. She had family, friends, coworkers, people who cared about her. The police were looking for her by now, of course they were. She just had to hang on until they came.

Remembering, she clapped her hands, and when the light came on, she let out a long breath. She saw breakfast — some sort of cereal in a bowl, a disposable container of milk, a cup of what would be — it always was — orange juice, another that would be coffee — probably cold now. That was fine, she never drank it because it had a hard, bitter taste she suspected came from drugs.

He always woke her — if she wasn't awake — when he brought breakfast. Why was this different?

She started to sit up, and the ugly headache had her letting out a moan.

Her brain felt too big, and somehow clogged.

But she remembered, at least a little.

He'd brought her dinner — chicken fingers, some kind of fake chicken, with soy fries, green beans. Well, more gray than green. A tube of water, a cup of tea.

Then he'd sat in the bolted-down chair. He'd actually asked if she'd had a good day.

160

She'd wanted to hurl the food back at him, but she'd eaten the food — stay strong! — even complimented it, which made him beam at her.

She tried telling him how the wrist cuff hurt. But he'd just smiled and said she had to wear it to stay safe. She'd pushed a little, as carefully as she could manage. But he'd gotten that look in his eyes, the one that warned her.

She would have dumped the tea, but he sat, and sat, and gave her no choice.

And she'd felt the world slipping away.

Now her head hurt from whatever he'd put in the tea, and she felt vaguely sick to her stomach. It was sore, too, and when she started to press a hand against it, she felt a dull pain. And the silver ball in her navel.

He'd pierced her! He'd violated her body while she'd slept — helpless under his goddamn drugs.

The outrage shot her to her feet, pain screaming. She nearly grabbed the ball, ripped it out. Then she stopped herself, stood, breath heaving. She'd hurt herself — then he'd hurt her. He'd put it back in.

Then she saw the two little cups — like they put meds in for people in the hospital. One held some sort of white cream, the other a clear liquid. Her hand shook as she reached for the carefully handwritten note beside them.

Mommy, use the cream on your pretty butterfly spreading its wings on your back. Use the other on your pretty new earrings and belly button when you turn them. Be gentle!

I knew you needed your beauty sleep, so I left you breakfast. Have a good day! Your baby darling.

'Oh my God, oh my God, what butterfly?' But her hands shot first to her ears. He'd pierced her there, too.

161

Multiple times. She felt the soreness as she clamped her hands over the little studs.

Tears spilled as she shifted, tried to run her hands over her back. She felt the slight difference, traced it as best she could.

'Jesus, it's huge. He pierced me, he tatted me. He's making me her.'

But he wouldn't. She wouldn't become somebody else no matter what he did.

She was Mary Kate Covino.

The tears fell and she went through her routine of naming off her family, her friends, what she did, what she liked. And she used the hydrogen peroxide on the piercings, did her best to smear the cream on the tattoo she couldn't see.

Then she banged on the pipes, banged and banged until she finally heard the answer.

Not alone.

★ ★ ★

Eve decided to take the roommate first. When you lived with someone, they knew stuff. Often things family might not.

A good building, she noted. Again Lower West Side. Definitely his territory. The obviously well-rehabbed redbrick building had door cams, an intercom for buzzing in, and required a swipe and a code for entry otherwise.

'She's a subway ride or a fifteen-to-twenty-minute walk from her workplace,' Eve calculated. 'The boyfriend's bar's only about two blocks away. So he stalked her coming and going from the bar. Tells me she must've had some sort of routine.'

She walked to the door, mastered in. 'Let's see if the roommate confirms that.'

'Sixth floor, 608.'

Since Eve judged the elevators in the small lobby, recently cleaned from the smell of it, likely reflected the maintenance of the building, she pressed a call button.

'Family's in Queens. Data says she's lived here for three years — with the same roommate. Worked for the marketing firm for going on four — right out of college. No criminal bumps.'

They stepped into the elevator — one that didn't make strange noises — and Eve called for the sixth floor.

Peabody read off the data. 'Roommate, Cleo Bette. Sous chef at Perfecto. That's like a block from the bar — upscale place.'

They got out on six.

Good soundproofing, Eve thought. Or everybody was out. She buzzed at 608.

'Margie, I said I'd let you know when —' The woman who yanked open the door stopped. 'Sorry. I thought you were my neighbor a couple floors down. Look, it's not a good time, so —'

She broke off again when Eve held up her badge. 'Oh, thank God.' She grabbed Eve's arm, all but pulled her into the apartment. 'Did you find her? Is she okay?'

'I'm sorry, we just got the report. Lieutenant Dallas, Detective Peabody.'

'Oh. I was hoping . . . Wait, wait. I know those names. We saw the vid. Mary Kate and I. Oh Jesus, you do murders.'

'Ms. Bette.' Peabody stepped up in her soothing

163

mode. 'We don't know that anything's happened to Mary Kate. We're here to help find her. Maybe we could sit down.'

'Okay, yeah, sorry.' She closed her eyes a moment, a tall, mixed-race woman with a lot of curly brown hair bundled back. She wore gray sweatpants, a black tank top, and looked terrified.

But she gestured to chairs in a small, very tidy, very female living area. 'I'm sick,' she went on, 'because I didn't know. I thought she was . . . I have to pull it together.'

'Why don't you start at the top,' Eve suggested. 'From the beginning.'

She clasped her hands with their long, slender fingers and short, unpainted nails. 'Mary Kate was supposed to take a trip to the beach for a few days. With Teegan Stone. They've been seeing each other for a few months. She was kind of . . . okay, she was dazzled. He's gorgeous, right? He owns Stoner's, a bar over on Seventh. I didn't see when she left because I was at work. I work most nights. I know she planned to take her rolly — her suitcase — with her, go down to the bar, spend the night with Teeg, and leave first thing the next morning.'

'When was this?'

'Um. Um. June third. I mean that's the night she went to the bar. I didn't think anything when she didn't tag me, because dazzled. I just figured she was having fun, all into him.'

'But she wasn't?' Eve prompted.

'They didn't go, and she didn't stay there that night. According to that shithead Teeg. See, she was supposed to be home last night — work night for me. I saw she wasn't here when I got home, and figured

164

she'd stayed at his place. I was tired, and I just went to bed. But I tried to tag her this morning, and I got nothing. No connection, so I tried Teeg. He was pissed at me because I woke him up, and he said he hadn't seen Mary Kate since she left the bar the night before they were supposed to go, how she'd gotten too pushy and clingy, and he cut her loose. And he said her stupid suitcase was still at his place, and tell her to come get it, and, if she didn't get it, he was just going to set it out on the street.'

Her eyes filled. 'Shithead.'

'Sounds like,' Peabody agreed.

'I told him how she hadn't been home, and he's all that's not his problem. I told him to get fucked, and I called the condo she'd booked at the beach. That's when I found out they hadn't shown, and she hadn't canceled, either. She'd've canceled, and she'd have come home so we could bitch about the shithead, so I could let her cry on my shoulder.'

'You're good friends.'

Cleo managed a smile for Peabody. 'Really tight, yes. Lucky. I wanted this apartment, but I needed a roommate so I could afford it. It's really close to work, it's a nice place, good neighborhood. She answered the ad, and we clicked. We really clicked. Like I said, I work most nights, but when we have a day off, or I have a night off, we'd hit the vids, or a club. Stoner's for a drink. Then he wound her in — he's got a way. She'd go down there four nights a week, sometimes five. She'd bus tables or serve drinks — for free.'

'And stay the night?' Eve asked.

'Nope. Never. He'd take her up — he lives over the bar — for a quickie sometimes, but no sleepovers. His rule, right? She'd head over there about eight and be home about midnight.'

'Four or five nights a week.'

'Yeah. I'm going to say I didn't like it. He was using her, but all that dazzle.' To illustrate, she did jazz hands by the sides of her face. 'The trip was her idea, and she made all the arrangements. She was really excited about it, then he dumps her like that? Shithead.'

'Was the night he dumped her one of her usual nights?'

'Sure, yeah.'

'Did he ever walk back here with her?'

Cleo snorted. 'No.' After pressing her fingers to her eyes, she rubbed her face, hard. 'I'm going to say we came the closest we ever have to a serious fight when I said he treated her like crap, and started pointing out how.'

She dropped her hands. 'I backed off because things were going to blow. You don't want to blow up with a friend over some asshole guy. She just had to get through it and over it.'

Now she smiled, just a little. 'She's the most sensible person I know, but she had it stuck that she was going to be the one to change him. Things were going to be different with her. Do you know what I mean?'

Peabody nodded. 'Yeah. Most of us have been there.'

'Maybe he did something to her. I mean, I don't see how, but —'

'We'll talk to him,' Eve said. 'Did she ever mention being uneasy about the walk home? About anyone bothering her?'

'No. And she's careful. A lot tougher than she looks. Teeg found some weak spot, because it wasn't really like her to get walked over like that. She wouldn't take

166

off, either. She wouldn't. I had to tag her mom, just to be sure she didn't go home. To be sure. Now her family's half crazy, too. They haven't seen or heard from her. She'd never do that. I called her boss, too, and nobody's heard from her.'

'Okay. Can we see her room?'

'Oh, sure.'

The two bedrooms faced each other down the short hallway that ended with the shared bathroom. Cleo gestured to the room on the right.

Eve saw neat, organized, and again female in the quiet pastels, the mountain range of fluffy and fancy pillows on a bed covered with a pale blue spread. Thin curtains in a peachy tone framed the single window — for decor, Eve decided. The table, painted the same blue as the spread, stood in front of the window and held a mini data and communication unit, what Eve took to be a family photo — all smiling faces and a tree loaded with lights and ornaments — and a small, slender vase swirling with pastel tones.

An oval mirror, framed in pale green, stood over a pale blue dresser with drawers painted to alternate the peach and green. Atop ranged a trio of fancy bottles, a faceted glass box, and a slim tray holding little candles.

No sign, Eve thought, of packing for a trip, outfits considered, tossed aside.

'Would you say this is how her room typically looks?'

'Oh, absolutely. If a hurricane blew through, M.K. would have everything back in its place within an hour.'

With a quick laugh, Cleo pointed across the hall to a room with bold, bright colors and cheerful disorder.

'I'm the hurricane. M.K. — sorry, Mary Kate and

167

her sister, Tara, helped decorate my room, and the rest of the place. They've got vision, and Mary Kate needs order and, well, pretty, like she needs to breathe.'

Eve imagined Mary Kate felt short of breath at the moment, but didn't say so. 'We'd like to look through her things. I know it's an intrusion, Cleo,' Eve continued when she saw Cleo's anxiety, 'but any detail can help us find her. I'd also like to send someone from EDD to take her D and C unit in, run a thorough search.'

'That's for work. I mean to say, she's really strict about that. Anything personal, she used her 'link or tablet. She wouldn't even contact her mom from her home comp.'

'And still,' Eve said.

'Okay, yeah. Anything.'

'Thanks. Peabody, contact EDD, have this unit picked up.' As she spoke, she opened the closet door.

They spent an hour, and while they found nothing that pointed to where Covino might be, or the identity of who held her there, Eve added to her picture.

Girlie, organized, and — from her scan of the computer — hardworking. Family and friend oriented, and with a strong enough personality to have her less tidy roommate keep their shared space in order.

'Let's walk down and have a conversation with the boyfriend.' Eve scanned the block when they came out of the building. 'Plenty of places along here to keep tabs on the building. Shops, restaurants, and with the good weather, sitting outside having coffee or whatever. Still, he had to see her to want her.'

'The bar.' Peabody fell into step beside her. 'Elder and Hobe both worked at bars, and Covino started hanging out in one, pitching in because of asshole boyfriend. He's trolling bars looking for women who tick off points on his list.'

'Which means he's been at this for months, most likely, not days, not weeks. This takes time. There'll be others who didn't make the cut, but it took time to eliminate them and select the ones that clicked for him.'

'Others,' Peabody agreed, 'who wouldn't be as easy to grab. They walked home or to transpo with somebody, or he found out they carried a sticker. Or . . . none of the three we're looking at had kids. Yeah, young for it, but it happens.'

'Good point. His mother's *his* mother, and nobody else's.' She paused at a shop with an outdoor flower cart, then with a gesture to Peabody, went in.

Your basics, as Eve saw it. A small produce section, a tiny dairy one offset with shelves of dehydrated milk, eggs, soy products.

Candy, snacks, general household stuff.

She walked to the counter, where the clerk finished ringing up a sale. 'Enjoy the day,' she said to the departing customer, offered Eve and Peabody an easy smile. 'Help you?'

'Maybe.' Eve held up her badge and the photo of Covino on her 'link. 'Do you recognize this woman?'

'Why?'

'She's been reported missing. We're looking for her.'

'Oh my God. No. I mean, yes, I recognize her. M.K., she's in here several times a week. As nice as they come. But, wait, when she was in last — I guess last week — she said she was going on a little trip so wouldn't be in.' The clerk, a tiny Black woman with a tat of a sinuous branch of ivy running from the inside of her elbow to her wrist, let out a huff of relief. 'She

169

went on a trip.'

'No,' Eve said, 'she didn't. She came in here regularly?'

'Yeah, yeah. For flowers once a week for sure, and just for this and that. Are you sure she didn't go on that trip? She was awfully excited about it.'

'Yes, ma'am.'

'Ivy, I'm Ivy. I don't know what to think. I'd hate for anything to happen to that girl. Nice as they come.'

'Did you ever notice anyone, maybe who came in when she did? A male, likely Caucasian and in his sixties?'

'I get customers like that, sure, but nobody I noticed especially. If I'd seen anybody giving her the eye — the wrong kind of eye — I'd've said something. A sweetheart's what she is. Takes time to chat a minute. Most are too busy or just don't bother. She asks how I'm doing. My grandson — he works now and then after school or when I can squeeze him into it — he's got a little crush on her.'

Ivy immediately looked horrified. 'Zel would never —'

'Relax. Do you think Zel might have noticed someone you missed?'

'I can ask him. I can sure ask him. He's coming in soon. Should be here any minute.'

'We have another stop to make in the neighborhood, then we'll be back. We'd like to talk to him then.'

'Absolutely. I hope nothing's happened to that girl. I'm going to say prayers for her.'

'Makes sense she'd use that shop,' Peabody said when they walked outside again. 'And if he was watching her, getting her routine down, he may have gone in after her, at least once.'

170

'She talks to people — the shopkeeper, the grandson. I'm betting the glide-cart operator where she got her street coffee, or the bakery clerk where she picked up bagels or muffins. Let's pull in a couple uniforms to hit the shops and restaurants along this stretch — from her subway stop to her apartment, and to the bar. And we'll check the same from her workplace.'

'I'll get that started.'

While Peabody arranged it, they took the turn to the bar. A lot of people out and about, Eve thought, enjoying the cafés, breezing in and out of shops, just strolling, enjoying the weather.

'Perfect time of year for it,' she commented. 'Did he wait, I wonder, for the weather? So he could sit outside and watch, or wander along behind her? Why trudge along in the cold when you can stalk in the warm?'

When they reached the bar, Eve stood a moment, studying it.

'Night spot, doesn't open until five, and that's to grab the drink-after-work crowd. We'll try upstairs.'

She mastered through the door to the apartments over the bar. In this case, she didn't give the single gray-doored elevator with its frowny-face graffiti an instant's consideration.

They took the stairs to the third floor.

She noted Stone's apartment door had double security locks and a cam.

She buzzed, waited a few beats, buzzed again, then just leaned on the buzzer.

'Maybe he's not in there,' Peabody suggested.

'Cam light blipped from red to green. He's home.'

The door banged open a half inch to a double secu-

171

rity chain. 'What the fuck?'

'The fuck is this.' Eve held up her badge. 'We'd like to speak with you, Mr. Stone.'

'Then come back when I'm not sleeping.'

'Happy to, with a search warrant, and we can have this conversation at Cop Central.' She turned away.

'Wait a damn minute.' He slammed the door, chains rattled. He yanked it open again and stood in a pair of black boxers that showed off a tanned, buff body. He swept a hand through a lot of disordered hair — milk-chocolate brown with a lot of sun-kissed highlights.

'I'm not even awake yet. I own the bar down below. I work nights. What's this about?'

'Mary Kate Covino.'

'For Christ's sake. Whiny woman goes off to sulk somewhere, and I get harassed over it? I need some goddamn coffee.'

'We'd like to come in, Mr. Stone, unless you'd like to have this conversation in the hallway, or down at Central.'

He made a come-ahead gesture, slammed the door behind them, then stalked off in his boxers to, Eve assumed, get his goddamn coffee.

The elevator and stairwell might be dicey, she concluded, but Stone lived lush.

Snappy furnishings in manly browns and blacks, slick double-size gel sofa, roomy leather chairs, an entertainment screen that spanned an entire wall.

His dining area held a glossy black table, with some sort of ornate copper centerpiece. A serving bar displayed several fancy decanters with the glass doors under it showing off sparkling glasses and a full wine fridge.

172

He stalked back out with a large white mug.

'Look, I'll tell you what I told her nosy roommate. I don't know where she is, and I don't care. Guess what? It's not my problem.'

Eve held up her badge again. 'Guess what? I'm making it your problem.'

11

He walked over, dropped down in one of his leather chairs. Gulped coffee.

'So check the half crap of a condo she rented on the Jersey Shore. Her idea of a freaking love nest. She probably went there to cry in her pillow.'

'Gee, why didn't we think of that?' Eve let the sarcasm drip. Stone just shrugged. 'You have a lot of contempt for a woman you were recently involved with.'

'*Involved*'s a strong word. We had sex once in a while, for a while. It ran its course, and I showed her the door. Arrest me.'

'If there was a law against being a complete dick, we would.'

Eve raised her eyebrows at Peabody's comeback, but said nothing.

'Unfortunately,' she continued, 'there are so many we'd run out of room for them.'

'Listen, sister —'

'Detective.' Eve stepped closer to stare him down. 'Detective Peabody and Lieutenant Dallas, and I believe my partner has just let you know you're nobody special. You were in a sexual relationship with Ms. Covino.'

'We had sex, not a relationship.'

'Several nights a week, she worked in your bar.'

'She helped out — her idea. And she takes all that and blows it up into something. Not my problem.'

'Yet you agreed to take a trip with her to this half-crap condo on the Jersey Shore.'

He shrugged. 'So I didn't say no right off. I was thinking about it. Maybe I even said sure, we'll do that, fix it up. I changed my mind, and she couldn't handle it. Dragged her dumbass suitcase into my place, puts it in the back like she owns the joint. Pissed me off.'

'Did she help you out in the bar that night before you changed your mind?'

'Sure. I was busy. I run a popular place, so I didn't get around to it for a while. I tried letting her down easy. Told her I wasn't going to be able to make it, and she got pushy. Not my problem she took off work, not my problem she put down a deposit. I can see she was going to make a scene out of it, so I cut it off. We're done, there's the door.'

He shrugged again. 'Women just can't take the moment and move on. We had some fun, that's it. It's why I've got a firm policy none of them stay the night. Makes them get too cozy. And what do they do? Leave something — a scarf, a hair thing, lip dye, whatever, so they have an excuse to come back. Pathetic. Like I don't get that?'

Idly, Eve wondered why so many ugly people had beautiful faces.

'What time did she leave?'

'How the hell do I know? I didn't clock her out. About midnight,' he said when Eve stared. 'Left her damn suitcase.'

'Did you try to contact her so she could come back for it?'

'Hell no — that's what they want. I give it a week, then I toss it — whatever they leave.'

'Did you notice anyone in the bar when she helped you out? Male, White, in his sixties, probably alone?'

'Hell, we get plenty of those. It's a popular place. If

175

they're not causing trouble, I don't pay much attention to old men. Look, she's just trying to get my attention. That's what they do.'

'Do they? Well, in this case, she has ours. Where is Ms. Covino's property?'

'Where she left it. Like I'm going to drag it up here, give her an excuse to come to the door.'

'Put some clothes on, open the bar. We'll take it with us.'

'You expect me to get dressed —'

'Since I can't arrest you for being a complete dick, I'd be thrilled to arrest you for indecent exposure. You've been flashing your actual dick since you sat down. While it's not very impressive, I could make a case. Put some pants on. Ms. Covino's suitcase is evidence.'

He went from slouch to poker straight. 'You've got no business talking to me that way. I pay your fucking salary.'

'Dallas, Lieutenant Eve. File a complaint — but put your pants on first, and give me my evidence.'

He pushed up, stormed to a closet in the hallway off the bedroom, came back with the suitcase.

'Evidence, my ass.'

'Funny, this doesn't look like the back room of your bar.'

'So I forgot I brought it up here to get it out of the way. When she comes slinking back after her snit, I'm going to demand an apology from all of you.'

'Good luck with that.' Eve pulled up the handle, rolled the suitcase to the door. 'Thanks for your time, and for revealing yourself to be an asshole.'

She shut the door. 'Let the roommate know we have the suitcase. It's now evidence, and we'll return it as soon as possible.'

'I'm so steamed.'

'Shake it off.' Eve shoved the handle down, hefted the bag up — it had weight! — to carry it down the stairs. 'He's nothing. I did admire your remark about not enough cage room to arrest complete dicks.'

'It just popped right out. The way he demeaned her, well, all of us, women in general.'

'It'll catch up with him. Sooner or later he'll pull that shit with the wrong woman. But for now, Mary Kate Covino's a lot more important than he is.'

'He lied about bringing the suitcase up there just to give us grief. I mentally kicked him in the groin, several times.'

'Good target, since that's where he lives. I feel there's another way. Like doing a search on former female employees who have either quit or been fired. Wouldn't it be fun if we found some who had a story about leaving his employ due to his sexual treatment of them?'

Peabody said nothing for nearly thirty seconds. 'Dallas, Lieutenant, sir, you are my hero. I am mentally kissing you on the mouth.'

'Keep it in your head or my boot meets your ass.'

'It might be worth it, but my admiration at this moment is too deep to cause your wrath. Can I do it, please, please? I can ask McNab to help. Off duty. Our own time.'

'It's all yours. What do you suppose she packed in here?' Eve wondered when they reached the street. 'It weighs a freaking ton.'

'Oh shit, and I didn't even offer to carry it.'

'So noted.' She pulled up the handle, pushed the case at Peabody. 'Take it to the car, seal it, log it.

Contact Covino's boss, tell them we're coming in. I'll stop by the market and talk to Zel if he's there.'

He was, and as upset and cooperative as his grandmother. But he couldn't add anything. Still, Eve left a card and a request to contact her if they remembered anything or anyone.

They hit the marketing firm next.

Eve found a high-energy atmosphere in the converted warehouse. Lots of open space with splashes and slashes of color in contrast, likely deliberate, with the industrial framework. She might have equated the sound and movement to EDD, except the denizens weren't dressed like circus performers.

What passed as the lobby area looked more like a loungy living area in someone's upscale home. Sofas, chairs, tables arranged in conversational groups, a bar area offering choices of water and soft drinks, coffees, teas, lent an air — certainly deliberate — of casual hospitality.

A man and a woman worked at the counter, chatting away on earbuds. The woman said, 'Hold please,' and tapped hers as Eve and Peabody approached. 'Hi! How can I help you?'

Eve held up her badge, and the woman hopped up before she could speak.

'You're here about M.K. Is she okay? Sly! It's about M.K.'

Her coworker's eyes widened as he ended the call. 'Is she okay?'

'We haven't located Ms. Covino. We'd like to see her work space and speak to her immediate supervisor.'

'I'll take you right up. I've got this, Andi. We only heard about her being missing a little while ago.'

178

He led them to a freight elevator. Eve looked long-ingly at the iron steps leading up to the open upper floors, but got in.

'Were you and Ms. Covino friends?'

'We're all friends here. We all thought she was at the beach for a few days with her boyfriend.'

'Has anyone come in asking about or for her?'

'Her roommate, Cleo, called this morning, and a detective from the police a little while ago.'

'Before that. In the last few weeks?'

'No. I mean, clients, accounts, that sort of thing. Her sister, her brother, or her mom or dad drop in now and again. And Cleo — her roommate — some-times. Linny's chill with family or friends visiting.'

The elevator door clanked open into spacious work areas. No cubes so staff mixed and mingled as they worked. Offices had doors open. Sly led them to one with a corner view.

The woman behind the desk had her feet, clad in red sneaks, on it and her eyes on a screen where what looked like a family of four enjoyed a rollicking break-fast.

'Linny, sorry, the police are here.'

'Hold vid.' Linny swung her feet off the desk, rose to a good six feet in height.

She wore her ink-black hair in a skullcap, had a tiny red stud winking on the right side of her nose and enormous silver hoops in her ears.

She thrust out a hand. 'Linny Dowell, thank you so much for coming. I've got this, Sly, thanks. And close the door.' The minute it did, her brisk welcome turned to fear. 'I recognize you. Mary Kate . . . please say it fast.'

'Ms. Dowell, we haven't located Mary Kate. We're

here because her possible abduction may be connected to another case.'

'She's not dead. You're not here because she was murdered?'

'The NYPSD is actively looking for her.'

'All right.' She pressed her fingers to her eyes a moment. 'When I saw you . . . Roarke Industries is the Holy Grail of any marketing firm, so I recognized you, and thought . . . Please sit down. Can I get you some coffee, a soft drink?'

'We won't keep you long.'

'Whatever you need. We all thought M.K. was on her little vacation.'

'We're just following up, and we'd like to see her work space, have a few minutes with her supervisor.'

'You could say I'm everyone's supervisor, but you'd want Jim — James Mosebly. Accounts manager, and M.K.'s mentor. Hold on.'

She went to the door, poked her head out. 'Hey, Nat, go grab Jim for me, would you? They just nailed down a major ad campaign,' she told Eve. 'Jim, M.K., Alistar, and Holly. Jim took M.K. under his wing when she came on board, and he heads most of the projects she works on.'

'How about outside the office?' Eve asked. 'Any socializing?'

'Sure, and quite a lot actually. We're a friendly group here. My philosophy is community and cooperation over competition. When we hire, we don't just look for talent and work ethic, but personality. Will this person fit? No sharks need apply,' she added with a smile.

'I worked at a firm for eight years, and that tank was full of sharks. You couldn't be sure, from day to

180

day, if somebody might swim up and bite your leg off. I climbed out of the tank, juggled finances, talked the bank into a start-up loan — and I talked Jim and Selma into coming on.'

'It looks like it worked out,' Peabody commented.

'We're small, but happy. Hey, Jim. Jim Mosebly, Lieutenant Dallas and Detective Peabody.'

Eve gauged Linny at mid-fifties, and put her colleague about fifteen years her senior. He had flyaway gray hair crowning a round, cherubic face. He wore baggy jeans and a royal blue polo over a solid, sturdy body. Like Linny, he wore sneakers — his on the battered side.

'Mary Kate,' he said in a voice with the faintest drawl. 'You found her.'

'We haven't located her as yet.'

'What can I do? What can we do?'

'You worked closely with her. Did she ever mention anyone bothering her?'

'She didn't. She was wrapped up in that slick bar owner. Stars in her eyes, and it wasn't like her.'

'How so?'

'She's grounded. Smart, steady. He's just a blip. Not that I said that to her. You don't hear sensible advice when you're in a haze.'

'You met him?'

'Stopped in for a drink a couple of times so I could, well, size him up some. We look out for each other here. We're family. Didn't like the look of him. He has user all over him. I'd hoped this trip with him would clear the haze. If he's hurt her —'

'We don't believe that's the case. When did you last see or speak with her?'

'Ah . . . June third — the last day before she started

181

her vacation. The team had wrapped up the Nordo campaign, so I was taking them out for a little unwind time, but she ducked out. She and the bar guy were due to leave the next morning and she wanted to finish packing. She said,' he continued with a smile. 'Believe me, someone as organized as Mary Kate would have had everything in place. But she opted out. We all walked out together, a little after five, I think, and she peeled off at her subway station. She was lit up,' he added. 'Just lit up.'

Mosebly let out a breath. 'I wanted her to see him for what he was. Not that I didn't want her to have a good time — she deserved one. But I wanted her to come back shed of him. And all this time. Dear God, Linny.'

'She's smart and she's strong. We're going to find her.'

'We'd like to see her work area, and have a word with Alistar and Holly.'

'Of course. I'll take you. She's a pretty thing,' Mosebly said as he walked them out, headed for the stairs. 'Young, pretty. I didn't like the idea of her walking home, even just a few blocks, so late at night from that bar.'

'You knew about that, her routine?'

'I did.' He moved briskly down the stairs, a man in good physical shape who likely used them often. 'She mentioned she enjoyed helping out at the bar, meeting people, having a little time with what's-his-name.'

'Teegan Stone.'

'Right.' He moved through a maze of workstations and activity, paused at one. 'I know Holly had a few things to say when it came out she didn't stay the night, *and* he couldn't be bothered to walk her home.

182

But Mary Kate brushed that off. I don't want to tell you how to do your job, but I'm going to tell you anyway. I think he's a man who could hurt women as well as use them.'

'We're looking at him, Mr. Mosebly.'

'All right, okay. This is Mary Kate's work space. It reflects her.'

'Does it?'

'Organized, efficient, but not rigid.' He brushed his fingers over a paperweight that showed a cow jumping over a crescent moon.

Other than that and her D and C, there sat a placard that read:

WORK SMARTER.
BITCH LESS.

'Her motto. And, as you can see, she kept her area clean — another motto.'

'We'd like to have her comp and any devices in her desk taken in to EDD for analysis.'

'You'll need to clear that with Linny — she's the boss — but I can't imagine her standing in your way. Let me round up Alistar and Holly for you. And if there's anything else I can do, please let me know.'

'Appreciate it. Do you live close by?'

'Actually, I live downtown. Mary Kate and I often took the subway together. Just give me a minute.'

'Run him, Peabody,' Eve ordered when he walked away.

'Yeah, on that. He checks some boxes.'

They talked to coworkers, arranged for the electronics pickup, and left with a suspect on the list.

'He's awfully invested in a coworker under his

supervision who's young enough to be his grand-daughter.'

'And checks more boxes,' Peabody said as they settled into the car.

'Lives alone, a couple of blocks from Elder's apartment. No marriages, no children. No criminal.'

'Tell me about his mother.'

'Getting there. Adalaide Mosebly, née Rowen, died last February at the age of a hundred and six. She'd been a resident/patient for the last sixteen years at the Suskind Home, on Long Island. That's a retirement and elder care facility. Full medical care, including mental and emotional.

'Prior,' Peabody continued, 'she was a home-maker and church secretary and helpmate — it says helpmate — to her husband, Reverend Elijah Mosebly — deceased November 2038. They lived in Kentucky until his death. Two years following that, she moved to New York — James Mosebly's address.'

'She doesn't sound like someone who'd dress up like our first victim. But Kentucky's not all that far from Tennessee, where that spangly top came from. And maybe she lived a different kind of life before hooking up with the reverend. When did they hook up?'

'Married May 1985. Ah, so she'd have been about thirty. Could've lived a different sort of life in her twenties — which is where our victim falls, and the abductions.'

'Theory.' Eve played it out as she navigated traffic. 'Little Jimmy loves Mommy. Mommy's pretty strict — preacher's wife. Maybe they even — what's the expression? — use the rod, control the child.'

'Spare the rod, spoil the child. Either way, it's nasty.'

184

'Maybe he blames Daddy for it, or maybe it's just how life is. But sometime in there, he learns Mommy liked to dress up and party. How does he feel about that? Excited, appalled, interested? However he feels, she's the center. Maybe she indulges him, spoils him — or the opposite, because some kids learn to love the boot when it's all they get.'

'He moved to New York in 2004 — at eighteen. I've got sketchy employment and residence until 2008. Enrolled in community college, add night school, part-time work at what looks like a pizza joint. Got a degree in marketing with a minor in sociology. Took him five years. Landed an entry-level at someplace called Adverts Unlimited, five years there, and he bounced to Young and Bester Marketing, seven years, climbed up to junior exec before shifting to Digby — that's where he'd have met and worked with Dowell — where he kept climbing to department head until he left to join Dowell's start-up. Wait, there are a couple of gaps.'

Eve pulled into Central's garage. 'What and where?'

'Three-month gap, from what I can tell. From April through August of 2031, then another in '38.'

'When his father died. We'll look, but maybe the father got sick in '31, he went back home to help out. Then he goes back when his father died.'

'Digby hired him back, both times, but again what I'm seeing? He took a salary cut. Talk about sharks.'

'And when did Dowell start up?'

'In 2046.'

'We're going to take a deeper look at the parents, get a good round picture. He hits too many points not to push on it.'

'But?' Peabody asked as they got on the elevator.

'He works with Covino, hangs out with her now and then outside the office. He knows her routine. But he doesn't grab her first. Okay, maybe her plans for the trip gave him the opening he was after, but he couldn't know those plans would blow up.'

'She'd never spent the night at Teeg the Dick's apartment before. He counted on that.'

'Yeah, maybe.' Hands in pockets, Eve jingled loose change. 'Timing feels off. What did his mother look like? Young.'

'I'll find that once we're upstairs. There wouldn't be national ID back when she was in her twenties, even thirties.'

'Right. Dig there. I'm going to shift over to Hobe, see if I can find any other way she could have crossed with Mosebly.'

And she had to push on Roarke's list. Wouldn't it be damn handy if Mosebly's residence was on it? Another box checked.

As they walked toward Homicide, Jenkinson and Reineke headed back from Interview with springs in their steps.

'We bagged one.' Jenkinson held out a fist for his partner to bump. 'Guy's just trying to teach his girl-friend a lesson, right? Just give her a little tune-up.'

'And what does she do?' Reineke picked it up. 'Why, that salty bitch shoved him, even slapped him, tried to run. What the hell else was he supposed to do but give her a good beatdown?'

'During which he cracked her skull like an egg, left her dying on the floor in puddles of her own blood and puke, and went out to have himself some waffles.' Jenkinson cast his eyes heavenward. 'Frigging waffles.'

In their practiced rhythm, Reineke ran the next.

'Comes back, finds her dead, and tries to cover it up by busting the door lock — from the inside — and calling it in like somebody broke in and beat her to death.'

'He still got her blood spatter on his shoes,' Jenkinson added. 'Changed his shirt, but shoved it into the recycler. And his knuckles are all torn up. His cheek's got her nail marks from eyeball to jaw where she got a piece of him.'

'So he changes his story to add how he saw the guy running out of his place, pursued, got into a tussle. Big guy, like six-six, this mope claims. And how when he ran back to the apartment, he found his dead girl-friend.'

Eve considered. 'So did he spill the truth because you scared him out of it with that tie?'

Jenkinson gave a closed-lip grin and fluttered the orange tie covered with purple insects with bugged-out eyes. 'It didn't hurt, but we broke him down with our exceptional interview skills.'

'His dumb-ass stupid didn't hurt, either.' Reineke held out a fist for a second bump.

'So you're clear.'

'Soon as we write this puppy up.' Jenkinson smoothed down his tie.

'Do that, then pull the file on Anna Hobe. Missing person, fits the profile for abduction by an unsub who shackled and held Lauren Elder for ten days before slitting her throat.'

'The body on the bench near Mavis's new place. And yours,' Jenkinson said to Peabody.

'That's right. If he's got Hobe, he's had her for eight days. Her clock's running down. Take a look. I could use fresh eyes.'

'You got it, boss.' Reineke turned to Jenkinson. 'Ready to roll on?'

'Always ready.'

'Dig deep as you can,' Eve told Peabody. 'And when you find a photo of the mother in the age range, send it.'

'Getting my shovel.'

Eve hit the AC for coffee the minute she walked into her office. With it, she sat down to update her book and send a fresh report to Mira, including her outline of data, her impressions of James Mosebly.

'A lot of check marks, Jim,' she muttered, and printed out his ID shot to add to her board.

When she completed her board, she sat again, brought up the list Roarke had sent while she'd been in the field.

And checked off another. Mosebly's residence was on it.

Took the team out to celebrate, she thought. Like family. Not a one-off with that. As head of the department, he took out his team regularly, she'd bet on it.

Maybe most often in the area around the firm, but wouldn't he branch out? His own neighborhood — which included Arnold's and Mike's Place, Stoner's.

She hadn't asked about a man of his age coming in with a group rather than solo. She'd rectify that.

He could have seen Hobe that way, noticed her, fixed on her. The same with Elder.

Took care of his mother, she thought as she got up to pace. Brought her to New York to live with him after she was widowed. Set her up in a facility for elder care . . . .

She sat again, searched for data on the facility.

188

Expensive. She could see that just from the photos. Round-the-clock professional care — body, mind, spirit, they claimed. Gardens, recreation area, therapists, nutritionist.

She scanned the options for apartments.

Okay, he hadn't cheaped out on taking care of Mommy — and for a dozen years.

She considered the drive time to Long Island, and decided to take a chance over the 'link first.

She got the initial and expected runaround, but eventually pushed her way to the director.

'Elise Grommet. How may I assist you, Lieutenant Dallas?'

'I'm investigating a homicide and the abductions of two women. I'd like to have some basic information on a former resident-patient.'

'Former?'

'She died last February. Adalaide Mosebly.'

'I see. You realize privacy laws —'

'She's dead, and I'm not going to ask, at this time, about treatments. It would be helpful to my investigation to know her basic condition upon admission, her cause of death.'

'I can tell you Mrs. Mosebly died of heart failure.'

'She had a heart condition?'

'No, Lieutenant, her heart simply stopped beating. She was a hundred and six. She hadn't left the grounds for more than ten years, and, given this, I can't see how she could have anything to do with your investigation.'

'Was she healthy otherwise? It seems like she was in your facility for a lot of years.'

'We have many residents who remain at Suskind Home for that long, and longer.'

'Why? That's not a privacy violation, it's a basic question. Why would someone remain in your facility for a decade or more?'

Grommet had what Eve thought of as a prim sort of mouth. Small, habitually pressed so it poked out a little.

It poked out now.

'There are many reasons. The individual may no longer wish to or be capable of living alone.'

'What if they weren't living alone? If they lived with a family member before coming to you?'

'It may be the family member no longer felt able to provide the necessary care and attention required. We provide both.'

'At a price — that's not a dig. I've got your website up, and you have what looks like an expansive, well-run facility. But it has to be less costly to, say, hire a health aide or companion. Did Mrs. Mosebly require more than that?'

'Lieutenant —'

'Two women are being held against their will. He's killed once, and will again. I need to pursue every angle available to me to save them. What you tell me may help me do that.'

After a long pause, Grommet cleared her throat. 'I'm speaking in generalities, you understand? Explaining as I might to anyone inquiring about trusting us with a loved one. We are fully staffed with skilled and caring professionals. When you can no longer care for a loved one, and home help is no longer an option, we offer a safe place, a loving place, a professional place to treat cruel conditions such as advanced dementia, which often includes paranoia and violent outbursts. A loved one may no longer recognize you and become agitated and distressed. We treat both the condition and the individual, and are dedicated to helping them feel safe.'

'Okay. Under those general conditions, would a loved one be allowed or advised to visit?'

'Of course. We also offer individual therapy and can recommend groups for those family members who are dealing with the pain and frustration of having a loved one who no longer recognizes them, who can't remember, or only sporadically remembers the life they had together.

'I'll add, as I can't see it infringes, that Mrs. Mosebly was very fortunate to have a loving, devoted son. She was well loved by him, and by our caregivers here.'

'Thanks.'

'If you want more it will require a warrant, and our legal team will vet same.'

'Understood. Thank you.'

'I hope you find the women you're looking for.'

'Yeah, me, too.'

Eve clicked off, then sat back to study her board.

A devoted son. A mother who no longer knew him, so no longer loved him. That could mess you up, couldn't it? Then she dies on you.

Maybe you want to bring her back, and bring her back when she's young and vital — as you see it.

It could play.

191

12

She pulled up a map, began to highlight the buildings on Roarke's list. Mosebly's residence — a semi-detached townhome, two-story with full basement — fit right in. She might have wished for fully detached, and/or a garage, but it still worked.

Others — townhomes, brownstones, warehouses, private garages, an old converted church now a privately owned residence — also worked.

And when she went through the owners or tenants, she gave Roarke points.

All of them could work.

Not all hit the profiled age range, but all were single occupancy.

She started a run on each and began to arrange them in order. She put one last on the list — male, thirty-eight, sales exec, transferred from Chicago to New York five months ago, after a divorce.

Not impossible, but unlikely.

As she started on the next, her incoming beeped. Before she could retrieve it, she heard Peabody's boots.

'Got her! I am so good! I'm so good I should have coffee.'

Eve just gestured to the AutoChef and pulled up the data and photo.

'This is an old mug shot. You said no criminal.'

'Expunged.' Peabody programmed coffee for both of them. 'And since it was eighty-four years ago, in Arkansas, it was basically poofed. Who cares, right, about a ding for possession of a few grams of coke eight decades ago.'

'Possession, use, and resisting.'

'Yeah, yeah, she partied, got stoned, got busted, tried to take a swing at the officer. And did her court-directed rehab. Her parents had enough money and influence to have it all wiped.'

'How do you know all that?'

'I found an article written at the time — gossipy. Her dad was a city councilman, and her mom's family had deep pockets. Anyway, that's her.'

'She's got the right coloring. Shape of the face is close enough. Hair's wrong. Blond, yeah, but what do you call it? Platinum, and with a lot of roots. Add it's long, and all fuzzy.'

Frowning, Eve kept studying. 'No distinguishing marks, so no tat.'

'She could've gotten one later.'

'Yeah. She's the type. We can say she's the type. The clothes, Peabody. This would be years earlier than we dated the ones on Elder. This is from 1977. Did they wear the same sort of thing?'

'Shit. I don't know. I'm betting not. Okay, but try this. He wasn't even born for another nine, ten years. Then you have to add a few years for him to fix a memory. Maybe it's a more adolescent memory, and he pictures her how he sees women — young women dress.'

'Does that work, or are we trying to make it work?' Eve printed out the photo and the attached gossip piece for the board. 'I don't know. Book us a conference room.'

'Really?'

'I want to set up three sections, one for each

woman. I've got Roarke's list of properties, and I'm running the occupants. I'm going to have Jenkinson and Reineke head out, start checking them. Let's get a room, spread this out.'

'I'll take care of it.'

'Let Jenkinson and Reineke know I'm pulling them in.'

Out of curiosity, she did a search for fashion from 1975 to 1985.

Her jaw dropped.

'Seriously? What's wrong with people?'

She closed it off before her eye started to twitch.

'Conference room B.' Peabody's voice came through the interoffice comm. 'I'll transfer the files.'

'I'll be right behind you.'

On the off chance, she shot a memo to Mira.

Briefing in CR B if you have time. New data, new questions.

She turned as brisk steps came her way, and waited until Officer Carmichael stood in her doorway.

'Sir. We'll be writing up the results of the canvass in the two areas designated. But I wanted to let you know, we found plenty who recognized Covino, but no one who remembered anyone who appeared to follow her or make recurring stops when she did.'

'Yeah, he's too careful for that — or he blends too well. Thanks.'

'People had a lot of nice things to say about her.'

'Yeah, I'm getting that.'

'Sorry we couldn't find more.'

'Even negatives are details.'

He cracked the faintest smile. 'That's the truth.'

194

Eve gathered what she needed, downed the last of the coffee, then headed to the conference room.

She found Peabody already setting up, and Reineke and Jenkinson looking hopefully at the AutoChef.

Jenkinson sent the hopeful look her way. 'Don't suppose you put any of your coffee in here, LT?'

'Up-class the coffee, spoil the cop.' Then she considered what that made her. 'Peabody, do that thing you do with the AC.'

'Score.' Reineke pumped a fist in the air. 'Jenkinson did the report, so I familiarized myself with the Covino case. You're thinking she's this guy's number three.'

'Lauren Elder,' Eve began. 'Last seen May twenty-eighth leaving Arnold's, a bar, her workplace, approximately zero-two-thirty.'

She read off the details while Peabody continued to set up. She moved to Anna Hobe, then began on Mary Kate Covino when Mira came in.

'I had an opening — not a wide one. Is that your coffee?'

'I appreciate the time. Jenkinson, get Dr. Mira some coffee.'

'Sit, sit.' Mira waved him down. 'I have it. Don't let me interrupt.'

She finished the briefing, filling in the newest data and statements.

'Our only suspect at this time, James Mosebly, fits, but not cleanly. He left home young, then floated around New York, as far as we can tell, for a couple of years before he decided to pursue additional education and a career. Makes me wonder where and how he floated, and that's a question I'll ask him.

'His attachment to Covino came off very sincere.

She's important to him. His attachment to his mother is illustrated by shelling out over five and a half million dollars in the last sixteen years of her life for her care and housing. He could have chosen less expensive options for her, but he didn't.'

'If his mother suffered from dementia as the director alluded,' Mira said, 'it would have been painful for him. Possibly traumatic. If she died without remembering him, without being able to say goodbye, mother to son, it may have caused a psychic break.'

'And he's got a replacement right under his nose,' Eve finished. 'But why doesn't he go for her first? That's a major hitch for me. Was Elder practice? Doesn't feel like it.'

Eve paced in front of the board. 'Then there's the timing of her trip. Maybe she didn't tell him she'd planned — hoped — to stay at the jerk's place. Maybe. But it feels strange he'd wait until that night, knowing she was planning a trip. Doesn't quite gel.

'And the clothes. Have you seen what they wore in the late '70s, early '80s?'

Jenkinson snorted. 'How old do you think I am, boss?'

Mira just laughed. 'I've seen pictures.'

'The hairstyle, the clothes he used on Elder are twenty years later — fashion-wise. His mother wouldn't have been in her twenties but her forties by that point. So —'

'You're talking yourself out of it,' Mira concluded.

'I'm looking at the flaws. Yeah, he's in the right age group, race. He obviously had a deep attachment to his mother, and some trauma due to her illness — prolonged, it seems — and her death. More, he lives alone, has never married or had a registered cohab.

196

He owns a semi-detached townhome.

'Peabody, I have a map. Put it up on-screen.

'Highlighted in red are the residences and work-places of the three women. Highlighted in yellow are buildings with occupants who fit the parameters.'

'Got a lot that fit,' Jenkinson commented.

'Yeah. And the one in green is Mosebly's town-home.'

'Convenient,' Reineke commented. 'Pretty damn convenient.'

'Yeah, it is. And it sticks out for me. He could have seen these other two women on the street, at their work. He's from the neighborhood, so others who are, are used to seeing him. Think nothing of it.

'He doesn't own a vehicle — or none is registered in his name. But he does have an up-to-date driver's license. No garage, which is a disappointment, but he's sturdy and solid, moves well. He could transfer a hundred-and-fifteen-pound woman from a vehi-cle at the curb to the house, late at night, choose his moment.'

'I'd like to know more about his relationship with his parents. No siblings?' Mira asked.

'No. Only child.'

'Yes, I'd like to know more.'

'We'll find out more. Meanwhile, Detectives, I want you to pay a visit to those residences highlighted. Get inside if you can, get a read on the occupant. Show the photos of the three women, get a reaction.'

'We got it.'

'I'm going to take Mosebly,' she added. 'He knows me, and I can call it a follow-up. I'm going to take Roarke, if he's free. Peabody, I want you to shift over to Hobe. Her time's ticking away. If we missed anything, find it. Talk to her coworkers again, canvass the neighbors. It's been done and done, but do it again. If McNab's free, take him with you.'

She checked the time. 'I'm authorizing OT. Let's get as much of this done tonight as we can. Peabody, shoot the map to their portables.'

'Already done. I'll check with McNab, and get started. Do you want to keep the room?'

'Yeah, let's hang on to it for now. Good hunting.'

As the others went out, Mira rose and walked to the board to stand beside Eve.

'I see why you're looking at him, and why you question yourself. It's not a clean fit but they aren't always. He has gaps, and you need to fill them to get a clearer picture.'

'What's your probability on him?'

'Mmm, I'd like to know more, but I'll say sixty percent.'

'Yeah, that's about where I land, too. It was higher before Peabody found the photo of his mother. There's a basic similarity, but the three women look more like each other than they look like her. To my eye anyway.'

'He's looking through his own. I have to get back, but I'd like your impressions after you speak to him, inside his home.'

'You'll get them.'

'Give my best to Roarke.'

'Hmm? Yeah, thanks.'

Distracted, Eve kept scanning the board, waiting for pieces to line up. When they refused, she pulled out her 'link.

Roarke answered himself. 'Lieutenant.'

'Hey. I've got to head out to the field to interview a suspect in about an hour. Some stuff to clean up here

198

first. Interested?'

'In spending time watching my cop grill a suspect? Always.'

'I'm not grilling him. Yet. Probably.'

'In any case. I'll meet you in the garage in an hour.'

'Good. Great. And I'm sort of thinking about talking to you about a real estate deal.'

His eyebrows shot up. 'Now I'm fascinated. What sort of deal?'

'We'll talk about it. And thanks for the list.'

'My pleasure. An hour.'

An hour, she thought as she pocketed the 'link. Time enough to clear her head and work on how to handle James Mosebly.

★ ★ ★

It took just over that hour for Eve to finish up, and when she scanned her desk for the last time, she compared it with Covino's pristine workstation.

'Show-off,' Eve muttered, then grabbed her file bag and jacket.

She shrugged into the jacket as she walked. She spotted Santiago and Carmichael in a huddle at Carmichael's desk. Either working the jumper/throwee case or debating where to grab an after-tour brew. Either way, Eve kept going.

She was already late.

With that in mind, she ignored the elevators. Cops coming on, cops heading home or, like her, back into the field meant packed cars and stops on every damn floor.

She took the glides, jogging down when she hit a clear stretch, then hit the stairs down to her level.

Roarke leaned against her ride, fiddling with something on his PPC.

Possibly buying one of those rings of Saturn.

'Sorry. Took me longer.'

He slid the device back in his pocket. 'I occupied myself well enough.' He lifted a hand to stroke her cheek. 'You look harried, Lieutenant.'

'Maybe a little. I feel like we moved a few steps closer, but it's not close enough. You drive, okay?'

She climbed in the passenger seat, programmed Mosebly's address.

'Not far, I see.'

'No, not far. Mosebly, James, Mary Kate Covino's supervisor and so-called mentor. She's been missing since June third.'

She gave him the basics as he maneuvered through downtown traffic.

'So she makes three, and this Mosebly fits your profile.'

'Most of it. His place is on your list. They're in this area, Hobe and Covino. I know it. If you can't find a street spot —'

She broke off when he hit vertical, did a neat airborne one-eighty, and dropped into a stingy spot between a mini and a glossy sedan.

'Nice. Why does Peabody always go glassy-eyed when I do that?'

'I couldn't say.' He patted her hand before they slid out. 'He'll be a half block down.' And now, took her hand. 'Lovely evening for a walk.'

'If he's not home, we'll canvass the neighborhood, so that'll be a walk.'

Not so many tourists on this stretch, she noted. Mostly the after-work crowd, heading home. Almost all residential, pretty townhomes all in a row, some with window boxes or pots of flowers, some with fancy grids on the windows.

Mosebly's didn't particularly stand out. He had flowers, a lot of purple and red and trailing green spilling out of window boxes that gleamed copper.

The whitewashed brick had a soft look, offset by a bold red door and a stylized copper heart as a door knocker.

'Palm plate, code scanner, cam, solid locks. One-way glass on the windows. He can see out, you can't see in.'

She stepped onto the stoop, one painted to resemble a mat. The scrolled red letters read:

Always Welcome!

'We'll see about that,' she grumbled, and pressed the bell. 'He's got a full basement under here. Corner lot. And from the windows, he could actually have watched Elder walk to work. He could have watched her from the comfort of his own home.'

'You're leaning heavily in his direction.'

The house, the location — those pieces fit clean and snug.

'I'm looking at the setup here, and I'm leaning.'

Mosebly opened the door. He still wore his baggy jeans and polo, but had changed into house skids. Hope shined from his face.

'Lieutenant! You found Mary Kate.'

'No, Mr. Mosebly, we're actively looking. We'd like to come in for a few minutes. I have some follow-up questions.'

Even as the hope dimmed, he stepped back. 'Of

201

course, of course, please. It's nice to finally meet you.' He held out a hand for Roarke's. 'I've admired your work, and especially the school you've just opened.'

'Thank you.'

'Ah.' Mosebly brushed a hand at his flyaway hair. 'Come in, sit down. Can I get you something to drink?'

'We're fine,' Eve said, and saw why Covino worked well with him.

His living area, both simple and attractive, had nothing out of place. No single-man debris, no clutter. A conversation area, a semicircle sofa in pale gray, a pair of cushy armchairs in a subtle pattern of the same gray with hints of blue, centered around a whitewashed fireplace currently full of flowers and candles.

On the slim mantel over it stood more candles — slim white tapers in squat and colorful blown-glass holders — a photo in a dark gray leather frame of a man and woman holding hands in front of a white, steepled church, and some sort of earth-toned pottery vase or urn.

A rug that looked old and valuable lay over the polished floors.

Mosebly gestured to the chairs, then took a seat on the end of the sofa.

'I'd so hoped you'd found her. I know how hard you're working to do just that. I hadn't read *The Icove Agenda* — so distressing — but after meeting you today, I downloaded it. I've only just begun, really, but I understand you're very good at your work. How can I help?'

'You and Mary Kate are close.'

'Yes, we're a close-knit group at Dowell's. It makes it a pleasure to go to work every day.'

202

'And you often took her, and others, out socially — to celebrate, for instance, a successful campaign.'

'That's right. Team leaders often do, and we try to gather socially as a full team — the Dowell team.'

'I wonder if you brought Mary Kate, or others, to venues here, in this neighborhood, for those social interactions.'

'Yes, now and then.'

'Here, to your home?'

'Yes. No point in having a home you enjoy and not sharing it.'

Eve took out her 'link, brought up Elder's photo ID.

'Do you know this woman?'

He took the 'link, frowned over it a moment, then let out a gasp. 'This is the young woman who was killed. I saw the reports, saw this photo. It was so upsetting, I turned it off.'

'Have you ever seen her before the reports?'

'I don't think so.'

'Have you ever been in Arnold's — it's a bar in the neighborhood.'

'Yes, I know it. A few times, but it's a little . . . stiff, I want to say.'

Eve took the 'link back, brought up Hobe.

'How about this woman?'

'I don't know that I've — Oh yes! Yes, I recognize her. Mike's Place, such a good voice. Anne, Annie?'

'Anna.'

'That's it. I've dragged a lot of people onto the stage at Mike's.' He smiled at the thought. 'That isn't a stiff sort of place, and more the sort I'd take a team for fun.'

'Anna Hobe has been missing for seven days.'

'What?' He jerked back. 'No! Like Mary Kate?'

'You haven't been in Mike's in the last week?'

'No, no, not for a couple of weeks, at least. We were working on the campaign, and I brought work home. What does this mean? The first girl . . . '

His color went nearly as gray as his hair.

'Oh my God, you think that could happen to Mary Kate?'

'All three of these women live within blocks of here. You've lived here for a number of years. I'm sure people are used to seeing you, think nothing of it. You have a nice view of the street from those windows.'

He still held the 'link, and his hand shook as he stared at her.

'You think I . . . I'm a suspect? Why would I . . . I could never . . . I — I need a glass of water.'

'Why don't I get that for you?' Roarke rose.

'I — Thank you. Ah, the kitchen . . . '

'I'll find it.'

Mosebly closed his eyes when Roarke walked away. His rapid breathing worried Eve a little. She sure as hell didn't need a panic attack or a heart event on her hands.

'I've never hurt another person in my life.' Mosebly hitched in a couple more breaths, let them out. 'I avoid conflicts, to be honest. And hard news when possible. I would never harm Mary Kate. I love her.'

'Tell me about your mother.'

His eyes popped open. 'My mother?'

'Yes.'

'She — she died last February after a long, difficult illness. I don't understand what —'

'You loved her, too.'

'Of course. She was my mother.'

204

'She lived with you here for several years.'

'Yes. I convinced her to come to New York and live with me after my father died. I don't know what this has to do with anything, but if it somehow helps . . . '

'You left home fairly young, and there are some gaps in the first couple of years after you came to New York. Can you fill those in?'

He closed his eyes again. 'We can never escape them, can we? Never really escape the sins of the past.'

He looked at Eve again, and she saw sorrow, not guilt, not fear. He shifted when Roarke came back with a glass of water. Taking it, he handed Roarke Eve's 'link.

He drank slowly before setting the glass down on the table.

'I'm gay,' he said simply.

'Okay. That has no bearing on —'

'You wanted the gaps filled. It's unremarkable to you, my sexual orientation, but it was anything but when I was growing up, a PK in rural Kentucky.'

'PK?'

'Preacher's kid. All those years ago, Lieutenant, if you know anything of history, you understand homosexuality wasn't widely accepted. In that time, in that place, I was an aberration, a sin, a freak. I stayed closeted — my shame, my instinct to avoid confrontations. When I finally screwed up the courage to tell my parents, they were shocked, hurt, and couldn't accept me or support me. My father . . . '

He glanced toward the photo on the mantel. 'He said harsh things. It was a shameful, painful experience, but not all that atypical of those times.

'I left home with that shame and pain inside me. I had a little money, thanks to my grandparents —

205

maternal — who were able to accept and support. I came to New York — my vision of the polar opposite of where I grew up. The money didn't last long. I was angry, desperate, determined never to return home.'

He picked up his glass again, drank some more. 'I met a man. A wealthy, influential man with many contacts. He ran . . . we'll call it an escort service. I hope the statute of limitations on such things has run its course, as I don't want to go to prison for things I did so long ago.'

'I've got no interest in charging you with prostitution, which is regulated and legal now.'

'It wasn't then.' He smiled a little. 'I was very good-looking, and my inexperience actually worked in my favor. I made a great deal of money, and there was enough PK in me that I was frugal with it. I avoided drugs, drank rarely and always in moderation.'

He paused to drink more water, and to Eve's eye, steady himself again.

'I learned my grandfather had died a week after his funeral, and that he had left me money. And a request that I use it to better myself.'

He set the glass back down. 'I loved my grandparents, and he'd died without me being there. They'd stood by me when no one else had. My grandfather made one request of me. He and my grandmother never judged me, and he'd made that one request.'

'You enrolled in college.'

'I did. It occurred to me that I'd been marketing myself and very well, so I aimed there. I got out of the life, and got an education. When I graduated, I went home. I didn't intend to see my parents, but I wanted to visit my grandfather's grave. I even took my diploma to, well, to show him. My mother found me there. A small community, Lieutenant. Someone saw me, recognized me, told her, and she came. She hugged me, and she wept, and she asked for my forgiveness.'

When his eyes filled, Mosebly pressed his fingers to them. 'I can't tell you what that meant to me. She asked me to come with her, talk to my father. It was harder for him, but we reconciled. We made peace with each other. When he got sick, I went home to help. And we found something more than peace, we found family again. When he died, I was with him, as I'd been with my grandmother when her time came.

'She, my grandmother, left me everything. The house and land, her life insurance. Everything. So when my father died, and I convinced my mother to come live with me, I used the money I'd saved, money given to me, to make her a place where she could be comfortable, where we could be family. Where I could take care of her.'

'You gave her a home,' Roarke said, 'here. With you.'

'Yes, and she enjoyed the city more than either of us expected. The arts, the restaurants, the parks, the pace. Until. Until she became ill.'

Once again, he looked at the photo above the fireplace. 'It was slow at first. It's a creeping, vicious disease. When I couldn't care for her any longer — her mind . . . It's so cruel when the mind fails before the body. I couldn't care for her any longer, I found a place that could, and would care with compassion. I was with her when she died, but she didn't know me.'

He pressed his lips together. 'She hadn't known me for the last eight years of her life.'

'That must've been painful.'

'I think of the day she came to my grandfather's grave and put her arms around me. I think of evenings we shared, before her mind betrayed her, playing gin rummy, her telling me stories of her misspent youth, as she called it. Stories about my father, my grandparents. The Christmases we shared, and the dinner parties we hosted. I have good memories.'

Eve brought another picture up on her 'link, handed it to Mosebly.

He looked baffled for a moment, then simply delighted. 'Is this my mother? It's Mom. Oh my God, it's a mug shot.' More tears spilled as he laughed. 'She told me, but I didn't actually believe . . . She was a preacher's wife, and a good one. Not stiff-necked, not, well, preachy, but a good one. She changed her life. She bettered herself. But look at her here, so young, so screwed up, so pissed off!'

'Could we look around your house, Mr. Mosebly?'

'You want to — oh, search more than look around. You have to be sure. I'll give you a tour, and you can look wherever you like. You can go through my electronics if that's helpful, or anything else.'

He rose. 'I'd like to ask a favor, when you're sure.'

'What's the favor?'

'Could I have a copy of that photo of my mother? I know it's a strange request — a mug shot. But it's a moment in time — I didn't believe her when she'd said she'd been arrested and why, and that made her change her life. Now I do, and I'd like that moment in time.'

'When I'm sure,' Eve told him, 'I'll get you a copy.'

13

Roarke waited until they'd reached the sidewalk, started down it, then slid an arm around Eve's waist.

'It's understandable you're disappointed.'

'That's not really the word. Well, okay, I'm disappointed we didn't find Hobe and Covino in the basement so we could get them out. I'm not disappointed Jim Mosebly isn't a whacked-out, mommy-freak killer.'

'He strikes me as a very good man. One still carrying some of the scars from the era and its mores when he grew up.'

'Yeah, strikes me the same. Why in hell did some people get so bent because somebody fell for, wanted to marry, or just wanted to bang somebody with the same body parts?'

'Some always have and always will find ways to be intolerant of what they consider other, or outside their version of the norm.'

'Well, the world would be better off if more people minded their own business instead of trying to run other people's lives. Anyway.' She shook it off. 'Eliminating Mosebly's another step, but it doesn't get me closer to finding those two women.'

When he nudged her along, she looked over at him. 'Did you forget where you parked?'

'I didn't, no. We're walking on a very nice evening on the edge between spring and summer. It occurs to me Mosebly came to New York all those years ago for much the same reasons you and I did. We were all bearing scars, and all came here to find our place.'

'Down there?' She gestured down the side street. 'That was Elder's place. Now the guy who loved her lives alone. Hobe, down that way, Covino, up and over that way. Hobe, no real close family ties, and she liked living alone. Opposite for Covino. But they intersect, those three women. Probably passed each other on the street more than once. Maybe waited on line at the same time in some shop. Now two of them, unless I'm way off the mark, are being held in the same place by the same man for the same reason.'

'You're not off the mark.' He steered her around the corner, kept going.

'We might run into Jenkinson and Reineke,' Eve speculated as people bustled by — heading home, heading to dinner, heading to one more shop. 'Maybe they'll get a hit. Peabody and McNab are going to do a canvass so . . .'

She trailed off when she registered where they were. A few steps from the pizza joint, the one where she'd had her first slice on her first day in New York.

'You're always thinking,' she murmured.

'Of you.' He brushed a kiss over the top of her head. 'We'll have ourselves a meal, a carafe of wine, and some downtime. And when we get home, you can update your board and book.'

Instead of turning to the door, she turned into him.

'Thanks.' And kissed him. 'Thank you.'

She walked into the scents — yeast and sauce and spices and grilled meat — the noise of voices, a squeal from some kid, the clatter of dishes — and felt the tension melt from the back of her neck.

A waitress hustled right up to them. 'Hi. Good to see you again. Your booth's ready.'

210

'You called ahead.'

'Always thinking,' he answered as they slid across from each other into the booth. 'Do you need a menu?'

'Nope. Large pie, pepperoni,' Eve said to the waitress.

'Large?'

Eve smiled at Roarke. 'Did you want one, too?'

He smiled back. 'A carafe of the house red, a bottle of sparkling water.'

'Get that going for you.'

As the waitress hurried away, Roarke leaned over, took both Eve's hands. 'Now, tell me, as I remain fascinated, about this real estate deal.'

She laughed. 'Just a wild hare.'

'That includes three words I'm very fond of. Real estate and deal.'

'Okay, well, there's this building.' She rattled off the address. 'You don't already own it — I checked.'

'All right then. Should I?'

'Commercial street level — slick bar and a tony-looking salon. Apartments above. Eight units a level, six levels.'

'Square footage, exterior material, original build date, and dates of major rehabs?'

'Well, jeez, if you're going to have all kinds of questions.'

'There are countless more, but I can find the answers.'

The waitress came back with the water, the wine, glasses, poured both.

'Brick,' Eve said as she picked up her wine. 'Brick, and it looked pre-Urban to me. Crappy security on the apartment entry door, crap elevator — single. Decent soundproofing. That's all I got.'

'I'll get the rest — after you tell me why this property interests you.'

She sat back, gestured with the wine. 'I thought about how if you bought it, you could kick out the fuckhead who owns the bar and lives above it.'

'Could I?' Amused, Roarke gestured back at her. 'Has he committed a crime?'

'If being a fuckhead was a crime, I'd have to lock up half of New York. And occasionally arrest myself. He's Covino's ex-boyfriend, except he only qualified on the boyfriend scale in her mind. He's a smarmy — it's the word — womanizing, self-important fuckhead.'

'Ah, you said she'd planned a trip, and the boyfriend, such as he was, canceled — on the night she was taken. This would be that fuckhead.'

'The very same. I really wanted to look at him, but he's covered, as he was working in the bar until two. Plus, he's too busy looking for the next quick bang to bother with Covino. And he doesn't care enough about anybody but himself to go to all this trouble.'

'So not a suspect.'

'No. I brought her suitcase into evidence. She'd packed all these girly beach clothes and sexy stuff, a bottle of sparkling wine, those little candles,' she added, making a circle with her thumb and index finger.

'It makes you sad.'

'Maybe. Some. Everyone says she's smart, stable, sensible. She wasn't about him. She's not the first to go off the tracks over some asshole with a good line and a pretty face.'

When Roarke grinned, and laughed, she shook her head. 'You're hardly ever an asshole.'

'Flattery like that will get you a pepperoni pizza.'

And he'd timed that comment perfectly, Eve noted, as the waitress set the pizza on the table rack. She set out the plates, topped off their water glasses.

'Enjoy! And let me know if you need anything else.'

Roarke slid a slice onto a plate, passed it to Eve, then took one for himself.

'This is the hardest part,' Eve said. 'Waiting for it to cool enough so you don't burn off the roof of your mouth.'

She glanced around. 'The first time I came in here, sat at the counter in front of the window, everything was new, and everything was possible. I was free, and I was going to the Academy, and I was going to be a damn good cop.'

'And so you are, a damn good cop.'

'Never figured on you. What I got there was a damn big bonus.' She picked up her slice, calculated she had about twenty more seconds left to avoid a scorched mouth. 'So did Mavis's place pass the inspection deal? What?' she demanded when he cocked his head. 'I pay attention.'

'More than many realize. It did, yes, and so the walls are going up. The landscape crew started some of the plantings, though the new owners and tenants want to do considerable themselves. And Peabody sent me very impressive, detailed plans for a water feature, asked about ordering the stone and pump and so on for it. She intends to build it as a thank-you to Mavis and Leonardo.'

'She's really going to do that waterfall thing?'

'Apparently. The design's creative and flawless.'

'I pay one visit to a retiring mob boss and my partner's replicating his waterfall thing. And you're buying his construction business.'

213

She tried a bite, let that warm, delicious comfort fill her senses. 'Perfect,' she said, and took another.

* * *

When they got home, Summerset waited.

'Did you enjoy your evening out?'

'Judge for yourself.' Roarke handed him a small take-out box. 'A midnight snack for you, and you'll find it well worth it.'

'Thank you. I'm sure I will.' Since Galahad reared up to sniff at the box, Summerset looked down. 'You've had your meal, but perhaps someone will find a small treat for you in a bit.'

Too blissed on pizza to take a swipe, Eve just headed upstairs.

Board and book, she thought, coffee and a write up of the interview with Mosebly. She'd check in with her detectives. A hit meant they'd check in with her, but she'd still tag them.

As she updated the board, the cat wound between her legs.

She crouched down to give him a rub, and the bite of pizza she'd folded into a napkin in her pocket.

'That's all you get.'

When Roarke came in twenty minutes later, suit replaced by jeans and a T-shirt, she'd moved from board to book.

'Elder's the only one who belonged to a gym,' Eve began. 'They didn't go to the same salon, use the same bank, medical provider, and no cross in circle of friends I've found.'

'Yet when you showed the photos to our wait-ress — and she called others over — the staff recognized Elder and Covino, and believed they recognized Hobe.'

'Good pizza gets a rep in a neighborhood. There'll be other places they cross. I still think he lives in the neighborhood or close. I think that's going to pay off. But he may have seen them elsewhere.'

She swiveled in her chair. 'The thing is, Covino didn't work in the neighborhood. So she probably used some shops in her work area. I found her market — where she bought her flowers — but they didn't recognize the other women.'

She pushed at her hair. 'I'm going back to the makeup. A lot of damn makeup.'

'I'm going to say the T word.'

Eve shook her head. 'It's not high-dollar stuff. It's stuff you buy in the drugstore. Trina would look down her nose. Anyway, how did he learn how to apply it — so exactly? Did he practice? Does he work in that area — theater, entertainment?'

'What about the top — from the Nashville store — you told me about?'

'Yeah, that. Can't track it down. We wound back to vintage shops again, but . . .'

'Finish the thought.' Knowing her, he programmed coffee for both of them.

'He didn't plan this yesterday, right? Nor a week from yesterday. Weeks at least, and more like months. So I don't think he bought all the clothes, the makeup, the damn shackles right before he grabbed Elder.'

Roarke handed her coffee, sat at her auxiliary station. 'For a few days, he had three women.'

'Yeah, thought about that, too, and it weighs on me. Now he has two. Does he need the three? Is he going to grab somebody tonight? I've got extra patrols in the area tonight, in case. But I can't keep that up indefi-nitely.'

She blew out a breath. 'Otherwise, holding three women — feeding them, toilet facilities.' She pushed up to pace. 'McQueen, he held more at a time, but he didn't give a rat's ass about feeding them. It was the having them, then raping them, then killing them. This one had another purpose.'

'Does he keep them together or separate them?'

'McQueen kept them together, chained up, desper-ate, terrified. But this is different.'

Around and around the board.

'He can't keep them together. How could he main-tain the illusion any one of them is his mother — or will become her — if they're together, if they talk to each other? He has to keep them separate, has to keep a wall between them — for them, for him. Has to have a big enough space.'

She turned back. 'Good job, pointing me at another angle. Maybe a big basement, maybe he keeps them on separate floors. But he's got to have those toilets. You can't keep three people chained up for days and days and not provide a john. Who wants to clean up the mess? And he likes things clean. Elder was clean. Body, hair, nails, the clothes. All perfectly clean.'

She wound around again. 'No signs of dehydration with Elder. She'd had a good last meal. Eat, drink, you gotta eliminate.'

She sat again. 'Planning. He took the three too close together not to have planned for at least three. Maybe he had to have those toilets installed. Yeah, he could've had them already. Hell, he could keep one of them locked up in a bathroom. As long as there's no window. But —'

'I can do some digging on permits. The houses on the list, additional plumbing in the last, what would you like, twelve months?'

'Yeah, yeah, that's a good one. That's a solid maybe.'

'I'll just do that here then.'

She picked up the coffee she'd forgotten. 'He's two people,' she said aloud.

'You think two are working together?'

'No, not like that. He's two people inside one man. The planner, the calculating adult, and the needy, angry child. Both of them are killers, both of them are crazy. But the adult maintains, he can contain, he can look and act sane. He'd have to, wouldn't he?'

She kicked back, put her boots on the counter. 'Yeah, he would. Eccentric at worst, people would think. But not overly because nobody notices him. Does that piss him off, or is that how he likes it?'

She saw Roarke watching her. 'What? Sorry. Just thinking out loud.'

'And it's fascinating. You're building him.'

'A potential him. Just more maybes.'

'Don't stop on my account. Keep building.'

'Well, if he's somewhere in his sixties or seventies as we profile, we'd say he has the maturity of his age and experience. But that inner brat's all impulse and rage. Plenty of rage in the man, too, because he doesn't have what he wants, because he's been disappointed, maybe mistreated. Probably mistreated. But he's got that control.'

Studying the board, she let it come.

'Mosebly was let down, and damn well mistreated. He escaped — with plenty of anger. But he had the grandparents, and, without that better-yourself message, he may have kept going down a hard road. When

217

his mother asked for forgiveness, he gave it. And the years after, reforming his family.

'This guy doesn't have any of that in him. When I saw Stella, recognized her —'

'Eve.'

'No, no guilt here. I would never have forgiven her, and never have reconnected. But I didn't wish her dead. I live with death, work with it, and I don't wish it on anyone. This guy? He has to kill. He kills what . . . disappoints him again.'

She tilted her head, narrowed her eyes. 'He sees, he imagines and needs, so he plans. Every step. It takes time and patience — and money, too. He has to make an investment. He watches, waits, and he takes.'

She sipped coffee. 'He doesn't physically or sexually assault — that would be . . . disrespectful, unseemly? They must beg him to let them go — it's human nature. And that's going to piss him off.'

'Why?'

'A mother wants to be with her child. This hurts his feelings — but he doesn't strike out at them. It's why he needs more than one. One of them will understand. One of them will become, and stay and love him.'

'He can make them like her — physically,' Roarke put in. 'The tattoo, the piercings.'

'That's right, and that's important, but he can't change who they are, or make them who they aren't. So, he'll end up disappointed again.'

She shifted her gaze from the board to his.

'But under it all, Roarke, he doesn't forgive her for what she did or what he perceives she did. So he'll kill her, and go on killing her.'

'You'll find him. You'll stop him.'

'We'll find him. We'll stop him. I just don't know if we will in time to save those two women on the board.'

She worked, and touched base with Peabody, with Reineke. When Roarke found a house on his list with a permit for rehabbing a laundry area, adding a bathroom, she passed it to Reineke and Jenkinson.

'We'd never get a search warrant — way too thin,' she told Roarke, 'but we can see how the occupant reacts when asked if a couple of cops can take a look at their basement.'

'At this time of night, said occupant may be less than hospitable.'

She frowned at her wrist unit. 'It's not that late. It's not even really twenty-three hundred.'

'It's ten past that.'

'See, not even barely there. And I told them this is the last one tonight. They can hit the others tomorrow. They got to a solid third of the list tonight.'

She rose, walked to the board one more time. 'If none of those properties pan out, we'll have to widen the area. I'm not wrong about the damn house. Okay, okay, what if he has the place, but he didn't put it in his name? Maybe the mother's name, or a family name, a place name. A combo.'

'I'll agree to set up a new search, put it on auto, if you agree to shut it down for the night.'

'I'll shut it down as soon as Reineke and Jenkinson check back in.'

'Deal.'

At midnight, because a deal was a damn deal, she slid into bed. 'I can't believe I'm obsessing about toilets.'

'It's a necessity.' Roarke wrapped an arm around her. 'As the man Jenkinson and Reineke talked with who had one installed in the basement he's turned into a media room understands. I wonder if we should add a media room.'

'I like stretching out on the sofa and watching vids in here.'

'As do I. Which is why I've gone back and forth on the idea. Now turn off that relentless cop's brain and sleep.'

In a minute. Or two. 'If he comes out to hunt tonight, and the patrols spot him —'

Roarke rolled over on top of her. 'I see what needs to be done.'

'Sex isn't the solution to everything.'

'But it does solve a multitude of problems. Now quiet down,' he said, and closed his mouth over hers.

He went the dreamy route — she knew his ways.

And they worked.

She heard the *thump* of the cat jumping off the bed, imagined him stalking away in annoyance. Then forgot him as the dreamy spread through her.

Soft and slow, lazy and sweet, Roarke relaxed her muscle by muscle. He found the places, all the places that needed to melt, the places that wanted to ache.

He slid her nightshirt up, inch by inch, over her head and away.

And she was away, with him, body against body, pulse against pulse, mouth against mouth.

He felt her yield, not just to him, but to the moment. The way that relentless cop gave way to the woman who loved. And like her, he yielded to her, to the moment. To the stroke of her hands on his skin, the warmth of her mouth answering his.

When he slipped inside her, she was warm and wet, and when she moved under him, he lifted his head to watch her watching him.

He whispered to her in Irish, heard her sigh in response. She laid her hand on his cheek, so he turned his head to press his lips to her palm as they moved together.

Slow and easy, easy and slow, no hurry, no time, no worry. Even as the need built, as the aches spread, as pulses beat, they clung to the moment, to each other.

And they held tight even when the moment blurred, and beyond it.

So she slept, and, when he knew she did, he joined her.

She dreamed, something in the dark, searching in the dark, following voices crying for help. Whenever she got close, they faded. When she called out to them, they sounded from a different direction.

No matter where she looked, she couldn't find them.

She woke with a start, her communicator beeping.

'Crap!' Dragging herself out of the dream, she grabbed for the communicator. 'Block video,' she ordered as Roarke called for lights on at ten percent. 'Dallas.'

Dispatch, Dallas, Lieutenant Eve. See the officers at twenty-one Leonard. Possible Homicide.

Already up and bolting to the closet for clothes, Eve snapped, 'Is the DB female?'

Affirmative.

'Copy that.' She dragged on trousers. 'Dallas out.' She grabbed for a shirt. 'Damn it, damn it, damn it.

221

It's going to be Hobe. He's had her the longest. What the fuck time is it?'

'Half-four.'

After shoving her feet into boots, she snagged a belt, a jacket. When she came out of the closet with them, a fully dressed Roarke handed her coffee.

'How do you *do* that?' She gulped down coffee before reaching for her weapon harness.

'I'll go with you. I'll drive.'

'I don't need you to —'

'I'll go with you,' he repeated. 'And I'll drive, then find my way back.'

He'd have to, she thought, as the black tee and jeans didn't meet his emperor-of-the-business-world standards.

'And you'll be tagging up Peabody and alerting Morris.'

Since that's exactly what she planned to do, she didn't argue.

He pulled on a black leather jacket; she did the same.

'At least you can't ding me for wearing black, since you are.' She shoved what she needed in her pockets. 'Damn it, Roarke, he didn't give her the ten days.'

The cat jogged down the stairs with them, then made a beeline for Summerset's quarters as they went out the door where her DLE sat waiting.

'Twenty-one Leonard.'

'Yes, I heard.'

She hit the lights and sirens.

He punched it.

As she brought up a map on the dash screen, she tagged Peabody.

'Peabody.' Her partner answered with video

222

blocked. 'Oh hell, Dallas.'

'Twenty-one Leonard, female DB. Looks like he went just a little outside the area we'd blocked for the body dump. Get up, get dressed, get there.'

'Got it. On my way.'

She tagged Morris next.

He didn't bother to block video, so in the dim light she saw him sit up in bed. The sheet, snowy white, covered — barely — anatomical parts she had no business seeing.

His sleepy eyes blinked once before he shook back his long, loose hair. 'Who started off the day dead?'

'Not sure yet, on my way to find out. But the DB's female, and the area indicates she's going to connect to Elder. It's him, Morris. I need you to take her.'

'I'll be waiting for her. Give me the address, and I'll arrange for her transportation when you've finished your on-scene.'

'Appreciate it. Sorry to call you in so early.'

'Dead cops, dead docs. Time means nothing to us.'

Since he started to toss the sheet back, she signed off quickly. 'Dallas out.'

She programmed coffee for both of them as Roarke sped through the city.

'I saw Jake Kincade's bare ass.'

'I'm sorry, what?'

'Not on purpose. When Nadine was on tour, I tagged her — and it was that earth-rotation deal wherever she was, so she's in bed. With him. It was when I wanted her to dig on that asshole from Oklahoma — Quirk's battering bastard of an ex. So she doesn't block video, and Jake just gets out of bed, and there's his bare ass as he walks off-screen.'

'All right.'

'It's a damn good ass, okay, but . . . And here's Morris. Doesn't block video and he's clearly naked in bed. And his works are under the sheet he's about to toss off. It's not like he's a flasher perv, he — like Jake — just doesn't think a thing of the naked parts.'

Roarke reached over to give her hand a squeeze. 'I love the things you find to be a prude over.'

'I'm not pruding. I mean, Morris has a tat of the Grim Reaper guy on his upper thigh. Should I have that information? Never mind.'

She saw from the map they'd be on scene in minutes. She decided to continue her streak, and ordered up the sweepers.

Roarke pulled up behind the police cruiser.

The uniforms had taped off about six feet on either side of the body. One stood with the body, and another sat on a stoop outside the barricade with a male. A teenage male, Eve noted.

Eve held up her badge.

'Lieutenant. Officer Kotter.' He rose, a hard-packed, mixed-race cop in his middle fifties. And kept one hand on the shoulder of the very pale kid who got shakily to his feet. 'This is Kylo Grishom. He discovered the body, and called it in.'

Kylo gripped a tube of water in both hands. 'Am I going to be in trouble?'

'Did you kill that woman?'

His eyes went to bugged-out saucers. 'No. Me? No. Holy shit!'

'Then why would you be in trouble?' Eve asked.

'Well, because I . . . Well, okay, I snuck out. See, I live right down there, and I snuck out to, you know, with my girlfriend. Her parents aren't home, right? So, well . . . um. You know.'

224

'Did you walk by here on the way to your girl-friend's?'

'Yeah.'

'What time?'

'Um, about midnight, I guess.'

'What time did you leave your girlfriend's?'

'Right around four. See, my mom gets up around five, and she gets my older brother up because they work the early shift. And she, for sure, gives me a quick shake before they leave because school's out and I watch my little brother and all. So I wanted to get back before she got up.'

'Where's your girlfriend live?'

'On Duane, right off Broadway. She's not supposed to have anybody over when her parents aren't home, but we, well . . . um.'

'I follow, Kylo.'

'See, I don't want to get her in trouble. I don't want to get in trouble, either, right? But when I saw the lady . . .'

His eyes had stopped bugging out, but he continued to vibrate like a plucked string.

'You were walking home from your girlfriend's and saw the body?'

'Yeah, yeah, see, I was walking, and I thought, at first I thought she was just a, you know, a sidewalk sleeper. But she didn't look like it in the clothes she has on. And I thought maybe she was just passed-out drunk or stoned. But she didn't look right. She was just staring and staring, and I thought, oh shit, she's, like, dead.'

He squeezed the tube so hard, Eve prepared for it to pop.

'I was going to just run, you know? I was, I even

started to, but . . . '

'You did the right thing.'

'I guess.'

'You did the right thing, Kylo. Did you touch the body?'

'Oh man, no. Uh-uh. Negativo plus.'

Eve checked her wrist unit. 'Your mom's going to be up by now. If I were you, I'd tell her exactly what happened.'

'She's gonna ground me for a month.'

'Maybe.' Eve dug out a card. 'You give this to her, and tell her I'll be contacting her, to congratulate her for raising a son who does the right thing.'

His eyes bugged again, but in shocked joy. 'You will? Serious?'

'I will.'

He smiled a little. 'She'll really and totally lap that one up. Thanks.'

'Go home. We'll be in touch. And thank you for your cooperation. Officer, why don't you walk Kylo the rest of the way home?'

'Yes, sir. Let's go, Kylo.'

Eve looked away from them and toward the body. She took the field kit Roarke handed her, and ducked under the tape.

14

She looked down at Anna Hobe.

You called me in the dark, I think. And I think some part of me knew I wouldn't find you in time.

She turned to the female uniform with her cap squared away over a bowl cut that reminded Eve of how Peabody had worn her hair back in her uniform days.

'Officer.'

'Pinsky, Lieutenant. We got the call from Dispatch at zero-four-nineteen and responded. Sir, we were part of the patrol in your investigation, but this was about a block out of the sector.'

'I'm aware.'

'Yes, sir. When we arrived, approximately two minutes later, the witness was sitting on the curb there, head between his knees. He was shook up, Lieutenant, and my partner stayed with him while I verified we had a DB. We secured the scene, and called it in.'

'Anyone else around?'

'No, sir.'

'Okay. When your partner returns, start knocking on doors.'

'Yes, sir.'

Eve glanced up at the sign over the steel-gated entrance.

EXPLORATION STATION

'Pinsky, do you know this place?'

'Yes, sure, it's a hands-on educational complex for kids. Toddlers to teens. Fun place. My kids like it.'

'Thanks.' Opening her field kit, she looked back at Roarke. 'It's Hobe.'

'Yes. And, in a way, another playground.'

She sealed up, and stepped to the body.

He'd laid his second victim out as he had his first. This time in the wide doorway. He'd styled the hair, made up the face much as he had the first, but Eve saw some subtle differences.

Different shades on the eyes, the lips.

He'd dressed her in a skirt — very short, denim, with flowers running down one side. Low on the waist again, Eve noted, to show off the bright red ball in her navel. The shirt — also red — left her shoulders bare and ended just under her breasts.

He'd gone for heels again, red ones this time, with pointed, open toes. He'd chosen a dark blue — nearly black — for the polish.

He'd printed his message in red crayon on white construction paper.

Bad Mommy!

She heard Peabody's fast walking and McNab's quick bounce down the sidewalk, and Roarke's greeting to them.

Eve crouched down, took out her Identi-pad to take the print and officially make the ID.

'Victim is Hobe, Anna. Female, Caucasian, age twenty-four. Reported missing on June one.' Peabody crouched behind her. 'Seal up, Peabody.'

'I did.'

Eve bagged the sign.

'Check under the neck ribbon.' Eve got out her gauges.

'Throat slit, and sewed. Precise stitches. It looks like the same thread, same type of ribbon used on Elder. Lab to confirm.'

With flat voices, efficient moves, they did the work.

'TOD, twenty-forty-six. Contusions and lacerations, right wrist and left ankle, indicate the victim was restrained.' She leaned down close. 'Perfume. Same scent he used on Elder.'

Though sure of it, she took a sample.

'Navel piercing, the multiple ear piercings, the same as Elder. The body's clean. No signs of other offensive or defensive wounds.

'Let's roll her, Peabody.'

When they had, Eve studied the butterfly, wings spread over the small of the back. 'Same tat, same precise work, but . . .'

She ran a sealed finger over the image. 'It's still a little, what, scabby. Not as much healing time as Elder's.'

She shifted to take a look at the neck wound herself.

'Angle's different. You see that? The angle's . . . From behind.' Eve took a fistful of Peabody's hair, pulled her head back, mimed slitting her throat with the other hand.

'Not an impulse this time, if the first one was. But this wasn't. Planned. From behind. See how it goes up at this end?'

'I do now.'

'Not arguing, not face-to-face. Come up from behind, yank her head up to give you a clear target. Swipe. He was done with her. Knew he was done with

229

her. He's either grabbed another we don't know about yet, or Covino's working out so far. Maybe both.'

'I think there's more bruising, deeper lacerations on her wrist than on Elder.'

'Yes, there is. Why do you think?'

'Maybe she struggled more. I think . . . ' Peabody took microgoggles out of her field bag. 'It looks to me like the more are fresher. Like she started struggling more in the last day or so.'

'Why do you think?'

Peabody sat back on her heels. 'She might've figured out she wasn't getting out alive unless she got herself out.'

'That, or she and Covino figured how to communicate. Hope tends to make you fight harder. Or she saw some way to get out. Could be any or all of that.'

'Should I contact the morgue, the sweepers?'

'I did on the way here. Gave Morris the heads-up. See this? The skirt, the shoes? Just a little big on her, where the jeans and the shoes were a little snug on Elder. He gets close though. He gets close.

'Stay with her. I need to go have a word with the mother of the nine-one-one caller. Lives right down there.'

'Okay. His mother?'

'He's about sixteen, snuck out to have a bang-o-rama with his girlfriend. But he called it in and stayed with her, so I'm going to have a word with his mother.'

She rose and spotted McNab and Roarke leaning against her ride drinking coffee.

'Dallas, I'm here to serve.'

'No e's on her,' she told McNab as she locked her field kit in the trunk. 'There's a door cam, but he's going to be smart enough to have jammed it. Still, get whoever runs this place down here to open up and let you check the feed.'

'You got it.'

'I need to talk to the wit's mother a minute.'

Roarke pushed off the car. 'I'll walk down with you.'

He didn't take her hand for comfort — she wouldn't want it. But as they walked down the block, he glanced down at her.

'Is there a point in me reminding you that you did all you could?'

'Wasn't enough.' She shook her head. 'And I know doing all you can isn't always enough. Can't be. I just feel I went in the wrong direction with Mosebly, and ate up that time.'

'You didn't. You eliminated him, as you needed to.'

'I did. You're right. You have to look at it straight on and, when I did, I knew if he upped his schedule by even one damn day, we wouldn't have enough time. He did. We didn't.'

She turned to look back down the street at the scene. The dead wagon pulled up. A couple of people poked their heads out of their doors to watch.

'Just outside the patrol area. Is that bad luck for me, or smart planning for him? Anyway, I'm going to go into Central when I'm done here.'

'I've a car coming.'

'Figured you would. Shit, you were running that search overnight.'

'And I'll send you the results.'

She took another moment. 'Wow, it's like — how do you say it? — about half-five. Well heading toward six now. I bet you missed buying a whole chunk of the universe already this morning.'

'The lovely thing about the universe is, it's still

there. Take care of my cop,' he said as an elegant black sedan slid to the curb. 'And feed her.'

'Right. Sure.'

He walked to the car, and she walked to Kylo's door.

Ten minutes later, Eve walked back to the crime scene with a fat, still-warm blueberry muffin.

McNab stood jawing with one of the sweepers who must have rolled up while she'd been inside.

'I got to the director,' he began, then sniffed the air. 'Is there a bakery?'

'No.' She'd already known this was coming, so split the muffin in three parts. 'Apparently the wit's mother makes them on the weekends, stocks the AC, so her boys don't starve to death in the mornings.'

'Thanks. Good,' he said as he popped his third into his mouth. 'Director's coming in. She's all whacked about having a body in front of the place. You know, kids.'

Eve nodded to where Peabody talked to the morgue team. 'It won't be here long.'

She popped her own share, and McNab was right. Good. 'Let me know if the gods smile on us and there's anything on the feed.'

'Old cam, not much range, and an easy jam. But you never know.'

Eve walked to Peabody, handed off the last of the muffin.

She spoke with the head sweeper, the dead-wagon driver, and had a word with the two uniforms when they came out of a neighboring building.

So far, the gods hadn't smiled enough to land a witness in her lap.

'He dumped her after midnight and before zero-four hundred,' Eve said as she got in the car. 'I'm

232

putting the probability at closer to the four hundred than midnight. It took time to clean her up, dress and make her up. Plus, you aim for somewhere around three in the morning, most bars have closed, most people who hang for last call or work closing shift are home by then. In bed by then.'

'You're still risking an insomniac, somebody with a kid or baby who's having a rough night. Or somebody like the nine-one-one caller, heading home after a let's-bang session.'

'Calculated risk. He's got to make his point, doesn't he? Either Mommy took him to places like this, or she should have.'

'He switched up the shades in the makeup,' Peabody pointed out.

'Yeah, I noticed that. Different nail color, different belly ball, different earrings. He's got a supply.'

'Size small on the label on the top and the skirt. I didn't recognize the brand. Labels were pretty faded out.'

'Old. Like the others. He's got a supply there, too. Clothes, shoes, everything. He's aware enough to understand he'd never hit the one he wants right off. And he's prepared to keep trying until he does.'

'He could have grabbed another. Someone who hasn't been reported yet.'

'Yeah. Contact Norman. Give him another hour, then bring him up to speed.'

'Mosebly checked a lot of boxes.' Peabody yawned, shook it off. 'Somebody else will. Somebody's going to check all of them.'

Eve turned into Central's garage. 'Roarke ran another search overnight, widening the potential properties. He damn well knows the area, and too

233

well not to live here.'

She got out, headed for the elevator. One advantage to catching a case so early was the lack of bodies crowded in the car. While they rode up, she laid out her toilet theory.

'That's good! He has to give some sort of bathroom privileges, and he wouldn't want them together. Talking, pooling ideas on how to get away. Could use chemical toilets though, like some people take on camping trips.'

'Why would any sane human being want to sleep outside in some tent or pod?'

'We'd make our own graham crackers and chocolate and marshmallows, then make s'mores. It's kind of fun, sitting around a campfire, eating s'mores and telling stories.'

'Stories about what fun it is to sit and sleep somewhere you're lower on the food chain than the big-ass bear who decides you look tasty?'

'Well.'

'Or those fun stories about how something decides to slither into your tent while you're sleeping and coil around your throat?' Eve cocked her eyebrows at Peabody. 'Those stories?'

'We liked ghost stories when I was a kid and went camping.'

'You could tell them about the ghosts of the people who got eaten by bears or strangled by snakes because they thought it would be fun to sleep in a tent.'

'I could, but now I think I'll never see the fun in camping again.'

'You're better off. Hobe's mother lives upstate, and her father in Ohio. I'll take care of the notifications. Send a memo to the lab,' Eve continued as they turned into the bullpen. 'I want priority on this. And one to Mira for a follow-up.'

In her office, Eve grabbed coffee. Considering the time, she thought she could wait a bit longer to tell Anna Hobe's parents their daughter was dead.

She worked on the board and the book, wrote the report, and copied Mira to go along with the memo from Peabody.

Then she sat, studied the board again before she closed her eyes.

Had she looked so hard at Mosebly because she'd wanted him to fit? Or because he shared some traits with the killer — or how she'd built the killer?

Not the killer trait, but others.

The right age group, single, never married or attached. Only child. Estranged or a history of parental difficulty. Lived alone, private residence.

Could she add a good, responsible job? How did you buy or rent a private residence unless you had the money to pay for it, maintain it?

Inheritance?

She opened her eyes again.

'Did Mommy die and leave you a big house and a bunch of money?'

Could be, she considered. Could definitely be. But then why was he pissed?

Because under the obsession, the need, was rage. The kid inside was pissed.

And why the need to replace her with a woman in her twenties?

'Because that's when it happened. Whatever the hell it was. Maybe she dumped you back then, or screwed up enough Child Services took you. Maybe she went to jail, or got sick, or died.'

235

Eve pushed up to pace. 'If she died, why wait so long to be pissed? That one doesn't fit. Except . . .'

She turned back to the board. 'You're fucking crazy. But you've got money, you've got means. Hell, maybe she pissed you off and you killed her, and that's when the rest broke down. You just want her back. Back when you remember happier times.'

She shook her head again. 'You don't dress Mommy like that to remember happier times. You're dressing her cheap, low-rent-hooker cheap. Maybe that's what she was.'

Once again, she put her boots up, closed her eyes, and let it all sift through.

She heard Peabody's clomp, heard her take a step away.

'Thinking, not sleeping.'

'Okay. I came to beg for a cup of coffee.'

Eve waved her in. 'He's going to be somewhere between sixty and seventy-five. I'm thinking on the lower side now. White male, or mixed race, as we have no data on the father. He lives alone, in a private residence, and likely has a solid job or career. He has a good intellect for a crazy son of a bitch, and skills. He's precise, he's neat, controlled, and a planner. You don't see crazy son of a bitch or killer when you look at him. I'm betting no one who works with him or for him, none of his neighbors would describe him as a man with a temper. And I'm going back to what I wondered from the start.

'Did they know him? Maybe not his name, but his face. That nice older guy who comes into the bar now and again, or who takes a walk every evening, who I see at the market or the glide-cart.'

'Familiar.'

236

'Familiar enough, harmless-looking enough that if they saw him for an instant before the grab, the fight-or-flight wouldn't kick in.'

Peabody set fresh black coffee on Eve's desk.

'I follow.'

'Follow this,' Eve told her. 'No like crimes, nothing pops. So as Mira profiled, something more recent caused the snap. I'm thinking he not only hasn't killed before this, he hasn't broken the law. Precise, careful, and so on. Maybe, until this point, a kind of rule-follower.'

'He's damn good for a novice.'

'He's taken his time, worked it all out. Inside, he's broken, a snotty kid, but the other part of him knows how to think, control it, cover his bases, take the time to.'

'Maybe, like you thought with Mosebly, he goes into the bars in a group.'

'Maybe, but . . . I think I was off there. He's a loner. At the core of him, he's a loner. Probably friendly enough with coworkers if he has them, and neighbors, but not the social type. It's the quiet life for him, especially in these last months. It takes plenty of alone time to plan all this out, to set all this up.'

Playing with angles and aspects, she took her coffee as she rose to walk to her window. 'He documented their routines, but he didn't know them — not in a genuine personal sense. If he had, he wouldn't have staked out Covino on that night. He'd have known she planned to stay with Asshole Boyfriend, or considered it. So he's not a friend, but yeah, familiar.'

She turned back to the board. 'I've got Yancy's projections of what the mother looks like at eighty, at seventy, at sixty — and he's working on the younger

237

decades. So far, no hits on face recognition.'

Turning, she eased a hip on the desk to face Peabody. 'Long shot there anyway, not only because it's a projection — no matter how good he is — but they're not the mother. They're just the type, the physical type.'

'It's still a good angle.'

'It is, and we'll keep running the program. But we need to ID the mother. If we're right and Elder was his first kill, the break happened within the last year. Longer than that isn't logical. Whatever triggered it, it's this time period he's fixed on.'

She tapped the photos of the two signs left with the bodies. 'Childhood. Young childhood. Even I know that's not the printing of, say, a ten- or twelve-year-old.'

'Four or five would be my guess. Maybe six.'

'So something happened during that period of his life, with his mother. Why does he want to go back here, to give up the freedom and choices of adulthood?'

'Maybe because of that. Young childhood means you don't have to make decisions, work for a living. Somebody else is in charge, takes care of everything. They feed you, clothe you, protect you.'

'That's good, but what if they do a crappy job of all that? Lots of parents and parental figures do a crappy job, and worse. Whether she was good at it or crap at it, he wants to go back there. That needy kid is still in there, but in this case, he's doing the feeding, the clothing. He's making the decisions right alongside the adult portion.'

'Are you thinking split personality? Multiple personality disorder?'

238

'MPD's rare, really rare, and I'd only buy into it here if he hasn't kept his job since the split or break. Not impossible,' she added, 'but we're not going to find that out until we find her.'

She tapped the signs again.

'Finding an unidentified woman of undetermined age, alive or dead unknown, place of origin unknown, current residence, if any, unknown.' Peabody pushed at her red-tipped hair. 'Good luck to us.'

'Screw luck, we work the case. She looked enough like these women — as he created them — to give us a sense. We extrapolate she was in her early twenties, like his vics, when he was between four and six. That means if she's the bio mother, she gave birth between the ages of — we'll call it seventeen and twenty-one to make it stretch. He dresses her like a party girl, so we have that. He hunts bars, so we again extrapolate she worked in one or frequented same enough to keep that stuck in his head. We have the tat, and it matters. Why go to the time and trouble to ink her with that exact symbol if he hadn't seen it on the mother?'

'They called them tramp stamps,' Peabody put in. 'I found that when I was researching. Tats on the lower back of a female, that's what they called them in that era.'

'Really? Pretty fucking sexist, but a good angle if we follow it. And we will because it's what we have. Maybe she boosted her income with prostitution, but if she got busted, we haven't turned up anyone with that tat.'

'Lots of years, lots of jurisdictions, and not all from back then are going to be in a database.'

'You're right about that, too.' She checked the time. 'I need to make the notifications, then we'll hit the

239

morgue.'

'I can take one of the notifications.'

'No, I got it. Send a memo to Jenkinson and let him know we'll be sending him and Reineke an expanded list of properties. And start a search for male children between four and six — no, make it seven — given up for adoption, abandoned, taken by Child Services in the time period we're speculating. Mother early twenties, Caucasian. Start in New York, all boroughs.'

'Holy shit.'

'Yeah, but it's going to be something like that. It just follows.'

'I'll set it up. I can keep going while we're in the field, and send alerts on any hits.'

'Do that.' Eve sat, engaged her desk 'link.

Anna Hobe might not have maintained close ties with her parents, but Eve knew when she ripped the heart out of two people.

After documenting the notification, she scrubbed her hands over her face, and put it aside.

Peabody shot up a hand when Eve walked into the bullpen. 'Two seconds, let me remote it. I'm getting hits,' she added as she finished, then popped up. 'So I'm filtering the alerts to bar workers or alcohol issues or other addictions, prostitution pops. I can go through the rest when we're back, but those filters might narrow it.'

'Good thinking.' She risked the elevator again. 'I doubt Morris will find many deviations from the first victim, except the big one. He killed Hobe from behind. Covino suits him better and, for her sake, I hope she keeps doing just that.'

'No fresh missing persons that fit. It's early, but if she does suit him better, maybe he won't grab another.'

240

'Aren't kids usually greedy?'

'Oh, well,' softhearted Peabody began, 'I don't know if I'd say that.'

'Sure they are. It's a natural state until you're taught about sharing and all that. The man plans, the boy wants. And the kid's inside a man who knows how to take. Covino won't keep him satisfied for more than a few days because she's not Mommy. But she can buy us time.'

She pulled out her signaling 'link. 'It's Mira,' she told Peabody, and answered as they came to a stop on her garage level. 'Dallas.'

'I've just read your report. I can come in early, within thirty, to consult.'

'I'm actually on my way to the morgue, then the lab.' She wondered how long Mira had been up, and how much time it had taken her to make her hair perfect. 'It may take more than an hour.'

'All right then. Why don't you —'

Mira paused as Dennis Mira came on-screen, pressed his cheek to his wife's. And smiled with his hair going everywhere at once and his eyes still a little sleepy. Eve accepted it when her heart just melted.

'Good morning!'

'Hey. Sorry to interrupt your morning.'

'Oh, that's all right. I'm going down and scrambling us some eggs, Charlie.' So saying, he kissed Mira's cheek.

'That would be great, Dennis. I'll be right down.'

'Don't you work too hard,' he told Eve, then shuffled off in a green bathrobe that looked like it had seen a dozen years of early mornings.

'Why don't you tag me when you're back at Central. I'll make time.'

'I'd appreciate it.' Eve got into the car. 'If you could come to the conference room when I tag you? I think it would be more useful for you to see the board, hear anything Peabody's dug up.'

'Just tag me, and I'll come to you.'

Eve thanked her again, clicked off. As she drove out of the garage, she considered. 'It's still early. Go ahead and program some eggs for Morris, and coffee. I got him out of bed with this.'

'Nice. And, ah, got me out of bed, too, so . . .'

'Fine, fine, whatever — just eat yours fast.'

'You want?'

'I don't —' Then she remembered she'd told Roarke she'd eat, and didn't think a third of a muffin qualified. 'Egg pocket.'

15

Once again, Eve walked the white tunnel, this time with Peabody carrying a go-box.

'I gotta say, I don't know how anybody could eat in a room with bodies on slabs and in drawers.'

Eve glanced over. 'Do you eat in the bullpen?'

'Well, yeah, but —'

'Work's work. You don't see the bodies when you eat, but you're standing for them.'

She pushed open the doors and found Morris standing for, and over, Anna Hobe.

'The saying is the early bird catches the worm,' Morris began.

'I guess that means the bird starts the day with murder,' Eve finished, and made him laugh.

'I suppose it does. Hers ended before this one dawned, as you know.'

'We brought you some breakfast.' Peabody made a wide circle around the slab and the body on it to set the go-box on his counter.

'That's very considerate of you, and I'll enjoy it when we're done here. Your on-scene observation on the wrist lacerations coincides with my exam. You also note the fresh lacerations and bruising don't appear on the ankle.'

'Yeah. I thought.' Eve pounded a fist in the air. 'Maybe beating on something, because they don't look like she got them trying to pull out of the cuff.'

'Indeed they don't. *Bang, bang, bang* — sharp movements that had the cuff slapping against her wrist. Pounding against a door perhaps, or wall, and over the last thirty-six hours before TOD.'

'Why'd she wait? That's the question. Wouldn't you start off with the beating and pounding? 'Let me the fuck out!' Then gradually give it up? She tries to pry off the cuff, pull her hand through, you can see the marks, but she gave *that* up to start pounding something.'

'You have a theory.'

'I wonder if we'll find something similar on Covino when we find her. Maybe they started banging on a door, a wall, something to try to communicate with each other. He has to have them separated, but in the same place. Nothing else makes sense.'

'A good theory.' With his protective cape over a pale gray suit with brighter, bolder needle stripes of blue, Morris studied the body.

He hadn't braided his hair, Eve noted. Hadn't had time — it must take a lot of time — because he'd come right in. He had it pulled back in a sleek tail instead.

'She had a meal at approximately nineteen hundred thirty. Pasta primavera, about four ounces of water, and another six of ginger ale. I don't have the tox report as yet. I sent samples — makeup, hair, and so on — to the lab, flagged for the same techs who worked on Elder's.'

'Appreciate it. How long ago, do you figure, he inked her, pierced her?'

'No more than five days. It's the same precise work, as is the stitching on her throat. I would say the same thread, but the lab will tell that tale. The wound, however . . .'

'From behind.' Eve held up her left hand, yanked it back, sliced the right. 'One hand pulling her head

244

back for a bigger target, the other — the right — making the slice.'

'Yes, I agree with your on-site there as well. From behind, slightly above. I would say he struck quickly and, again, precisely. She didn't have time to struggle, or, if he dosed her, may have been too passive to do so.'

'I'm going with the second choice. He doses his victims to keep them in line. If he's going to get that close, with a weapon, he wanted her dulled up — probably put something in the food. She's got a free hand, right, he only cuffs one. Why risk her struggling and maybe, just maybe, getting that free hand on the blade, using it on him?'

She studied Hobe. 'He knew he was going to kill her, but he fed her.'

'Barely an hour between the meal and TOD,' Morris agreed.

'That's a waste unless you consider it as a vehicle. Something to put the drug into, to keep her complacent. There's a coward in him. He doesn't just cuff a hand to keep them in place, he drugs them, and he cuffs an ankle. That way, he can stay out of their reach, doesn't risk them taking a punch at him.'

'I'll rush the tox through for you. Otherwise, I can tell you she was healthy, no signs of alcohol or illegals abuse. She bit her nails.'

'She what?'

'She'd — recently, since her abduction — bitten her nails below the quick.'

Morris lifted one of Anna's hands, showed Eve the nail of the index finger. 'I removed one of the replacement nails he'd applied and painted — sent it to the lab as well.'

'I missed that on scene.'

'It's precisely and perfectly done. I imagine an expert could have done no better.'

'He couldn't know she'd bite her nails, and he wanted to paint them, have them look good.' Eve felt a crack open in the wall she felt she'd been pushing against.

'He had to buy the replacements within the last week, more likely the last couple days. We can work with that.' She looked at Peabody. 'We can work with that.'

Because as Eve said, work was work, Peabody approached the body, studied the hand. 'The other nine are perfect, and look completely natural. Trina does this kind of service in her salon. To get that kind of precision, I'm betting he had to use salon grade. Not the sort of fakes you can pick up in a drugstore. I've used those before and they never look that good.'

Eve had already grabbed microgoggles for a closer exam.

'Not just good. Perfect, like you said, Morris.

'That's a mistake,' she said as she straightened. 'That's a big mistake. He needed perfect, and she bit her nails.'

'I'll remove the others as well, but you can see from this one, he smoothed where she'd bitten, then roughed up the nail bed.'

'Yeah, you've got to do that to get a good adhesion,' Peabody said. 'Then, at least for the cheaper ones, the do-it-yourself kind, you paint on the glue, fit the nail on. You have to give the glue time to set, then you shape it the way you want before you add color.'

'Okay, good, let's give this a hard shove at the lab. This is a break, Morris. Thanks for coming in to take

246

her. Her parents will contact you. They're divorced, but they're both coming to New York.'

'I'll have her ready for them to say their goodbyes. Thanks for breakfast.'

'You more than earned it. Peabody, with me.'

Hustling to keep up, Peabody sent Morris a wave. 'The salon grade are a serious sting.'

'They hurt?'

'The wallet,' Peabody explained. 'What I'm saying is the drugstore brand would've done the job. I mean, it's not like she was going to mess them up, right?'

'Looking for perfect, willing to pay for it. Add he might have thought we'd miss them. I didn't spot them on scene. Less expensive makeup, hair stuff? I'm going with it's the sort of thing his mother used. Probability is Mommy didn't bite her nails and buy fakes to cover it.'

'Follows. I'll tag Trina first, ask where you'd get them. I don't know if salons sell the kits to regular people.'

'Had to be in the last few days. Had to be. Elder's nails . . . ' She opened the car door, pushed her mind back to her board. 'On the short side, neat and even because he'd manicured them after he killed her. Hobe's were longer. Not crazy long, but longer, because he was working with the fakes, had more to work with. So it's not the length, it's the look.'

Tuning out Peabody's conversation with Trina, she drove through building traffic.

She parked again, and Peabody continued to talk as they got out of the car.

'That'd be great, big help.'

'No prob for me.' Trina's voice popped over the noise of downtown. 'Catch that murdering bastard,

Peabody. And tell Dallas — I know she can hear me — she's overdue for a trim. And it's been weeks since her last facial. You get one freaking face, so you gotta take care of it.'

Eve kept walking.

'You bet. See you at the house maybe this weekend. Cha, Trina.'

As she had before, Eve bypassed Berenski's station and headed straight for Harvo's.

Purple still ruled the day, but Harvo married it with candy pink in baggies with purple cuffs that folded inches above her ankles and showed off purple high-tops with pink laces.

She sucked something from a jumbo go-cup through a straw and waved them in.

'Figured I'd see you. Pushed this through as soon as my ass hit the chair. Easy one, as I already had the baseline from Elder on the hair products. You got the same deal with your new vic.'

Because she'd expected it, Eve nodded, hooked her thumbs in her belt loops. 'How about the clothes?'

'I'm kinda scooping on the skirt. Old-timey, sure, but it's got some zing. It's ninety-five percent cotton, with three percent spandex, two viscose. Little bit of stretch, see? The embroidery's machine done, poly-neon thread. That's for the shine and color pop. Size small. I'm working on reconstituting the label. It's mostly faded out, but I should be able to get you a brand.

'Top's ninety-two rayon, eight spandex. Snug and stretchy. I took a quick gander, and back in the day, these would've been easy to come by without much of a sting.'

'Relatively inexpensive, easily accessible.'

248

'And recently laundered, same deal there. Size small. Label's Looloo, which — another quick gander — was a store brand for AllMart. They're still going strong — every fricking where in the 'burbs and such — but they killed the Looloo line in 2009.'

'That's good data, Harvo, and fast work. Thanks.'

'That's my rep. Gotta keep it. Do you need me to show you where to find Dawber and the Dezi?'

'No, we got it. Thanks again. Vintage shops,' Eve continued as they walked. 'We keep pushing on those. It seems to me both outfits were in too good condition to have ended up in a down-market thrift store or flea market sort of thing.'

She paused at Dawber's area, where he sat studiously working on a comp. Eve rapped her knuckles on the doorframe.

'Sorry to interrupt,' she began.

'Not at all. I'm just sending you the completed report from Victim Elder. There were so many products, you see, and shades.'

'Understood. Have you started on Anna Hobe?'

'Only just. I've been running some analyses while I complete this report. Just let me . . .'

He swiveled around, gave his chair a little push to send it to another work space. He swiped at the screen, entered some sort of code on the keyboard. Then made unintelligible noises as he studied the screen.

'All right, yes, there we are. The two-in-one tinted moisturizer. The same brand as Elder, and, yes, the same shade. It seems — ah — I see. We have a concealer — Toot Sweet brand again. Found under the victim's eyes, and along the left cheek beside the nose. A scatter of broken blood vessels, you see, from the morgue photo Dr. Morris provided.'

'Used to cover them?'

'Yes, indeed, to cover minor flaws, and some dark circles under the eyes.'

'Stress, not sleeping well.'

'Ah, possibly, yes, but I couldn't confirm something like that. I'll analyze the other products.'

'I need you to give the nail priority.'

'The nail?'

'The fake fingernail sample. I need that at the front of the line.'

'Oh, all right.' He looked a little nonplussed. 'I generally complete a category, but I can interrupt the facial enhancements.'

'Do that. I need everything you can tell me about that sample as soon as you can.' She throttled back on the tone. 'You and Harvo make a good team.'

'Oh, she's just brilliant, and so charming. You don't always find those two qualities in one person.'

'Guess not. We appreciate your work, Dawber.'

'And I yours, of course.'

Eve backed out, aimed for the shoe guy's area. And found Berenski, hands on hips, in the doorway.

His eyebrows beetled together over the beady eyes in his egg-shaped head. The mustache he'd decided to grow looked like a smooshed caterpillar over his tight, turned-down mouth.

'You're doing end runs around me to nag at my people?'

At his station behind Berenski's back, Dezi frowned ferociously and waved jazz hands.

Eve kept her face as stony as Dickhead's. 'You can call it an end run. I needed to talk hair and fiber, so went to the queen, where you'd have sent me. Saved

250

us both time.'

'Then you're on Dawber's back, and Dezi's.'

Dezi made pistols out of his fingers, shot them in all directions, then slumped as if struck with a ricochet.

'Harvo said Dawber and Dezi had the evidence samples.'

'I'm head of this lab.' He poked himself in the chest with his thumb.

'And I'm head of this investigation. Two dead, another very likely on deck.'

'You come to me, or you wait for the freaking reports.'

Dezi mimed strangling someone, then wrapping a noose around his own neck and hanging himself. And Eve was pretty sure he ended with committing hari-kari.

'Your people complaining?'

'Not the point. We got a system. I'm the system. And I got the jewelry from Hobe, and you'll get the freaking report when I finish and send it.'

When Eve took a step forward, she watched Beren-ski's eyes jitter, just a little.

'Mary Kate Covino, age twenty-five. Missing for six days. She's got shackles digging into her wrist, her ankle. He held Elder for ten days before he sliced her throat. He moved up the timeline a day with Hobe. If you sit on that report, on any of the reports that pertain to this investigation, I'll pop out your eyes with my thumbs and make you eat them like gumballs.'

'Back off, back off. Nobody sits on anything around here. I'm not having my people harassed because you want to cut the line.'

'Mary Kate Covino, age twenty-five. Missing for six days. She won't get another six. If you don't want

251

me talking to your people, who work for the same city I do, fine. You tell me about the shoes found on Anna Hobe's body.'

'Dezi's got the shoes,' Berenski muttered.

A bare instant before he turned to Dezi, the tech stopped mugging monster faces and sat quietly. 'Where are you on the shoes, Dezi?'

'Just finished, Chief.'

'Give her what she needs. Don't like end runs,' he said, jabbed a finger at Eve, then stomped off.

'You're a card, Dezi.'

'You gotta make your own fun. Hey, listen, Dickhead can be just that, but things hop around here, and he keeps it going.'

'I got that. What've you got?'

'Size seven and a half, open-toe pump, four-inch stiletto-type heels, three-quarter-inch platform, polyurethane upper, synthetic sole — I'll have all the data in the report. Style was called Andrea, under the City Styles brand. They named their shoes, see? This style was available from 2002 to 2004 in this shade — Ruby — and in black. It's in excellent condition for a shoe that old. Some scuffing on the sole, but not much. I'd say it wasn't worn much. Probably hurt like hell.'

'Good data, thanks. And for the show.'

'Hey,' Dezi called as Eve walked off, 'I'm here all week!'

'Why say you're a card when you mean funny?' Eve wondered. 'What's funny about a card?'

'I guess, maybe, I don't know. Jokers. A joker's a card,' Peabody said.

'Nobody uses jokers. She must've ditched the drugs whenever possible,' Eve continued. 'Dark circles under her eyes, so maybe from lack of sleep if she managed to ditch the drugs. Nail biting — you don't do that when you're drugged out or zoned by them. The indications she beat or banged on something.'

'And the shoe size, same as the first victim, but they were loose, like you said on scene. She was a size seven, Elder more like an eight. So you have to figure the mom was a seven and a half.'

'He used concealer stuff — she had to be perfect. No flaws. Mira and the other shrinks are going to have a field day with this guy when we get him.'

Out of the lab and back in the car, Eve sat a moment. 'Let's get all this added to the board in the conference room. I want Mira to have all the data.'

She pulled out, eased behind a delivery truck, biding her time. Then zipped around it, punched it, and squeezed through a light an instant before it turned red.

A couple of pedestrians trying to advance ahead of the Walk signal shook fists at her back bumper.

'Trina came through during the Dickhead show. I've got a list of outlets that sell directly to salons. She says you have to have an account.'

'We don't have the readout on the nail yet, but it's going to be a new account. Got to be in the last week. Make it two for a buffer. Start on that, and I'll set things up.'

She pulled into the garage. 'Wouldn't it be a kick in the ass if a fake fingernail breaks this?'

Her 'link signaled as she got out of the car. 'And Roarke came through with the list of additional properties.'

'He copied me, too.' Peabody nodded at her handheld. 'I'll send it to Jenkinson and Reineke.'

They got in the elevator, and Eve started her mental checklist. Cops and support staff shuffled or clipped off. As she worked on that list, she calculated she could handle another couple of floors before bolting for the glides.

When the doors opened again, she spotted the wild eyes of a junkie at the peak of a high, caught the whiff of urine, which explained the dark spot spreading at crotch level and the stream of wet in his wake. As the two uniforms flanking him began to perp-walk him toward the elevator, she bodily blocked the door, said, 'No.'

The junkie grinned; one of the uniforms said, in aggrieved tones, 'Come on, man.'

'He just pissed himself,' Eve added.

When the doors closed on the junkie's high giggle, the other passengers applauded.

With that success, she handled the elevator the rest of the way up.

'I'm going to update in my office, then tag Mira before I update in the conference room. You can take ten more on the salon venues once I head down to the conference room.'

Coffee first, always, and, with it in hand, she wrote up her notes, updated her book, then her board. She took a moment to study Roarke's expanded list, to familiarize herself with it, then sent Mira a text.

As she passed through the bullpen, she called out, 'Ten minutes, Peabody,' and kept going to start the next task on her list.

BEFORE

Violet had three children, and her love for them often made her heart ache even as it soared. Sometimes she looked in on her daughter, her two sons when they slept. No matter how many squabbles she'd dealt with during the day, those moments brought such peace.

In the twelve years since she'd collapsed, lost, frightened, nameless, in the road for Joe to find, she'd found peace, her place, her purpose.

She believed with everything she was that Joe had been meant to find her. They'd been meant to find each other, to make this life, to have these beautiful children.

She'd become an avid gardener and a good cook. She had twice-a-week help with the housework, but she and Joe had both agreed they didn't want any live-in help.

The house, one they'd pampered and preserved and repaired, was only theirs.

Now that their youngest had started school, she took more time for volunteer work. She chaired the garden club, and enjoyed it, prized the friendships she'd made through it. She organized an annual fashion show with the profits earmarked for women in need, and was so, so proud of the work.

Joe held the vital and difficult job of chief resident in the ER, yet another source of pride for her. She'd considered working outside the home, but the home, and tending it and the children, gave her such satisfaction, such joy.

They had two dogs, a cat, and the three goldfish won at a local carnival to round out the family.

The summer before they'd bought a vacation home

in Hilton Head, and she looked forward to years of memories made there.

Her life was all she could want.

Except for the occasional nightmare. She hadn't told Joe — didn't want to worry him when she woke shaking, her head pounding.

Terrifying dreams, even if she couldn't really remember them clearly. Just the sensation of drowning, a child screaming. Screaming for her? A feeling, such a strong feeling of utter despair.

But they passed, they always passed. And in the morning everything was just as it should be.

Her life was far too busy and full of light to worry about those rare moments in the dark.

NOW

She woke in a different room, and, for a moment, Mary Kate thought she'd come out of a horrible dream. But it wasn't her room. It wasn't her apartment.

The horrible dream remained her reality.

But he'd moved her, she realized. He'd drugged her and moved her to another space.

No windows again, but a larger space with more furniture, and a small kitchen area. Not that she could reach it, because the chain shackling her to the wall was too short.

But she could move to a sofa — bolted to the floor — and noted rather than the cot she now had an actual bed. Also bolted down.

More lights — some in the ceiling, some bolted down.

On dim, those ceiling lights, but when she called for lights on full, nothing changed. She clapped her hands, and the three lamps came on.

She had a rug, she saw, on the concrete floor, what her grandfather called an easy chair, as well as the sofa. Books on a shelf, and she could reach them.

Old books, many yellowed with age, a lot of children's books with them.

A bathroom area — toilet, sink, shower. She could have wept at the idea of a shower. A single towel, a washcloth, a tube of liquid soap, another of shampoo, conditioner.

No door, but she'd long passed the point of modesty. In any case she'd wait until she heard him leave before trying the shower.

And hunting for weapons.

She saw clothes folded on a table, but a set of stairs had her heart tripping.

Stairs led to a way out. She just had to find a way to get to the stairs, to find something to break the goddamn chains and get to the stairs.

Locked door, absolutely locked, but if she could get that far, she'd be damned if a locked door stopped her.

She heard those locks *clink* open, heard the sliding *snick* of a bolt, and he came down.

He carried a tray. Her breakfast, she assumed. She held back her rage, her fear, her hope, and smiled at him.

'Good morning, baby darling! What a nice room.'

'I knew you'd like it. I knew it!' His pleasure beamed out as he set the tray on the table by the easy chair. 'We can spend more time together now, and have snacks! I can't stay now, but we'll have dinner together tonight.

And you can read me a story before I go to bed.'

'I'd love to do that. Will you be gone very long?'

His eyes narrowed, sparked at her as the man swallowed up the little boy. 'Why?'

'Because I'll miss you, of course.'

'I have to go do my chores, but we'll spend lots of time together when I come home. I made you a nice breakfast.'

'You're so good to me.' You rat-fucking son of a bitch.

'We have to take care of each other. Mommies and their baby darlings have to take care of each other.'

He started for the steps, started up them, turned. The man looked down at her, sly and smiling. 'You're number three and the third time's the charm.'

She heard the locks fall into place, the bolt slide home.

And waited, waited. She heard him walking over her head, thought, as she strained, she might have heard a door slam home. But she didn't hear the rumbling sound.

A different part of the basement, she concluded. He's gone, she told herself. I know he's gone.

But she forced herself to wait, counted to a hundred five times before she rose to examine every part of the room she could reach.

She spotted a pipe, not unlike the one in her first space, one she could reach.

She started to strike the wrist cuff against it, then spotted the scratches, the tiny nicks in the metal. Like the ones she'd put on the pipe in the other room.

'God. God. Anna.' She banged and banged, shouted, pleaded.

But there was no answer.

'He moved her, too, so she can't hear me. That's all.' But when she rested her forehead on the pipe, she knew better.

Third time's the charm, he'd said.

He'd done something to Anna.

'Don't lose it, don't lose hope, either. Hang on, M.K., just hang on.'

She breathed her way through it. She'd figure out how to take a shower with one hand and one ankle chained. She'd eat because she'd stay strong. And if she couldn't find a weapon, by God, she'd be the weapon.

She wouldn't live the rest of her life here. She wouldn't let him end her life here.

'I'll kill him if I have to,' she mumbled, staring at the locked door. 'I'll do what I have to do.'

16

By the time Peabody came into the conference room, Eve had nearly finished updating the board.

'Pull up the map,' she told Peabody, 'add the second crime scene, and leave it on display.'

'I hit some new accounts. One wholesaler had fourteen in the last week. The thing is,' Peabody continued as she worked, 'you can't just buy, like, one nail kit or whatever. There's a minimum purchase. But there are also — from Trina's list — some brick-and-mortar locations. You have to be a licensed salon owner or tech, but you can go in person, and there's no minimum.'

'There's where we focus when we ID the brand. Fake the license, go in, get what you need. Mistake, and a stupid one, but it plays in with obsession.'

She turned as Mira walked in.

'Question,' Eve said. 'How deep is his need for precision, perfection?'

'It's one of the drivers of his psychosis.'

'Okay. The second vic bit her nails. He used what we believe are salon-grade fakes, precisely. So precisely, I missed it on scene. To get them, he'd have to forge a license, then create or open an account, either order — what's the minimum, Peabody?'

'At the wholesalers I got to, two grand for an initial order, new account, and fifteen hundred thereafter.'

'He'd have to do that,' Eve continued, 'or go, in person, to one of the brick-and-mortar vendors who don't have a minimum.'

Mira walked closer to the board in a pair of needle heels with open toes and backs that matched her canary yellow suit.

Her nails, Eve noted, sported a summer-sky blue — that matched the hint of lace under the jacket.

'The kit likely runs about a hundred, a hundred and fifty, I'd think.'

'Depending on the brand and the level of the kit, they go from ninety-five to three-fifty wholesale,' Peabody told her.

'So the minimum requirement would be wasteful. It would be difficult for him to tolerate such waste, unless he could make up the minimum with other, useful products.'

'He's already got the other products, but . . . Peabody, can you buy the cheap stuff at these places?'

'Not the really snooty ones, but I'll check on that.'

'Yeah, we'll cover it, but it's going to be in person. He had to move on the nails fairly quickly, and have time to study how to apply them.'

'I'm going to agree with you. She bit her nails,' Mira mused. 'That would have upset him. Terrible habit, he'd think. And ruins the illusion. It may have been something that minor that caused him to kill her.'

'It's a mistake. The illusion, as you put it, that's paramount. The clothes, the shoes — all the mother's sizes. The shoes and the jeans were both snug on Elder, and the shoes and skirt both a little loose on Hobe. So he either knew what size the mother wore, or he's decided on it.'

Mira lifted a finger, ticked it at Eve. 'That's good, the deciding. It may very well be that. He placed the second victim at another venue for children. She broke the illusion — didn't qualify so had to be eliminated.

But he left her, with that illusion — where parents, where, for him, mothers take their children.'

Walking to the AutoChef, Mira programmed her flowery tea. 'He makes her — to his eye — beautiful, then lays her near a playground, a child's center. Because there's love. But he does all of this because there's also hate, and there's rage, and pain. Who can cause us more pain than the people who brought us into the world?'

Mira took her tea, and, turning a chair around, sat facing Eve and the board. 'The child wants love — for her and from her. The man feels the rage and the pain. He can't stop himself from this quest to re-create her, as he wishes her, and the women he takes can never be who he wishes.'

'What are Covino's chances?'

Like Eve, Mira studied Covino's ID shot. 'She may prolong the inevitable. The illusion may hold awhile, but it will shatter. When it does, he'll kill her.'

'He wants to kill her as much as he wants to re-create her. He's punishing the mother every time he chains one of these women up, every time he kills.'

'Yes,' Mira agreed. 'Create and destroy, that's the cycle. The man can look back at who she was — at this age — and judge her. Bad Mommy. Whatever disappointments, failures, difficulties he's experienced in his life all, to his mind, come from that. Something, and something traumatic, happened at this particular time in his life and hers. So now, after something related to her, to that, to them happened and caused this psychic break, he's compelled to go back to that time. Or rather just before. Before the trauma. With this second victim, the pattern's very clear.'

'The map.' Eve gestured so Mira turned in her

chair to study the screen. 'The highlighted locations are the two crime scenes, the victims' — including Covino's — residence and workplace. Dotted lines are their routine routes to and from work — or in Covino's case, the subway.

'Computer, highlight properties from first list of same generated by Roarke, mark those eliminated. You see private homes and other properties that fit the parameters,' she told Mira. 'Owned, rented, and/ or occupied by single males. We're doing door-to-doors, and have eliminated those so marked.'

'A considerable amount of legwork,' Mira commented.

'That's why cops have legs. Computer, highlight properties from the second list generated by Roarke. We expanded,' Eve explained. 'Single occupancy, but owned or occupied — on record — by a female, couples or families, or a group or a company. We're starting more door-to-doors.'

'I absolutely agree this is his hunting ground. He lives or works there, perhaps both.'

'I think —' Eve broke off as Nadine walked in, along with Quilla, her teenage intern.

'Nadine, we're in the middle of a consult.'

'So I was told when I asked in the bullpen.' Nadine shook back her sleek and streaky hair. 'We've got something that's going to add to that.'

Eve knew Nadine well enough to recognize the smug. She had a moment's tug-of-war regarding Quilla, then let it go.

'You got something on the unsub's mother.'

'I got her.' Nadine reached into her ten-gallon bag and pulled out a disc.

'Son of a bitch. Peabody.'

Peabody hustled over to take the disc.

'I expect coffee, and not the bullpen sludge,' Nadine told Eve. 'And my young apprentice prefers Coke.'

'Just wait a damn minute.'

As she spoke, Jamie swaggered — no other word for it — into the conference room. 'Score! Hey, Dr. Mira.'

'Scored what?'

'Got your tattooed mom.' He held up a disc.

'Jesus. Peabody.'

'Got it, got it. I can run simultaneous, split screen. Need a second. Holy shit,' Peabody said.

'Hi, Nadine Furst, right? Really like your books. The vid topped it out,' Jamie gushed.

'Thanks. Quilla, this is Jamie Lingstrom. Captain Feeney's godson.'

'Hey,' Jamie said in response. 'The hair's chill.'

Quilla reached up, skimmed fingers through the oak brown with its candy-pink bangs and crown. 'Thanks, I'm, ah, Nadine's intern.'

'Yeah? Also chill. I'm interning up in EDD.'

'About that coffee.'

'Just wait!' Eve snapped. 'I don't know how to get it from my AC to this one, and Peabody's busy.'

'I can do it. What? You want Dallas's high-test?'

'Yes, please, with a little cream,' Nadine said to Jamie. 'And a Coke for Quilla.'

'Coming up.'

'How did you find her?' Nadine asked him.

'Well . . .'

Dallas gave him points for not blurting it out, but looking to her for guidance.

'Go ahead. She found her, too.'

'Yeah? Good work. Took some doing with the thin

264

data to pull on. Had to go back to 1994.'

'Busted for solicitation at age sixteen, Arcadia, Tennessee. Expunged and sealed after completion of court-mandated counseling and community service.'

When Quilla rolled off the data, Jamie offered her a Coke and a grin.

'She already had the tat,' he continued. 'And this little bumfuck town actually preserved the records from the way back.'

'How'd you get the data?' Eve asked him.

'Had a hunch on it — the when, the where — and when I dug up a photo of her — driver's license — the look of her. So, I did a search, found a judge down there, gave him the what's what. He didn't decide until this morning — wanted to review the file and all that — but he unsealed the records, and bang. They had the tat listed as identifying mark.'

'You?' Eve asked Nadine.

When Quilla started to speak, Nadine put a hand on her arm. 'Something like that,' she said. And fluttered her lashes.

'Say no more. Peabody, for Christ's sake,' Dallas snapped.

'It's coming. The unit's having a moment doing the duet.'

'I'll get it.' Jamie strolled over, tapped a few commands. The split screen — identical — came on-screen.

The mug shot showed a thin-faced blond girl with defiant eyes. The mascara and whatever else she'd piled on those eyes had run, leaving clumpy shadows under them.

The profile shot revealed the multiple ear piercings.

'And there you are, Lisa McKinney. Younger here

265

than our age range, but yeah, fits the type he's grab-bing. Height, weight, coloring. What else do we know?'

Jamie started to speak, then gestured to Nadine. 'You can take it.'

'That's sweet. Actually, as part of the research team on this, Quilla has a report.'

'I can start, and then you can pick it up,' she said to Jamie.

'Good deal.'

'Okay, Lisa Evangeline McKinney, born in Bigsby, Alabama, September 8, 1978, to Buford McKinney and Tiffany Boswell McKinney — both eighteen, which is just whacked. The Tiffany came from Arca-dia, but moved to Bigsby when she was a kid. So they busted up in 1984, *quelle surprise*, right? Anyway, dead now, but both got hooked up again — her twice — and he had two more kids with the second wife.'

She took a second to gulp down some of her Coke.

'Tiffany went back to Arcadia in 1991 — took Lisa — that's where she hooked up with husband number three in '93. That busted in '95, but in the meantime, Lisa has some sketchy attendance in school, did the runaway thing a few times, got busted. She finished high school — barely — and worked a series of jobs, nothing more than a few months. Then in November of 1998 . . .'

She paused, looked at Jamie. 'You can take it.'

'Thanks. That's when she had the kid,' Jamie con-tinued. 'Baby boy. No name, no father listed. Did you get the car wreck?'

'What? No.' Quilla blew annoyance at her pink bangs. 'What'd we miss?'

'She was in a vehicular accident in '99. She wasn't driving, but the driver — a Marshall Riggs — was

266

charged with DWI. She ended up with a concussion, a dislocated shoulder, a busted wrist, and a couple of cracked ribs. She lived — maternal grandmother's address — in Arcadia until 2000, then it looks like she took to the road. What employment I found — again sketchy — bar work, cocktail waitress, did some stripping. No address or employment I could find from early 2002 on. But she had a car registered in her name — had to be a beater.'

'Anything on her or the kid from Child Services?' Eve asked. 'Social Services?'

'Nothing I found. And there's nothing, Dallas, like poof, after 2002. I got this picture — ad for a strip club, Nashville, 2002. Computer, display doc McKinney 3-A.'

Working. Displayed.

She had her head thrown back and her arm around a pole. She wore a G-string, pasties, and looked worn around the edges to Eve.

'Magnify her face.'

When Jamie had, Eve studied it. 'Yeah, a resemblance, a type, more pronounced with the shorter hair. She's on something. I can see user on her. She's what — damn math.'

'Like twenty-four,' Quilla said.

'Yeah, like that, has a kid about three or four, and she's riding a pole, living off the grid to stay ahead of Child Services, doesn't stay in one place long. She tried selling herself at sixteen, so there's probably that. But she either took the kid with her when she hit the road, or paid him regular visits.'

Mira nodded. 'While he could have become

obsessed due to the absent mother, and formed the illusion, there are too many details to his re-creation attempts. The trauma occurred sometime after she left Arcadia. They had a relationship. And I would say, in her way, she loved her son. Easier, by far, to have walked away, left him with the grandmother.'

'Let's be sure she didn't.'

Nadine set aside her coffee mug. 'According to Lisa's half brother — who still resides in Bigsby, she didn't. I contacted him first thing this morning. He remembers Lisa's mother calling his father when Lisa left and took the child. He doesn't remember the name of the child — the son of the half sister he didn't really know wasn't part of his life. But he remembers hearing his parents arguing about it, as his mother was very upset about the situation.'

'You've got more. What else does he know?'

'His mother didn't like the fact that his father had, essentially, cut ties with his daughter. And his father didn't like the fact that his mother kept pushing him to try to reach her — Lisa, and his grandson. His father claimed Lisa was a junkie whore, and he was done with her. He remembers that clearly, as his father didn't use that kind of language. So I'd say you're right, and she was on something in Jamie's photo.

'I also have his sister's contact information, but haven't contacted her as yet because she lives in Oregon, and it's too early.'

'Is the info on the disc?'

'It is.'

'We'll take it. This is good work, all around.'

'And my one-on-one?'

'We're trying to save a life here. That life.' She pointed to the board and Covino. 'If we go public with

268

this before we find her, he'll kill her. You'll get it, and if I were you, when this is wrapped, I'd do a segment on how a couple of young interns helped break a case, save a life, and find a killer.'

Nadine smiled. 'Already on my agenda. You'll have an on-air conversation with Quilla, won't you, Jamie, about how the two of you assisted in finding information that led to an arrest?'

'I — yeah, I guess.' He managed to look surprised, delighted, and embarrassed all at once. 'Yeah. Could be frosty. I'd want a go on it from the captain.'

'I could interview him,' Quilla suggested. 'I think, maybe, as a journalist, I shouldn't be part of the story, and discussing the research on our end comes too close to revealing a source. Sort of.'

'Listen to you, telling me exactly what I'd hoped to hear. What's like a fish without gills, Quilla?'

'A journalist without integrity. They both sink to the bottom of the tank — but the journalist had a choice.'

Nadine draped an arm around Quilla's shoulders. 'That's my girl. Let's go be journalists. One-on-one,' she said to Eve, and, 'Intern interview,' to Jamie. 'Catch that bastard,' she said to the room at large, then started out with Quilla.

Quilla threw a look at Jamie over her shoulder. 'Nice meeting you and all that.'

'You, too. I gotta get back. So you'll keep me in the loop, right?'

'You're in it. You did damn good work, Jamie. Now beat it.'

'Beating it.' He swaggered out.

'Quilla gave him the flirt eye,' Peabody commented, and Mira laughed.

'Yeah, I saw it. She's just a kid.'

'She's a bright, healthy teenage girl,' Mira corrected. 'If I were a bright, healthy teenage girl, I'd give him the flirt eye. He's adorable. However.'

She rose to stand with Eve at the board. 'A sad life. Lisa McKinney, that's a sad life. Her parents married, according to the data, six months before her birth. Some that young and in those circumstances make it, build a solid life. Most won't. The mother moves out of state with the child, with no recorded custody battle there. They'd have found it if there'd been one.'

'Yes, they'd have found it.'

'He had another wife, other children. For whatever reason he closed the door on his oldest daughter. She makes bad choices, a pattern of them. Her addiction? Possibly, even probably, began or escalated after the car accident. Painkillers, from that era oxycodone would be my first guess.'

She glanced at Eve. 'You could compare it with street Bliss. In any case, Lisa's mother went from man to man, and — as she lived with the grand-mother — that relationship wasn't strong, unlikely healthy. History of truancy, of running away, then pregnancy. An unhappy young woman.'

'But she didn't terminate the pregnancy.'

'Someone — her own — who'd love her.'

Eve looked over at Peabody.

'Keep going.'

'Just from everything we've got now, it seems like she might have wanted the child because it would be hers. The kid would love her. Her father didn't — or not enough. Her mother, there's something there, too. A kid may run away once in a snit, but she was a repeater. And she's busted for prostitution in her own

270

small town.'

'Wanted to get busted,' Eve concluded.

'A cry for help. It may have been,' Mira agreed, 'and one she didn't feel — right or wrong — was answered. I think she and the child loved each other, in their own ways. But she was a troubled woman, an addict, estranged, it seems, from her own family. Just the two of them.

'The trauma happened sometime after 2002, sometime when he was still dependent and attached. Just the two of them,' Mira repeated.

'If she OD'd, there'd be a death record. She could've ended up dead and dumped, and her body not found or ID'd, that's possible. Or, addicted, she chose her drug of choice over the kid, dumped him.'

'If any of those, there should be a record of him — his name — taken into the system. Not by a relative from what we know.'

'I'm going to confirm that. Maybe he was too young to know her name. She's just Mommy, or the trauma wiped it out for him. But we've got enough here to dig. We know his age — he'll be sixty-three this November. Let's see if Yancy can do another projection, since we have the mother's face now.

'I'm going to contact the half sister in Portland, see if she can add anything. Peabody, contact Norman to catch him up, start working the brick-and-mortars for the nail thing — and give Dawber a push on the details.'

Eve turned to Mira. 'Thanks. Between this, and you, I've got a clearer picture.'

'As do I. I think we'll find there's a history of mental illness here, and that it likely went untreated. Something triggered a violent aspect of his.'

'He'll get treatment when I stop him.'

And she would, Eve thought. Before he claimed another victim.

She went straight to her office, tagged Yancy.

'I'm sending you a mug shot — age sixteen — of the suspect's mother. Can you age it? Say, ages thirty-five, fifty-five, eighty-five.'

'I can start that, sure.'

'Send me what you have when you have it — don't wait for all of them. I'll start running them.'

'No hits on the others?'

'No, but you'll see there's distinct differences. They're a type, you might think cousins at best.'

'Send it on. I've got some clear time this morning.'

'Thanks. I owe you.'

She sent the file, then pulled up the information on Lisa McKinney's half sister.

Irene Jasper, age seventy-four, married to Phillip Jasper, two offspring. Freelance photographer.

Irene answered on the second ring, a sharp-featured woman with a disordered crown of maroon hair. 'Police,' she said in a raspy voice with a lot of drawl. 'New York. This must be about Lisa and her boy.'

'Yes, ma'am.'

'My brother just filled me in. Good thing I'm an early riser, but I don't know how I can help you. I met Lisa exactly once, when my mother insisted we drive up to Tennessee so Harry and I — he'd have been three, I guess — could meet our half sister. I don't remember much of it other than a lot of shouting, and hearing words I was, at that time, unfamiliar with.'

She smiled a little. 'I do remember we stayed in a motel that had a swimming pool — the height of luxury for me. And that my mother cried that night

272

when she thought Harry and I were asleep. He was, I wasn't.'

'You never had contact with her again?'

'I didn't, no. My mother pushed for it off and on later, when Lisa had the child, but my father was adamant. And, to be honest, I was fine with that.'

'Do you know her son's name?'

'I don't. If I ever did, it's long gone. My father died ten years ago, and Mama left us this past winter. They might have known, I suppose they did, but there's no asking them now. I can tell you, it's clear — from what I heard growing up, and the usual gossip in a small town where I grew up — that my father's first wife was a wild one. Trouble in school, liked the fast times, the fast boys, and drank and used as much as she could get when she could get it. About the opposite of my own. Mama was a rule follower, as softhearted as they came. My daddy's estrangement from his oldest child troubled that soft heart.'

'Did Lisa ever try to exploit that?'

Irene pursed her lips. 'Now, that's a thought, and I'll admit it would have been easy enough. I don't think so. Mama would've told me. Maybe not when I was a young thing, but later on. Now, I do know Lisa's grandma divorced her grandpa before Lisa was born. He liked his drink, and chasing the ladies, wedding ring or not. He even did some time for beating some guy — and this is after, the story goes, he gave his wife a taste of it more than once.'

Irene lifted a bright red mug of something, chugged as she angled her head and thought back.

'I heard tales of Big Beau Boswell plenty, as when they locked him up a second time — for putting his hands on a woman who objected — he got himself beat to death in prison.

'Lisa would've been a baby, I expect, when her grandma married again and she moved back up to Tennessee. So when my daddy divorced Lisa's mama — and she married and divorced right quick after — she moved on up there, too. Shook small-town Bigsby off her high-heeled shoes. Married again, I'm told, and that didn't take. Don't suppose it's a wonder Lisa was a wild one.'

Irene paused. 'I expect you're thinking her boy's more than wild.'

The boy, Eve thought, had over six decades under his belt. 'He's a suspect in two murders and at least three abductions.'

'I'm sorry to hear that. I'm sorry to know that somebody who came from my daddy would turn out so wrong. My daddy was a good man, a good father. Funny and hardworking. Could be stern, but could be sweet, too. I know that first marriage had some ugly moments, things he never spoke of — but small towns have big ears and bigger mouths. And I'll tell you, word was maybe the baby was his, maybe not. She was wild, Lisa's mama, and enjoyed the back seat of many a car, so the stories say. But Daddy married her, and was a father to that girl until they took off.

'I believe Daddy's first wife died some thirty years back or more. Pills and liquor, word was.'

'Do you know if there were any photographs of Lisa and her son?'

'I never saw any. The fact is, I couldn't tell you what she looked like, even from meeting her that one time. I remember that swimming pool, and my mama crying that night, but I can't get myself a picture of that girl's face.'

'Any other family you know of? Aunts, uncles, cousins?'

'I don't know of any other family, so I don't know what would have become of photos or anything else. The last I knew, Lisa took off with the boy. He couldn't have been but three or four, I guess. It's been a long time. She was ten years older than me, Lieutenant Dallas, and if her name came up, a cloud fell over our house.'

Now she sighed. 'I'm gonna confess. When my daddy got sick, and we knew he didn't have long, Mama wanted to try to find her. She even talked about hiring a private eye and all that. I took Daddy's side — or what I knew would be his side if he knew what she was thinking. I told her no, and I told her flat, and I said some hard things. And she let it go. Maybe I should be sorry for that, but I'm not.'

'I don't think I would be, either. If you think of anything else, any detail at all, please contact me.'

'I surely will. Sorry I don't know more. I hope you find him, Lisa's boy, before he hurts anyone else.'

'Thank you.'

Eve wrote up the gist of the call.

Then looked up the data on the cast of characters Irene had given her.

Maternal great-grandfather — a drunk, a womanizer. Wife-beater, con, dies in prison — second stretch.

Maternal grandmother, slept around, liked to drink and use illegals — busts for destruction of property, underage drinking, possession, disturbing the peace, disorderly conduct. Dead at sixty-one, overdose of barbiturates mixed in vodka.

Mother, busted for solicitation as a juvenile, had a male child at the age of twenty — no father listed — possibly addicted to painkillers, uneven employment and place-of-residence history. No records after 2002.

Could've worked off the books, Eve thought. Worked the streets. Could've drifted from place to place.

Dumped the kid maybe. But not through channels, or there'd be a record. Sold him, dumped him, died on him.

But she hadn't dumped him with the grandmother when she'd taken off, so why dump him later? Why not take him back?

She studied her notes again. Harsh DNA in there. Dark and harsh blood running through.

Violence and addiction and self-destruction.

But murder was a choice. It was always a choice. And he'd chosen.

17

After she checked in with Jenkinson — no hits in the field — Eve started to call in Peabody to brief her. Then she heard the cowgirl boots on their way.

'I haven't hit with the nail kit yet,' Peabody told her. 'But I talked to Dawber at the lab. Short delay, comp glitch, but he's back on it. He should have the sample analyzed and ID'd within thirty.'

'I've got Yancy working on the age projection sketches, and I spoke with McKinney's half sister. There's history on McKinney's maternal side of alcohol and drug abuse, violence, and indications that could weigh in on Mira's supposition re mental illness. I'm sending you and Mira a copy of my notes. But here's the thing.'

Eve sat back, gestured to the AC so Peabody could get them both coffee.

'The half sister lives in Oregon, but my search shows she's the only family member to relocate north of Tennessee. How and why did McKinney's son end up in New York? Did she bring him — break that generational geographical habit?'

'Possible,' Peabody speculated. 'She comes off as a drifter — no real employment skills or ambitions, no close family ties. Could be an: I'm done with this place. I need action, bright lights.'

'Possible,' Eve agreed. 'But it takes guts to make that dramatic a change. Small to smallish southern towns to big-ass big city in the North. And funds. Costs more to live in New York, especially with a kid in tow. Even unhappy people cling to the familiar.'

Rising, Eve paced with her coffee. 'There's nothing to indicate she set her sights on New York, or the North. She took off, more than once as a teenager, but she didn't get on a bus or stick out her thumb and head to a big city, or travel outside that — in general — familiar area. Every time she was picked up within a fifty-mile radius of home.'

'But he's here.'

'Yeah, he is. She dumped him or died, that's how it looks for me. Dumped him when she just couldn't hack it anymore, or OD'd, met a bad end, or self-terminated.'

Eve paused by the board, looked into the young Lisa McKinney's eyes. Pissed and defiant.

'She could've sold him — and that would suck for us, as we'd never find him in the system, and it's already a crapshoot finding a John Doe minor, between age four and six — and we'd need to add a year on both sides to cover any discrepancies or miscalculations, in the Southeast.'

'If she abandoned him or died, he'd have told the cops, the social workers, his name.'

'Not if he didn't know it. First name, highly probable — she called him something even if it was *asshole*. But last? I was older, and didn't know mine. It wasn't just the trauma,' she added. 'They didn't give me a first name, and I didn't know from last names. So say you've got this kid, most likely under the age of seven. Ends up on the proverbial doorstep, or scooped up by somebody when the mother dies or doesn't come back.'

Eve sat again. 'That's how we look. I've got a search running now in eight states from 2002 to 2006 for a

Minor Doe, male in the age range, taken into the system. We didn't hit before, in the broader search, but maybe we have better luck narrowing it.'

'It's a shot,' Peabody agreed. 'The records from back then are so damn unreliable. But with a narrower focus, it's a shot.'

They both turned to Eve's comp when it signaled an incoming.

'Dawber beat the thirty?'

'No, it's Yancy. We've got his first image. Lisa McKinney, age thirty-five.'

'Damn, that's good!' Peabody leaned closer. 'You can see how he aged her, even changed the hairstyle some to go with, I'm guessing, what was in.'

'It is good.' Eve studied the face, the subtle signs of a decade of time around the eyes, the mouth. 'The unsub couldn't replicate like this. We were never going to get a hit using the victims. They're not the real deal, just the best he can do.

'Computer, begin face recognition program on displayed image, searching for matches from the years 2012 to 2022.'

Command acknowledged. Searching . . . .

'Keep it narrow,' Eve muttered. 'We'll keep each image he comes up with to a ten-year span. Something's going to hit. Unless she's been dead all along.'

'Why don't I start a secondary search? Use the same image, skip to 2023, do, say five more years.'

'Yeah, go ahead and try that. And if Dawber doesn't come through inside the thirty, push him again.'

When Peabody left, Eve rose again to go to the window with what was left of her coffee.

He was out there, she thought. On the street, in an office, in a house, a market, a meeting. Maybe drinking coffee as she was now, but he was out there.

And they were closing in. She could feel it. She could feel the pieces fitting together. The mother had always been the key.

Now they had her name, her face, her hometown.

'Lisa McKinney, where did you go? What did you do?'

She thought of herself, a child, wandering the streets of Dallas, bloodied, broken, too traumatized to remember the last rape, the last beating, or anything that came before it.

'But it hadn't been like that for you,' she murmured. 'No, not like that. You wouldn't want her back if it had been like that. She didn't beat you, or you'd have beaten the replacements. She fed you, clothed you — and you do the same for her, your projection of her.'

She dumped him, sold him, or died, Eve thought again. And all of those equal, to his mind, leaving him. Abandoning him. Bad Mommy to leave your little boy.

Eve glanced back at her working comp. And if she'd died during his early childhood, the search for Lisa McKinney would lead nowhere.

No death record meant no body found or the body went unidentified. But she'd had a car and a license in 2002, so . . . .

Still plenty of ways for a person to die, go undiscovered, or remain a Jane Doe.

When her comp signaled another incoming, she pounced on it.

'Okay, Dawber, I don't have to head over there

280

and kick your ass into gear.' She bypassed the — to her — unintelligible science stuff, and went straight to the meat.

'Nail It by Adora, salon grade, professional use only. Color On a Moonlit Sea — who comes up with this shit? Acrylic Monomer (liquid), Crystal Acrylic Powder, Ultra Nail Prep and Ultra Bond, Adora Total Max Nail Glue. Blah blah blah,' Eve finished.

Peabody came hustling back.

'He copied me,' Eve said.

'I plugged it into the search. That's one of the top brands, and a deluxe kit. Goes for over four hundred wholesale.'

'And all that for freaking fingernails? Who wants all that stuff gunked on their fingernails?'

'It'd cost you double to get the service in a salon. He had to buy the color separately, because the kit doesn't include.'

'For four hundred, you don't get the stupid polish?'

'And you have to use the Adora product made for the kit. I checked with Trina on that when I was setting up the first search. So I've plugged in the kit and the color. Even if he paid cash — and probably — they're going to have a record. This is going to pay off.'

'All because she bit her nails. Let's pull out some of the vendors, do this face-to-face.'

'I'll set it up to alert me on any hits,' Peabody began, and Eve's comp signaled again.

Initial match on search, ninety-eight-point-two probability.

'Display on main screen,' Eve snapped. 'Fucking A! That's her. Changed her name, but that's her. Violet

281

Blank Fletcher, in the damn system, driver's license, passport, even a social security. Age listed as thirty-four in 2014. Married Joseph Fletcher, MD — three offspring, two sons, a daughter. But wrong ages there for our guy. Too young, born after she poofed. Poofed to Sylvan, Louisiana. Computer, display map of Louisiana, highlight Sylvan.'

'Oh, oh, look! It's not far from New Orleans! Are we going to New Orleans?'

'Throttle back, Peabody. Computer, full data on Violet Blank Fletcher on-screen.'

Acknowledged.

'Married the doctor in May of 2004. Doesn't list her place of birth, her parents, any employment — or any offspring before the three with the doctor.'

'Because Violet Blank Fletcher didn't have any,' Peabody concluded.

'She sure as hell didn't. And it also lists her date of death, last September. Accidental overdose of sleeping pills. I'm taking a wild guess here that it wasn't, given her history, her family history, an accident. And somehow her death was his trigger.'

'He's not listed, no child from before her marriage is listed.'

Eyes narrowed, the hunt bubbling in her blood, Eve nodded. 'Bet that's a pisser. Marries a doctor, has another family, and he's not part of that. We'll find out why and how. She gave him up, changed her name.'

'You were right about the geography, too. She stayed in the South.'

'Look at the other data here, Peabody. Not just a doctor — he ended up a big-shot ER doc, and there's

282

family money. Gooey piles of old money. She died rich, seriously rich. He predeceased her, the husband, just six months before.'

She ordered a split screen with Joseph Fletcher's data.

'Okay, a lot of family money,' Peabody noted. 'And he's taken out by a drunk driver.'

'Tell Yancy we've got her, and I'll fill him in later.' Eve called up the data on Violet Fletcher's children.

'Look here,' she said as Peabody contacted Yancy. 'Daughter's chief of surgery, same hospital where Daddy headed up the ER. Older son's a writer — looks successful.'

'Chasen Q. Fletcher? Very. I've read his books. They're really good.'

'Younger son went into law and is now the senator from Louisiana. All three are married — once each — have children, and continue to live in the same area of the state — with the writer and his family residing in the house where they grew up.'

She studied the ID shots.

'Peabody, we need to have some conversations.'

'I'll say. I guess we're not going to actually have them in New Orleans.'

'No. Keep the search for the nail crap going, and we'll hit the field after the conversations, but let's find out what the unsub's half sibs know. Start with the writer. I'll start with the daughter. The politician's bound to be more slippery with anything he knows about his mother's former life. But we'll get to him.'

'It's moving now,' Peabody said as she hurried out. 'It's really moving.'

Damn straight, Eve thought, and contacted Dr. Joella Fletcher's office.

She got the runaround, as she expected, but wouldn't relent.

'Dr. Fletcher may be saving lives there,' Eve said to the third person she'd been passed to, 'but I'm trying to save one here. Ask the doctor if she wants to be responsible for the murder of Mary Kate Covino, age twenty-five, because she's too damn busy to come on the 'link.'

The woman on-screen smiled and, in sugary sweet Southern tones, said, 'There's no need for rudeness, ma'am.'

'Tell that to Mary Kate — and it's Lieutenant, not ma'am. She talks to me now, or I get on a shuttle, come to her. And I'll charge her with obstruction of justice.'

The smile vanished. 'Please hold.'

The screen went to blue and drippy holding music. But this time the doctor herself came on.

'What in the world is this about? I had to leave a vital meeting of —'

'I don't care. I'm investigating two murders, three abductions.'

The woman who looked to be wearing a sharp red suit stared back at Eve with Lisa McKinney's eyes. 'You do realize I'm not in New York City?'

'Your half brother is, and he's my prime suspect.'

Joella Fletcher brushed at her perfectly groomed auburn hair around a narrow face — like her mother's — and cast her eyes skyward. 'I don't have a half brother. I have two brothers, and neither of them are in New York. Now, Lieutenant —'

'Your mother was Violet Fletcher?'

'Yes.'

'Before she became Violet Fletcher or Violet Blank,

284

she was Lisa McKinney, born in Bigsby, Alabama, in 1978, and gave birth to a male child in 1998.'

'That's ridiculous.'

'It's fact.'

'Lieutenant, my mother, Violet Blank Fletcher, was born in Tennessee. Her parents were drifters who moved around, taking work in housekeeping, lawn maintenance. Handyman stuff. They were killed during Hurricane Opal.'

'Her parents were Buford and Tiffany McKinney. Violet Blank didn't exist before 2004. What did she say her parents' names were?'

Eve actually heard Joella's nails drumming impatiently on her desk. 'She didn't, that I recall.'

'Where did she go to school?'

'I don't know. I don't know if she went regularly because her parents moved around so much. She didn't like to talk about it. She often said her life really began when she met my father.'

'I bet. And how did they meet?'

'He hired her to help with the house, the gardens. It's an old family plantation house that came to him from his grandparents. They fell in love, married, raised a family there. A happy family that has nothing to do with murders in New York.'

'Your mother died last fall of an overdose.'

'Accidental,' Joella snapped. 'She was grieving for her husband, my father. His death was so sudden, so hard. It's still hard. She couldn't sleep, and she became disoriented and took too many pills.'

'Doctor, I believe up to now you've told me the truth as you know it. It's not the truth, but it's what you were told, and why would you question it? But you just lied to me, and that tells me your mother

285

took her own life.'

'I have nothing more to say to you.'

'I believe she contacted this individual, her first child, perhaps to try to make amends in some way. And that contact triggered a psychic break. I have the top profiler and psychiatrist in New York City, if not the damn East Coast, who will confirm this. He's killed two women with strong resemblances to your mother at the same age.

'You're a scientist. There were a lot of blanks in her past — before your father. Including the name she chose. Blank. You never questioned that?'

'She had an unhappy childhood, and wanted to put it behind her.'

'She did have an unhappy childhood, just not the one she created for you. And from what I've learned today, she created a new life, and a good one, was a good mother, a good wife. She loved you. She left a note for you before she took those pills.'

'It was an accident.'

'Dr. Fletcher, by trying to save your mother's memory, to spare the shadow of suicide, you're blocking any detail that might help me find and stop this man. Look at this.'

She turned to bring up Elder's crime scene photo. 'Her name was Lauren Elder. She had a man who loved her, a family who loved her. This is what he did to her because she bore a resemblance to your mother.'

'My — my mother never looked like that. She never.'

'She had a tattoo of a butterfly on her back, wings spread. Lower back.'

'She had it done when she was a teenager. I don't

see what —'

'Wait.' She shifted to the photo of Elder's back. 'This is the tattoo he put on Lauren Elder, and on Anna Hobe, his second victim. It's the same, isn't it?'

She watched some of the color drain out of Joella's face. 'A lot of women get butterfly tattoos.'

'It's exactly the same, isn't it?'

'Yes. Yes. I don't understand it.'

'This is Mary Kate Covino. She's alive, being held, but alive. He's probably put that tattoo on her by now. You're a doctor. Help me save her life.'

'I don't know what I can do.'

'She left you a note. Was there anything in the note, anything she said to you that, knowing what I'm telling you now about having another child, applies?'

'I can't help you.'

'If you refuse to, I promise you I'll have your mother's death investigated. You could lose your license over this, and you know it. Your brother the senator will have a major scandal on his hands. Help me, and we let her rest in peace.'

'You'd threaten to —'

Fuck this, Eve thought. 'Mary Alice Covino's been held, shackled like an animal, for almost a week. The time's coming up fast when he'll slit her throat. I need the truth from you, so I'm telling you that what I'll do if you continue to lie isn't a threat. It's reality. She left you a note.'

Joella pressed her lips together. 'She left a note for each of us. For myself and each of my brothers. We decided not to tell the authorities about the notes, and to push the accidental overdose.'

'I don't care about that, and there's no reason I can see why that has to be in the record. I care about what she might have told or written you.'

'She had blanks, that was clear, but I thought — we all thought — it was because her childhood was difficult. I thought most likely abusive. She overcame it.'

'I believe she did.'

'She was joyful, active, giving. She did occasionally have trouble sleeping. When my father died, so much of the joy went out of her. She had insomnia — chronic — headaches, listlessness. Then she seemed to get better, a little better. She went to our house in Hilton Head for a week. She said she wanted to walk the beach, and have some alone time.'

'She went alone?'

'Yes, she insisted. But we talked every day, it was only a few days, and she'd seemed better. We had a big family dinner a few weeks after she got back. She seemed better, steadier. Happier.'

Joella paused to gather herself. 'I believed, we all did, she'd found her peace. My husband and I stayed the night, and I found her in the morning. Found her and the notes. She said, in my note, she was sorry. She knew this would cause me grief, but she was with Daddy now. She couldn't go on without him, and she couldn't face the before him. She'd done the best she could for all her children. She loved all her children, and asked forgiveness. She asked for understanding. She said her life began on the night my father saved her, and to believe she was at peace now, with him.'

'She said specifically 'all her children,' not, for instance she'd done her best and loved you and your brothers?'

'Yes, she wrote 'all her children.' God. Dear God.'

'And she wrote about the night your father saved her.'

'Yes, I thought she was confused. As he'd hired her to garden and house clean, and . . . '

'I understand this is difficult, but it's very helpful. If your father had come across someone in distress, in pain, or who needed help of some kind, what would he have done?'

'Helped.' Those eyes, so like her mother's, gleamed behind a sheen of tears. 'Done whatever he could to help. He wasn't just a doctor. He was a healer. He devoted his life to helping and healing. Lieutenant, if my mother had a child before us, my father would have accepted that child, raised that child as his own. He would never have turned his back.'

'It's possible he didn't know.'

'No — I don't see how. You have to understand how close they were. No secrets. They were united. And my mother? Children were her greatest joy. It's impossible to believe she would have cut herself off from a child. There has to be a mistake, another explanation.'

'If there is, I'll find it. I'm going to ask you for two more things. First, my partner should be talking to your younger brother now. If it would help smooth the way, I'd like you to contact your youngest brother, and convince him to speak honestly with me. And second, if you would send me a copy of the letter your mother left for you. I won't log it into the file. You have my word.'

'I need to know the answers. I need the truth.'

'When I have the answers, you'll get them.'

Eve wrote up the conversation, copied Mira. Then she pushed up from the desk, started to head to the bullpen. And waited when she heard Peabody coming her way.

'You talked to the writer.'

'He was really forthcoming. Still a lot of grief there — losing both parents within a year — and that may have helped open him up. He didn't know anything about his mother having another kid, changing her name, any of it. I believe him.'

'Same with the sister, and agreed. Did he admit to the suicide, tell you about the notes she left?'

'He did, and he's sending a copy of his. Dallas, when he talked about his mother, there just wasn't any Lisa McKinney in there. No trauma, no addictions, no wild side. Rock-solid family, happy.'

'I got that.' Eve started to continue, then stopped. 'What's your take?'

'They didn't know. She was Violet Fletcher. She was Mama. From everything he said, it feels like she would have told her husband, but from everything he said, it jars they didn't keep her son, or get him back if she'd lost him or dumped him. So that bugs me, but it's pretty damn clear she remade herself, had a strong marriage, a loving family, a good home, did good works.'

Eve waited a beat. 'And?'

'Okay, well, listening to Chasen Fletcher, and what he told me about the letter she left, it's like her world, her life, started with Joe, and then ended when he died. Going on sixty years is a long time to maintain an illusion, but if that's how it really was for her, maybe his death broke the spell. What if, during that six months between Joe's death and her suicide, she contacted the unsub, her first child? Lisa McKinney's son.'

'And,' Eve continued, 'he learns the mother who abandoned him, one way or the other, had almost six decades of happy — add rich on top — and three other kids. Kids she tucked in at night, but not him. Kids she helped with schoolwork, but not him. Kids who had her love and attention, who blew out birthday candles and opened Christmas presents in a big house with flowers in the yard. It would just burn your ass, wouldn't it?'

'He dresses her the way she was when she was his.'

'And kills her. His mommy's the Bad Mommy. Chains her up — can't walk away this time. He wants what she gave to others all those years.'

'You'd think he'd go after the siblings, want to kill them.'

Eve shook her head. 'Give him time. But he came first. She's his. She's what matters most. Love and rage, warring. Send your notes to Mira, you can write it up when we get back.'

'Nails?'

'Nails,' Eve confirmed. 'You drive.'

After Peabody picked her jaw up off the floor, she hustled after Eve. 'You want me to drive?'

'I'm going to go through all this with the third sibling, and it might take some doing to push on a United States senator. So you drive.'

She ignored the elevators completely for the glides. 'We'll start in Brooklyn. If I were a crazy, mommy-obsessed killer who wanted to cover my tracks when I bought a fancy fake nail kit, I'd go over the bridge to do it.'

'I'm driving to Brooklyn!' Because Eve was slightly in front of her, Peabody risked a butt wiggle.

'I saw that.'

'You couldn't have seen that. Only moms have the metaphorical eyes in the back of their heads.'

'Moms are just cops with kids.'

Peabody started to object, but rethought it. 'Huh. They sort of are. I wonder what it was like for Lisa-slash-Violet. Did she ever think about her other life? Did she keep tabs on the child she had in that other life? Could she really just erase all that?'

'Why not? You can take the cynical route. She's broke, pissed off, dragging a kid around, giving BJs, and working the pole. Decides it's time to look out for number one, dumps the kid, and that makes things easier, but she needs to find a way out of the life. And here's this young, good-looking, rich doctor. Find a way to get into his life, clean his house, pull some weeds, whatever. Make yourself over some, whatever it takes to get him in the sack. Maybe use the old damsel in distress thing. He's a doctor, a healer according to his daughter. Work it so he wants to heal you.'

'It didn't sound like that,' Peabody said when they switched the glides for the stairs to their garage level. 'It sounded romantic, and sweet.'

'Maybe. Maybe it started out cynical and turned real. If it had been a game, if he'd just been a mark, she'd have gotten all the money she could out of him and booked it. But she didn't.'

Eve got in the passenger seat while Peabody wiggled her butt in the driver's seat.

'She'd been a drifter, working the low life. You don't raise three kids to successful adulthood, stay with the same man for decades unless you want to or you're forced to. And there's nothing to indicate force here. She wanted that life, that man, those children, and she made it all hers. You can't fake love, not for half a century.'

'He knows that,' Eve added. 'Number one son

292

knows that, knows she gave that love to others and not to him.'

As Eve pulled out her 'link, Peabody finished programming their route and stops. 'How about a nice cold drink!'

So saying, Peabody programmed for two tubes. Diet and regular.

'Road trip!'

Eve just cast her eyes to the roof of the car. 'She's not even out of the garage, and I already regret this.'

18

Eve concluded the senator's older sister had greased the wheels, as it only took plowing through three staffers to reach him.

While he proved more evasive, less conclusive in certain areas, the winding conversation confirmed everything his siblings had stated. He spoke of a halcyon childhood, noisy family dinners, catching his parents kissing in the kitchen, of his mother squealing, then laughing as their old hound Cecil managed to drag a whole baked ham off the kitchen counter.

'Our house was always open to friends and family. It was the center,' he added. 'She was the center of that. She was always there. My father's work sometimes prevented him from being there, but we knew if we couldn't go to him, we could go to her.'

He took a breath. 'They were beautiful together. Their devotion and respect for each other never wavered. Did they disagree at times, even argue? Of course, but never with rancor. He was her hero. She said that to me more than once.

'Whenever I felt my daddy was being too hard, too strict, expected too much — and during my teenage years, there were plenty of times I felt that — she'd tell me he expected much because he loved much. He was what I should aspire to be. A good man, a compassionate one, who never failed to reach out a hand to help another. She'd say he was the foundation for what we'd all become, just as he'd been hers.'

'The foundation for what she became?'

'As you know, my mother had a troubled child-hood. It wasn't something we talked about, not often. It seemed so distant. I've always felt she credited my father for helping her put that behind her.'

As Eve wound the conversation up, Peabody — who in Eve's opinion drove like an old lady past due for her biannual vision adjustment — pulled up at the first stop.

By the third stop, Eve had time to write up the conversation, and start to play with another theory.

She had time to roll it around, touch base with Reineke — still no hits — and study the incoming lab reports on the drive back, with two more stops along the way.

'Maybe he ordered the kit online,' Peabody said as she chugged behind a line of traffic. 'Do you want to keep going? We've got more in Manhattan, one in the Bronx, more in Queens, and —'

'The way you drive, we'd get to the Bronx by Tuesday.'

'So that's a no.'

'Head back to the house. We're coming up on end of shift, and most of the vendors are hitting end of business day. We'll try a few more by 'link.'

Internally, she imagined whipping around the all-terrain in front of them, then skimming by the mini, snaking through the Rapid Cab and sedan.

'Have you noticed I haven't brought up the work on the house all day?' Peabody asked. 'Not once.'

'Which causes me to assume you intend to do so now.'

'Just for a minute. The drywall's going up so fast, it's like magic, and our kitchen cabinets are coming in by the end of the week. My beautiful bright red cabinets.'

'Red? I thought you went with — you said soft blue. Or green. Soft something.'

'You paid attention! I wanted to see if you paid attention, and you did! My sweet soft blue cabinets are on their way. Mavis's are going to take a few more days, so they're starting to install some of her studio equipment.'

As if she only had that single minute, Peabody spoke a lot faster than she drove.

'Roarke said she could even try it out next week, just test it in case she decides she wants to change anything. And since Leonardo wants to keep the exposed beams in his big attic studio, they're going to start installing there. And McNab and I are abso-poso going to nail down our decision on the powder room and guest bathroom tile tonight.

'We pinky swore.'

'Well then. Roarke said you ordered a crap-ton of rocks.'

'Oh, the stone, for the waterfall feature.'

'He said it was a solid design.'

'He did?' Peabody's face lit up like a candle, and she still failed to pass the AT. 'He told me it was, but I thought he could've just been being nice, you know? But if he told you, he must mean it. I want it to be just mag. Mavis, I know she wants, like, a fairyland, the flowers and veg, the trees, all of it. I really want to help give it to her. She and Leonardo are doing so much for us. We're going to have a house and a yard, gardens, space, stuff it would've taken years if ever for us to manage, and —'

'Stop. Yeah, they're doing a lot for you. You're doing a lot for them. You're giving them security, and that means it's all right there. You're giving them companionship, which for some reason all of you need on a constant basis. Mavis never planted anything in her life before you, now she's all about it. They're about to have their second kid, and what have they got, readily installed? A couple of people they trust absolutely who won't mind if Bella goes running around their space looking for a cookie.'

'I'm always going to have cookies. Thanks.' Peabody had to blink back the sheen in her eyes. 'I get a little — a lot — overwhelmed sometimes with all this. Buzzed and overwhelmed and teary and everything at once. Like when I fell for McNab. It's all: Is this really happening? I can really have this?'

'Looks like you can, and you're stuck with McNab's skinny ass.'

'Last night in bed —'

'Oh no. No.' Grim, Eve flipped back her jacket, laid a hand on her weapon harness. 'I will draw my weapon, place it between your eyes, and fire. At the rate you're driving, no one's going to notice when we come to a dead stop.'

'Not that part — this was after that part. He said how he felt he'd rubbed a lamp and the genie gave him three wishes. The first was the job, because he got that before me. So I was the second wish, and the best. And the third was happening now, with the house, with the home we were making for each other.'

She sighed, hugely. 'Saying stuff like that's why I love his skinny ass.'

Finally, finally, Peabody pulled into the garage. She parked meticulously, turned to Eve, and smiled.

'Then we had sex again. Slow, yummy sex.'

She bolted from the car before Eve followed through

on the threat.

'Anyway.' She tried the smile again. 'I'm torn here. I really thought we'd hit with the supply vendors, then we'd go bag the bastard, save Covino, fry him in the box, and call it a damn good day. But I still feel up because McNab and I are going to walk over to the house and look at the progress.'

'We are going to hit. Before you go anywhere, you're going to contact more vendors — and so will I — before they close for the day. I don't see him onlining this. Can't pay cash that way, and it'll leave a bigger trail. If he did, we'll find him that way. We'll push there tonight after the brick-and-mortars close.'

They got in the elevator.

'He didn't have them on hand, and had to buy or order them in the last few days. That specific brand, that specific color. He remembers she liked to wear color on her nails. Not like pink or red or clear. Bolder, weirder. He remembers a lot. She's fixed in his brain — an image, indelible to him, from a specific time in his life.'

'Age five. Old enough to have images, memories cement. I remember — I must have been about five — and I was crying because Zeke broke the wheels off this little blue truck I had. He didn't really mean to. My dad hauled me up onto his shoulders, bounced them until I laughed — it always worked.

'His hair smelled like sawdust, and he wore it long. I grabbed it like reins and he galloped around the yard making horse noises while my mom fixed the little truck.'

She shuffled over as more cops loaded on. 'I can see exactly how they looked, remember the sun was hot and my mom wore shorts she'd cut off from an old pair of jeans.'

When the car stopped again, Eve escaped with Peabody in her wake. 'I don't remember being five.'

'I didn't mean to —'

'No.' Eve stopped her as they jumped on a glide. 'Not what I mean. You've got a solid memory — lots of them — and you like to pull them out. Good times, good family. I got the same from McKinney's three adult children. The good can etch things in the memory, and so can the traumatic. The traumatic can also erase them. Or block them.'

'True. My cousin Janis fell out of a tree when she was about seven. Broke her arm, knocked herself out. She doesn't remember even climbing the tree, much less falling.'

'Which is more likely? A woman maintains a fake name, a life, a family for sixty-odd years without, as far as we can tell, a hitch, or the woman doesn't remember the life that came before?'

'Amnesia? I sure hadn't gone there. It's kind of, you know, vid of the week.'

'I'm going there.' Because vid of the week or not, she'd been there herself. 'Trauma. Some john beats the crap out of her, she OD'd and they pull her back, she wrecks the car, sells the kid — something. Maybe an attempted suicide — it's the way she went out in the end. She might have tried it before. In any case, she's blank — just like the name she gave herself. What do they call it — tabula rasa. And maybe that suits her just fine. Maybe there's enough in her to see it as a second chance.'

Switching glides again, she angled toward Peabody. 'Now you've got a doctor — ER doc — who by all accounts is compassionate, dedicated. He tries to help her. You don't get the kind of fake ID she had without a lot of money. Maybe she paid for it by selling the kid. That would do it. Or maybe the rich young doctor who fell for her financed it.'

'I can see how maybe.'

'There's nothing in her background that makes me believe she could run a solid con — dupe the doctor into marrying her, financing her. She was a loser, a drifter, an addict. But if all that's gone, if she doesn't remember it, you can reinvent yourself.'

They got off on the Homicide level, and Eve pointed. 'Conference room. I want to see it all laid out, one big picture. She lives a happy life,' Eve continued. 'A good life. She is Violet Fletcher. Maybe she gets flashes now and then of McKinney, of the kid. You get flashes, but they don't stick. Can keep you up at night, bring on hard dreams and cold sweats, but you shove them aside, and get on with your life. Because you're not ready or not willing to go back.'

When they walked into the conference room, Peabody cleared her throat. 'Do you want coffee?'

'Not yet, and stop worrying. It's useful to have some personal experience, and I'm thinking about this angle because I know how it works. Print out her ID shot — the license for McKinney. Print out Violet Fletcher's first and last ID shot with it. I want them on the board.'

She started to pace. 'Nobody looks for McKinney — why would they? She's been drifting with the kid for a year or two. Nobody knows the kid. She's all he's got.'

'Maybe we should ask Mira to come up.'

'Not yet,' Eve said again. 'I didn't try to get out because how do you know what's on the other side

300

of the door isn't worse? Especially if they keep telling you it is. Maybe she did that. Or maybe, maybe because she had it in her, she did her best to take care of him. Maybe she loved him, and he felt that. Don't you know when they love you just like you know when they don't?'

'Yeah. Yes, I think you do.'

'She left him, and gave that love to other kids. Left him and didn't come back. Maybe she left him when she worked the streets or the pole. Maybe gave him a little something to make him sleep, or hired another stripper to watch him a few hours. But she always came back. Until she didn't.'

Eve stepped to the board, tapped the photos. 'She went from this, to this, and ended here,' she said, tapping the final ID shot of a pretty older woman with happy eyes and an easy smile.

'Trauma. The man she loved for more than half a century, the one who helped her become Violet, gave her a home, a family — all the damn wishes in the genie lamp — is gone. So the foundation breaks under her, her world crumbles. And so does the block. She remembers. She remembers it all, and the child she left.'

'She went to Hilton Head — to their vacation house for about a week. She checked in every day, and I followed up. She did book a shuttle from New Orleans to Hilton Head.'

'A quick trip. I checked from there while you were creeping your way back to Central. She booked another shuttle from there to New York City, leaving the night she arrived in Hilton Head. Return trip three nights later. She spent three days in New York.'

'She came to New York.' Eve's theory started to gel

301

for Peabody. 'I never thought to look for that.'

'That's why I'm the boss. We'll run a search on hotels, but the question is, did she go to see him, talk to him? At the very least she found him and checked to see what kind of life he had, how he looked. She's his mother, she had to at least look at him, at the man he'd become.'

She wanted coffee after all, gestured to the Auto-Chef. 'Is mine still in there?'

'Yeah, Jamie programmed it for as long as we have the room. I'll get it for both of us.'

'According to their statements, she seemed better when she got back. I don't see that if she'd found him, and he'd been some lowlife, scraping by, or another addict, another loser.'

'She sees him, a grown man, doing okay. He did okay without her.' Peabody passed Eve her coffee. 'Do you think she contacted him then, went to see him, told him what happened? Apologized?'

'I don't know, but she did before she took the pills and ended it. She'd have to. She couldn't end it, claim she was at peace, until she made some sort of amends to her first child. And that's what snapped him. Whatever she told him, he could find out all the rest, the life she'd led without him, once he had her name. And rather than giving him comfort or settling his mind, it woke the rage. It was always in there, but now she's gone — way beyond his reach.'

'He has to re-create her.'

'That's right. Down to her goddamn fingernails. We've got a little time to push that now. Let's hit the 'links. Any venue that's closing,' Eve continued as they left the conference room, 'we nag their asses to stay and check the records. Otherwise, we dig into the

302

online angle from home.'

'Jenkinson and Reineke didn't hit yet, but that doesn't mean they won't.'

'If it's not a residence, maybe a business. Maybe one he owns and has an area he can block off. A warehouse, a storage facility.'

Too many possibilities, Eve thought. And time wasn't on Covino's side.

'I'll take the first three we have left, you take the next. We'll run over end of business day by the time we get through them, if not before.'

In her office, Eve sat, called up the list, and got to work.

She ran up against close of business when she reached the third, and pushed hard against the unfortunate clerk.

And got nothing for the effort.

'I appreciate your time. You have my contact. If you find or remember anything, please contact me.'

She clicked off as Roarke walked into her office.

'Are you supposed to be here? Do we have a thing?'

'We have many things.' He crossed to her, tipped up her chin, kissed her. 'And there's one. But I had a meeting in the area, chanced my luck on catching a ride home with you. But I see from this, and Peabody at her desk, you're not done.'

'Pretty much am. We thought we caught a major break with fingernails. Fake fingernails. But we're crapping out.'

'There's considerably more on your board for crapping out.' He looked closer. 'You found her.'

'Yeah, Lisa McKinney, who became Violet Blank — ha ha — who became Violet Fletcher when she married a rich doctor. She spent the last sixty years as Violet, living in a big old house outside New Orleans, raising a family — one of her sons is Senator Edward Fletcher of Louisiana. I'll fill you in on the rest, but she died — swallowed pills — last fall, six months after her husband died in a car wreck. Her other son — got a doctor daughter, too — is some writer dude, and he's living in the big old house with his family now.'

'Chasen Q. Fletcher? He's excellent.'

'Yeah, fine.' Frustrated, she swiveled back and forth in the chair. 'She had to contact her firstborn, had to. I'm thinking maybe she blocked her former life — something happened, big trauma, blocked it, forgot about the first kid. I've got reasons, and I'll go into them later. But she had to. And now I'm just thinking, big old house. You live in the same place for over half a century. That's a lot to go through, a lot of stuff. Maybe there's something there that connects. She wrote notes to her three kids — with the doctor. Maybe she wrote one to her first kid from before. Maybe there's a copy. Or she talked to him. Maybe they still have her 'link.'

She hissed, pushed up, paced. 'I don't want to take the time — Covino doesn't have any to spare — but maybe we should go down to New Orleans after all.'

'*Laissez les bon temps rouler.*'

She stopped, stared. 'What?'

He smiled. 'We'll have to go down for Mardi Gras one of these days.'

'Yeah, that's what we'll do. Go party with the drunks, the street thieves, and the half-naked people riding on those — whatever they are.'

'Floats. Should I arrange for a shuttle?'

She rubbed her eyes. 'Damn it. It's a stone, and

you've got to turn it over. It just feels like I'm not going to find anything under it but those creepy bugs.'

'Ants are industrious and useful.'

'No, not those. Those little white wriggling — never mind,' she said when her 'link signaled. 'Dallas.'

'Oh, hey, um, Lieutenant Dallas, this is Darci at Salon Pro. You and Detective Peabody came in this afternoon. I got all flustered because I just so hearted the Icove vid.'

'I remember.' Just as Eve remembered the squeals emanating from the perfectly coiffed and made-up twenty-something assistant manager with the enormous, emeralds-on-steroids eyes. 'Did you find something on the nail kit?'

'No. I mean I didn't. I'm going to get flustered again! We don't have a record of a sale of the Adora Nail It deluxe with the On a Moonlit Sea polish, but my friend Carrie — she's salesperson of the month — we were just talking about it because she totally hearted the vid, too. And she was all sad she was on a break when you and Detective Peabody came in so she didn't get to meet you and —'

'Darci.' For the sake of her own sanity, Eve interrupted. 'Do you have any information for me?'

'Okay, well yeah, that's the thing. We're talking, Carrie and me, when we're closing up for the day, and I'm telling her, and she says how it's abso on the weird that she sold this old man, I mean this older gentleman, a Lovelle Pro Deluxe Faux Nail kit with the choice — it has a deal where you get one choice of standard Lovelle color, or a discount on the Super — and he got the Super in Midnight Madness.'

Eve stabbed a finger at Roarke, said, 'Peabody.'

'She said how she thought oh crap when he came

in because it was pretty close to closing, but he knew just what he wanted. The brand, the color, so it was just peasy, right? I mean it's not the kit and color you said, but the thing is,' Darci went on, 'there's not a whole lot of difference in the product. I mean to say, they're, um, comparable, so we sort of wondered if maybe there was a mistake on the brand.'

'It's possible.' Comp glitch, she remembered. Convenient.

'When did he come in, when did he buy the kit?'

'Oh, just yesterday, Carrie said, and I went ahead and checked the receipts. Cash purchase at, um, four-fifty-eight. He had a pro license and everything.'

Peabody came on the run, with Roarke and McNab behind her. Eve held up a hand. 'You have in-store security feed.' She'd seen the cams.

'Oh yeah, sure. You gotta.'

'Do you have the feed from yesterday when he was in?'

'Uh-huh.'

Eve doubted two syllables had ever brought her such pleasure.

'We loop it back every forty-eight hours, so —'

'I need to see that feed, Darci. I'd rather not take the time to come to you, so I need you to send me the feed.'

'Oh, I mean, I know the boss would want me to do whatever, but I don't know how to do that. It's just me and Carrie here now, and —'

A second woman shoved her face next to Darci's and waved frantically.

'That's Carrie, and it's just that we don't know how to do that.'

Before Eve could yank out her own hair, Roarke

nipped the 'link out of her hand. 'Hello, Darci, why don't I walk you through how to do what the lieutenant needs?'

'*Oh! My! God!*' The squeals followed, in stereo, and knowing his wife's threshold for such things, Roarke strolled out into the hall.

'He's the right age. Run Dawber, Peabody.'

'You think — Jesus. Dawber — do we have his full name?'

'Fuck me.' Eve squeezed her eyes shut, took herself back to the lab, to Harvo, to the walk to Dawber's area. 'Andy. Try Andrew. Dawber, Andrew. See if he was adopted or in the foster system.'

'Dallas, if I can have your desk unit, I can set it up for what Roarke's having them send you.'

'It's yours,' she told McNab. 'Son of a bitch, it could be the son of a bitch. Under my damn nose. Works for the cops. Forensic chemist. Knows just what to do, how to do it. How not to leave a trace of himself on the body, how to choose the products, the clothes that make it close to impossible to track back.

'Except for the nails.' She paced as well as she could with two other people in her office. 'Had to have the perfect, the exact, and didn't have time to cover it well. Went to Brooklyn, but that's not enough. Gave us the wrong data, wasted a day there, but that's not going to be enough.'

She whipped back to McNab. 'How long is this going to take?'

'You're set, and it's not that complicated on the other end, but they're already buzzed out and they don't know the system, so it might take a few minutes to baby them through it.'

She checked the time. 'He'll have clocked out of the

lab. He's with her now or on his way. I didn't see it. I looked right at him, and I thought: You'd be the type. The right age range, the quiet type, perfectionist, the type who blends so people don't really see him.

'Son of a bitch.'

'Dallas, he went into the foster system as John Church in 2003, in Baton Rouge, Louisiana. Age five, no parents or guardians on record, found wandering alone in a church yard. Adopted in 2005 by Elyse and Lloyd Dawber. I've got his education, medical, criminal — and at a glance, nothing pops. He moved to New York in 2016 to attend Columbia, got his advanced degree in forensic chemistry, and has worked for the NYPSD lab since 2025.'

'Address.'

'Yeah, Lower West. He could walk to the lab.'

'What kind of building?'

'Take me a minute.'

Roarke walked back in, still talking on her 'link. He gestured to McNab, got a nod. 'You've done very well indeed. The feed's on your screen now, cued up as we discussed.'

'Uh-huh, uh-huh. This is so exciting. Your accent just slays me.'

'You and Carrie have been an enormous help. You have the code for the lieutenant's unit in the corner there for receiving, so now you only need to click send.'

'Here goes! Did it work? Did it work?'

'It certainly did, and thank you. The lieutenant's going to be busy for a while yet, but she'll contact you tomorrow.'

'This was fun!'

Eve ignored Roarke as he stepped out again to end

the conversation, and watched the feed.

'Son of a bitch,' she said yet again as Andrew Dawber walked into view.

He looked harmless with his round face, his pressed khakis, the shy cherub's smile. He went directly to the nail products — no browsing, no distractions. Eve watched Carrie — salesperson of the month — cross to him.

Need any help? Eve thought. Can I show you something?

Quick, friendly conversation, and she found the color for him. She gestured, probably trying to make an upsell, but he just smiled, shook his head.

Back to the sales counter, check his license — chatting, her chatting, him smiling — take the cash, make the change — bag it up.

'In and out in under four minutes. He doesn't waste time. Friendly, but not memorable. But Carrie remembered enough.'

'It's an apartment building, Dallas. Multiunit, a deli and a convenience market street level. He's on the fifth floor. I don't see how he got three women in there and held them.'

'A basement, maybe he has access to the basement. Rents it so he can close it off.'

But it didn't feel right.

Yanking out her communicator, she contacted Jenkinson.

He said, 'Yo.'

'We've ID'd him. Andrew Dawber, lives — Peabody!'

Peabody rattled off the address.

'Hey, not Andy Dawber the lab nerd?'

'Yeah, him.'

'Well, son of a bitch! I know that son of a bitch. He's worked for the department as long as I have. Maybe longer. You want us to go get the fucker, boss?'

'No. I want you to back us up when we check out the apartment building. One possible is he has the basement for his prison. He'd need to get them in and out, hold up to three women there.'

'Doesn't gel.'

'No, but we check it out. Where the hell are you?'

'At the Blue Line. We just ordered burgers. We'll put a hold on that, meet you there.'

'Ten minutes.' She clicked off. 'McNab, suit up, and get a vest for the civilian while you're at it.' She considered a moment, then tagged Feeney.

He also said, 'Yo.'

'I've got an ID on the whack job — the investigation I had Jamie work on.'

'Boy did all right.'

'More than. I need a van. I've got two e-men with me. I want eyes and ears. I've got an address, but it doesn't feel right. We need to cover it.'

'I'll get you one. Who's your man?'

'Dawber, Andrew Dawber from the freaking lab.'

'Andy? Are you fucking kidding me? Goddamn it. I'll meet you with the van in the garage in ten.'

'I've got Roarke and McNab. You don't need to —'

'I know that son of a bitch.'

When her screen went blank after Feeney's outrage, Eve shrugged. 'Okay, we've got three e-men. Ten minutes,' she muttered, and contacted Mira.

She said, 'Eve, what can I do for you?'

'We've got an ID — solid. I've got a team heading out to his residence in ten — but it's an apartment building, and he's on the fifth floor.'

310

'Does he have a private entrance, adequate space?'

'Fifth floor, so doubtful, but we'll check. It's Andrew Dawber.'

'Why is that name vaguely familiar?'

'Forensic chemist, employed by the NYPSD.'

'Ah, of course, I've seen his name on countless reports. Forensic chemist. Precise, focused, while he works with a team, he does his work primarily alone. He'd know how to prepare a body to remove any trace evidence that could lead back to him. I'm just pulling up at home. Do you want me to come back?'

'Not until we have him. I'm hoping that's tonight. If he slips by us, we'll take him when he gets to the lab in the morning. I'm hoping tonight.'

'I'll join that hope, and I'll be there when you have him. Covino will, undoubtedly, need some counseling. Good luck to you and your team.'

'We'll take it. Let's move out,' she said when she clicked off. She looked at Roarke. 'You'll be taking a little detour before I give you that ride home.'

19

She contacted APA Cher Reo on the way to the garage. 'I need warrants, search and arrest.'

'Elder and Hobe?'

'Yeah. We've ID'd him, and we're on our way to his address of record.'

'How solid?'

'It's a fucking rock. We've got more to add to the reports I've sent you. He was found, abandoned, at age five some miles from where the mother ended up living the rest of her life. He fits the profile down the line. And we have him on security feed purchasing the nail kit and color with a fake license from a vendor in Brooklyn yesterday. That's after he gave us incorrect data on said fake nail.'

'What do you mean he gave you the data?'

'He's a forensic chemist at the lab.'

'Son of a bitch!'

'Phrase of the day,' Eve agreed as she tried to ignore the cops crowding on the elevator. 'Andrew Dawber.'

'Dawber? Seriously? We've used his testimony more times than I can count — and that's just since I came on. He's the perfect expert witness! Jesus, we're going to have a slew of defense attorneys filing to have his testimony tossed.'

'That's a problem for later.'

'Oh yeah, it is. I'll get the damn warrants. Fucking Dawber.'

Eve nodded at her 'link when the screen went blank. 'She's displeased. Crap, I'm going to need to

312

brief Whitney.' She slid a glance toward Peabody, who immediately hiked her shoulders to her ears, aimed puppy dog eyes, and shook her head.

'I'll do it, I'll do it.' But Eve blew out a breath first, then took another. Let that one go before she made the contact.

She saw, immediately, he was in some fancy bar. She heard the murmur of other patrons in the background, the laughter around his own table.

He might have appeared relaxed, but he still radiated that force of command.

'Lieutenant. Excuse me,' he said to his companions, and leaned over to kiss his wife's cheek (she also looked displeased). 'I'll only be a minute.'

He rose, began to walk through the bar, a big man with wide shoulders, dark hair cropped close and threaded with silver.

'I'm sorry to interrupt your evening, Commander.'

'I assume you have reason to.'

'Yes, sir.' She waited while he made his way through the bar area of a restaurant where everyone looked elegant, and some guy in a tux opened the door to an outside area where other elegant people sat with sparkling drinks.

Whitney stepped away from them.

'And it is?'

'We've identified the suspect in the Elder and Hobe abductions and murders and the Covino abduction. I have a team ready to go, and APA Reo is securing the proper warrants. I'll update my report to you with the additional evidence that led to the identification.'

He nodded. 'Very good. I'll pass this along to Chief Tibble. We're having drinks, or will be. Is there a reason you need to inform me of this, at this moment?'

'Yes, sir.' Finally, Eve got out of the elevator and into the garage. 'We have considerable and I believe conclusive evidence the target is Andrew Dawber.'

'Excuse me?'

'Dawber, sir. Forensic chemist in our lab. And one assigned to analyze evidence in this investigation.'

Whitney said, 'Son of a bitch!'

Roarke waited until she'd finished, until they stood by the van parked behind her car.

He gave her shoulder a quick rub. 'That went well enough.'

She rolled her shoulders, circled her head. 'Okay, that's done.'

She looked at Feeney with his baggy brown suit, his crooked tie with its latest stain, his hound-dog face and explosion of ginger hair.

And the bright neon light of Jamie beside him.

'Really?'

Feeney jerked a thumb at grinning Jamie. 'He earned it.'

'He earned it,' Eve agreed. 'Now I have four e-men and four other cops to take down one crazy, mommy-whacked scientist.'

'Where are the other two?' Feeney asked.

'Probably sitting on the apartment building by now. Jenkinson and Reineke. Everybody in, let's move. They're not going to be there,' she said as she boosted herself into the van. 'It doesn't play out. Unless . . .'

She shook her head as Feeney took the wheel, Jamie got in beside him, and the others settled into the back. McNab and Roarke at the equipment.

'No, hold on. Jamie, come back here and do the e-thing with McNab. Roarke, start running another search on properties. Same basics with the building,

314

but plug in these names or derivatives. Lisa McKinney, Violet Blank, Violet Fletcher, John Church, Andrew Dawber. Could use place names, maybe. Bigsby, Arcadia, Tennessee, Alabama, Louisiana. Peabody, dig up the name of the church where she left him, and we'll try that, too. He could use Andrew McKinney, or Lisa Church, any combo. Okay?'

'I've got it. Setting it up now.'

'I want to look for heat sources in this building. Focus on the basement if it has one, and in this sector it's likely. Also focus on Dawber's apartment. If we hit, we'll need eyes and ears. We need to move him away from Covino — or any other woman he might have grabbed since. We secure the civilians, secure the suspect.'

'Short drive,' Feeney announced. 'I'm putting us at max distance for the heat search. He'd recognize an e-van, or give it a hard eye if he spots us.

'You got it, Jamie. Run it.'

'Frosted!'

'Your detectives coming up on the cargo doors, kid.'

At Feeney's alert, Eve got up, opened them. 'Inside.'

'No movement we've seen in the apartment windows,' Jenkinson told her as he parked his butt on one of the bench seats. 'We've been here maybe five minutes. Guess you're sure it's him.'

'Damn sure.'

He shook his head. 'You think you know somebody.'

Since his tie — wildly colored gumdrops over blinding white — hurt her eyes, she focused on Jamie.

'Anything?'

'Got a basement, got one heat source northeast corner. Moving around and . . . walking — carrying something by the arm position — west, and up.'

'Laundry or storage area,' Reineke said. 'Or both. Betcha.'

'Following the heat source, and it's heading straight up. I'd say an elevator now. Exiting, third floor, moving north, turn, and into a space with three other sources. Two of them probably kids from the size.'

'No keeping women shackled up in an area with that kind of access. Move to his apartment.'

'Fifth floor,' Jenkinson told Jamie. 'Front facing, on the right over the deli, second and third windows.'

'Changing scan. Nobody's in there.'

'There's the warrants. Peabody, with me. Jenkinson, you and Reineke take outside doors, in case. Feeney, if you spot him heading home, beep my comm twice.'

'Will do.'

She hopped out the back, then pointed at Jamie. 'You, put on a recorder. Grab a can of Seal-It, and bring it along.'

His eyes popped. 'I'm going in? Woo!'

'If you're looking at this like an adventure, toss me the sealant and stay in the van.'

His Christmas-morning eyes went immediately sober. 'Got it. Sir.'

The target wasn't on the premises, Eve concluded, so he had another hole — a bigger one, a private one. And that made the warranted entry and search a training exercise.

'Record on. We have a warrant to arrest Andrew Dawber, and to enter and search his residence — and his lab space when we get to it. Entrance has pass-coded locks and cams. We'll want that feed.'

She mastered through the locks, ignored the elevator in the small, tidy lobby, and hit the stairway.

'Heat source scan showed no occupant in Dawber's

316

apartment. Heat source scan indicated community area, so not conducive to hiding and holding abductees. Conclusion?'

'Me?' Jamie blinked. 'Okay, I'd conclude the suspect isn't here, and has access to another property where he's holding Covino, and held Elder and Hobe.'

Used their names, Eve thought as they reached the second level, continued up. Good.

'If he's not here, why are we going in?'

'To see his space, how he lives, and, more important, to look for evidence of the abductions, the murders. Most important, to find anything that leads us to where he's holding Covino. Finding her and getting her to safety is numero uno.'

'Affirmative.'

When they came out on five, Eve turned to him. 'We knock, announce ourselves. And we go through the door exactly as we would if the suspect were inside. Which means Peabody and I take the door, and you come in behind us.'

'Because interns aren't issued weapons.'

'Affirmative. You stay behind Peabody while we clear the apartment.'

At the door, Eve kept one hand on her weapon, knocked with the other. The door across the hall opened, and a woman with a pudgy little dog with bulbous eyes and pointy ears stepped out.

The dog yipped once, wagged its stub of a tail.

'He's just saying hello.' From the open doorway behind her came the sound of pipy voices — kid voices — arguing passionately. 'Our boys, having their nightly battle. Pugs and I are leaving the field to their dad and escaping. Anyway, Gina and Jan aren't home. They went out to meet some friends for dinner.'

317

'We're here for Andrew Dawber.'

'Mr. Dawber?'

Jamie caved, crouched down to pet the dog, who'd pranced over to sniff his kicks.

'He moved out months ago. Sweet man, quiet, but never complained about the noise the twins can make. And he always had a treat for Pugs.'

'He no longer lives at this address?'

'Not since . . . ' She pushed at a mop of disordered brown hair. 'Well, before Thanksgiving anyway.'

'Do you know where he went? Did he leave you any contact information?'

'No.' Belatedly, she closed the door at her back, and her eyebrows drew together. 'Why?'

Eve took out her badge. 'NYPSD. We need to speak with Mr. Dawber.'

'Well, he works with the police, right? Science stuff.'

'Yes, he does. This is the address he has on record.'

'Oh. I guess he didn't change it. Strange, as he seems so organized. Sorry, I just know he moved out — you know, I think it was before Halloween now that I look back. Yeah, sure it was. Because Gina and Jan got all costumed up, and had candy for the twins before they went to a party.'

'You haven't seen or spoken to him since he moved from the building?'

'No — I . . . Not spoken to him, but I saw him out walking, maybe from work. He liked to walk around the neighborhood. He was across the street though, so I didn't talk to him.'

'Does he have a vehicle?'

'You're not going to tell me he's in trouble. He's such a nice man.'

The dog, now blissfully on his back, got an enthu-

318

siastic belly rub from Jamie.

'Ma'am?'

'Sherry, Sherry Wozinski.'

'Ms. Wozinski, it's important we locate Mr. Dawber as soon as possible. Does he have a vehicle?'

'No. At least I never saw him driving. I don't know why he'd have one, since he can walk to work in a couple of minutes, and otherwise, he didn't go out much except to take his walks, go to the market, the usual.'

'Did he have visitors?'

'I — no, not really. I don't remember seeing anyone go in or come out but Mr. Dawber. What do you think he's done? I can't imagine him doing anything against the law.'

'Was he friendly with anyone in the building, the neighborhood that you know of? Someone who might know his new address?'

'No, not really. He was the quiet type, kept to himself, and . . . ' Her whole being went from baffled to panicked. 'Oh God, that's what the neighbors end up saying about ax murderers.'

'Could we speak to the twins' father a moment, in case he has any information?'

'Yes, sure. I don't think he does, but . . . ' She pulled a key out of her pocket and, unlocking the door, poked her head in.

The fight had turned to hysterical laughter. Wozinski lifted her voice over it. 'Brad, come here a minute, will you?'

Eve ran through the same routine, received basically the same responses.

'Mother died in September,' Eve said as they started down the stairway. 'Rich mother, guilty mother, suicidal mother. I bet she left the three children she had

319

as Violet really well-set. And I'm betting she did the same for her firstborn.'

'Enough for him to buy a house — something private,' Peabody said. 'Something with a basement or attic or an area he could use as a prison.'

'It's going to narrow the search. He moved in before Halloween, and she died September eighteen. That's the window now.'

She signaled to Jenkinson as she headed back to the van. When she stood on the sidewalk, thinking before she briefed them, Roarke, Feeney, and McNab got out to join them.

'He moved out before Halloween. Neighbors don't know where, but the woman across the hall saw him walking, she thinks maybe to work, after he moved out. He didn't move too close or they'd probably have seen him more than one time. They said he liked taking walks, and they have a dog, so walks.'

She scanned the buildings up and down the block. 'It's not going to be too close to his old place, but close enough he can still walk to work if he wants — and it's familiar — the Lower West is familiar. He got a place — the private residence — between September eighteenth and the end of October.'

'Mommy left him some scratch,' Feeney put in.

'I'm betting on it. Finds himself a house. Could be a warehouse, a storage facility, but why? Why not be comfortable? House is still first on the list, but the search is for ownership to begin in September.'

'I'll adjust it,' Roarke told her.

'If we hit on anything tonight, I'll pull you back.'

'Are you working from home?' Peabody asked her.

'Central for now. I need to —'

'Central it is.' Jenkinson jabbed a finger. 'Boss,

you're going to work it, we're going to work it. That girl's been locked up a damn week. We got a chance to find her tonight? I want to take it.'

'Go get your burgers, and I'll keep you in the loop.'

Even as Jenkinson folded his arms, put on his just-try-to-budge-me face, Roarke stepped in.

'It happens we own a pub right down the block there and around the corner. I'll wager no one's had a meal as yet, so I can work on this search, the lieutenant can do what she must, and all can have that meal. Together,' he added with a glance at Eve. 'So it saves time when we locate him.'

Feeney punched Roarke's shoulder. 'The Dubliner? That's yours? Why don't you tell me these things?' he asked Eve. 'Prime eats, prime brew. It makes sense, kid. Good time management.'

'Fine. Leave the rides here — On Duty. He's not on this block. If we don't hit by the time we've had the prime eats, everybody goes home.'

'Hey. What if he's still at the lab?'

Eve flicked Peabody a glance. 'He clocked out at sixteen-forty-three. I checked with security before we moved out.'

'Oh. Well. Sure.'

'So. We've got ourselves a good deal.' Jenkinson looked back at Roarke. 'I don't guess they have actual cow meat.'

'They got it,' Feeney answered first. 'Costs your right nut, but they got it. They do one hell of a fish and chips.'

'My pub, my treat,' Roarke said as they began to walk.

'You should come on ops more often,' Jenkinson told him.

'Yeah, he's got nothing better to do. We're going to need a table where we can bounce things around as they come. And I need to update my —'

'We've a nice roomy snug.' Roarke snagged Eve's hand before she could stop him. 'Not to worry.'

'*Roomy* and *snug* are opposites.'

Feeney just shook his head at Jamie. 'You've got a lot to learn, boy.'

They rounded the corner. 'So, can I get a brew?'

'No,' Eve and Feeney said together.

'You're underage. Too young,' Feeney said, 'and you know it.'

'If we're working, nobody gets a brew.'

At Eve's statement, Feeney sighed. 'That's a damn shame.'

People packed the outdoor tables, and the interior hopped. The music piping through the speakers plastered a grin on Feeney's face. And the air smelled of prime eats.

A waitress with a bright red braid and a face full of freckles paused with a tray of pints on her hip.

'Good evening to you! We've got you all set up in the snug, sir. I'll take you back as soon as I've served these pints.'

'I know the way, thanks.'

'Well then, I'll come around and take your orders before you know it.'

'Is that accent real?' Eve wondered as Roarke wove the way through tables and around a long, busy bar.

'It would be, yes. She's from Cork if I remember it right.'

He opened a door, herded them in, closed it.

The noise level dropped by half.

It proved a roomy snug, with what looked like three

smaller tables pushed together to make one. The space included a one-person workstation, a wall screen, a wing chair, and a low sofa — the sort that whispered: Nap here.

The table already held two boards with rounds of brown bread, dishes of butter, three large bottles of water, and wedges of lemons and limes.

'Okay, I get roomy.' Jamie immediately attacked the bread. 'Why is it a snug?'

'A cozy sort of place,' Roarke told him. 'And private. Well back in the day a place where those who didn't want to be seen lifting a pint could drink. An old tradition, mostly abandoned now, but I liked the idea of it for this place.'

'Frosty.' He slathered butter on the bread, devoured it, then grinned at his godfather. 'Prime.'

Eve sat, took out her PPC, and got to work.

'I can write it up.'

She shook her head at Peabody. 'I've got it.'

'Then can I take five minutes to consult with McNab on the tile so we can put the order in and not break the sacred pinky swear?'

Without looking up, Eve held up five fingers while the other cops — and the intern — talked about the menu.

The waitress popped in. 'I'm Morah, and Jack — who'll be along — and I will be serving you tonight. Now, what can I get you fine officers of the law to drink this evening?'

'Coffee, black,' Eve said, again without looking up.

As the orders went around and Morah gave her spiel about specials, Jamie dropped into the chair beside Eve.

'So, what's the story with Quilla?'

'Why?'

'Wondering.'

Now Eve looked up. 'You're too old for her.'

'Come on. Too young for a beer, but too old for the cute girl?'

'Yes. Go away. Working.'

By the time she'd written the report, sent the update to Mira, the commander, and Reo, the waitstaff had not only served the coffee but brought in a coffee service for easy refills. And were busily taking orders.

'And what's your pleasure tonight, Lieutenant?'

She hadn't thought about it, or glanced at the menu. 'Burger's good. Burger and fries. Thanks. He'd want top security,' she said to Feeney. 'Anyplace he'd use to hold these women, he'd need it secure. Maybe he had a new system put in, or added to one.'

'We can work with that. Jamie, start looking for permits, issued after September eighteenth, on security systems. Start top-line, work down. Stick to the sector, then spread out.'

Eve looked down the table at Roarke, who seemed deep in a conversation with Reineke that didn't look like cop work.

'The search.'

'It's running. You should try the fried clam table appetizer,' Roarke advised. 'It's lovely.'

Eve looked at the trio of nearly depleted dishes, considered what clams looked like before frying.

'No. There's the plumbing angle, too.'

Roarke poured himself more water. 'If I wanted to cover my tracks, remain as much off the grid as possible, and needed such things as new security and plumbing, what have you — and had the resources of someone who'd worked with the police for near to

324

four decades — I wouldn't go through proper channels. If I couldn't manage the work myself, I'd hire those who wouldn't quibble about permits and such.'

Jenkinson gestured with a fried clam before he popped it in his mouth. 'That's a point.'

'Crap. It's a good point.'

So good, she had to stand up and pace.

'Yeah, yeah, he knows how not to leave a trail — or to cover it up, make it hard to spot the tracks. And yeah, he's worked with cops, observed cops, knows the process. But he's not a cop. And he's pretty damn new at being a murderer. He slipped up with the fake nails, then he had to regroup and try sending us in the wrong direction.'

She grabbed her cup, walked over to refill it from the station.

'He slipped up once,' Jenkinson said. 'He slipped up somewhere else. We just haven't hit it yet.'

'Damn right. He's a creature of habit, a perfectionist, obsessive. He plans and plans — carefully — but the plans have to fit the obsession. He saw these women *because* of his habits and routines. He likes to walk. He could have seen Covino countless times given where she lives in connection to his apartment, his workplace. The other two, still Lower West, but a longer walk east. Possibly he didn't spot them until he moved.'

'Putting his new hold farther away from the lab,' Feeney put in.

'He likes to walk, and he'd have more reason to after September, after the break. Now he's hunting.'

She started to ask Roarke to put the wall screen on so she could bring up a map and look again. And the food came in.

Let it sit, she ordered herself, just let it work around in there until something else breaks through.

For a few minutes while the waitstaff served, the snug turned as noisy as the main pub. And she had to admit, the smell of food — those prime eats — rang all the happy bells in her empty stomach.

She sat again, loaded her food with salt before taking a bite of her burger. She pointed at Feeney, who was digging into his fish and chips. 'You know him — work know him. First word that springs to describe him.'

Feeney swirled a forkful of fish in tartar sauce. '*Nebbishy* — that's the word.'

'It is?'

'Like, you know, timid on the geek side. You asked.'

'I did. Same, Jenkinson.'

'*Reliable*. Always came through with the goods. I get the nebbish, but it's a Yiddish deal that can mean indecisive or awkward. Awkward fits well enough, but not the indecisive part. Timid, awkward yeah, and reliable.'

'Okay.' She ate a fry, decided it was a potato miracle, so ate another. 'How about you, Reineke?'

'First two are taken, so I'm saying *exacting*. Couldn't rush the guy, but when he finished, you had it all spelled out.'

'And Reo said he's a stellar witness in court. Peabody?'

Peabody paused over her own fish and chips. 'I only met him those couple of times, but I'm saying *soft*.'

'Soft?'

'Soft eyes, soft smile, soft voice, kind of a soft manner. And no accent. He's from the South, but not a trace of it.'

'You don't blend as well with an accent.'

'I guess you don't. Have you got a word?'

'*Alone*. The way he got flustered when Harvo went into his space in her Harvo way. He's used to being alone. So . . . a soft, nebbishy, precise, reliable loner.'

'He has to keep them in a separate space.' Jamie had nearly polished off a burger the size of Kansas and seriously depleted his mountain of fries. 'You put all those words together like you did? He can't have them in his space — he needs his own. He probably has a routine worked out with them. Feeding times and all that. He'd need to spend time with them, or what's the point? But they're not in his space, his area.

'Basement's still the best bet.'

Feeney smiled a proud smile over his chips.

'Agreed. It's a damn house with a damn basement and damn good security.'

Roarke picked up the PPC he'd set on the table, studied it. 'I believe it is, yes. And we've a solid hit.'

'You found him.'

'I have. I agreed with your conclusion that someone so obsessed would have to use his mother's name, or some derivative of it, but found nothing there. Then it occurred to me,' he continued, rising to set up the screen, 'that someone like him, as you all just described, might be clever enough to hide that. An anagram. I ran for anagrams of his mother's birth name.'

'Anagram? Mixing up words to make other words?'

'And Lisa McKinney becomes Cami and Ken Snily — so a couple, rather than a single.' He brought up the map. 'Cami and Ken Snily are the owners of record, as the property transferred into those names on September twenty-fifth from a trust held by the

327

law firm of — ha — McKinney and Son.'

'He did the anagram, and one of them made up the name of the law firm — likely him again.' Eve studied the map. 'Highlight the other areas — crime scenes, residences. She wanted to make it up to him, somehow. She came to New York, bought the house for him, and sent him the paperwork before she took the pills. I'm betting Cami and Ken also have a fat bank account, opened around the same time. She'd want to give him money to maintain the house, to make up for all those years.'

'Already looking for that,' Feeney told her. 'Didn't want him to have to pay estate taxes,' he continued as he worked, 'or wait to claim the house until the estate settled. That's my guess.'

'And didn't want her other children to know,' Eve finished. 'Couldn't face that, even at the end. Can you get blueprints?'

Roarke sent Reineke a put-upon look. 'And listen how she insults me after we've had such a pleasant meal.'

'No permits applied for,' Jamie said, 'not for that property. Roarke probably hit that one. He slid around permits.'

Moments later, the blueprints flashed on-screen.

'Fucking A, look at the size of that basement! What's the date on these?'

'March of last year, when they were generated for a rehab. A house sale, I'm thinking. And on the market, I'll wager we'll find, just in time for his mother to buy it. You see there's a small kitchen on the basement level, and two full and two half baths as well. One of the baths to make a master's suite. No windows but for this eastmost wall in that suite area — must have that for code, you see. There's your way out in case of fire, for instance — and I expect your way in.'

'He may have blocked it off, or it's something she can't reach, something she can't get to. Blocked off, maybe, privacy screened absolutely. Don't want anyone getting nosy enough to look in. Stairs leading up, almost center of the big-ass basement. Doors on the main level, front, back, both sides, another door second level to a porch thing, deck thing, stairs down to what looks like a little walled-off courtyard.'

'Yes, it's a very nice property.'

'Okay, okay, he's going to have cams, solid security. He's crazy, but he's not stupid.'

She stood a moment, hands in pockets, studying the blueprints, working it out in her head.

'All right, here's how we take him down.'

20

BEFORE

She couldn't sleep, not with the bed so empty beside her. She was a doctor's wife, and had often slept alone when Joe's duties had kept him late into the night.

But he'd always come home, and she'd always waked, at least enough to turn to him, to reach for his hand.

He'd always come home.

Until that horrible night.

How could she sleep knowing he'd never come back to her?

Everything about her had been wrong before Joe, she knew that now. Everything wrong, everything bad, every mistake — so many, too many — had rushed back into her. And all of it so raw, so real, flooding over her like the waters of the lake where she'd tried, and failed, to end her own life.

She'd left her little boy. She'd actually thought to kill him, to take him with her into the dark. Oh God, oh God, what did that make her?

The sweet, sassy baby darling she'd failed in so many ways.

No, in every way, she thought yet again as she stared out the bedroom window at the gardens she and Joe, then their children with them, had tended for so long.

So many years among the flowers, under the Spanish moss, in the beautiful old house. Breakfasts in the kitchen. Off to school now, learn something today!

Sweet tea on the veranda, picnics on the lawn.

Quiet nights loving Joe while the children slept.

Birthdays and skinned knees, squabbles and bed-time stories.

Graduations and weddings, her babies' beautiful babies.

And she'd left her little boy alone.

She'd washed his face and hands in a service station bathroom that smelled of piss-soaked heat because she'd traded her body for pills instead of a motel room.

He'd been angry, whiny so her head felt as if it would split.

Why shouldn't he have been, when instead of a bath and bed, she'd taken the Oxy and gas money so she could move on? Just move on.

How could she have loved — and she had, oh, she had loved her little boy — and been such a terrible mother?

Because everything about her had been wrong.

She'd known it, finally accepted it, and determined to end it.

But she hadn't taken him with her. She'd left him at that church. There'd been hope. She hadn't killed her baby.

Only left him, and forgotten him. Forgotten it all as if it had never happened, as if Lisa McKinney had never been.

And been reborn, with Joe. By Joe, for Joe.

Now he was gone, and all the years, so many years, she'd been a good wife, a good mother, a good per-son, a caring, loving, productive woman? Gone with him.

Violet had been stripped away to Lisa. Lisa didn't deserve those years of joy and comfort and love. The selfish, foolish, reckless girl who'd abandoned her own child deserved nothing.

And the Violet who remained couldn't live with it. How could she tell her children, their children, she'd built their lives on a lie?

Maybe, maybe if she'd remembered it all when Joe had still been alive, they'd have found a way. He always found a way. But he was gone, her North Star had flickered out, and she couldn't find her way any longer.

She wandered the room, touching photographs and the memories they held. The candlesticks that had been Joe's grandmother's — a strong, proud woman who'd given her a pair of diamond teardrop earrings on her wedding day as something old.

The vase she'd found in Venice on their honeymoon, the trinket box — wonderfully gaudy — the children had given her for Mother's Day so, so long ago.

Precious things, those pieces of the life she'd lived. Violet's life. But Violet couldn't exist, not really, without Joe.

She'd walked the house earlier, before all the children came for dinner. A last supper, she thought. She couldn't do so now, not with Joella staying over. If Joella heard her, she'd try to comfort, and she'd worry.

But she'd walked the house, the gardens, said her goodbyes. She'd fed her children, a big, happy meal. She'd hugged them, held them.

Now, she set out the letters she'd written each of them. They'd grieve, she knew. But they'd forgive her. Forgive Mama. And their lives would go on. She could be proud of that, proud there had been something strong and good in her, something Joe found in her that helped her raise such fine children.

Nothing of Lisa in them, she thought. Only Joe and Violet.

She'd written to her son, her firstborn, the little boy she'd deserted. So strange, so odd, so disconcerting to see him, a grown man, a gray-haired man.

A scientist!

She'd thought to go to him, to speak to him, to tell him everything face-to-face, but she hadn't found the courage.

But she had to leave him something, had to make up somehow for all the lost years, for the fear he must have felt, waking alone on the steps of the church.

She'd bought the house — not as big as the one where her other children had grown up. But a lovely old house, a solid house, still close to where he worked.

She'd opened a bank account for him, and arranged it all so he could simply move in — or sell the house if it didn't suit him.

She'd sent all the paperwork just that morning, with a letter confessing, explaining — or trying to.

Would he forgive her? Maybe one day.

But she felt Violet had done all she could for Lisa's baby darling.

She was a doctor's wife, and knew how many pills to take. She got into bed, the bed she'd shared with Joe for a lifetime, and began to take them. One at a time, letting each one settle.

When she felt drowsy, she took more. When it was enough, she set the glass aside.

When it was enough, she lay down, stretched a hand out to Joe's side of the bed, imagined him taking that hand in his.

She sighed once, said, 'Joe,' and finally slept.

NOW

Mary Kate heard the footsteps overhead. He was back.

Very deliberately, she sat in the reading chair, picked up a book. She accepted Anna was gone. He'd moved her, or he'd killed her.

He'd do the same to her eventually, unless she found a way out — and she'd gotten nowhere on that — or held him off long enough for someone to find her.

Holding him off meant placating him, playing him, playing a role. She'd damn well do just that.

If she could find a way, she'd kill or disable him, and pray he had the key to her chains or a 'link she could use to call for help.

She had food, she had water, she even had a decent bathroom.

And she had, she constantly reminded herself, a brain and a spine.

So she sat in the French-cut pink T-shirt and cropped pants. Not her style, a little on the rich-matron side for her, but comfortable. She had white skids — no laces.

If she'd had laces, she might have tied them together and tried to strangle him with them.

He'd probably thought of that.

He had a brain, too, but there was something really wrong with it. He'd grown up in the South — she'd figured that out. The man didn't have an accent, but when he reverted to the kid, the kid did. A twangy one — whiny and twangy.

Maybe she could use that. Maybe.

What she'd decided she could use, and would, was her own mother. How her mother handled her and her siblings.

Patient, firm, some humor, and a lot of: Don't push it, kid, or pay the price.

When she heard the locks give, she gripped the book tight, made herself breathe. Made herself smile.

He had a sour look to him, but she kept the smile bright.

'Hi! Welcome home. How was your day?'

He stared at her, and the sour look deepened. 'I had a very difficult day.'

'Oh, I'm sorry to hear that.' She set the book aside as if she wanted nothing more than to talk to him. 'Tell me all about it.'

'Why would you care?'

'Of course I care, baby darling. You know what you need? You need a snack. Let me fix you . . .'

She started to get up, trailed off, then settled again. Added a self-deprecating laugh.

'Sorry. Tell you what. Why don't you fix us both a snack, and you can tell me what happened to make you unhappy?' She lifted her free hand, waved a finger. 'No sweets now, not this close to dinner.'

He continued to stare at her, but she saw what she thought was interest — and a touch of slyness come into his eyes. 'I want a cookie.'

She let out a big sigh. 'Was it really that bad a day?'

'Yes.'

She held up the finger again. 'One cookie.'

The sour look vanished.

He went into the kitchen, opened one of the cabinets. From her angle, she could see he'd loaded it with snack food — kid food.

Bags of cookies, chips, candy bars. He took a bag of cookies out.

'How about a nice cold glass of milk to go with it?'

At her suggestion, his face went fierce — and the accent crept in. 'I want a *soda pop!*'

Fear clawed in her belly, but she channeled her mother, sent him a cold stare. 'I understand you had a bad day, but you'll watch your tone with me, young man.'

When he goggled at her, she inclined her head as her mother might have done. 'Now apologize, and ask properly.'

'Don't wanna.'

'Then we have nothing more to say.' With her heart pounding against her ribs, she picked up the book and pretended to read while the words blurred.

In the silence, she heard his rapid breathing, and forced herself not to look up when it dragged on.

'I'm sorry, Mommy.'

She looked over to see his head hanging. Chastised.

'Can I have a soda pop? Please, please?'

It took her a moment because her throat didn't want to work.

'Just this once because you had a bad day.'

'Yay!'

He went to the mini-friggie. Some juice, she noted, a container of soy milk, and heavy on the soft drinks.

'Aren't you going to get me one?'

He bounced on his toes like a child. 'What kind do you want, Mommy? We got all kinds!'

'Hmm.' Tilting her head, she tapped a finger on her chin. Watching him, watching his every move and expression. 'Well, since we're going to have ourselves a little predinner party, I should have my favorite.'

'Cherry Coca-Cola! You like that best.'

Despised it. 'I sure do.' She got up, moved to the

bed. And patted the space beside her. 'Now, you fix us a nice snack, then come on over here and tell me all about the bad day.'

''Kay. It was bad, and they keep asking questions. I did everything right.'

'Of course you did.'

The man came back, and she found herself much more frightened of the man.

'I did it all perfectly. Why do they care about a fingernail? Why did they even notice when I did it all perfectly? It had to be perfect, had to be right. I take pride in my work.'

'Of course you do.' What did it mean? Keep him talking. 'You're so good at it. You're the best.'

The man looked at her with glittering eyes. 'How do you know? You went away. You left me.'

'I'm so sorry, baby darling. I'm so sorry I went away, but I'm here now.'

'You left me, and I couldn't find you.' He began to tap his fist on the counter. 'You forgot me. You never tried to find me.'

'I'm so ashamed.' It wasn't hard to work up tears. 'I'll never forgive myself. How could I forgive myself? All I can do is try to make it up to you. Try to be a good mommy and take care of you, and be here, and listen when you've had a bad day.'

'I had to pretend to make a mistake. I don't make mistakes.'

'But it was just pretend. It's okay to pretend.'

'I don't make mistakes,' he repeated, 'so they won't find out because they'll believe what I said.'

'Absolutely.'

'They'd be mean to me if they knew. But the others, they were wrong. *They* made mistakes, so I knew they were wrong.' He studied her like something smeared on a slide under a microscope. 'Maybe you're wrong, too. There's another. I'll bring her home tonight. She could be the right one.'

Mary Kate went with instinct, took the risk. 'What a thing to say! I said I was sorry, I'm trying to make up for it. But you're hurting my feelings anyway. I'm the only one.'

She knuckled a tear away. 'I made an awful mistake, but I'm trying so hard.'

'Don't cry, Mommy.'

'I just — I want us to be happy together again, and for you to believe me, and let me fix you snacks when you come home.' She looked over at him. 'Let's not be mad at each other. Let's have our party. You don't have to talk about the bad day because we're going to have a good one. You and me.'

'Do you promise?'

She patted the bed again. 'Come on over here for our party. We'll play a game!'

'A game?'

'Let's see, what kind of a game should we play?'

The boy was back as he hurried over with the cookies and soda. She wondered what sick war raged into his head to cause him to flip back and forth.

But she thought — hoped — she could handle the boy. She nibbled on the cookie, though her skin crawled when he snuggled up beside her.

'We could play See It. Remember when we drove and drove and we'd play See It? I see a red car! I see a flagpole!'

'That's a good game.' She took another bite of the cookie. 'We could use things in this room, and . . . Oh, I've got a game! A memory game.'

Like a child, he ate the cookie greedily. 'A memory game.'

'This'll be fun. A test of my powers.' She wiggled her eyebrows, laughed. 'I have to close my eyes, and you take everything out of your pockets and put it all on the table there, by the chair. Then I get to look for three seconds — you count it off. Then I close my eyes again, and have to say everything you set out.'

'What's the prize! What's the prize!'

'Well . . . Okay, if I don't remember every single thing, you . . . get another cookie!' Holding back disgust, she tickled a finger at his ribs.

'What if you do?'

'Then I get another cookie, of course.'

'I want the cookie!'

'Then you have to play the game.'

'I'm gonna win! Close your eyes. No cheating!'

'No cheating,' she promised, and saying a quick prayer, closed her eyes.

★ ★ ★

In the van, well out of camera range, Eve studied the screen while McNab ran the heat source search.

'Two, basement. Almost dead center. Run the whole place,' she told McNab, 'but that's going to be Dawber and Covino. If he'd grabbed another, she'd be down there somewhere. Roarke?'

'Finishing the analysis on the security system, but yes, we can take it down.'

'He'll be smart enough to have an alert down here, or on a 'link or device, if anything goes down, glitches. We don't risk that when he's with her. Christ, all but in her lap from how it looks.'

339

'Sitting,' McNab confirmed, 'hip-to-hip. No other sources down here, none on the main level. Moving up.'

'Jenkinson, Reineke. Are you in position?'

'Back wall, out of cam range, but we've got a decent angle on the house,' Jenkinson answered.

'Hold there until the go. We need to get him upstairs, away from her. Then take down the security. Covino's priority. You can get over the wall?'

'I can scale a damn wall.' Jenkinson's insult came through as clearly as his voice.

'She's center of the basement level now. If that changes, we'll relay new position. Get over, get in, get to her when I say go.'

'The house is clear, Dallas. It's just the two of them in there. He's moving. Just a few steps.'

'Jamie? If you've got a single doubt, say it.'

'I'm good. I've got this.'

'He's going to see you, watch you. Maintain. You get him up to the door, we shut down security, we move in. And you get out of the way.'

'Copy that.'

'Jamie's a go.'

He picked up the stack of flyers they'd designed and printed out. After getting out of the van, he walked up the sidewalk into camera range, then turned to the house.

'Feeney —'

'He'll handle it. He's the only one of us we know Dawber won't recognize. Doesn't look like a cop yet. Cop's in there, but doesn't show yet.'

'Everybody hold.'

* * *

340

In the basement, Mary Kate scanned the items on the table. A 'link, a set of old-fashioned keys, a swipe, an ID card, and Jesus, a mini-Taser. A folding knife, loose change, wallet, a white handkerchief.

'Three! Close your eyes. Close them, Mommy.'

She even put her free hand over them.

'Okay. Boy, three seconds isn't long.' She remembered every damn item, but drew it out. 'Um . . . A 'link, a wallet, a hankie, keys on a ring, a swipe . . . Oh, I know there was more. Wait, wait . . . Um. Darn it!'

'I won! I won!'

If there was anything stranger than seeing a grown man with a little pudgy middle dance and spin in circles, she'd yet to see it. He dashed over to the kitchen for his prize.

She had to get the 'link. The keys. The Taser, the knife. Keep him occupied.

'Let's play again. It can be your turn to test your powers.'

She jolted when something gave out a loud buzz.

'What's that? Scared me. Anyway —'

'Someone's at the door.' His voice had gone flat.

She had to stick her hands under her legs as hope trembled through them. 'Oh, one of your friends? Maybe they want to play, too.'

'I don't have any friends.'

'Because they're not worthy of you. Go on up now,' she said when the buzzing came again. 'Tell them to go away. We don't need them, right?'

'They'll go away. I won't answer.' He stepped over, brought up a small screen. 'It's just some boy. He'll go away.'

But the buzzing came a third time.

'Baby darling, go up and tell him we're busy. Go on

now so I can set up for your turn.'

'He needs to go away!' Dawber stomped to the stairs and up. The minute the door closed, Mary Kate leaped on the 'link.

Security locked. She dropped it, grabbed the keys. One of them had to open the shackles, if she could just stop shaking long enough to use them.

★ ★ ★

'He's heading up, Jamie. Get ready. Roarke, the minute he opens the door.'

'You'll have it.'

Jamie heard the locks turn. The door opened a crack.

'Go away!'

'Sir, sir!' He added a southern drawl to his character. 'I'm sorry to disturb your evening, but Pepper's missing. My dog. She's just a little dog.' He held up a flyer, let that southern boy's voice shake with tears. 'We just moved in today, down there?' He gestured.

'I'm not interested in —'

'Moved from South Carolina.' Jamie rolled right over Dawber, talking fast, looking directly into his eyes. 'And she's lost. She doesn't know where she is. I'm afraid something . . . Please, mister, would you take a flyer, please? Pepper, she's still just a puppy really, and it's my fault she got out. Please, sir.'

'I haven't seen your dog.' But Dawber opened the door another inch to take the flyer.

'Thank you, sir. Thank you so much.'

And Eve kicked the door all the way open. 'Police. Put your hands up, Dawber.'

He shrieked. And ran across a dimly lit, empty foyer.

She could have stunned him with the weapon in her hand, but opted for a short chase — he had some speed.

He whipped left, into a big, empty room, toward a side door. Her hard tackle had him skidding over the dusty floor.

'Mommy! I want my mommy!' He beat his fists, kicked his feet, shrieking in a voice she wondered didn't shatter glass in a radius of ten miles. 'She's gonna beat you up.'

'Yeah? I don't think so.' Eve yanked his arms behind his back, slapped on the restraints. 'Andrew Dawber, you're under arrest for the murders of Lauren Elder and Anna Hobe, for the abductions of same and of Mary Kate Covino.'

'I *hate* you. You're a bad girl.'

'Bet your ass I'm bad.' Rising, Eve stared down as Dawber sobbed and thrashed. 'Got him, Peabody?'

'Yeah, I got him.'

'Jenkinson, target secure. I'm heading your way.'

'Copy that. Had to bust the damn window, but we're through. Mary Kate! Mary Kate Covino. Police! We're the police.'

She stood, shackles on the floor, keys clutched in one hand, the little Taser in the other.

And looked ready to use it.

Jenkinson holstered his weapon, held up his badge as his partner did the same. 'It's okay now, Mary Kate.' Jenkinson softened his tone. 'We're the cops. It's okay now. You're safe now.'

Her breath heaved and hitched before she dropped the Taser. She made a limping run to Jenkinson, threw herself at him.

'Please, get me out of here. Get me out.'

343

'That's what we're going to do. Don't you worry.'

Eve reached the steps to see Jenkinson stroking Covino's hair as she wept on his shoulder.

'Bring her up this way. It's clear.'

Still clinging to Jenkinson, Mary Kate whipped her head toward Eve. 'Did you catch him? Did you find him? He's insane.'

'We have him,' Eve assured her. 'He's secured. We're going to have you transported to the hospital, and —'

'No, please, no, please. I don't want to go to the hospital. I want . . . God, I want my mom. I want . . . ' She buried her face in Jenkinson's shoulder again.

'Mary Kate.' Eve came down a few steps. 'Cop Central's not far.'

'It's not? Where the hell am I?'

'About six blocks from where you live. How about we take you to Central, and I contact your mother, your family, your roommate, anyone you want. We can have a medical look you over there.'

'Please. Okay, please. Can you take me out of here?'

'Jenkinson, take Mary Kate into Central, stay with her. Ah, cloak the board in the conference room, use that. Reineke, I'm going to need you here on the search for now. Start on the second floor.'

'You'll stay with me?'

'Sure I will. I bet that ankle's sore. You lean on me now.'

With a sob that ended on a sigh, Mary Kate leaned on Jenkinson. She looked at Eve.

'There was another woman here. At least one other. Her name was Anna, that's all I could hear. I think he killed her. I'm afraid he did.'

'We'll talk about it.'

Eve walked down as they walked up. When Roarke

came down a few minutes later, she stood at one of the cells. 'I'm going to contact Louise — she's closer than Mira for a physical exam on Covino. Mira'll handle the rest, but her wrist and ankle looked rough. Three cells. Two more like this.'

She gestured. 'And he'd have used the bath in the bedroom suite deal to clean them up. He has a work space set up in there — a long table, all the hair stuff, makeup, the tattoo kit, and so on. Wardrobe in the closet.

'She got the keys from him. I need to ask her how the hell she managed to get him to set down the keys, a knife that's likely the murder weapon, a Taser — a mini, wouldn't do much, but still. How the hell did she get him to leave all of that within her reach?'

'She must be a very clever woman. She outwitted him. So did you.'

'On our part, good cop work. On hers? That's grit. Smarts, yeah, but grit. I have to go in, talk to her. I may want a pass at Dawber tonight, we'll see. Either way it's going to take awhile.'

Because she had her recorder on, and he knew her standards, he didn't touch her. 'You know I'm going with you.'

'Figured, but just wanted to point all that out.'

'Dallas?' Peabody called from the top of the stairs. 'He has an office set up on the second floor. He had more targets lined up. You're going to want to see this.'

'On my way.' She looked again at the windowless room with its narrow cot, the shackles bolted to the wall.

'Grit,' she repeated.

21

As she walked from the basement level to the second floor, Eve contacted Louise Dimatto.

'Hey,' Eve said when Louise, blond hair loose and wavy, came on-screen. 'I need a favor.'

'I'm in a very good mood, so inclined to give one.'

'Where are you?' Walking, Eve observed. Street noises.

'Enjoying a slow walk home after a lovely dinner with my sexy husband.'

Louise aimed her 'link over and up so Charles came on-screen. 'Hey back, Lieutenant Sugar.'

Good moods all around, Eve concluded, for the doctor and the former licensed companion turned sex therapist.

'How about grabbing your medical bag and making a detour to Central?'

Louise angled the 'link back, and the dreamy light in her gray eyes vanished. 'Who's hurt?'

'Female victim, Mary Kate Covino. Minor physical injuries, primarily contusions and lacerations on her wrist and ankle. I could call the MTs, but she's going to feel more comfortable with you.'

'Is this connected to the two women who were murdered?'

'She would've been number three. We've got him.'

'Good. We're nearly home. I'll get my bag.'

'Thanks. I'm putting her in a conference room on my level, and Jenkinson's with her. Peabody's going to clear it so you can go straight to her. He had her a

346

week, Louise.'

'Understood. Mira —'

'I'm calling her in.'

'Also good. I'll see you soon.'

'Peabody, clear them through,' she said when she clicked off.

She stepped into a large room with an attached bath. It had big double windows, privacy screened, facing the street.

She wouldn't have called it an office, but an HQ.

He had boards set up, one for each victim. Photographs of them at work, on the street, shopping, drinks with a friend. Time sheets, she noted, studying them one by one. Logging each woman's routines, work schedules, days or nights off. A list of family, friends, coworkers, shops and restaurants most frequented.

Very, very thorough, she thought.

He'd taken photos of them as they slept in captivity, photos of the tattoo he'd replicated — included precise measurements of the butterfly, the colors of inks used.

He noted down what they'd eaten and when, what drugs he'd given them and when.

And he'd taken more photos after he'd killed them, cleaned them, dressed them, styled their hair and face. Included a list of the products, the wardrobe chosen for each.

'Cops should avoid terms like *slam dunk*,' Peabody commented. 'But.'

Eve just nodded. 'Numbers instead of names. And it looks like he worked in groups of three. He had four, five, and six lined up.' She moved closer. 'And he had four ready to go. See this? He completed his research, had his plan for number four. He planned to grab her tonight.'

She moved across the room, bypassing, for now, the workstation and electronics for the board devoted to Lisa McKinney/Violet Fletcher.

'Got her mug shot, the stripper ad. Date of birth, all family connections. The date she disappeared. Clippings of her wedding to Joseph, and plenty of others through the years. Charity work, garden clubs. Birth announcements — and you can see he's documented Violet's three children over the years. He'd have gone after them eventually.'

She turned back to the victim board. 'If one of them suited him, or well enough, if one of them worked, he could shift his focus to his mother's other kids. She should never have had them. They got her, and that big house, the good life.'

As she took another turn around the room, Roarke watched her face.

'The lieutenant's considering another angle of approach on your slam dunk.'

'Yeah, I am. Look at this — and tag Baxter, Peabody, I want him and Trueheart in here to help Reineke and the e-team. We're going to go over every inch of this place. But look at it. The precision, the details, the focus, the skill. Timelines. He's even got the patrols, the beat cops assigned to the area he hunted. I'm betting everything he purchases — the clothes, the makeup, everything — is logged on that comp. The where he got every item, the cost, the date of purchase.'

She turned to Roarke. 'I'm going to have his electronics from the lab brought in, and every single device from this house. Maybe you want to give Feeney a hand with all that.'

348

'I would, yes. An entertaining evening for me, I expect.'

'Yeah, a geek party.'

'Sorry, boss.' Reineke stepped in. 'We got a safe in the bedroom back here, the one Dawber used. Feeney said Roarke could probably get into it quicker than he could.'

'More fun for me.'

'The other thing. Guy's got Spider-Man pajamas. Four pairs of Spider-Man pajamas.'

'Spider-Man?'

'You know, Loo, the Amazing Spider-Man. Friendly neighborhood Spider-Man.'

'I know who it is because —' She jerked a thumb at Roarke. 'Kid size?'

'Nope. For himself.'

'According to the police report, that's what he was wearing when they found him.'

'Bowlful of nuts,' Reineke said as he went out again.

Roarke gave Eve a light rub on the shoulder. 'I'll go have my fun.'

'Do that. I want to get to Covino, get her statement so we can send her home.'

'Let me know when you leave. I'll stick with Feeney and company.'

Eve nodded absently as Roarke left the room.

'Maybe we give Dawber a round tonight. I want Mira in the box with us on this one. We'll keep Reo on tap, but I don't think we'll need her right off.'

'Because?' Peabody wondered.

'Is he going to lawyer up? We'll see. But look how smart he is — how smart he thinks he is. How careful, how attentive to details. I'm betting we find contingency plans on the comps. Plan A goes wrong — not because he screwed up, not that, because it's never going to be his fault — but the target changed some element on the target date. He'd factor the variables.'

'Okay.'

'Jesus, Peabody, open up.' Eve gestured to encompass the room. 'So he's crazy, and he's got some nasty little five-year-old demon inside him. But you can't look at all this and conclude he doesn't know right from wrong. Insanity defense? That's a legal deal, and we're going to rip that to shreds with all this. He knew exactly what he was doing, how he intended to do it. He had six women — so far — as targets, and disposed of them when they didn't fit his criteria.

'The why he did it? Yeah, that's the crazy. But it's not going to be enough, even if the shrinks and the courts give him the insanity, we're going to make damn sure he's held responsible. No five or ten years of treatment and therapy, and he's all good to go again.'

She saw her way, saw some angles. 'Let's go talk to Covino.'

As they started out, Jamie came running, an evidence bag in his hand.

'Man oh man, Roarke cut through that safe like a katana. Just swipe, slash. I gotta learn how to do that.'

Ignoring the intern's dazzle over the skills of a former thief, Eve pointed to the bag. 'Is that for me?'

'Reineke said to get it to you asap. It's a letter from Dawber's bio mom, dated a couple days before she self-terminated. Bunch of paperwork and docs in there, too. Deed to the house, bank accounts, tax stuff. He said they'll bring it in, but you'd want this now.'

'He'd be right.' She took the bag and the handwritten pages inside.

'You should've seen it. I mean, it's like he had the

combination in his head.'

'I bet. Tell Reineke to call in the sweepers, and that Baxter and Trueheart are coming in to help with the search. I'll send Jenkinson back once I get to Central. I want all the e's taken in, and Feeney needs to send someone — ask for Callendar — to get Dawber's work e's from the lab. You got all that?'

'Yes, sir, I got it. This night rocks up and down and sideways.'

As he took off at a run, Eve passed the evidence bag to Peabody.

'Take it out, read it out loud on the way. Let's see what Mommy had to say.'

'I did a quick walk-through of the house,' Peabody told her. 'Looks like he used the kitchen in the basement, not the really mag one on the main level. And only used the two bedrooms — one for his office, the other for sleeping. Mostly the house is empty.'

'He had other things on his mind, no time or interest in furnishing, or really living in this place. Read.'

Baby darling, Peabody began, *I wonder if you remember I called you that. I wonder if you remember me at all. A part of me hopes you don't, that you've long ago forgotten me, all I did, all I didn't do. Every part of me hopes you've had a happy life with a loving family, with caring friends.*

I know you're a scientist. A forensic chemist! You were always so smart, so full of questions, so insistent on answers. And there were so many answers I couldn't give you. I understand now I was so very damaged, so lacking, such a selfish and reckless woman. No matter how much I

351

loved you, and I did love you, loved only you, I wasn't a good mother to you. You were so young, you couldn't know how I craved the pills, and the craving made me only more lacking, selfish, reckless.

And so, so unhappy.

I would tell myself that the next town, the next stop, the next day, I would do better by you. I'd find a place, find a decent job, give up the pills, the life I led and made you lead. But I was too weak, and the next was always the same until I lost everything. Living in the car, you sleeping in the back seat while I traded my body for those pills or enough money to buy them. Again and again.

Still I clung to you. Instead of doing what I could to see you had a good life, I chained you to mine and, yes, lost everything. My health, my reason, my mind. But the most precious thing I lost was you.

The morning of the last day I had to try to clean you up in a filthy gas station bathroom. You were so angry you fought me, struck out at me. Bad Mommy, you called me, and you were right.

I bought you chips and candy, whatever I thought would keep you happy in that damn back seat while I drove and drove and drove. Nearly out of money, nearly out of pills, and completely out of my mind.

I was broken, my baby darling, and saw no way out but to end it. And God forgive me, for I cannot, I clung to you still and thought to take you with me. I see you now, in that back seat in the Spider-Man pj's I stole to make you happy. I see you as I stopped because you were thirsty and very cranky, and my head really pounded. I went inside the mart — the air was extremely warm and thick — and bought you a soda pop, and slipped one of my last pills into it so you'd sleep. So you'd just sleep and somehow we'd wake up together in a better place.

As you slept and I drove — half-crazed — planning to take both our lives, I saw a light. A church. I stopped and, weeping, carried you to the door, left you sleeping there.

Someone would find you, and give you the good, happy life I never could.

I left you, my precious, under that single light in the dark. I drove and drove, and I saw the lake. I didn't hesitate, but drove straight into it.

I don't remember fighting to get out of the car — only vague terrors of water pouring over me, of swallowing it. I don't remember clearly dragging myself out of the water, or the days — I think two, at least — of fever and chills and fear that I spent wandering the swamps.

I remembered nothing, not what happened to me, my own name, not you. It was gone, just gone. I was alone — I was no one — and sick, hurt, terrified.

Joe found me. He took me in. He's a doctor, and he took care of me. He gave me my way when I begged him not to call the police or take me to a hospital. The fear was all I remembered from before.

He named me, and when we fell in love, gave me a life I now know I never deserved. We had three children together. You have a sister and two brothers, nieces and nephews. But I stole all of that, the life Joe would have given you, when I left you under that single light on the church steps.

I didn't remember, and I've lived all these years in a beautiful home with a beautiful family.

Joe was killed, a drunk driver took him from us. And I think of all the times I drove with you in the back seat while I was high on pills. I might have taken some good man from a family who loved him with my recklessness.

And in my grief, my terrible grief, it all flooded back on me, like the water in the lake. All of it, all I'd done. The child I'd abandoned and forgotten.

Though I know now you were taken in, adopted by good people, had a good home, a good life, I can't and won't ask you to forgive me. I nearly decided to leave this world, one I can't live in with these memories, without Joe beside me, never writing this letter. Never telling you.

But it feels, once again, like taking the coward's way. You deserve to know.

And I know I can't make up to you what I did, and the years between, but I need to give you something, some part of what Joe gave me. I'm enclosing the deed and all the paperwork to a house in your city, and have opened a bank account in your name. I do this to provide for you, my son, what I should have throughout your life.

I'm sorry, my baby darling. Please know that when I remembered all that came before, my first thought was of you.

Here, I'm weak. Too much of Lisa, not enough Violet, so I need to go to Joe.

I love you,

Mommy

As Peabody finished, a little teary-eyed, they stepped out of the elevator on Homicide.

'A lot of it's what you thought might have happened. She blocked it all out, or the trauma did it for her.'

'Wandering around some swamp, no sense of time, fever, chills, detoxing off the pills cold turkey. Rough. Then she hits pay dirt.'

'It didn't sound like she thought of it like that.'

'Not her, Peabody. Dawber. How he thinks of it, of her. She ditches him and lands in the bed of roses. Now she thinks she can buy him off? Ditch her guilt like she ditched him for a house and some money? Then she takes herself out? She never paid, never will.'

'So he replicates her so she will.'

'And that's how we play him. I'll take Covino. You check, see if he's saying lawyer. If not, we'll take a run at him tonight before he changes his mind. If he is, tag Reo, and we'll go from there.'

Eve continued to the conference room as Peabody turned into the bullpen.

She found Charles standing outside the door.

'I didn't think I should go in,' he said. 'I did raid your office AutoChef on doctor's orders. She said I'd find a lot better than at Vending, and she wanted Mary Kate to have some food.'

355

'That's fine. You can wait there, or in the bullpen. I appreciate you both coming in so quickly.'

'No need for appreciation. This is what she does. Let her know I'm in your office, helping myself to some of your exceptional coffee.'

She went inside to find Mary Kate with her roommate sitting beside her, and Jenkinson on her other side. Louise, in a fancy lace dress the color of her eyes, sat across from them.

Mary Kate had clean, white bandages on her wrist, her ankle, good color in her cheeks, and spooned up what smelled like chicken soup.

'This tastes like heaven. Not only because it doesn't come from him, but because it tastes like heaven.' When she spotted Eve, she set down the spoon.

'Go ahead and eat. Jenkinson, they could use you back at the crime scene.'

He gave Eve a nod, but turned to Mary Kate. 'You're going to be okay now.'

Eve watched him blink in surprise when Mary Kate took his face in her hands. And when she kissed him, saw the faint flush rise up the back of his neck.

'Thank you. I'm never going to forget everything you did. Never.'

He gave her an awkward pat. 'You're a strong, smart woman.'

He rose, gave Eve another nod, and headed out.

'He said you're the boss. I'm going to say you're lucky to have someone like him on your team.'

Eve sat. 'I couldn't agree more.'

'Okay.' Mary Kate let out a long breath. 'Anyway, thanks for not making me go to a hospital, and getting Cleo here so fast. Louise said I'm in pretty good shape. Just . . . you know, from the cuffs. No infection

from the tat or the piercings. I really want this off —'
She pointed to her belly. 'And the damn earrings, but
she — Louise — said we should wait for you. Can she
please take them out of me?'

'Yeah, but I need to get them on record first.'

She rose, turned, hiked up her shirt to reveal the
butterfly. 'God knows what it's going to take to have
this removed. I'm not thinking about it yet.'

'M.K.'s family's on their way,' Cleo told Eve. 'But
I'm going to thank you first. You got her out. You got
her out safe.'

'It's what I do, but from what I hear, she was working on that herself. Got the tat, can you turn around?'

Mary Kate turned, still holding up her shirt. 'The
other detective — Reineke — I'd like to thank him
again. I cried all over Detective Jenkinson. He made
me feel so safe.'

'Reineke's still in the field, but I'll pass it along.'
She got out two small evidence bags. 'Are your hands
sealed, Louise?'

'They are, of course.'

'Go ahead and take the rings out, place them in the
bags.'

When she had, Mary Kate sat again, began to cry.
'Sorry. Second.' And turned to wrap herself in her
roommate's arms.

'It's okay now,' Cleo soothed while Eve sealed and
labeled the evidence, put it out of sight.

'I know. I know. Okay.' She pulled back, swiped at
the tears, then looked at Eve. 'What's next?'

'I need your statement, on record, with as much
detail as you can provide. Can you tell me if you knew
or had contact with Andrew Dawber before your
abduction?'

'Is that his name? He insisted I call him baby darling. Made me sick, but I did it. No, I didn't know him. I don't think I'd seen him before, but I'm not absolutely sure. When he first came into that horrible little room, I was sort of sick and dizzy, and I thought he looked a little familiar. But I don't know, and I don't know that name.'

'Okay. Why don't you . . . ' Eve broke off when Mira came in. Rather than one of her fashionable suits, she wore slim black pants, a flowy white top with a black linen jacket over it. 'Mary Kate, this is Dr. Mira.'

'I get two doctors?'

'I'm very glad to meet you, Mary Kate.' Mira extended a hand. 'I work for the NYPSD.'

'Shrink. Head shrink,' Eve supplied.

'Oh. Okay.'

'Dr. Mira's profile helped us identify and apprehend Dawber.'

Mira bounced off Eve's statement as she sat. 'You've been through an ordeal.'

'I get a little shaky, but mostly I'm just really pissed off.'

'Sounds healthy.'

'I'd like Mary Kate to start at the beginning, take us through it. As many details as you can,' Eve reminded her.

'All right. I planned this romantic getaway with this jerk dog of an asshole I got stupid over.'

She had a good head for details, Eve concluded as Mary Kate told her story, finished the soup along the way.

How he'd looked, how he'd sounded, what he wore. The rumbling sound that signaled departure or return. Garage door, Eve thought.

358

They took a break when Peabody escorted her family in. Eve stepped away from the tears, the embraces, gave them the space they needed.

'He hasn't asked for a lawyer yet,' Peabody told her. 'But he's finally stopped yelling for his mommy and crying. He's just sitting quietly in his cell now.'

'Good. I'm close to letting Covino go, then we'll bring him up.'

'The search turned up a case of pressure syringes locked in the van — loaded ones. Zip ties, a stunner — police issue — a gurney, a ramp. And he put together his own lab on the third floor of the house — probably to make what's in the syringes, and whatever drugs he put in their food. McNab says he kept really good records in there.'

'He would. He wouldn't be able to help himself. Contact Dickhead.'

'Crap.'

'Yeah. He's going to go off about this — Dawber worked under him. Shut him down, tell him to get his ass into the lab, and identify what's in the syringes, what we send him from the home lab. If he gives you any grief, tell him the commander and the chief are already informed and involved — and you're happy to inform them of his lack of cooperation.'

'That actually might be sort of fun.'

'Take what you can where you find it. Book an interview room first, and have Dawber brought up. He can sit in the box while we finish up.'

Eve walked back across the room.

'I'm sorry to interrupt, but I'd like to get the rest of Mary Kate's statement so we can let her go.'

Mary Kate's mother leaped up, threw her arms around Eve, and basically squeezed the breath out of her.

'You saved my girl, my precious girl. You're an angel. A goddess!'

'I'm a cop, Ms. Covino. If I could just —'

Ms. Covino pulled back, eyes very like her daughter's, red-rimmed but fierce. 'I want you to hurt this man who took my girl.'

'I understand, but we're the police. I'm not allowed to physically harm a suspect.'

Now Ms. Covino gave Eve a poke. 'I saw the vid. Twice!'

'Mom. Let Lieutenant Dallas finish.'

'Finish him,' the woman whispered in Eve's ear, then went back to stand behind her daughter like a palace guard.

'All right, Mary Kate, you said tonight when he came into this new space where he'd put you, he was in a bad mood, but you were able to placate him.'

'That's right. I'd decided I had to do whatever I could to string him along until somebody found me, or I found a way out. He went into that little brat mode — with the accent like I told you before? And he got mad at me. So I pulled this one out.'

She reached up for her mother's hand. 'Used that 'watch it, kid' mom tone, then ignored him. It worked on him just like it worked on us, and he got sulky, then cooperative.'

'How did you get him to take the keys, the 'link, the rest out and leave it where you could reach it?'

'I said we'd play a game. He was still in creepy kid mode, so he jumped on it. A memory game — I've got a good one.'

'So I've noticed.'

'I'd close my eyes and he'd take everything out of

360

his pockets and put it on that little table he'd bolted down. I got to look for, like, three seconds, then if I couldn't name everything, he got a cookie.'

'A cookie?'

'It worked. I wanted to see what he had, what I could use if I could get to it. So I lost on purpose, and he went tearing over to get the cookie. That's when the buzzer — the doorbell — went off.'

She ran through the rest up until she'd managed to unlock the shackles, grab the Taser and the police had come in.

'Then I cried all over Detective Jenkinson, you came down, and they took me out. Detective Reineke found me some tissues.'

Eve sat back. 'You're in marketing, right?'

'Yeah.'

'If you ever want to change careers and try the cops, I'll get you into the Academy and into this division.'

Mary Kate gave a watery laugh. 'I think I'll stick with marketing.'

'I may have follow-up questions tomorrow, but you should go home, get some rest. I can arrange for transportation.'

'We have cars.' Ms. Covino rubbed her daughter's shoulders. 'We'll all go to the house tonight, everyone. You, too, Cleo. We'll have a lot of wine.'

'We'll talk soon, Mary Kate.'

She nodded at Mira. 'Yes, thank you. And thank you,' she said to Louise.

'Glad to help. Use the medication I gave you and change the bandages in the morning. The piercings will close, but if you have any issues, contact me or your family doctor.'

'I will.' Rising, she reached out, took both of Eve's

hands. 'Don't let the little boy fool you. He's as vicious as the man.'

'I know. I'd tell you to take care of yourself, but you've already proven you know how.'

When they'd all filed out, Eve sat. 'Louise, is she as stable physically as she looks?'

'She needs about twelve hours' natural and deep sleep, probably another few good meals — and the wine won't hurt. If she's vigilant about the medication and bandage changes, she shouldn't have any scarring, or very minimal.'

'She'll be vigilant. Dr. Mira?'

'Strong-willed. She'll have some bad moments — but the support of family, of friends will help. And she's very open to counseling.'

'Will she handle giving testimony in court if this goes to court?'

'I have no doubts there. Strong-willed,' Mira repeated.

'Good. Louise, I'm cutting you loose.'

'Happy to be cut loose.'

'Charles is probably in my office, waiting for you.'

'I'll find him. Let's all take a page from the Covinos and have a lot of wine sometime soon.'

When Louise left, Eve got up, uncloaked the board.

'You've had a very long day,' Mira pointed out.

'I think I can finish it by finishing him. Not by punching him several times the way Ms. Covino might like, but in the box, within the law. I can get to him. Both sides of him. I could use your help.'

'You have it. What do you have in mind?'

'Let me get Peabody in here, and we'll talk it through.'

22

After she had Dawber brought up, Eve let him cook in the box for about forty minutes, while she conferenced with Mira and Peabody, and Reo by remote.

She put her heel down hard on the possibility of a deal, and got no substantial argument from the APA. They had a witness in Covino with a strong handle on details, and an entire mountain range of evidence.

The sticking point was, and would be, if Dawber proved mentally capable of understanding his crimes, and could be held responsible for them.

With what continued to come in from the search of his house, the updates on his electronics from EDD, Eve pushed hard on the: Hell yes.

In her office, Eve put together a few fat files to take into Interview. Peabody would take in the box of carefully selected evidence removed from his residence. And Mira would serve as the expert shrink, evaluating Dawber's mental status.

Mira wouldn't be the last of those, Eve knew. If and when Dawber said *lawyer*, any capable defense attorney would arrange for an outside psychiatric eval.

Even if he didn't, there would be other evaluations. So they had to nail it, and nail him.

Ready, she turned toward the door just as Roarke stepped in.

'I hear everybody else, and nine times out of ten I know who's coming by the sound of their walk. But you slide around like your feet don't touch the ground.'

'Darling, I walk on air when I'm near you.'

When she snorted, he stepped to her, cupped her chin in his hand, skimmed a thumb over the dent in it. 'You should be exhausted, but you're not.'

'No, not tired. Revved. Murder cops don't often get to watch a live one — a tough, smart live one like Mary Kate Covino — walk away with her family to go drink a bunch of wine. He took two, and we're going to make him pay. But she walked away.'

'I've more here that may help with the payment portion.' He handed her a file and a disc. 'Knowing you prefer paper copies, we generated those. You have the disc if you want to put it on the screen in the box.'

She set down the files she carried to open the new one.

'Jesus, he journaled every target, by name. This is gold. Detailed notes on his hunting and stalking phases, dates, times, his conclusions, going back to last October.'

'You'll see he had two other potentials he dropped during his research. One he learned had a black belt in karate, the other he learned had a cop for a father.'

'Shit, this is Redman from Special Victims. I know him a little.'

'His daughter, age twenty-four, is a grad student at NYU and lives in Dawber's hunting grounds, where she also works nights tending bar.'

'Crossed them off the list. The first, he had to calculate her reaction time, her fighting instincts and skills — not worth the risks. The second, snatch the kid of a cop? Too much risk there, too. And this is gold because it shows calculation. And back to all that careful planning with these log entries.'

'One more thing that you'll find useful? You'll see

he did considerable research on his half siblings, their spouses, their children, and so on. One of the younger generation, named after her grandmother, also bears a striking resemblance to her namesake. He took particular interest in her.'

Eve flipped through until she found the data — along with the ID shot. 'Okay, yeah, she looks more like Lisa/Violet than the women he killed or captured. And she's in the age range. Single, an intern at the same hospital where her grandfather worked, her aunt works now. Looks like he's done a thorough run on her.'

'You'll find her in his journal notes as well, including a trip he took to see her for himself last December. He had when he applied for the vacation time, booked the trip, where he stayed over that three-day period — what and where he ate. But more, her routine.'

'Yeah, yeah, I see it. Find out if he's put in for more time off.'

'Feeney's anticipated that, and is already digging for it. But we thought you'd want this right away.'

'Yeah, I do. He's got a potful of money now, thanks to Mommy.' Considering, she eyed Roarke. 'You know, it'd be interesting to see if he looked into real estate down there. Purchase or rental, private property. Maybe he just wanted to kill her, but pattern says he'd want to play with her for a while first.'

Smiling, Roarke tapped a finger on Eve's head. 'Always thinking. And it would be interesting. I'll have a look for that myself.'

'Good. I've got to get to this, but did Callendar get the work e's?'

'She did, and so far there's nothing but official work on his work unit. All very precise again, and very like

365

his personal records in the setup. Jamie's working on his other devices. He used his 'link to take pictures of his targets — which include his niece. He then transferred those to the computer in his home lab, deleted them from the 'link. But of course, Jamie dug them out.'

'Also good. That calculation again. We're in Interview A. Anything else that adds weight, have McNab text Peabody. She'll judge when she can step out of Interview to get it.'

He cupped her chin again, and this time kissed her lightly. 'When it's done, why don't we go home, open a bottle of wine, and take it and ourselves for a walk to sit by the pond in the moonlight?'

'I could get behind that. I could seriously get behind that.'

'A date then.'

He walked out with her, continued on while she stopped at Peabody's desk. 'We've got more.'

'McNab gave me a quick rundown. I passed it on to Mira.'

Eve glanced over where Mira, at Jenkinson's empty desk, slid the PPC she'd been working on into her jacket pocket.

'It's going to add weight,' Eve said. 'Peabody, if they get more that does the same, McNab will text you. You pick the time to step out, get the information, bring it back in.'

She heard someone stomping their way toward Homicide, and turned as Dick Berenski barreled in.

'What the fuck, Dallas! You have Peabody try to tell me you've dragged Dawber in here on some nutball charge. Then you send your storm troopers in to clear out his lab. And I don't find out all this bullshit about

366

the storm troopers until lab security lets me know. What the fuck!'

'I'll tell you what the fuck. Andrew Dawber's charged with three abductions, three counts of involuntary imprisonment, multiple charges of forcibly injecting or otherwise inducing controlled substances, and two counts of murder in the first.'

Berenski slammed his fisted hands on his hips. 'This is batshit bullshit! Have you met Andy?'

'Yeah, and the last time we met, I tackled him during his attempt to escape while two of my detectives secured the safety of the woman being forcibly held and restrained and drugged in the basement of his house. And I need the contents of the syringes found in his van, the contents of his home lab analyzed, and now.'

'I put somebody on the lab work. You think you can threaten me like that?'

He moved up, got in her face, and tempted her to punch the anemic caterpillar over his sneering top lip.

'Screw all that. And screw this bullshit. Andy doesn't have a house. He lives in a damn apartment a spitball away from the lab.'

'Not since September, when his bio mother left him a three-story brownstone — with full basement — and six million in the bank. Don't tell me it's bullshit,' she snapped before he could. 'I've got two bodies, I've got the statement from the third woman he held. I've got his own records, the evidence from his home lab, the loaded syringes and zip ties in his van.'

'He . . . he doesn't have a van.'

'Didn't have.'

Berenski dragged his hands over the slicked-down hair on his egg-shaped head. 'I've known Andy more than twenty damn years. Sure he can be a little weird, but . . .' He looked toward Mira. 'Are you saying what she's saying?'

'Yes, and we have more than she's told you. I'm very sorry, but there's no question of his guilt.'

'Lemme talk to him.'

'No.'

At Eve's flat refusal, he swung back to her. 'I want to hear his side. For Christ's sake. He's one of mine. How would you feel if all this was coming down on one of yours?'

'Pissed and shitty, which is why instead of escorting you the hell out of here, Peabody's going to set you up in Observation. I can't let you talk to him now. That's our job. At some point down the road, I can arrange it, but not until we close this. Peabody.'

Peabody rose, crossed to the doorway.

'You've got the wrong guy,' Berenski claimed as he followed Peabody out. 'That's on you. You got the wrong guy.'

'It's difficult.' Mira rose, walked over to Eve. 'Brutal, I'd think, to know someone, work with them for so many years, then learn they're not who and what you believed.'

'Yeah, that's why I'm cutting him some slack. That, and the fact he came in here to stand up for one of his people. That counts.'

'Some of the brass will want to know how the lab chief didn't see the psychopath in his house.'

'Hell.' She hadn't thought of that, and now she had to. 'They're going to make me stand up for Dickhead.'

'As will I.'

Peabody came back. 'It's starting to hit him this isn't a mistake. And he looks a little sick.'

'It's about to hit harder. Let's go have a chat with Andy.'

He sat quietly, hands folded on the table in front of him. Eve wondered how he felt feeling the cuffs at his wrists and ankles.

'Record on. Dallas, Lieutenant Eve; Peabody, Detective Delia; Mira, Dr. Charlotte entering Interview with Dawber, Andrew.'

She read off the case numbers as she and the others took their seats.

'Mr. Dawber, you were read your rights at the time of your arrest. I will again inform you on this record.'

She recited the Revised Miranda.

'Do you understand these rights and obligations?'

'Yes, yes, of course. But I'm very confused. I think there's been some mistake.'

'Yeah, you made several of them. Underestimating Mary Kate Covino's the biggest.'

'I'm sorry. I don't know who that is.' With a worried look in his eyes, he tried that vague smile.

'One of the three woman you hunted, stalked, abducted, and kept chained in your basement. The one who's still alive.'

Those worried eyes widened. 'Oh my goodness! I would never — could never. What basement? There's been some terrible mix-up.'

Liar, Eve thought, calculating liar.

'The basement in your brownstone.'

'Brownstone.' He laughed a little. 'Lieutenant Dallas, how could I afford a brownstone on my salary? I live frugally, but —'

'Deeded to you last September.' Eve took the copies of the documents out of the file, pushed them over the table, where Dawber hunched over them, brow furrowed.

'This isn't my name. It's —'

'An anagram of your birth mother's name. Lisa McKinney, who bought it for you, sent you the paperwork, deposited six million in a brokerage account for you, and informed you of same in this letter sent just before she took her own life.'

'No, this can't be. I've never seen any of this. I haven't seen my birth mother for decades. I barely remember her. I . . .'

He looked up, and his face crumbled. 'I want my mommy!' The twangy screech echoed in the room. 'You're mean and ugly and I don't want you. I want my mommy now.'

'Knock it off,' Eve snapped.

'She's gonna beat you up!'

'Dead. Tough for her to manage that.'

'Is not, is not, is not!' He beat his cuffed hands on the table, kicked his shackled feet while tears streamed down his reddened face.

'How old are you, Andy?'

At Mira's question, her quiet and pleasant voice, he snarled at her. 'I'm not Andy. Andy's a stupid head. I'm baby darling, and I want my mommy.'

'Where is your mommy?'

'She's waiting for me.'

'Where?'

He turned sly. 'I'm not gonna tell. I want a soda pop!'

'What kind do you want?' Peabody spoke now, kindly. 'If you ask nicely, I'll get you one.'

'I'm thirsty. Get me one right now!'

'I bet your mommy taught you how to say please and thank you.'

370

His bottom lip poked out, a strange look on a man of sixty. 'Maybe. Please can I have an orange soda pop?'

'Sure.'

'Peabody exiting Interview,' Eve said for the record. 'Where do you live?'

'In the car. We have adventures and don't need anybody else. We sing songs and play games and I can have candy when I want it. I want candy now.'

'No. And try screaming again you won't get the soda, either.' Eve leaned closer. 'You're not five years old, and you're nobody's baby darling.'

He tried to lunge at her; she didn't flinch.

'I hate you, hate you, hate you!'

'Yeah, that hurts my feelings.'

'What did your mother call you when she got upset with you?' Mira asked him.

'Johnny, you stop that right now!' And he giggled. 'But I'm baby darling and she loves only me. Just me. And I want her now!'

Eve slid Elder's crime scene photo across the table.

'That's not my mommy.'

'No, so you had to kill her. What did she do to make you so mad you slit her throat?'

'I don't have to tell you.' He used a singsong voice now. 'I don't have to tell you.'

'Peabody reentering Interview. He doesn't get that until he stops being an asshole.'

'You said a bad word because you're a bad girl.'

'But you're a good boy,' Mira said. 'You try to be a very good boy.'

'I'm the best boy. Mommy says, and one day we're going to live in a big house and eat ice cream all day. I want ice cream now!'

371

Mira smiled at him. 'You can have your soda, and maybe some ice cream if we can talk to Andy.'

'Chocolate ice cream!'

'A whole bowl.'

Like a light switch, Dawber's face changed. He blinked his eyes. 'I'm sorry, what was I saying?'

Mira looked at Eve. 'You were right.' Then she folded her hands, addressed Dawber. 'That was much too rushed. Scientist to scientist? I have no doubt you're aware that multiple personality disorder is very rare.'

'I don't know what —'

'Quiet,' Eve ordered. 'Let her finish.'

'There are cases, of course,' Mira continued. 'Well-documented, carefully studied. And I'm sure, Mr. Dawber, with some careful study, we'll find the neglected and unhappy child you were has great influence on the man you are. It may be that you find some emotional release by allowing yourself to behave like that child, permitting the child to say and do what the mature and disciplined man can't, or wouldn't until last fall.'

'I don't know what you mean. Dr. Mira, I know you have a sterling reputation.'

The meek and mild might have worked, Eve thought, but he piled it on too thick. Desperate — and she saw the desperate — to compensate.

'I think — I admit that over the past months I've had some incidents. Some gaps in memory, but . . . '

'You moved out of your apartment and into the brownstone on October first,' Eve repeated. 'Explain.'

'I didn't. I don't . . . I don't know.'

Eve shoved the log, his own log, detailing his travel, his hotel in New Orleans. 'Explain this. Explain the trip you took to Louisiana in December of last year and the information, including photographs, of this woman. Your niece.'

'I don't have a niece. I'm an only child. I certainly didn't go to Louisiana. I have very bad memories of that area. I was found there, at age five. I was a foundling, and put into the foster system until I was adopted.'

Another mistake, Eve thought. A bratty five-year-old couldn't book the travel, take the trip, document it all.

'You have three half siblings. After your mother tossed you aside, she hooked a rich doctor and had kids she decided to keep.'

His head snapped back as if she'd slapped him, but he couldn't quite disguise the fury that burned in his eyes.

'That's a vicious thing to say. You're a vicious person. Something happened to my mother, that's the only explanation. She would never have left me if she had a choice.'

'Shakier ground,' Eve said, because his hands had started to tremble. 'She didn't want you, couldn't wait to ditch the whiny brat holding her back. So she dumped you and drove away. Never gave you another thought.'

'That's a lie!'

There you are, Eve thought, when the fury, full-blown now, raged in his eyes.

'Pure truth. Who wants to listen to some snotty brat throwing tantrums, demanding candy and ice cream? Tossing you aside was her best shot at real freedom. So she walked away, and probably wondered why she hadn't done it years before.'

'Lies! Lies! She loved me. She was young and weak,

373

an addict, but I'm the one she loved. She left me to save me. She was wrong, wrong, wrong, and I can have her back my way. I deserve it. She thought she could make it up to me — all those years — with a house, with money. She was supposed to stay with me, look after me, and I'll fix it so she has to. I deserve to have my mother.'

Peabody shot Eve a look, then rose.

'Peabody exiting Interview.' Eve pushed the tube of soda toward Dawber. 'It must have been a hell of a shock, getting that letter.'

He cracked the tube, drank thirstily. He smiled, but the calculation showed through. 'What letter?'

'The bullshit letter she wrote you to try to ease her guilty conscience before she swallowed a bunch of pills. Killed herself, not over you, Dawber, but over the father of her real children.'

He heaved the tube at Eve. She snagged it in mid-air. 'That's a weak arm, pal. No wonder she shrugged you off.'

'I'm her son. I'm her only. The rest are fakes and lies.'

'She doted on them, but not you. She cared more about getting high than you, more about living her new life than you.'

'I want my mommy.' Pulling out the little boy again, Dawber laid his head on the table and wept. 'I want my ice cream, I want my mommy.'

'Peabody reentering Interview.'

Eve took the file Peabody gave her, listened as Peabody leaned close to her ear.

'McNab said they had to dig this out. He'd deleted it, but left enough markers for them to dig.'

With a nod, Eve opened the file. After she'd scanned

it, gotten the gist, she passed it to Mira.

'You're not getting a damn thing. If you want to keep playing this game, that's just fine. What did Lauren Elder do that prompted you to take out the knife and slice it across her neck? I already know the bulk of it. She didn't work out for you. She didn't know how to play along. She kept begging you to let her go, and it just pissed you off. Pissed off the brat, and the scientist calculated that experiment a failure. You had the other two, and they looked more promising.

'You'd spent months setting it all up, getting the wardrobe, the makeup, the perfume, all of it. You set up your own lab, set up an HQ, invested in security.'

'I don't like you.' He muttered it as he closed his eyes. 'You're mean and nasty.'

'You'd expected — a scientist, a precise sort of man — to have some failures. But one of them was going to work. One would be your mother, your slave. One would pay for years and years and years for what Lisa McKinney did. Never leave you, never leave that basement. Always be there. When you wanted to be a little boy, she'd play with you or sing songs, whatever. When you didn't, you could look at her and know she paid and paid.'

Wearily, Dawber lifted his head. 'I don't know what you're talking about. I think — I'm afraid — something's wrong with me. I haven't been myself.'

He appealed to Mira. 'At work, it's all as it should be. But when I leave, I . . . I don't clearly remember. Not until I'm at work again. It's like I step out of myself, or into something else. It's all a blur. I need help. Can you help me?'

Mira studied him with her soft blue eyes. 'I'd certainly try. If any of that were true. I see here you've done considerable and thorough research on MPD. Documented cases, debunked cases. And you added your own notes, I see.'

'Somebody who's worked with the cops as long as you,' Peabody commented, 'should know what EDD can do. You thought you were smarter. You're not.'

'I researched it because I had concerns about my mental health.'

'Maybe.' Eve leaned back. 'Maybe a grain of truth in there, but what you did was expand on it, calculate how you might use it if you ever ended up where you are now. You selected, stalked, abducted, chained, and emotionally tortured three women, killed two of them. You did that with a cold, clear mind. You killed them, dressed them like her because it was always her you needed to punish.

'Bad Mommy.'

'She was.'

Eve nodded. 'No doubts here she fucked up and was fucked-up. Predisposed it seems to addiction, like her mother, her grandfather. Like you.'

'I am not an addict.'

'Yeah, you are. Lisa McKinney's your addiction. Was she always? What about the mother who raised you?'

He looked away to stare at the wall. 'She was not my mother. She was never my mother.'

'Why? Because she didn't push you out of her vagina?'

'She wasn't my mother!'

The anger came back, and Eve gauged it was time to push on it.

'Did she beat you, starve you?'

'I was a child, a frightened little boy, and they put

376

me with strangers. Do you know what that's like? Foster homes with social workers sniffing around, then they just give you away to someone. A fake family. And they were old! Already in their late forties, and took me as a substitute because they couldn't make their own child. They changed my name, and then it was: No sweets before dinner, Andy. Wash your hands, Andy. Time for school, time for bed. Rules, rules, and rules.'

'You followed the rules,' Mira said. 'You did what you were told, studied hard, did what was expected of you. You didn't love this family, but you needed them. You didn't want to be left alone again.'

'They were *ordinary*. My mother wasn't ordinary. They tried to make me ordinary. My mother knew I was special. I got away from them as soon as I was of age. I looked for her for months and months. But I couldn't find her. Nobody could find her. And she was right there the whole time.'

'Right there,' Eve repeated. 'It made you mad when you found out she'd lived in a big house, had a big family, a happy life without you, all those years.'

'She left me, and I looked for her, and she was right there.' Chains rattling, he pounded his fists again.

'I studied in college, so hard, and every break I looked for her. I went back to Louisiana, but nobody knew where she was. Nobody cared.'

'You cared, and deeply.'

His eyes went hot when he looked at Mira. 'She didn't care about me. Left me, tried to kill herself rather than take care of me. And she couldn't even do that right. Then she's rewarded for it while I'm with strangers? And in the end, she does kill herself. Takes her own life rather than open that life to me. Tell me she didn't deserve to be punished.'

'Lauren Elder, Anna Hobe, Mary Kate Covino.' Eve waited until he shifted his gaze to her. 'They didn't deserve what you did to them.'

'Careful selection. I selected them carefully. All they had to do was meet the criteria, and they would have been housed, clothed, fed.'

'You gave each of them the tattoo your mother had, the same body piercings.'

He sighed, wearily. 'Of course. They could hardly be her without them.'

'Why did you kill Lauren Elder?'

'She didn't meet the criteria! She refused to cooperate. She shouted at me, called me vile names. She slapped me! She made me very angry. She wasted my time, my good work. But even then, I took care of her. I bathed her, and dressed her, did her hair, her makeup, her nails. I made her perfect. I took her where mothers take their children.'

'You left a sign on her. Bad Mommy. Why?'

He sighed again. 'She didn't meet the criteria,' he repeated. 'The mother who left me was bad. The one who'd stay would be good.'

'Okay, let's go back. Tell me how you selected Lauren Elder.'

His eyes glinted. 'Maybe I'm too tired and thirsty.'

'We can put you back in a cell. Solitary, I think. Suicide watch?' Eve glanced at Mira.

'Yes, I'd recommend that.'

'Or we can get you another soda, and you'll walk us through it.'

'I want grape this time. And some ice cream. Chocolate.'

'Fine. Peabody, will you take care of that? Peabody

378

exiting Interview. Now, tell me about Lauren Elder.'

He was a man of details and precision, and relating all those details took a long time — as well as two more sodas, ice cream, gummy candy, and a bag of chips.

He bounced back and forth a few times, back to that little kid twang, but they got every detail on record. A full confession.

Eve didn't miss the sly look he snuck toward her as she arranged to have him taken back to his cell.

'He thinks he's going to cop to insanity, get off with a few years — even up to ten — in a minimum-security facility, with therapy, regular evals, and all that. He's crazy,' Eve said to Mira. 'When this started, I figured something along the lines he's thinking — though a solid twenty to twenty-five inside a supermax.'

'You don't think that now.'

'I'm hoping you'll tell me in your expert opinion you don't, either.'

'He's a psychopath. I suspect if his mother hadn't left him as she did, he'd have grown up to embrace his psychopathy much sooner. He buried it — primarily out of fear of abandonment — and strapped himself into the world of science, of rules, of logic. But as we see, he never made or kept friendships, relationships. If you develop relationships, you risk abandonment, disappointments. These are intolerable for him.

'He's a psychopath, one with obsessive-compulsive tendencies, a malignant narcissism he releases through the persona of the child he was. He isn't sane, but while we'll do other, deeper evaluations, in my opinion he won't reach the threshold of legal insanity.'

'If he got the chance, he'd search for, select, and kill his mother again.'

'I have no doubt of it, and so I'll say in my report. You handled him well, as did you, Peabody.'

'He thinks he played us. I could see it.' Peabody rolled her tired shoulders. 'He didn't.'

'Go home, get some sleep. I'll write it up.'

'No, I'll write it up. You get to deal with . . .' Peabody nearly said *Dickhead* before she remembered they still sat in Interview. 'Berenski.'

'Right. You write it up. I appreciate you coming in for this, Dr. Mira, and sticking.'

'A fascinating interview from my end. I'll write up my initial evaluation. I suspect he'll call for a lawyer once he realizes he didn't win this game.'

'Yeah, but it won't matter. He'll get the ward for mentally defective, but in a supermax, and for three life terms — or at least two and a solid twenty for Covino. That's what matters.'

Eve rose. 'I'll text Reo so she does her own lawyer thing in the morning. Good work, all around.'

She stepped out and walked up to Observation. It surprised her to find Roarke with Berenski, then realized it shouldn't have.

They sat drinking what she knew from the scent was real coffee. And Berenski looked exhausted.

Roarke stood. 'I'll leave you two alone.' He brushed his hand over Eve's arm as he left the room.

'Decent son of a bitch for a rich bastard.' Then Berenski waved a hand. 'Sorry.'

'He is decent, he is rich. And he can be a son of a bitching bastard when he wants.'

Berenski let out a short laugh before he scrubbed a hand over his face. 'Nearly half my life I've known Andy. I never saw what was in him, never saw what I saw in that room when you took him apart. I'd've sworn on a case of prime Kentucky bourbon Andy Dawber wouldn't hurt a fricking fly.'

'He broke. Whatever chains or restraints or control he wrapped around what was in him broke. Maybe if his mother hadn't tried to do what she thought was right in the end, they'd have stayed in place. He wasn't right, he was never right. I don't think he was right before she left him at that church. And he just couldn't hold it back anymore.'

'What he did . . . He's going to need a lawyer.'

'Don't. Stop,' she said before he could speak. 'You're thinking he's one of your people, and he's not. Not anymore. You're a fucking dick, Dick, more than half the time, but you're a good boss from everything I've seen. More, you're not responsible here. Harvo flirted with him the way somebody like her flirts with a guy old enough to be her grandfather. She's not responsible, or any of the others who worked with him.'

'You could toss some of the blame on me.'

'Could I?' She angled her head. 'Tempting. But no, no I couldn't, because none of it belongs on you. It's his. Go home. You're going to have to talk to your people tomorrow.'

'Yeah, I am.' He set the mug aside, rose. 'But I'm going in now. Likely we've got the analysis you need, but I want to double-check it.'

'Appreciate it.'

'Yeah, yeah. You know, next time you want priority treatment in my place, you should bring some of that coffee.'

'Get out of my house.'

He let out a bark of laughter. At the door he paused. 'Thanks.' He didn't look around. 'Just thanks.' And went out.

In the bullpen she saw Peabody working and McNab sitting on the corner of her desk.

In her office, Roarke did the same on hers.

'Good work, Lieutenant. Very good work.'

'All around, including our expert consultant, civilian. Peabody's writing it up, but I've still got some things to tie off.'

'So I understand.'

'Listen . . . I appreciate you hanging with Dickhead.'

'It seemed the thing to do. I saw about the last three-quarters of an hour of the interview. Dawber is a very twisted man.'

'Yep.' She sat. 'But not, in Mira's opinion, crazy enough to meet the legal threshold for insanity. So I'm closing this out in a damn good mood. I'd be in a better one if somebody got me coffee.'

'I can do that. In EDD it ended on fizzies. Many large fizzies.' He set a mug by her elbow. 'And with tonight's adventures I've come to accept I'll never pry Jamie from EDD. The boy's a bloody cop to the marrow.'

Eve didn't bother to hide the smirk. 'Could've told you.'

'Best I saw it for myself.' He kissed the top of her head. 'My loss, your gain. I'll find a place to wait for you.'

'Roarke?' She reached up and back to grab his hand before he left. 'It's late, I know, but are you still up for the wine, the walk, and the pond when we get home?'

'I am, if you're included.'

'Good, I could use all three. And you.'

'I'll be waiting.'

She turned to the work, but took a moment.

382

They had that coming, she thought. A good way to end a long day — or to begin the next, considering the time.

She glanced at the board, at the dead and the living. 'We did our best,' she murmured.

Then turned to finish the work.

Other titles published by Ulverscroft:

FORGOTTEN IN DEATH

J.D. Robb

Lieutenant Eve Dallas hasn't even arrived at work when her first call of the day comes in. Alva Quirk — 46 years old, sidewalk sleeper — was beaten to death with a crowbar. Eve has barely had time to examine the crime scene when her second victim of the morning is discovered just a block away. Make that second and third. Jane Doe — a well-dressed young mother and her baby shot and buried over 40 years ago. Two very different victims in the same location with no one to claim them. To uncover the truth Eve must delve into a world of family businesses, Russian mobsters and shady dealings.

FAITHLESS IN DEATH

J.D. Robb

It's a beautiful Spring day in NYC when Eve Dallas gets an early morning murder call. A talented young sculptor hasn't had such a perfect day in May. Killed by her own hammer, it looks like an argument with a jealous partner at first, but it soon becomes clear that there is much more to this case than a lovers' quarrel turned fatal. Eve finds herself drawn into the dark and dangerous world of a secret order. A world in which white supremacy, misogyny and religious fanaticism are everyday activities. Eve has dealt with some tough cases before but is it too much even for her to take on a wealthy, influential organisation with friends in very high places . . . ?

SHADOWS IN DEATH

J.D. Robb

When a night out at the theatre is interrupted by the murder of a young woman in Washington Square Park, it seems like an ordinary case for Detective Eve Dallas and her team. But when Roarke spots a shadow from his past in the crowd, Eve realises that this case is far from business as usual. Eve has two complex cases on her hands — the shocking murder of this wealthy young mother and tracking down the shadow before he can strike again, this time much closer to home. Eve is well used to being the hunter, but how will she cope when the tables are turned? As Eve and the team follow leads to Roarke's hometown in Ireland, the race is on to stop the shadow making his next move . . .